PRAISE FOR *THERE BUT FOR GRACE*

"Who wouldn't want to go on a Grace Winthrop Hobbes adventure? I loved following her through the streets of Cambridge, as she figures out sex, motherhood, friendship, and family, never knowing what will befall her next. *There but for Grace* is a lovely, witty, deeply absorbing novel."

—Margot Livesey, author of *The Road from Belhaven* and *The Boy in the Field*

"When Anne Whitney Pierce skillfully lures us into the life of Grace, newly divorced and open to experiences she's not dared dream of before, we are hooked. Grace's narrative is authentic, adventurous and sympathetic, laced with the truth about all that she endures. This includes errant men, grown children, and a difficult mother. We are with her all the way."

—Susannah Marren, author of *Maribelle's Shadow*

THERE BUT FOR GRACE

Anne Whitney Pierce

Regal House Publishing

Published by
Regal House Publishing, LLC
Raleigh, NC 27605

ISBN -13 (paperback): 9781646035571
ISBN -13 (epub): 9781646035588
Library of Congress Control Number: 2024935071

Cover images and design by © C. B. Royal
Author photo credit: Natalia Provencher

Regal House Publishing, LLC
https://regalhousepublishing.com

Printed in the United States of America

For all the cats I've ever loved

Fluffy, Percy, Raspberry, Bingo, Tyrus, Pebbles, Gracie,

Luna I, Edward, Maisie, Leo, Wolfie, Luna II, and Malcolm

1

"You broke the windshield," says Fuzz, the man with whom I just had sex in my car. So much for post-coital tenderness.

"What are you talking about?" Breathless and rumpled, I look up to see an enormous spider-web crack on the passenger side of the glass. "Oh my god. It must have cracked!"

"Brilliant!" He laughs. "And what made it crack, Sherlock?"

"We did." I lower my legs from the dashboard and straighten out my crooked shirt. "By my count, there are two of us in this car."

"But technically speaking, your feet were the culprits. Ow!" Fuzz hits his head on the rearview mirror while plunking back down into his seat. "My feet were nowhere near the scene of the crime."

"Where else was I supposed to put them?" I shimmy down my skirt and locate my underwear, which has somehow managed to wrap itself around the gas pedal. "You didn't exactly leave me any choice," I say.

"So we're co-conspirators." He reaches down to retrieve his glasses on the floor. On the way back up, his hand finds the smooth ridge of my calf. "It's hard to argue with someone who feels so good," he says.

My smooth legs, more than anything, remind me it's not the sixties anymore, which is the last time I had sex in a car, thrashing around with a certain Thaddeus Peacock in my rusty VW bug after a night of drinking Boone's Farm Apple Wine from a jug down on the riverbank outside of Harvard Square. In those days, it was a matter of honor; we let our leg and armpit hair grow wild. Never would we have shaved our legs for the sake of a guy. But that's just what I did three hours ago, before I ventured out to the Wonder Bar, went through two disposable razors and half a can of shaving cream, a nick on each ankle bone and an unsightly gash on my right knee to show for it all, not for any specific man, but for the notion of a man, a flesh and blood man. And now here he is, still half-naked, with his hand moving slowly up my thigh.

Fuzz's real name escapes me at the moment. He told me when we met earlier tonight at the bar. He was alarmingly good-looking in a Paul Newmanish way, chiseled features and a strong jawline, but only half as much hair. What was left was strawberry blond and cut close, giving his head the look of a ripening peach. From the start, I had an overwhelming urge to pet him, as I would my cats, Atticus and Maude. But I kept my impulses in check until the end of the evening, when he walked me to my car, where one thing led to another—the exchange of phone numbers, my offer of a ride home, the first fateful kiss…

Once we've pulled ourselves together, Fuzz and I sit side by side in the dark car. Luckily, I parked on Shepard Street off the main drag, and now, after midnight, the streets are all but deserted.

"I can't believe we just did that." I try to smooth down my hair, now a mass of frazzled curls.

"Well, we did," Fuzz says cheerfully. He fiddles with his glasses, which have taken a hit in the tussle.

"I don't even know you." I rub a mysterious tender spot on my left temple.

"You do now."

"I just don't want you to think—"

"Think what?" He snakes his belt through his belt loops. "That we're two healthy adults who just had consensual sex—hot, consensual sex, I might add—just like zillions of people do every day?"

"Not in cars," I say. "Not at our age."

"Sometimes in cars." He slides his glasses back on and checks himself out in the tilted rearview mirror. "Sometimes in even more interesting places. And what does age have to do with it?" he says.

His logic, at this moment, strikes me as unusually sound.

"My wife would never do anything but the missionary," he says. "For sixteen years, it was just me on top and her on the bottom. And always in the bed. I could never get her out of that goddamned bed." Fuzz looks over at me. "What's the weirdest place you've ever had sex?" he says.

My brain instantly freezes, knowing nothing I come up with will be able to top what he's about to tell me. I catch a glimpse of the Fresh Pond parking sticker on the back windshield. "On a golf course," I say, pushing my shirt sleeves up over my elbows. It's an outright lie.

"Nice." Fuzz pulls a small notebook out of his jacket pocket. "Want to know the kinkiest place I've ever had sex?"

I hate that word. Kinky. And all of its variations. "Sure," I say half-heartedly.

"Underwater," he says. "At Walden Pond."

"Wow," I say. "That would've given Thoreau something to write about."

"Good one," he says, with an approving nod. I'd like to ask if it's really possible to have sex underwater, but I don't want to hear all the gory details.

"I have to say, for first-time sex, that was pretty great." Fuzz starts writing in his notebook. "On a scale of one to ten, I'd give it, say, a seven."

"You're taking notes?" It's now clear that whatever game we're playing, there are points involved.

"What?" He looks over at me as if I'm the crazy one. "How would you rate it?" he says.

"Well," I stammer, not wanting to admit that I haven't had much to compare it to for a while. "I guess a seven sounds about right." I don't add that I've never been in the habit of evaluating my sexual encounters. Typically, I just try to enjoy them.

"With your feet up on the dashboard that way, your hips were at..." He tilts an outstretched hand. "I'd say about a forty-eight degree angle to my torso. That's just about perfect for optimal penetration. It gave me just the leverage I needed."

Oh my god, I think. Is this guy some kind of psycho pervert? And how often does he do this, anyway?

"And the corresponding angle of my Johnson allowed for the maximum semen flow through the vas deferens," Fuzz goes on. "I bet I came an additional ten percent above my normal ejaculation level. In fact, I think I may have counted five plumes. That would be a personal high-water mark."

As I sit there watching him scribbling away, I can't help but think it would have been a lot sexier if he just said something like, "Oh, baby, what you did to me!"

"Always working toward the ultimate orgasm," Fuzz says, closing up his notebook. "Not just for me," he adds quickly. "For you too."

"Thanks," I say, tucking in the rest of my shirt. I guess a psycho pervert wouldn't much care if I climaxed or not. And this is no time to mention that I didn't even come, that I can count on both hands the number of actual orgasms I've had in my life and that most of them were, shall we say, of my own design. But even so—men find this hard to understand—the sex still felt sublime.

"So, how 'bout that ride home, Sherlock?" Fuzz says.

"Grace," I say. "My name is Grace." I start up the car, thinking that if this guy had any sense of romance or chivalry, he'd slip me a signed blank check to pay for the cracked windshield and disappear after one last lingering kiss into the night. Instead, he jots down more notes as I pull out of the parking space and head toward Garden Street, not even bothering to try and make conversation. When we reach his apartment on Pearl Street, deep down in the Port, he caresses my thigh with one hand while reaching for the car door handle with the other. "How 'bout we meet at the Half Tone this Saturday?" he says. "Nine o'clock. Listen to some blues."

"Sounds great," I say, putting the car back into drive. This sounds more promising, more like a real "date"—whatever that means these days.

"Afterward," Fuzz says, stepping out of the car, "we can try for an eight."

Once I've dropped Fuzz off, I allow myself to explode. With what, I'm not sure—relief, adrenaline, euphoria? SEX! I've just had sex for the first time in three years! I had no idea until Phillip and I got divorced two months ago how much I'd missed it. Not the headlong, passionate sex that miraculously makes babies, or the weary-but-determined sex of the toddler era, not the comfortable, fuzzy sex of the middle years, and certainly not the few-and-far-between forays Phillip and I made into the bedroom toward the end of our marriage because it seemed so sad *not* to. What I've been craving since I became single again is the steamy, raw sex of my youth, the taste of a new mouth, the thrill of an unknown hand on my skin, a tensing thigh bone, the feel of a stranger pushing deep inside me.

I barely notice the roar of my sagging muffler on the way home. It's a warm September night and a cockeyed half moon hovers low. Search lights crisscross the western sky. The smell of burning leaves floats through my open window, but who burns leaves anymore? Didn't they ban that years ago? I sing "Afternoon Delight" off-key all the way down Broadway toward Harvard Square, hitting a glorious run of green lights. As I round the corner onto Yerxa Road in North Cambridge, I wave to my creepy neighbors, Alice and Franklin, who are out walking their dog, Albert the Third, even though it's well after one in the morning. But since the divorce, they no longer wave back, and I could swear Albert the Third has started to growl when I pass by.

Pulling into the driveway of my eggplant-colored house, I feel a rush of affection for Phillip, who gave me the house in the divorce and without a grumble found himself an apartment in East Cambridge. It would have broken my heart to have to leave this place. This is where we raised our twins, Max and El. This, for a quarter of a century, has been home.

The cats are waiting for me at the door.

"Big news, you guys!" I bend down to pet the haughty, long-legged Maude, who backs just out of reach, while Atticus, a handsome Maine Coon, flops down on his back for a belly rub. I look around my ramshackle living room, which I painted chartreuse green a few years ago to the horror of my entire family—at the saggy, wrap-around couch and the big purple armchair, the faded Persian rug, framed artwork done by the twins over the years, a few photographs of Phillip's prize-winning houses, the jade plants in the bay window, a string of hot chili lights, the small black-and-white TV with a fork sticking out of its broken antenna, and a hanging birdcage which has been empty since Tweetie Bird, the parakeet, flew the coop eleven years ago.

I head for the downstairs bathroom mirror to see how the tryst with Fuzz has changed me, expecting some kind of new radiance, a glowing, triumphant serenity. But the only difference—besides my wildly unkempt hair—is a rosy hue which might have been becoming had it not chosen to present itself in ragged patches on my face. I scrunch up my nose. Lookswise, I've never been anything special, but I'm not without a certain *je ne sais quoi.* A guy I once dated in college said I had *allure* and I thought that had a certain ring to it. If I had to pick my best feature, I'd say my hair, though I didn't always appreciate it. Fine, straight hair and pinned-back ears were the norm in my lineage—the true signs of good breeding, my mother claimed. My ears were practically glued to my head, so I passed muster on that front, but my hair was corkscrew curly and grew like ragweed, earning me the horrendous nickname of "Brillo Pad" in my family.

I offer up these frivolous details so you'll begin to understand the world I come from. Four letters of the alphabet pretty much say it all. W-A-S-P. It's an odd and complex species, call it a cult if you will, characterized by an intricate maze of moral, political, and social contradictions. Consider the WASP tenants on beauty. Appearances are important, but not in the way you might think. In my family, pretty was as pretty did. If you'd been born with good looks, it was your obligation to mute them, play them down. My mother always said of me that I looked "just fine," which was alternately mortifying and oddly reassuring. My younger sister, Nell, was often chided for being "a bit too pretty for her own good." To this day, this makes her uneasy. We're both still smarting from a comment a friend made at a party some years ago, that our older brother, Charlie, was the one who got the looks in the family.

Oh well. I peer into the mirror again. A major transformation was maybe too much to hope for. Get a grip, I tell myself, relaxing the muscles in my face. As Popeye would say, and who better to take counsel from, "I yam what I yam."

Maude jumps up onto the bathroom counter and meows. In that meow, I hear the voice of my mother, Celia, and what she's saying is: *What on earth have you done now, Grace?* And in that brief, wet-blanket moment, my euphoria is suddenly gone.

"What *have* I done?" I pose the question to Atticus, who's settled himself belly-up in the bathroom sink. I scratch under his upturned chin, which causes him to start drooling blissfully. My breath hitches as my brain does a complete one-eighty flip. OMG!?!, as the texters would have it. Did I really just have sex in my car with a man I'd met at the bar only an hour before? I remind myself there's a condom wrapped in a Kleenex in my coat pocket to prove it. How could I even have dared? Am I out of my middle-aged mind? Who *am* I anyway?

Here's what I can tell you. I'm Grace Winthrop Hobbes, a name that might bring to mind a crabby, dried-up spinster in a corset and chastity belt, which no doubt could describe any number of my female ancestors down the line. After all, on my family tree hangs not only a healthy smattering of Mercy's and Patience's, but an honest-to-goodness *Submit.* But I assure you, I'm not from that branch of the tree. I lost my virginity when I was fifteen with Crazy Legs Campbell behind the Harvard Stadium, just like in the Van Morrison song. By the age of sixteen, I was on the pill and buying nickel bags of pot in the girls' bathroom at school. I saw the Beatles at the Suffolk

Downs Racetrack and Bob Dylan at the Club 47 in Harvard Square. I was let into a Grateful Dead concert by none other than Jerry Garcia himself, who opened the back stage door and let a stampede of fans in for free. I smoked Camel non-filters and wore miniskirts up to my navel, as my mother liked to say. I roamed the Square barefoot at all hours of the day and night and smoked hash on top of the Lincoln statue in the Cambridge Common during the anti-war demonstrations. Mid-range baby boomer, stubborn rebel to the core, I couldn't possibly have ended up a prude—even with a name like mine.

Now it's 2005 and I'm fifty-three years old. How I got to be this alarming age, I can't possibly imagine. Back in the sixties, we were sure we'd all be dead by now. Miraculously, though, most of us are not only still alive, but kicking. I collapse onto the fluffy, zebra-striped toilet seat cover, overcome by a surge of embarrassment and regret. What on earth was I thinking? What I just did with Fuzz was undignified, beneath me—pathetic, even. People of my "vintage" simply didn't do such things. And what's more, I enjoyed it! *Act your age, not your hat size!*—it's one of my mother's favorite expressions. And maybe she's got a point. Forget about *fifty* being the new *thirty-five*. Fifty's old, sister, no matter how many expensive creams you buy, no matter how many hours you put in at the gym, more than halfway to the grave for most of us—sad but true. Everything starts to stretch and droop and wrinkle and ooze and you get a glimpse of the gruesome way it will all play out in the end. Gravity and time spare no one.

"Aaarrggggghhhhh!"

A startled Maude jumps up onto the windowsill and slides gracefully into a Cleopatra pose, one paw dangling languidly over the edge. "You wouldn't understand," I say, running my hand along the snow-white ridge of her back. "You'll always be beautiful, Maudie."

I decide a post-mortem of the Fuzz debacle with my friend Isabelle is in order. I know she'll still be awake, even at this ungodly hour. She's what I call an insomniac and what she considers someone who just doesn't need much sleep. She was with me at the Wonder Bar earlier tonight, but ducked out just before I met Fuzz. I know I can count on Isabelle, if not for comfort, at least for counsel. Three years ago, she turned forty, just as I was turning fifty. We both met our respective new decades head-on, with a growing terror of inertia and a yearning for a complete life overhaul.

"You did *what*?" For the ever-unflappable Isabelle, this is tantamount to flabbergast. "I leave you alone at the bar and you freaking go and get laid in your car?"

"Well, maybe if you hadn't abandoned me."

"Whoa. Don't try to pin this on me, Gracie. How did you end up in *coitus vehiculus* with a total goddamned stranger?"

"It's not as if I jumped him or anything," I say. "We had a nice conversation, he bought me a glass of wine, he walked me to my car and—"

"Yada, yada, yada," Isabelle says. "Damn. I have to say, Grace, I'm slightly impressed."

"You are?"

"Slightly," she says.

"Am I crazy, Iz? Does this make me, you know, a wanton floozy?"

"Wanton floozy?" Isabelle dissolves into a fit of laughter. "That's hilarious," she says. "You're the one who came of age in the sixties, Gracie. Weren't you guys all screwing like rabbits back in the day?"

"You're right," I say. "Back then, this would've been a drop in the sexual bucket. Another notch on the belt of free love."

"God, we're pathetic," Isabelle says. "We're three minutes into this conversation and we've already flunked the Bechdel test."

"What's the Bechdel test?"

"The premise of two women, with actual names. Talking together for five minutes. Without mentioning a man. Do you know how many frickin' books and movies—not to mention conversations—don't even come close to meeting those criteria?"

"Not many, I'm guessing," I say. "Who made up this test?"

"A cartoonist named Alison Bechdel. She grew up in a family of eccentric undertakers. Virginia Woolf gets credit for the original idea, but Bechdel's the one who ran with it."

"Well, she's right," I say. "We spend way too much time talking about men. Still, you don't think I'm out of my mind?"

Isabelle stifles a yawn. "People have sex, honey," she says. "It's no big whoop."

"No big whoop," I tell Atticus and Maude after hanging up the phone. I dance out of the bathroom feeling vindicated, the cats trailing behind me, with tails held high. Time to stop the guilt-ridden, self-loathing presses. Isabelle's right. Aren't I the one always ranting and raving about the number the culture has done on us older women?—not to buck all responsibility, but please! What chance have we had to age gracefully and with dignity, given the constant media hype around youth, beauty, and physical perfection? Somewhere along the line, I must have unwittingly bought into all that brainwashing. I look down at my two-pack abs and my crooked toes and all around my dark and musty house. And I wonder, whatever became of me, that carefree, bell-bottomed love child of the sixties?

Up in the attic, my keepsake box is calling me. I climb the creaky stairs. It's tucked under the eaves where I stashed it when Phillip and I bought the house back in 1980, an old Victorian that was "charming but needed work." And oh, man, did it ever. Phillip and I were the suckers who fell for all of its lopsided charm. And only half of the work ever really got done.

The box itself is an antique, a Brylcreem carton from the 1950s. It's labeled in black magic marker—GRACIE STUFF. First up is a handwritten list of the WBZ radio countdown of the 100 best songs of 1966. What a motley crop—I'd forgotten: "Hang on Sloopy, #19," "Paperback Writer, #3" "Walk Away Renee, #6" "They're Coming to Take Me Away, Ha Ha,"

#3—more a helium-fueled rant than an actual song. At #2 was the Stones's "Satisfaction," and at the #1 spot sat "Cherish," a syrupy love song oozing over that crusty heap of rock and roll. Talk about contradictions.

Bound in a droopy rubber band are all of my grammar school report cards. I open the one from seventh grade. Worst teacher ever—Miss Clutch. She looked like George Washington and had a verbal tic which involved the random and involuntary insertion of the word "group" into her sentences. We kept a careful tally on our notebook pages. Miss Clutch had it out for me, I swear. I was the first Hobbes ever to disgrace the family by getting Fs (for Fair, as in just barely better than P for poor) in the two main areas of the Comportment Section—Conduct and Self-Control. As punishment, my mother made me read Eleanor Roosevelt's *Book of Common Sense Etiquette* and write an essay on the "The Importance of Civility." And, to add insult to injury, I had to read it out loud at the dinner table.

I hold up a mini skirt I made in home ec class back in the eighth grade. Bright orange cotton with spirals of yellow dots, it couldn't measure more than ten by fourteen inches. *More cotton in the top of an aspirin bottle,* as the saying used to go. I could no more fit into this bizarre-looking article of clothing now than I could a pair of washcloths. I made the skirt from a piece of Marimekko fabric that I bought at Design Research back in the sixties in Harvard Square. The material was fifty-six inches wide, so in those days, one yard was enough to make two skirts.

I pick up my rare English copy of *Yesterday and Today,* with the Beatles dressed in butcher smocks amidst all the raw meat and gory doll appendages on the album cover. It's probably worth a fortune now. There's a pair of brown corduroy hip hugger bell bottoms I got in Greenwich Village on a family trip in 1968, worn threadbare at the thighs and ragged at the hems. And there's Al Pacino's autograph on a parking stub, which I got when we ran into him on MacDougal Street, a shaggy, dark-eyed troll holding hands with a six-foot blond.

Rummaging further, my hand unearths something soft and

white—my high school boyfriend's T-shirt that I held captive after we had sex one hot summer night. He regularly snuck up to my third-floor bedroom to ravage me, with my parents sleeping right below. Talk about *laissez-faire* parenting! It's amazing what we got away with in those days. If either of the twins ever tried a stunt like that, I'd be furious. I hold the shirt up to my face—it used to smell sweet and sexy, like my boyfriend, Floyd, but now it smells mostly like mold.

In the bottom corner of the box is something black and furry. At first, I think it's some attic creature that's crept into the box to roost or die. I jab at it with the Red Sox backscratcher I've also unearthed. Thankfully, it doesn't move. Dusting it off, I realize it's my brother Charlie's Beatle wig, which he pestered my mother to get at the Porter Square Star Market with S&H Green Stamps back in 1964. I slap the wig on my head and glance at myself in a tarnished mirror leaning up against the wall. Good gawd. I look like Mo of the Three Stooges in drag.

Wearing the mini skirt around one arm, I take out the last item in the box, a piece of paper folded up into a square wad and bound in ancient scotch tape. I remember right away what it is—a list I made after a fight with my mother one Christmas morning when I was eleven. Celia was insisting that Nell and I wear these hideous twin velvet sailor dresses with red bow ties for the family dinner. I vowed that day to be the opposite of my mother when I grew up, sure that someday, this would be my best revenge.

Peeling off the crackling yellow tape, which has long since lost any properties of adhesion, I smooth out the creased, lined paper.

READ IN THE YEAR 2000, it says, in jagged black letters at the top of the page. IF YOU ARE STILL ALIVE!

Things I Will Never Do When I'm a Grown-up

- *Straighten my hair even though Mother hates it.*
- *Let a boy kiss me unless I want to. Tyler Graham tried in the third grade and it was gross.*

- *Burn the bacon.*
- *Make my kids wear clothes they hate. (underlined in faded red)*
- *Tell my kids over and over again that hate is a very strong word. (We get it, already!)*
- *Or that they can't say "ain't." (It's in the dictionary.)*
- *Tell my kids they can't get a fish tank. (Even if they promise to keep it clean!)*
- *Wear a girdle or a garter belt. (Disgusting.)*
- *Tell my kids they can't believe in Santa Claus. (It's their right!)*
- *CHANGE MY MIND THAT GEORGE IS MY FAVORITE BEATLE!!!!*
- *Signed, (in my best Palmer cursive): Grace Winthrop Hobbes*

On the way back downstairs, the Beatles wig still perched on my head and the mini-skirt encircling one arm, I pass a descending row of photos of the twins on the wall. Both are seniors in college now. Our daughter Max, short for Maxine, is studying painting and sculpture at the Museum School in Boston. Eliot, long ago shortened to El, is a dance major up at Bennington College in Vermont. It's no surprise that Phillip and I spawned no stockbrokers or computer geniuses. He's an architect and I'm a writer, so the artist genes run deep. I stop before a picture of the twins building a two-headed snowman in the backyard at the age of six or seven, snow-suited, with mittens dangling on strings, cheeks flushed with cold, white gap teeth gleaming. My heart wobbles, remembering those happy, uncomplicated days.

As I make my way down the stairs, the kids grow older in each photograph—El mid-leap at a ballet recital, looking for all the world like a young Nureyev, Max dressed up like Groucho Marx for a school play, with a magic-marker mustache and bubble gum cigar hanging out of the corner of her mouth. At the bottom of the stairs is a photo of the twins hamming it up in caps and gowns, giving each other rabbit ears after their high school graduation.

Gazing now at the image of my almost-grown children, I mentally go through the points on my folded list, to see how

I'd rate as a grown-up and parent according to my eleven-year-old criteria. Well, I did pretty well with the Santa Claus situation: the twins were believers until the age of seven, when their grandmother Celia told them it was utter nonsense—the notion of a fat bearded man sliding down a dirty chimney was ludicrous enough, let alone with a sack full of gifts. And of course reindeer really didn't know how to fly. Let's see. I've never straightened my hair, even though my mother still can't stand it. Check. On the burned bacon front (not to mention the "hate is a very strong word" issue), there's no doubt I could've done better. But on the other hand, I never did let a boy kiss me unless I wanted him to after Tyler Graham chased me down in the schoolyard in third grade. And although it makes me crazy, I try extremely hard to refrain from correcting my children's grammar.

Settling into the purple armchair in the living room with a cup of ginger tea, I'm pleasantly aware of a pulsing sensation deep inside me, that rhythmic after-sex thump I haven't felt in so long. I remember how Fuzz lowered the front seat with a jolt and the tingling that began in my toes and made its way up my legs as he ran his hand low over my stomach. I feel the push of his warm body against mine and the sweaty soft bristle of hair at the nape of his neck as I peeled off his shirt. I feel his silky shaft getting hard against my thigh and the shift to find my center. And I remember how cool the windshield felt against the soles of my feet when he found it and I pressed hard. I remember how his head lifted up when he came. And how good that made me feel. How powerful. I don't know if the sex really did deserve a solid seven rating, but it sure did feel great.

My eyes make a sweep of the living room. At that moment, every object looks sacred and beautiful, for what it has been through, for what it has meant in the grand and sloppy scheme of things. I look up at the skylight we put in over the front hall table, and there it still is, that silver, cockeyed moon. I see the wobbly cat-food bowls Max made in her third-grade ceramics class, filled with bits of crusted salmon. I've never noticed how *big* this room is. Phillip and I filled it up so quickly, first with furniture and plants, and then baby toys and books and gadgets and sports gear. So much *stuff.* Now, with the twins away at college and Phillip moved out, I realize how much space I have. And it's mine. All that glorious room. All that freedom. To move, to breathe, to sit, to do absolutely nothing at all!

And with that rush of exhilaration comes a feeling of sheer terror that rocks me to my very core, the isolation that may one day be the tradeoff for divorce, the deep love I have for my children and what Phillip and I once had. The loss of the past and all that didn't go right and what couldn't be fixed, no matter how hard we tried. How we've fought and hugged and kicked and howled. But how, ultimately, we've survived. It's the first time it's ever occurred to me that freedom might be lonely.

Nevertheless, starting tonight, a new era has begun. I've been divorced for two months and I finally got up the nerve to go out on the town. I ended up having sex and though I may need some time to actually convince myself it's true, there's no reason not to celebrate that. No way Fuzz is sitting around feeling embarrassed or regretful. He'll no doubt be congratulated by his buddies on having "scored" on the first try, slapped on the back, punched in the arm, with an added, "You sly dog, you!" Well, slap me on the back and punch me in the arm too. Just not too hard. I bruise easily. Time to break the old double standard.

I'm fifty-three years old and I'm as free as Tweetie Bird, the parakeet, who took flight all those years ago and left the twins in mourning for weeks. It's not how I imagined my life would be at this point, but here I am. My kids are launched, my ex and I are on good terms, and I'm all alone in this big, empty house. I can let the dishes pile up and the dust balls grow big as grapefruits, sleep until noon if I want to, eat frosted Pop-Tarts for breakfast, lunch, and dinner, watch midnight movie marathons in my underwear. I can dance naked in front of the mirror, sing out of tune to my favorite songs at the top of my lungs. I can go to three movies in a row, or out to a show or a bar or walk on the riverbank at dawn. And I can have sex! With whomever I please.

Adjusting Charlie's Beatle wig on my head, I put *Meet the Beatles* on my old KLH stereo. The warped black disc wobbles round and round. Picking off a thick ball of dust, I place the needle on the shiny black line of the second song, "I Saw Her Standing There." Paul kicks it off with a countdown: *"One, two three, four!"* At that moment, 1964 doesn't feel like all that long ago—sitting on the sunporch on top of Avon Hill with Charlie and Nell, with a can of Fresca and a bag of Frito Lays, while our parents bickered down below, watching those four lads from Liverpool take the stage on the *Ed Sullivan Show* with their mop-top haircuts, in their natty suits and ties.

Ringo pounded away on the drums, shaking his shaggy head back and forth with a snaggle-toothed grin. Paul did his heartthrob thing, cocking his pretty head while his left hand strummed all those major chords, the girls in the audience screaming and crying, some even fainting. John stood tall and cocky, his face letting go the occasional smirk. His voice always held the edge.

I dance to "Hold Me Tight," "All My Loving," "Not a Second Time." I can identify each song after just one note; I know every single word. I dance all of the old dances—the Frug, the Pony, the Hitchhike and the hold-your-nose Swim, which then morphs into a frenzied Twist. Maude settles on the couch and turns her back on me, licks one slender, outstretched leg.

At fifty-three, I'm setting out to rediscover my bold, free-spirited sixties self, the one that somewhere along the line fell prey to the culture's vulture-like gender mandates. Time to find my way back to my inner, liberated self. After all, I was the one who seduced Crazy Legs Campbell behind the Stadium that night in 1968. He never would've had the nerve. And if I hadn't floated Fuzz that dazzling smile tonight at the bar, he never would have come over and sat down next to me. They don't call us the baby boomers for nothing. Come and get me, old age. I won't go gently into your dark night. Case in point.

It's way past my bedtime and I've just had sex in my car with a handsome, peach fuzz-covered stranger.

And one last thing. I never did waver from my vow that George was my favorite Beatle, even though in my heart of hearts, I knew it was Paul.

2

And so my life as a carefree divorcee has started off with a resounding bang—well, more accurately, a walloping crack. An empty house, a new outlook on life, and spontaneous, responsible sex on my first night out on the town. I'd be a complete idiot, not to mention a colossal hypocrite, to have anything but safe sex. Besides the obvious issues of STDs and sexual responsibility (which I've preached mercilessly to the twins), this is no time to make the front page of the *National Enquirer*—"Ancient hippie mom gives birth to Brillo Pad mutant." At fifty-three, when most women are done with "all that," I'm the lucky one who still gets the occasional unannounced, raging period.

I drive around the next day, admiring my shattered windshield and replaying the night's encounter. It must have been some sort of divine intervention, Fuzz appearing like that out of the blue. The evening began with hardly a whimper. I coaxed Isabelle out to the bar, not for companionship, so much, as courage. By nature, she's a bit of a recluse—and I try to respect that. Isabelle's single and likes it that way. "Let the biological clock tick on," has long been her dating mantra. A rare book librarian at Harvard, she's recently decided to try her hand at being an internet auteur, starting a blog for women over forty called *Squiggle Z*. Squiggle Z is the computer command that negates the last one made, a metaphor, I suppose, for second chances—taking back ourselves, from failed marriages, grown children, our hang-ups, obsessions, our ruts and rules. *Squiggle Z*. I think it's brilliant.

To save money, Isabelle recently moved in with her mother, who is, to put it mildly, a piece of work. Molly "Blow Torch" Murphy was a roller derby queen in the sixties and got pregnant with Isabelle when she was eighteen. Isabelle was raised for the most part by her grandparents in Medford and has never met her father. Molly claims not even to know who he is. She ran hard and fast in those days, she says matter-of-factly.

Somehow, this rather blunt explanation of Isabelle's conception has been easier for her to live with than there being an actual person out there she might have to reckon with some day, hunt down or care about or blame. Whoever this rogue man was gave her the gifts of mystery and dark beauty, the opposite of Molly—a short and brassy Irish blond. Isabelle's worked hard to cultivate an image of cool and calm. She has a graduate degree from Wellesley in the Classics and is one of the smartest people I know. The only thing that gives her away is her relentlessly foul mouth. She unapologetically spews forth the F and the B and the A bombs and all the others, liberally scattering profanities throughout her otherwise sophisticated vocabulary. It's effin' this and gd that. And bs to that mf. What an a-hole! I've gotten used to Isabelle's swearing over the years, but it throws most people for a loop—and she gets a kick out of that. Deep down, she's a Medford girl. Through and through. And she never wants you to forget it.

So I took full advantage of Isabelle's frazzled state last night, luring her out of the house with the offer of free drinks and an evening away from mother fatigue, a condition with which I'm all too familiar. We met at the Wonder Bar at eight o'clock, one of several neighborhood joints on Mass. Ave., in between Harvard and Porter Squares. It's been a restaurant-slash-bar for as long as I can remember—a wood-boothed Brigham's back in the late fifties, a Greek restaurant when I was a kid, a mediocre Italian joint in the seventies, Nick's Beef and Beer House in the late eighties (Ick's Eef and Bee Ho at the end of its reign, after certain of the neon lights on its sign went out and were never replaced). I know all this because I'm something of a local fossil, having lived in the same neighborhood my entire life. 02138. Most opinionated zip code on the planet, a local T-shirt reads. Can't say I disagree.

We ushered a trail of warm air into the air-conditioned bar. Isabelle was dressed casually, conservative chic, I guess you'd call it, in a grey V-neck sweater and black blazer, beige linen pants, the kind that only work on someone with her willowy build. Her straight black hair is cut at a slant just above the shoulder, with wispy bangs and stylish streaks of natural silver. Isabelle always looks neat and unflustered, well put together. Whereas I, in my red-and-black-striped boatneck shirt and dangly silver earrings, black jean skirt washed grey, unruly dark curls and no make-up, along with a pair of maroon faux snakeskin ankle boots from my admittedly unconventional collection of shoes, often feel like a fashion disaster. "Grace bears an uncanny resemblance to an unmade bed," my mother likes to say. This is supposed to be a joke.

We took two empty seats at the bar. Isabelle's neighbor was an older man, actually, on second glance, probably not much older than I was. He was nice-looking, compact, grey-haired with a handlebar mustache, wearing a tweedy jacket but no tie. On my left was a younger guy, with a cheerful round face and a buzz cut, busily scribbling on a bar napkin, nursing a foamy beer.

"How's your mother?" I ordered Isabelle a mojito. A cabernet for me.

"Certifiably nuts," Isabelle said. "She makes the Energizer Bunny look like a goddamned slug. I guess there's no second act after being on the derby circuit. She's tried it all—bowling, photography, Scrabble, pottery, laser tag. Everything's boring, she says. If her knees hadn't given out, I swear she'd still be out there ripping up the track and crashing into the boards. Last night she made me play air hockey for two frickin' hours. My wrists are killing me."

"Air hockey?"

"Never mind," Isabelle said. "So what's this sudden fascination with bar life, Grace?"

"It's not so sudden." I took a sip of my wine. "Phillip and I started going out at night after the twins left for college. He reignited his old love affair with Manhattans and I got to know my red wines. Any excuse not to stay home alone together. It was the beginning of the end, I suppose, even though we didn't know it then."

"And now?" Isabelle said.

"I like bars," I said. "It's free theater. Look at that guy over there with the combover. How long do you think it took him to get it just right?" I rested my chin on my hand. "It's kind of sad, isn't it? He hopes no one will notice but of course everyone does."

"Fascinating," Isabelle said. "Although for my money, his friend's rack of man boobs is way more impressive. That guy should either get his ass to the gym or buy himself a bra. Have a little frickin' self-respect, dude."

"Don't be mean," I said. "He's probably depressed."

"Well, he should get over it," Isabelle said. "Doesn't he know about all the starving children in the world? They've got *real* problems."

The more I looked at the combover guy, the more I saw the good effort he'd tried to make. "It really doesn't look that bad," I said.

"It looks like frickin' roadkill," Isabelle said.

"Listen to Valley Gal Sal over there at the end of the bar," I said. "She must've said *like* ten times in the last two minutes. It drives me crazy. Makes me long for the good old days of *um*."

"Even Terri Gross says *like*," Isabelle said. "Get over it."

"Well, I'm having, like, a mid-life crisis. Men are allowed to have them. So, like, why can't I? Like?"

"You can have one," Isabelle said. "But why would you frickin' want one?"

"I refuse to turn into some dried-up spinster who does word search puzzles and sucks on lemon drops all day." I sat up straight out of a slouch. "I just read about this woman whose skin started to fuse to her leather recliner because she was such a couch potato," I said.

"I doubt that will be your fate," Isabelle said.

"I like being out here where all the action is, the human drama," I said. "It's comforting somehow. You get to be part of the play."

"What play?" Isabelle scoffed.

"The neighborhood play. The play of life. Makes me feel like we're all in this together."

"The play of life?" Isabelle said sarcastically. "Really, Grace?"

"And when the music's good, it's even better. I've always wanted to have a corny soundtrack to my life," I say. "And even though I'm not necessarily looking for another guy, I'm not necessarily *not* looking either."

"But why would you look in a bar?" The last word dripped with disdain.

"Bars are melting pots," I said. "Level meeting grounds."

"If you say so." I noticed she was scrutinizing my face.

"What?" My hand sprang up to my mouth. "Do I have something in my teeth?"

"You need something," Isabelle said.

"What? What do I need?"

"Lipstick." She started rummaging in her purse. "It'll give your face a lift."

"My face needs a lift?" I pushed up my cheeks with my hands, then let them fall.

"Go," Isabelle said, smacking the lipstick into my open palm.

I went to the restroom to put on some of Isabelle's brick red lipstick. A no-makeup child of the sixties, I made a mess of it and had to do it over three times. And honestly, rather than giving my pale face a lift, I thought the lipstick kind of did it in. But I had to trust Isabelle on these matters. She was way more experienced than I was at being a girl. Celia had never gone in for all that feminine "nonsense"—makeup, shaving, plucking, primping. In the beauty department, Nell and I had had to fend for ourselves.

When I got back to the bar, Isabelle was deep in conversation with her tweedy neighbor. I looked over at her wistfully, so at ease with herself, so relaxed. People listened to Isabelle. She commanded attention, and got it. This is me, her regal bearing said. Like it or lump it. I, on the other hand, after years of ably navigating the social whirl as mother and wife, suddenly find myself with woefully inadequate social skills. I think it has something to do with coming of age in the sixties. As part of the stoned, roving masses, we never really learned how to be ourselves. Those who were born in the sixties, like Isabelle, are the ones who are really in charge.

The young guy next to me was still scribbling away on his bar napkin.

"What're you working on?" I said.

"Boston," he said. "*Did not sob.*"

"I'm sorry?" He was sporting a "Strawberry Alarm Clock" T-shirt and I gave him credit for that.

"It's perfect. So simple," he said. I noticed a slight Southern drawl. "I mean obviously, Boston backwards is *not sob*. You add the *did*, which is a palindrome itself. And presto, you've got the headline after the Sox finally won the World Series last year. 'Boston Did Not Sob!'"

"Oh, palindromes." I finally got it. "Like 'able was I…'" I spun my hand around, trying to conjure up the rest.

"*'Ere I saw Elba*," he said. "That was Napoleon's story after he got too big for his britches."

"*A man, a plan, a canal…*" I thought of another.

"Yeah, Panama," he said. "Those are the palindromes everyone knows. But there're so many better ones." He slid into a pirate voice. "*Murder for a jar of red rum*. Or…" He put his fingers to his chin. "*Do geese see God?* And then there's the all-time classic…" He finished writing with a flourish. "*Sit on a potato pan, Otis.*"

"That is a good one," I said.

Isabelle tapped me on the shoulder. "I'm heading out," she said.

"What do you mean?" I looked at my watch. "We just got here."

"I asked the mustachioed fellow if he'd like to go get a cup of coffee. He's kind of interesting. And the mojito's way too frickin' sweet."

"You're leaving me for the walrus guy?" I looked over at him paying his check. "Just like that?"

"Just like that," Isabelle said, slipping a ten-spot under her glass.

It was after Isabelle left that I first noticed Fuzz farther down the bar. He was almost too good to be true, sitting there alone, rakishly handsome in a crisp lavender button-down shirt, casual in a masculine way, and as far as I could tell unattached—no wedding band, no anxious glances at the door, no manic finger-play with his cell phone. Furthermore, and this was key—I figured he probably wasn't much younger than I was.

I caught his eye and smiled. He picked up his drink and came on over.

"Mind if I join you?" A sprig of reddish-blond hair sprang up out of his shirt, the same fuzz that covered most of his head. In contrast, his cool grey-blue eyes were disarming.

"Sure," I said. "What brings you out on this warm night?"

"Boredom," he said.

"Are things starting to look up?"

"They are now." His voice was so flat, it took me a second to realize he was throwing me a compliment.

"What line of work are you in?" If I knew one thing about men, it was that they liked to explain exactly what it was that they *did.* And Fuzz was no exception.

"I'm an international freelance marketing analyst," he said. "Which basically means I help global economies get their shit together."

"I always wondered who did that," I said.

He launched into an in-depth description of his job, something where the words *Market* and *Consulting* and *Research* cropped up often, and also *Green.* All initial caps, very PC. He traveled a lot, to Asia and Buenos Aires and various of the California "San's," sometimes just for a few days. From what I could gather, he was always needed somewhere more urgently than where he'd just been before.

"What about family?" I asked him.

"What about it?" he said, rather confrontationally, I thought.

"Do you have one?"

He gave me a withering look. "Is the pope Catholic?" he said.

"Unless he's keeping something from us." I took a sip of my wine. "I shudder to think what the old geezer's really up to over there in that creepy old Vatican."

He laughed. "Touché," he said.

I cringed. Did people actually say that in casual conversation and not just laugh-track sitcoms?

While Fuzz talked, I looked him over. Slender and fit, he leaned in close and I liked that. And I've always been a sucker for a man fresh out of the shower, still smelling of shaving cream and soap. Fuzz was recently divorced, he told me, no kids. He had adult onset ADD, and tapped his foot incessantly on the rim of the barstool, as if to prove it. "I'm one of five boys," he said. "The oldest. The overachiever. I'm the one who always had to fall on his sword."

"Ouch!" I said. "Wow, five boys! Your mother must have been—"

"Outnumbered," he said, and then, as if this was the last piece of personal information he was willing to divulge, he announced, "We come from a long line of Philadelphians."

"Philadelphians. Mmm…" I didn't know much about this town, but somehow this helped to account for this character trait in him—stuffy, though not in a Republican way.

"But enough about me," he said finally, but not with much conviction.

I started in on the more salient points of the life and times of Grace Winthrop Hobbes, beginning with the fact that I was a published writer. But before I'd even gotten a chance to brag about my children, Fuzz yawned.

"Bored again?" I said.

"Sorry," he said. "I just got in from Seoul. The jet lag's killing me. I'm wearing myself ragged. I've got insomnia and carpal tunnel syndrome. It's all starting to get to me." It was becoming clear that most of Fuzz's sentences were rife with first person pronouns.

Somehow, none of this boded too well. The guy was clearly full of himself. But hey, I reminded myself, this wasn't the old days of courtship—plotting, pining, praying. This was the here and now. The present. A man and a woman sitting next to each other at the bar. No spring chickens. No pretenses. Fuzz pepped up a bit when I told him I thought it was cool he was wearing a purple shirt, that it took guts for a guy and he looked terrific in it. He bought me another glass of wine and when his hand brushed my arm, I felt a jolt in my stomach. We looked each other straight in the eye. I'd read somewhere that a locked gaze between two people lasting longer than six seconds could only mean one of two things to follow—sex or murder.

We both knew what we were there for.

Turns out the broken windshield is covered by insurance. A repairman comes over a few days later to replace it. I meet him out on the street. *Mike,* the patch on his blue jacket reads.

"Wow. This is a doozy!" He lets loose a long, admiring whistle. Secretly, I'm pleased. Clearly, my crack is no ordinary, run-of-the-mill crack. My crack has made this guy's day. "We can usually identify the point of impact," he says, examining the damage. "But this baby's all over the place. Yowza!" He looks up at me, as if I can provide the answers to life's deepest mysteries. "How the heck did this happen, lady?"

"No idea," I say. Among other new personality traits I seem to have acquired lately is that of a bold-faced liar.

As Mike drives away in his truck, I'm almost sorry to have gotten the windshield fixed so quickly. I would've liked to gaze upon it for a while longer, as I drove around town, a testament to my rejuvenated womanhood, my unabashed and unassailable sexuality, a huntress hanging onto the gizzard of her prey, not for a late-night snack or anything twisted like that, but just for proof, you know, for show.

When I go back into the house, there's a message on my voicemail.

"Hi, Grace. Saturday won't work after all." Fuzz's voice is hard to read, level and calm. "Give me a call and I'll explain."

I catch him on his way home from work. "What's up?" I say.

"I wasn't quite straight with you the other night," he says. "There's this other woman—"

"Of course there is." I curse myself for the tug in my gut, for my sarcastic, defensive response. We're nothing to each other, Fuzz and I. A half hour of middle-aged hanky-panky in my car and already jealousy dared to rear its ridiculous head? Wasn't this supposed to be the beauty of older age romance—no strings attached, no hurt feelings, *que sera*? At my age, this should all be a piece of emotional cake.

"Go on," I say evenly.

"I've been trying to break up with her for some time now," Fuzz says.

"And did our little rendezvous in the car help or hurt the cause?" Sarcasm has always been my first line of defense.

"I've decided to give it one more try," he says. "But if it doesn't work out…"

I can't believe what I'm hearing. Some day down the line, Fuzz is essentially telling me, I may come up for readmission in his elite, selective school of L-U-V. Did I not perform well enough at my sexual "interview"? Score too low on perky breasts and six-pack abs? And what was all that BS about the angle of the dashboard and the seven rating for first-time sex?

"The sex was awesome, though," he says. "So maybe someday…"

"You can take me off your waiting list, buster." I somehow rally to have the last word, to at least pretend I have some dignity left. My clam phone shuts with a loud clap and I toss it onto the kitchen table, but it misses and clatters onto the floor. I get down on my knees to retrieve it and bump my head on the underside of the table on the way up. Noticing the cobwebs growing under the kitchen chairs, I feel the burn of approaching tears. His loss, I tell myself as I get back on my feet, furiously wiping my eyes with my shirt. In a few years, he probably won't have any hair left at all. And could he have been any more full of himself? Anyway, I reason, as I swat away the cobwebs with a dish towel, no way I ever could've gotten involved with a grown man who says "awesome."

Back to the bathroom mirror and scornful misery. I scrunch up my face, accentuating all of my wrinkles and age spots. And this time, it's a witchy hag out of an old Disney flick staring back at me. Crow's feet and worry lines. Saggy neck and frizzled hair. Even my nose looks as if it's suddenly grown pointy and crooked. And that may not actually be a wart on my chin, but it's definitely some kind of horrible old-age blemish.

Who but a woman on my side of the great half-century divide can understand this sense of urgency, this clarity of purpose? One thing I'm not willing to do at this point, is wait. At my age, and after such a long, dry spell, I've got no time to, well, screw around. I have friends who've given up on sex altogether, one claiming to prefer an evening with a bag of chocolates and a ceiling fan to a night of passionate romance and this terrifies me. How much longer will I be immune to Mother Nature's eventual betrayal?

I feel the grip of a panic attack take hold, the first tightening flutter in my chest. Was that one romp with Fuzz in my car just a fluke, no more than beginner's luck? Will all the men I meet from hereon in be at least halfway bald and dangling two women, maybe more? My preferred remedy for panic is Brigham's vanilla ice cream. I keep a ready supply in the freezer. Not French vanilla, no fancy variations; don't try and woo me with cookies and cream. It's another Hobbes family tendency, common to the WASP species. When we like something, we cling to it relentlessly. Phillip called it the "beat-it-to-death syndrome."

"Vanilla's not even a real flavor," he'd grumble. "Live dangerously, for cripe's sake, Grace. Try a freaking chocolate ripple or a pecan swirl." I can understand. He's one of seven kids in a raucous, opinionated, and always-hungry Italian family. In the Chicarelli household, whatever was put in front of you—you ate.

But I'm not with Phillip anymore. I can eat plain old vanilla ice cream until I'm blue in the face, without criticism, without derision. I plunk myself down in the purple armchair. For a while, watching Perry Mason re-runs, I'm comforted. Perry's deep, rumbling voice soothes me and I marvel at the workings of his steel-trap mind. Della Street is saucy, loyal, and smart as a whip—not to mention a snappy dresser. With these two in charge and a quart of ice cream at the ready, all is right with the world for a while.

But as darkness falls, the demons of the id come at me again with tiny stinging arrows of doubt and self-recrimination. *You should do things the proper way!* I hear my mother's voice haranguing me. I know very well why I don't. Because I hate both of those terms—proper and should—cornerstone words in the WASP Behavioral Manifesto. I made my peace with what happened in the car that night with Fuzz. As Isabelle said so eloquently, it was no big whoop. So why, now that he's dumped me, do I feel so vulnerable and inadequate? Why, all of a sudden, do I feel so ugly? My ire builds with each spoonful of ice cream and I eat until the carton's empty, refusing to look at the calorie count on the back, which is based on one five-ounce serving. So what. Who's counting? I've had six.

"The Case of the Terrified Typist" begins uncharacteristically—in the courtroom. Perry's client sits next to him on the bench, fidgeting, sweating bullets, waiting for the jury to file back in. She wrings her hands nervously, blouse all askew, but we all know that's just for show. The jury foreman rises with verdict in hand.

"We find the defendant—guilty!" he says. There's a horrified, collective gasp in the courtroom. Pandemonium ensues. The defendant's mother faints and the press storm the door, flashbulbs popping. Perry Mason has lost his first case! Della is dumbstruck. Even Hamilton Burger's too stunned to realize he's finally outwitted his nemesis.

Still, Perry leaves the courtroom with his head held high, vowing to clear his client's good name in due time. And suddenly I get it. In the end, it's about strength of character. If Perry can handle the tough days, so can I. He has faith in himself and never gives up. I'm better than these feelings I'm having. And stronger. I get up off the couch and do fifty jumping jacks, then twenty cheaty push-ups on the floor. And it's amazing how, from the throes of rejection and self-pity, the juices of self-preservation start to flow. After the quart of ice cream settles, the sting of Fuzz's rejection starts to ease. Isabelle calls and I fill her in on the latest.

"Can you believe this guy?" I do my best dry, boring nerd impression. "'But if it doesn't work out, Grace—'"

"Forget about that a-hole," Isabelle says. "In the end, he'll just be a tiny blip on the big screen of your life. Just think of him as the first freaking house."

"Which first freaking house?"

"You know how when you're house hunting, or looking at apartments? You fall in love with the first one you see; you absolutely have to have it. But then someone else comes along and makes a better offer or you find out the foundation's being devoured by a bunch of goddamned termites."

"Termites?" I say.

"That's right, termites!" Isabelle crunches celery on the other end of the phone—the only food you actually burn calories while eating, she claims. She goes on. "At first you're devastated, right? But after you start looking again, you begin to see all of the first house's drawbacks and flaws. And in retrospect, you're glad you saved your ass, that you didn't jump on the first piece of crap you saw."

"Good point," I say.

I decide to try and see things Isabelle's way. Fuzz is that first house and this other woman, whoever she is, is clearly one of the termites.

Which reminds me of a good joke…

A termite walks into a bar and says, "Is the bar tender here?" Practice this one carefully. As with romance, timing and inflection are key.

3

We should probably get it out of the way now, the rest of Grace Winthrop Hobbes in a nutshell. It pretty much boils down to this. Other than producing two great kids and writing a book about mushrooms called *Mycological Myths and Mysteries*, I've turned out to be quite unspectacular. I was the moody rebel in a family teeming with overzealous lawyers and dedicated teachers, all leaning toward sainthood. My brother Charlie is a senior partner in a downtown law firm and my sister Nell teaches fifth grade in a charter school in Mattapan. And then there's me, the middle child.

I was born in 1953, one of the charmed Eisenhower babies, into the sunny, post-war era of gung-ho optimism and ignorant social bliss—TV dinners and moon rockets red glare, mothers in maroon lipstick and belted seersucker dresses, squeaky clean dooby-doo-wah music and neatly mowed lawns. Nine years later, the Cuban Missile Crisis paralyzed the nation and then JFK was assassinated in 1963. I got my period two years later in the seventh grade, after which, as my father often lamented, everything started to go to hell in a hand basket.

Considered possibly brilliant as a child, I skipped the fourth grade, where, my third-grade teacher told my mother, I would simply be wasting my time. On the first day of fifth grade, one of the boys in my class—a certain bulldog-faced Curtis Hannigan—gestured to a book on his desk he claimed he was reading, *The Ugly American*, and then pointed straight at me. At ten, a scrawny upstart with messy braids in a moth-eaten Scottish kilt and a Red Sox cap, thrown into a pit of surly fifth-grade toughs, I was promptly put in my place.

I managed to hold my own in the fifth grade. But after that, I failed increasingly each year to live up to earlier great academic expectations. An inadequate number of genius-questing genes in my DNA, I've always maintained. And whose fault was that, I pointed out to my parents. Certainly not mine. A promising career in music went down the tubes when I was rude to my violin teacher, who didn't appreciate my "reworking" of yet another boring Bartok etude. I'd put a kind of salsa-y spin on it, *cha-cha-cha* style. "It sounds way better like this," I told her. Madame Van der Snitten "suggested" to my mother that I might prefer to play another instrument. I believe she recommended the oboe.

By age twelve, my elegant Palmer-style cursive penmanship, once passed around the class to be admired, had disintegrated into an illegible scrawl. I might have had a shot at the visual arts, but a dominant anal WASP gene killed all that. Sure, I could've been a stellar pupil at one of those matchbook schools of art, painting sunsets by number or Elvis portraits on velvet, but as for any real artistic talent? Zilch. Schoolwork wasn't much of a challenge, but I was lazy and chose to "get by" rather than excel, this perhaps the least forgivable crime in my over-achieving family—the plodding, uninspired pursuit of mediocrity.

Still, I managed to get into a college that didn't embarrass my family. Back in those days, the early seventies, it wasn't that hard. Majoring in English Lit, I read my way through those blissful four years, burrowed away in a bucolic little town in upstate New York, living on Lipton instant chicken noodle soup and gourmet jelly beans, dreading the day I'd have to go out into the world and put my expensive college education to work. At twenty-one, I emerged from the dank cocoon of nineteenth-century England, where I'd been dwelling contentedly with the likes of Heathcliff and Tess and Mr. Darcy and Emma. Ten pounds heavier and with only a piece of paper in my hand to show for it all, I had to come to terms with the possibility that the third grade might have been as good as it was ever going to get.

After college, I wrote a few articles for a local newspaper and then did a stint with the *Boston Globe* "obits," which was, well—there's no other word for it—deadly. In the late seventies,

I discovered there was money to be made in technical writing, which I could do at home on my self-correcting IBM Selectric II typewriter. Then along came computers and the tech world exploded. The work load tripled and I made good money. Phillip and I got married in 1978. We tried forever to get pregnant, six years before the twins were miraculously conceived. Just after we'd finally given up on having a family.

Then there's the mushroom book, *Mycological Myths and Mysteries*. I wrote it seven years ago. The twins were in middle school by then and I had more time on my hands. An editor I'd worked for occasionally recommended me to a photographer named Olga Sanoff. Her Russian grandmother had taught her everything she knew about fungi, and over the years, she'd taken hundreds of gorgeous color close-ups of every conceivable species of mushroom, from various angles and in different lights. Olga called to say she couldn't write her way out of a paper bag and was looking for someone who saw the exotic beauty of the fungi and could write about them in a vivid, original way. I spent one evening pouring over Olga's photographs. When we met, I threw out adjectives as she held up different images—"pouty," "intrepid," "stealthy," "smug"—and we made a connection. It was no lie when I told Olga that as a child, when other kids compared themselves to animals—chipmunks or panthers or deer—I'd often thought of myself as a toadstool.

The mushroom book reminds me that there's one last backpedal we have to make—to the divorce—and what set it all in motion. We can almost laugh about that day now—"Whack Sunday," as it's come to be referred to in our family. All of us, that is, except our daughter Max, who walked in on the tail-end of the scene. It was early last May and she'd come home for the weekend from her apartment in Allston, sick of her messy college roommates and craving some home-cooked meals. On Saturday, she and I watched Marx Brothers movies on DVD and ate our way through a batch of homemade chocolate chip cookies. Phillip made his famous chicken cacciatore for dinner and the three of us played Hearts into the wee hours.

Sunday was cold and gloomy, with a forecast of freezing rain. Phillip was watching the Red Sox lose to the Yankees on TV, which meant he'd be in a bad mood for the rest of the day. Max was doing laundry and talking non-stop on her new cell phone. I hadn't seen El since the winter holidays. The good news was that he loved college; the bad news was that he hardly ever came home. I had a salt and sugar hangover and was in a rotten mood.

In the afternoon, I walked into the Square to see a Russian movie at the Brattle Theater, *Oblomov,* the story of a wealthy and indolent man who lived in St. Petersburg with his grumpy, inept servant, Zakhar, and spent the lion's share of his life in bed. Overcome by the futility of modern endeavor, he retreated into the safety and comfort of childhood memories on his parents' idyllic estate. It was a concept I was seriously considering as I walked home from the movie theater that dreary day, climbing into bed and not getting up until the crocuses finally found the courage to poke their heads out of the ground. I'd been down in the dumps for months.

I must have been just rounding the corner onto Yerxa Road when it actually happened, but by the time our house came into view, all I saw was Max slamming the front door behind her and storming down the walkway barefoot in her running clothes. Her long brown hair swayed back and forth the way it did when she was either dancing or fighting mad. As always, I was struck by her dark, exotic beauty, which she'd clearly gotten from Phillip's side of the family, high cheekbones and wide-set brown eyes, a body as strong and noble as the bowsprit on a Viking ship. How Max sprang from my pale, WASPy loins, I'll never understand.

"Max!" I called out.

"Our family is so whack!" she yelled.

"What happened?" I said. "And where are your shoes?"

"Ask them." She jabbed her thumb back toward the house.

"Ask who?" I said, but she'd already stalked off barefoot down the street.

I walked into the house to find Phillip and my sister, Nell, sitting on either end of the living room couch. In and of itself, this wasn't so odd. Nell lived nearby and often stopped in unannounced. She was dressed in one of her matching pastel sweat suits, one of several she rotated like clockwork. There's no way to make this sound like anything but an insult, but my sister bears an uncanny resemblance to a slightly chubby Peter Pan—petite, snub-nosed, with green eyes and a pixie haircut. Phillip was his usual rumpled, handsome self, smoky-eyed and lean, wearing a green, long-sleeved Celtics jersey that had seen better days. He always has that just slightly holier-than-thou look about him, but without the chops to really back it up. I think being one of seven kids kind of beat the fight out of him early on and I always loved him for that.

But the way Phillip and Nell were perched on the couch that day was odd—straight-backed and silent. Unusually pale.

"Hi, guys." I threw my keys down on the hallway table and kicked off my shoes. "What's up with Max? And why is our family so whack?"

"Oh, Gracie!" Nell got up and came over to me and I could tell she'd been crying. "It's all my fault."

"No, it's not," Phillip said from the couch.

"I'm a terrible sister," Nell said.

"No, you're not," Phillip said.

"What's going on?" I was more exasperated by this time than worried. I'd seen Max in the flesh, so I knew she wasn't lying in a gutter somewhere, and if something had happened to her brother, she would've told me. As long as my kids were okay, I could handle just about anything.

"It didn't mean anything," Phillip said.

"But still," Nell said.

At this point, I lost it. "What the hell is going on?"

"Nell and I. . . ." Phillip started out.

But before he could finish, Nell had tackled me, the tears

starting up all over again. "We almost had sex, Grace. We didn't mean to. I swear. I know that's what people always say, as if that's any kind of excuse, and it isn't, but it's true..."

Almost had sex. As the three words crystallized, I felt instantly, oddly relieved. Something had gone wrong, but it wasn't the end of the world. And, more importantly, it wasn't my fault. From a deep layer of my consciousness came the quick spark of an elicit thrill, knowing that my life had just changed forever.

"What are you talking about?" Unsettled by my strange reaction, I fell into older sister mode, leading the teary Nell over to the purple armchair, while Phillip sat motionless on the couch. I knew I'd get the truth. It was a toss-up as to who was a worse liar, my husband or my sister.

"I came by to borrow that Alice Munro short story collection, *The Lives of Girls and Women*," Nell said between sniffles. "Remember, I asked you about it the other day? You weren't home, so Phillip said he'd help me. We were in your study, looking on the shelves. A book fell off and we both reached down to get it. When we stood back up, we bumped into each other. Phillip took my arm, just to steady me, and then..."

"We kissed," Phillip said quietly and then, as if to explain, "the Red Sox were getting creamed."

"It just happened," Nell blurted out.

"And then?" By that time, my hands were planted firmly on my hips.

Phillip looked increasingly withered and blanched, while Nell kept trying to explain.

"That's the terrible part," she said. "We didn't stop there. We went over to the couch." She jabbed one finger toward the offending piece of furniture. "And then..."

I raised my hand to stop her. "Just the upshot. Please."

"Nothing in the end." Phillip's voice came to me as if through a shell.

"Phillip finally said, 'We can't do this,'" Nell said. "And just as we came to our senses, Max came down to look for her running shoes..."

I looked over at Phillip. "How much did she see?"

He bowed his head. "Enough," he said.

"And what makes me feel even more guilty"—Nell has never known when to stop—"is how you've been confiding in me lately, Gracie, about not being happy in your marriage, so maybe subconsciously I—"

"What the—" Phillip's head sprang back up.

"Nell," I said, giving her a steely look.

"Oh god, I shouldn't have said that," Nell said.

"Time for you to go now." I led her to the door.

"Will you ever forgive me?" Nell's green eyes were rimmed with tears.

"How should I know?" I said to my sister, who'd just sort of almost had sex with my soon-to-be ex-husband. "Nothing like this has ever happened before."

"You're not happy in our marriage?" By the time I'd ushered Nell out, Phillip had forgotten his guilt and found his rage. I knew the look, when the purple bubbled up into his face and his fists clenched tight at his sides.

"Let's not lose sight of what happened here," I said. "You just kissed my sister, buster."

"Buster?" Phillip was beside himself. "Why are you calling me buster?"

"Lower case *b*. It's just an expression, what you say when you want to bring a point home hard."

"Not necessary," he said. Over time, Phillip had learned to control his temper, and by then, he was a bit calmer. "I know I just kissed your sister, Grace, and that was inexcusable. The only thing I can say here, and I don't know if it makes it better or worse, is that it wasn't so important that it was your sister. It could have been anyone."

"That makes it much worse," I say. "You make it sound as if you've been desperate to kiss anyone at all. Except for me!"

"That's not true…" Phillip's voice trailed off. "You're so good at twisting my words. You have to admit that you and I haven't exactly been intimate lately. For a long time, actually."

"Oh, so it's my fault, right? The old ball and chain won't put out, so what's a poor, neglected husband to do but...hit on her sister? Seriously, Phil?"

"Oh, Grace." He sighed.

"Don't 'oh, Grace' me. You haven't exactly been putting out either."

"I know," he said, his fists clenching again. "That's not what I meant."

"You know what?" I was suddenly overcome by a crushing fatigue. "We can't do this right now. We've got to find Max and drive her back to Allston. She's got an exam first thing tomorrow morning."

As if on cue, Max's face appeared around the front door. "Is it safe to come in?" she said.

"Nell's gone," I said.

"Max." Phillip looked pleadingly at her.

"Don't even try to explain, Dad," she said. "I can't believe what you just did. How could you? Mom would never do that to you."

They both looked over at me, catching me off guard.

"Right, Mom?"

"Grace?" Phillip said.

"This isn't the time or the place—"

Phillip's face pulled tight. "Is there something you want to tell me?" he said.

"Oh my god." Max threw up her hands. "You've both been cheating on each other? Jee-sus. That's just great."

"Max," we both chimed in.

She raised a hand to stop us. "This is totally whack. I'm getting out of here. Don't bother driving me back to my apartment. I'll take the T."

"Wait," I pleaded.

"I'll get my laundry later." She grabbed her sneakers and her purse and stormed toward the front door. "You guys have a busted marriage to fix," she said.

It was confession time then, time to spill the little grey secret I'd harbored for so long, one that lay so pure and sleepy in my memory, I honestly hadn't ever felt it was worth revealing. I saw then how cowardly this had been on my part. How could I have simply spirited this little "indiscretion" out of my consciousness, without the slightest prick of guilt? It was so un-WASP-like. The part of me that wasn't ashamed was rather impressed.

Seven years ago, just after *Mycological Myths and Mysteries* was published, Olga and I were invited to a literary conference up in Vermont in late October, featuring newly published books on the natural world. The twins had just turned thirteen and I was starting to get a taste of what lay ahead in the parenting department. Max was embarrassed to be seen within one mile of me and El had virtually stopped speaking at all. So I was thrilled to hand over the parental reins to Phillip for a couple of days.

As I drove north with Olga, I felt my whole body relax. The foliage was near peak bloom, deep yellows and blood-red oranges splashing a clear blue sky. After getting off the highway, we drove for miles along a winding road which bordered a rocky-bottomed river, listening to one lilting Chopin sonata after another on Vermont Public Radio. As we crossed over a rickety covered bridge into the little town of Dummerston, I felt as if I'd slipped for a brief, magical while into an alternate universe, where everything smelled like firewood and lilacs and damp moss, where there were no dour teenagers or overworked husbands or bills to pay.

I was one of five authors asked to read from their books that night. I'd brought my one nice dress, the little black one that's *de rigueur*. My hair was freshly cut and I felt pretty as I stood up on the open-air podium and read a passage on the deadly Autumn Skullcap, nicknamed the "Mad Dog" because Native Americans use it to treat rabies. I was inspired by the serene beauty around me, a stand of delicate birch at my back and the mountains in the distance, a creamsicle sun setting against a lavender sky. I was proud of the book I'd somehow managed to write with Olga, and filled with a vague and comforting love for my family, safely ensconced in our house back in Cambridge. I should have taken this overabundance of sentiment as a warning not to drink the wine at the reception.

But drink the wine I did—a spicy little pinot noir. And then some more at dinner, not as good a vintage, but it didn't much matter. The woman next to me talked my ear off about the water crisis on the planet and looked pointedly at me every time I took a sip from my glass. I caught the young man sitting to my right eyeing me in between forkfuls of fiddlehead risotto. His dark hair stuck straight up from his head, hedgehog style. He was probably no more than thirty-five to my then forty-six, fresh-faced and freckled, with a sexy gap between his two front teeth. He wore a long-sleeved paisley shirt buttoned up to his neck and I found that touching somehow.

"Trees," he finally said and held out his hand.

"I'm sorry?"

"My book's about trees," he said. "How about yours?"

"Ah, mushrooms," I said. "Nice to meet you."

"Oh, right…" He slid into a creepy, haunted-house voice. "The Autumn Skullcap, also known as the Mad Dog…"

"Good memory," I said.

Liam was his name, one I've always been a sucker for. Liam proceeded to tell me about the myriad varieties of pine trees and all of the diseases that could possibly ravage them, all the while stealing glances at my breasts. I told him about Boletes, the "Chicken of the Woods." As the wine mellowed me, I had a slow-burning desire to free him of that tight paisley shirt, button by button.

Liam told me tree jokes: "What did the tree wear to the pool party? Swimming trunks." "What did the beaver say to the tree? It's been nice gnawing you." I laughed. These were my kind of jokes. I threw out a few of my corny mushroom jokes. "What do mushrooms eat when they're sitting around the campfire? S'pores." I saved the best for last, the one about the drunken mushroom and the wobbly stool. At the end of the night, Liam walked me to the door of my room at the inn and asked if he could come inside.

"I don't think that's such a good idea." I held my shoes in one hand, now fully feeling the wine. "I'm married, Liam," I said.

He brushed the nape of my neck with one finger. "We're here at a conference on the wonders of the natural world. What could be more wonderful…" Lifting up my hair, he kissed me on my neck. "Or natural," he said.

At that tipsy moment, I couldn't for the life of me come up with a good answer. I opened the door with my key and let us into my room. He pushed me toward the bed with his hand on my lower back. We fell back onto the mattress and undressed each other slowly. The paisley shirt slid off his shoulders, revealing his slender, muscled frame. I was already wet and he was hard. He teased my breasts with his mouth, and then licked my belly low. His head inched lower and lower, until his face was in between my legs. I drew a sharp breath. I'd never once asked Phillip to go down on me and he'd never offered. Instantly, I had an inkling of what I'd missed. Liam's tongue knew just what it was doing. Arousal rushed up through me.

"Oh my god," I whispered.

"Good?" Liam said.

"Fantastic," I said. "Don't stop."

He came up slightly for air.

"But no actual sex, Liam." I raked my hands through his hair. "I'll never be able to forgive myself."

"No actual sex." He laughed. "What will we call it then?" His tongue slid back inside me and I groaned.

"Foreplay," I whispered, as I arched my back. "We'll just call it all foreplay."

But now, confronted by Phillip seven years later in our kitchen, I wasn't about to offer up this detailed version of the story.

"So, what do you want to tell me, Grace?" he demanded.

"I don't really *want* to tell you anything," I said. "But Max really put me on the spot. So here's the short version." I sat down at the table while Phillip paced. "Remember when I went to that book conference up in Vermont when the twins were thirteen? Well, that night I had a little dalliance…"

"Dalliance?" He stopped in his tracks. "Where do you come up with these ridiculous words?"

"Would you let me finish?"

"Dalliance," he muttered.

"I got a little boozy and fooled around with this guy. But we didn't actually have sex."

"What did you actually have?"

"Hey, Nell just told me that you guys 'almost had sex.' And I didn't ask for details. So we've both strayed a bit. Now we're even."

"I wasn't aware this was some sort of competition," Phillip said.

"But on second thought," I said. "We're not really even. Because you fooled around with my sister. At least I had the decency to do it with a stranger."

"Very thoughtful," he said sarcastically. "And you've been keeping this little secret to yourself for seven years? Jesus, Grace. Talk about a major breach of trust."

"You're right, Phillip, it was. I'm sorry. Listen. You're telling me that what happened with Nell meant nothing and I'm trying to believe you. So please try to believe me. I actually was thinking about you and the kids that night in Vermont, how much you all meant to me. I know that sounds sick, but it wasn't. It was just a random, meaningless…thing."

"Thing?" Phillip did laps around the kitchen table. "Just a meaningless thing? Don't you think we should consider why we both 'strayed,' Grace? To use your archaic word."

"It's human nature, don't you think?" I chose this unlikely moment to start emptying the dishwasher. "To be curious? To be flawed?"

"I think it brings up a much larger issue."

"What's larger than human nature?" A blast of steam escaped from the dishwasher door.

"It brings up the question of..." He tugged at his hair the way he did to try and keep his temper in check, to keep himself from exploding. "Are we, for lack of a better word—happy together?" Phillip said.

The heat of a steaming plate shot through my hand. Happy? I was dumbfounded. As a good WASP, I'd never felt I had the right to ask such a selfish question. After you'd made your bed in life, weren't you expected to lie in it forever? After all, the decision to marry Phillip had been made of my own free will. When we'd said our version of "till death do us part," I'd accepted this as part of the pact we'd made, to be married to one another, until the end of time. It wasn't until that moment in the kitchen that I considered there might be circumstances under which it might be all right to get up out of the bed you'd made, to flip or turn the mattress, or change the sheets, or god forbid, maybe even consider getting a whole new bed.

"Happy?" I looked into Phillip's tired brown eyes, hardly recognizing the man I'd been married to for twenty-seven years. "I have no idea," I said.

Phillip and I agreed to try and save our marriage. No matter what the outcome, we decided, the twins needed an explanation, something they could make peace with in the end. Kids these days need that kind of clarity. After an unfettered romp in the sixties, love is back to being a black and white affair, no longer the amorphous, psychedelic pastiche it was for our generation. But of course, we had to play it out for ourselves as well. We were nothing if not well-intentioned. The events of Whack Sunday had shaken and scared us both. We'd been so determined; we'd worked so hard. It didn't make sense that after all that time, we hadn't turned into a *bona fide* happy family, that the two of us wouldn't hobble contentedly into the sunset together.

Phillip and I talked throughout the last days of that cold,

dreary May and into a grudging June. We looked back, remembering how we'd gotten together in our late twenties, first as friends, then casual lovers. We'd been a comfortable, solid fit—same values, rhythms, life goals. We'd seen starting a family as a grown-up, rational choice. And we knew we could give it a good shot. We talked about how we'd never had much of a physical connection but made a conscious choice to proceed without that. Having come of age in the sixties, we both thought we'd had enough sexual experience by then to last a lifetime. But who has the foggiest notion, at thirty, how long a lifetime can be?

Looking back, I think the mistake Phillip and I made was believing we could rescue each other from our own worst selves. I hoped that Phillip's hot-blooded, impulsive nature might unleash the wild woman in me, allow me to free myself up and write a novel full of passion and abandon. And he in turn hoped that I would rein in his temper and his carelessness, make him a better candidate for the profession he had chosen, architecture—a world full of well-groomed, mannered, and uptight designers. But in an O'Henry-like twist, none of this ever came to be. And in the end, I think we both felt as though we'd let the other one down.

After Phillip and I were done looking backward, we looked forward. We admitted that we'd been kidding ourselves about enjoying our empty nest, that we were miserable, really, without the twins, missing the loud music and slamming doors, the heated games of Hearts, watching *Seinfeld* and *Simpsons* re-runs and lounging on the couch—all that lovely family chaos. We admitted how much easier it had become to go out at night than to stay at home together alone and we vowed to try and change that. We tried sex counseling, taking a vacation to Prince Edward Island; we even took tango lessons, hoping, with each new venture, to have found a way back. But something had broken irrevocably, and it wasn't just our petty infidelities. And the more we tried to bandage and salve and duct tape it all together, the more it seemed to crumble.

"Maybe we're trying too hard," I said to Phillip one Saturday morning in June.

He was pushing cold scrambled eggs around on his plate and I was on my fourth cup of coffee. We'd just come back from a rain-drenched trip to Canada and I had a bad cold. We had no plans for the day, or any part of the future. Phillip looked haggard and spent in the pale morning light.

"To do what?" he said dully.

"To figure this out," I said. "To fix it." I made small rips on the bottom of the newspaper's front page, giving it a fringe. "Maybe that's just not going to happen. And maybe…" I thought long and hard before I said it. "And maybe that's all right."

"Mmm." I saw a flicker of light cross Phillip's eyes, which were glued to the *Globe* sports page.

"I've been thinking lately," I said, "how I want to stop doing things that I only enjoy after the fact."

"What are you talking about?" He started tugging at his hair.

"Like exercise," I said. "I never actually enjoy it while it's happening. I'm only ever glad I did it when it's over. It's that whole, crazy future past thing. You know, *I will have enjoyed running around the reservoir after I've finished doing it.* So what's the point?"

"And how exactly does this relate to our marriage?" Phillip was starting to lose it again.

"I don't think we should stay in our marriage just so that when all is said and done, we can say that we did."

"What does that even mean?" Phillip gave me that crazed look of exasperation that came over him when I tried to explain how I was feeling. "When all is said and done, Grace, we'll be dead."

"Exactly!" I said triumphantly.

"I don't get it." He shook his head back and forth. "I never really get it, Grace." If I hadn't known him better, I would've thought he was about to cry.

"What, Phil?" I sensed that if I kept at him, he'd find the

words for both of us. "What is it?" I said. "What do you want to say?"

"All I know is..." He looked up at me with sad, tired eyes. "I don't want to live this way anymore."

I put my hand on his arm as the truth shook me hard. "Neither do I," I said.

We sat the twins down a few days later to break the news. El took it better than Max, who was still angry and tough as nails.

"Figures," was all our daughter had to say. "I knew you guys wouldn't be able to work it out. Are you happy now? You've ruined our family."

"Max." Phillip put out his hand, but she pulled away.

"Our family's not ruined," I said. "Your dad and I will always be there for you both."

"Can't you just forgive each other?" El asked.

"We have," I said.

"So what's the problem?" Max said.

"You're not in love anymore, are you?" said El.

It was painful to hear El reduce it to those terms, sad to have to tell him that the answer, though complicated, was, in a word—no. But my kids are half WASP and stoicism runs as thick in their blood as the high drama on Phillip's side of the family. The stiff upper lip phase kicked in soon enough. "Don't mope, deal," was my own parental version of my mother's "the show must go on." And the twins did deal and the family show, as fractured and haphazard as it had become, did in fact go on.

"Whatever," was Max's final word.

The twins took off on faraway jaunts—Max to England to work in summer theater in Penzance and El to help build a school in rural Guatemala. Who can blame them, for wanting to flee, for just wanting it all to be over? And by the end of July, it was done—the dissolution of the partnership Chicarelli & Hobbes through civil mediation, the elegant ampersand replaced by an unyielding *vs.* in the divorce agreement we signed before the judge, followed by a friendly, if fragile, dinner at Il

Panino, our favorite Italian restaurant in between Harvard and Central Squares.

It was almost two months ago that Phillip and I sat at that wooden table, the last supper, as it were. A warm breeze wafted in from the street, as we inhaled the delicious aromas of garlic, oregano, and melted butter. We listened to the cops shooting the breeze and the bull at the next table over, police radios crackling, the jaunty banter of the line cooks behind the counter. We lingered as we had so many times before, finishing the pizza crusts and one last Sunday *Globe* crossword puzzle together, the last cup of sludgy black coffee, the last cocoa-dusted cannoli, the last triumphant filled-in square.

"Well, I guess that's all she wrote," Phillip said, getting up from the table.

I got up and hugged him. "Take care of yourself," I said, and watched him walk out the door.

And then there it was, the empty feeling that inevitably followed, when you looked down at the puzzle you'd so painstakingly solved and wondered, for the life of you…now what?

53 across. One of the long ones. Seventeen letters. The clue was: DISAPPEAR. I'd written the letters in black ink.

V-A-N-I-S-H-I-N-T-O-T-H-I-N-A-I-R.

4

Are you dating yet, Grace?" my mother, Celia, asks me, over chamomile tea and raisin scones. We meet at Simon's coffee shop on Mass. Ave near Linnaean every Tuesday afternoon at four o'clock, pretty much rain or shine. And today, it's pouring out. Simon's is a long, narrow storefront lined with old movie posters and rickety wooden tables. When I was a kid, it used to be a laundromat. I can still picture the stacked washers and dryers and detergent vending machines, and the fading poster with the perky housewife in a belted gingham dress, wagging her finger at you on the way out. "Do you have all your socks?" her voice bubble read. Today, there's a pile of wet umbrellas in the corner by the door, and an odd-looking, babbling baby sitting in a high chair between two doting moms. The heavenly smell of fresh-baked cinnamon rolls wafts through the damp air.

"Dating?" I say.

"Or whatever they call the mating process these days." Celia brushes a crumb off her threadbare Talbots cardigan.

"For heaven's sake, I'm done mating, Mother," I say. "But I guess you could say I'm looking around."

"Where, for instance?" Celia's never been one to beat around the bush. I notice she's wearing two different earrings, one clip-on pearl and one turquoise teardrop.

"Out and about." I try to keep it vague.

"That's hardly an answer," she says.

I groan.

"I don't know why you just couldn't stick it out with Phillip," she goes on. "In my day, 'till death do us part' actually meant something."

"Yes, it meant a lot of people went to their graves miserable and sex-starved."

"Honestly, Grace."

"Well, it's true." I pick a raisin out of my scone and Celia swats my hand, causing the raisin to fall onto her plate. "Anyway, Phillip and I were married for twenty-seven years. I'd call that sticking it out. In the end, we realized we just weren't happy together."

"Happiness is a luxury." Celia tries to push the liberated raisin back into my scone. "That's what you young people don't understand."

"It shouldn't have to be," I say.

"I thought you hated that word," Celia says.

"I'm using it for good." I snatch up the raisin and pop it into my mouth. "Not for evil," I say.

Why is it that no matter how steadfastly we vow not to repeat the shortcomings and sins of our parents, we nonetheless consistently do? My parents stayed in their tortured marriage for "the sake of the children," long after we'd left the nest. Badly matched from the outset, they spent their last thirty years together alternately bickering and giving each other the silent treatment. How often did Charlie and Nell and I wish they'd break up, if not for their sake, we'd plead silently, at least for ours?

My father continued his WASPy life of martinis and bridge games and tennis and bow ties deep into the sixties, as if the walls weren't shaking and crumbling all around him. Celia, on the other hand, went to the opposite extreme, flinging convention to the wind—going to civil rights marches and making endless batches of homemade lentil soup, bell bottoms, Bob Dylan, peace, love, and even…marijuana. Essentially, she embarked on her second adolescence as I started out on my first. And frankly, if there's one person you don't want to go through puberty with—especially if you're a girl—it's your mother.

"Define out and about." Celia breaks off a piece of her poppyseed scone. It's clear to me now that my mother's brief dive into the subculture of the sixties yielded no permanent changes in character. For her, it was just a detour, a respite from my stodgy, stick-in-the-mud father, a mid-life romp. Since then, she's slowly morphed back into the feisty, stubborn, uptight, thrifty, liberal, maddening, no-nonsense, judgmental person I remember as a child. If you ever reminded her now that she used to smoke pot, she'd flatly deny it.

"I've actually been going out to a few bars," I venture.

"*Bars*?" Celia clutches at the neck of her cardigan. I might as well have announced I'd become a stripper down in the Combat Zone. "Isn't that a bit degrading at your age, Grace? Rather self-indulgent?" A huge black Newfoundland barrels into the coffee shop and the odd-looking baby lets out an ear-piercing shriek of delight. The air fills with the aroma of wet, panting dog.

"I don't think so." I try not to sound defensive. I won't fall into Celia's old maternal traps.

"Why don't you just go on the computer to solve your problems like everyone else does these days?" she says. "One of those dating services or something, although I find them so distasteful."

"And suffer through all those creepy, uncomfortable blind dates? No thanks. I don't need a computer to play matchmaker for me." I take a sip of my tea. "By the way, Mother, do you know you're wearing two different earrings?"

Celia's hands shoot up to her ears. "Am I?" I catch a familiar gleam in her eye that makes me suspicious. "Honestly, I'm getting so scatterbrained lately," she says.

"And in any case," I say. "I don't need a man."

"You're no spring chicken, Grace," she says.

"I'm aware of that," I say.

It occurs to me that having to share my teenagehood with my mother may be part of the reason that now, at fifty-three, I'm starting off on my second adolescence, because my first one was never played out completely, wasn't entirely mine. Maybe that's how Celia felt, too, with her mother. Maybe that's always the way it is. In the end—it's hard to argue Freud on this one—it really is all about your mother.

"And honestly, Grace, if you just did something with your hair—"

"We've been over this a million times," I say. "It's just hair, Mother!"

"All I'm saying is, you had a perfectly good husband."

"No, that's not all you're saying!" I try and stand my ground. "You're also saying that I'm over the hill and frumpy and selfish and by the way, none of this is helping the cause."

"I'm sorry." She pats my arm. "I'm sure you're doing the best you can, Rose."

"Your sister's been dead for twelve years now, Mother. Why on earth are you calling me Rose?"

"Poor Rose. She had the bad luck of a hat on a bed," Celia says, getting a far-away look in her eye. "I seem to get everything mixed up these days, don't I? I probably shouldn't be living on my own for much longer."

"You're fine, Mother," I say. I happen to know that her good friend, Martha Coolidge, just moved into a luxury assisted living complex out in tony Lincoln, and Celia's green with envy.

"That's just the way it started with Martha," she says. "She couldn't remember the word for saucer. She kept saying, 'You know, that thing you put under the tea cup.'"

"Martha Coolidge has full-blown dementia, Mother. She barely recognizes her own children. Be thankful you still have your wits about you and that you still *can* live on your own." Heaven forbid, I think, she should get any ideas about moving in with me.

Celia shakes her head as she finishes up her tea, as if to say she'll never understand her n'eer-do-well, Brillo-Pad, middle child. "Anyway," she says. "Now that you're without a husband, Grace, isn't it time you found a real job?"

And then I realize what's odd-looking about the babbling baby with two moms. He only has hair on half of his head.

On the final count, Celia's right. About the job, that is. I bought Phillip out of the house as part of the divorce settlement and that leaves me real-estate rich but cash poor. The mortgage is almost paid and I don't need much to live on, but I do need to eat. I've been doing the endless, stand-up, snacking routine that Cher did in *Mermaids* and it's not helping my bank account or my waistline. It's time to start making some money and buying some real food.

A few days later, I pull up to one of the local health food stores, the Mustard Seed, just as it's closing. I put my hands up in prayer to the man locking the door and he lets me in.

"Thanks so much," I say. "I just need a few things. I'm trying to get healthy again. I love those Turkish figs you carry."

"Take your time," he says. "I have to finish up these chalkboards before I leave." He sits down cross-legged on the floor in a spear of fading sunlight, a steaming mug of coffee by his side. He's writing the specials on the board, drawing pictures with pastel-colored chalks. I recognize him as a jogger I see occasionally at the Fresh Pond Reservoir, most memorable because of the fact that he's missing most of his right arm. He's nice-looking, late forties, I'd say, not exactly my type, too much like me, pale and thin, with an uneventful face, wearing jeans and an untucked, checked flannel shirt, the right sleeve neatly hemmed a few inches down from his shoulder, a solid head of dark brown hair. The missing arm is intriguing, though.

"Nice signs." I remember my once-elegant penmanship and a brief foray into calligraphy in my twenties. "Is that fun?" I ask him. "It looks like fun."

"It is fun." He finishes the word CANTALOUPE with a flourish of an *E*, then takes a sip of his coffee. "Mindless. Satisfying." He draws the curvy lines of a slice of melon with a bumpy, half-moon green skin. "But I won't be doing it for much longer."

"Why not?" I pluck a container of Turkish figs off a shelf in the bulk aisle.

"I've got to find a way to carve out more time." He makes a curlicued *K* to start the beginning of a kale sign, switching from light to dark green chalk.

"For what?"

"My family," he says. "My art. Myself, too, I guess. That's what the shrink says. Apparently until I learn how to take better care of myself, I won't be much good taking care of anyone else."

"It's true," I say. "You're an artist?"

"I dabble," he says. I know about this kind of vague answer. Sometimes when people ask me what I write, I answer, "Drivel, mostly."

"The store pretty much swallows me whole," he says. "I want to spend more time with my daughter. She's having kind of a rough time these days. And my painting. The shrink said I should get more in touch with the inner me. Not sure I want to, though." He shrugs and gestures to his sign. "First thing I've got to do is get better at delegating. Know anyone who might be good at this?"

"I might be, actually." I extend one hand, running the other through my hair the way I do when I'm nervous or excited, the result of years of Celia telling me to *tamp down that unholy bird's nest before you go out in public.* "I'm Grace, by the way."

"Otis." He turns the blackboard around and hands me a piece of chalk. "Okay, Grace. Let's see what you've got. Try..." He consults his price list. "Turnips. $2.14 per pound."

"I think I've seen you jogging around the reservoir." I sit down on the floor and start in on a peach-colored *T*.

He nods. "I try to make it over there a few times a week."

"I'm lucky if I manage two."

"Two's good," he says.

"I could really use this job." I'm trying to remember the difference between turnips and parsnips, which Isabelle refers to as the "brute" vegetables. "I just got divorced," I say.

"Join the club."

"You too?" He nods. "How long?" I say.

"Almost three years."

"Just a couple of months for me," I say. "How old is your daughter?"

"Seven," he says. "I was a late bloomer."

"I've got twins. Seniors in college," I say. "They're great."

"Mine's great too," he says.

I turn my finished sign around to face Otis. He nods and a thumb sprouts up from his left fist.

"Turnip masterpiece," he says. "You're hired, Grace."

"Just like that?"

"When can you start?"

"Tomorrow?" I raise my shoulders in a why-not shrug.

"Tomorrow it is."

"I love this store," I say, getting back up on my feet. "It must be hard to survive as the little guy, now that health food is a multibillion-dollar business."

"I've got a lot of stamina," he says. "And an incredible staff. Would you like a tour before you go?"

"Sure." I pretty much know where everything is, but I sense something is happening here, something pleasant and mysterious, and I don't want it to end. The produce section is a gorgeous array of bright colors—magenta beets and deep green broccoli, bright yellow lemons and orange peppers. We turn the corner into the frozen food aisle and I feel a bit of a shiver. And yet I could swear a thin line of sweat has formed on the nape of my neck. I watch Otis as he walks. I see the tight curve of his butt and the broad shelf of his shoulders. I see the sway of his left arm and instinctively look for the sway in his right. How odd that it's simply not there.

He shows me the newly opened Wellness Aisle—men's health on one side of a latticed wall, women's on the other. There are shelves and shelves of pills and lotions and gels. I pick up a bottle in the men's section and read the label.

"Mmm," I say. "'Enhances male potency.'" And just like that, I've begun to seduce him.

"Is that right?" Otis opens the bottle and takes out a pill. "I wonder if it works," he says, popping it into his mouth.

"Did you just really do that?" I laugh.

"Oh my god!" His eyes open wide. "It's working already. I can feel it happening as we speak."

"But how could it possibly…" And then I get it. This is no mystery. This is how it can happen, if you relax, if you don't overthink it, just like in the movies. Pure, unadulterated lust rising up from the dust of an ordinary day and working its magic, no harm, no foul. I think about Fuzz's phone call and Perry Mason and how peaceful it is here in the store, with the floating aromas of soap and incense and herbal teas and the soft warm light of the waning day filtering in through the windows. I think about how time flies and how nice it is that this man and I seem to have some sort of odd, muted attraction and maybe Fuzz is right, that it *is* boring always to have sex in a bed.

"Yep," Otis says, grinning. "It's working all right."

I look down at the ridge in his pants and by the time our eyes meet again, we've tumbled headlong into that comic scene in every grade-B rom-com—furiously kissing and trying to rip off each other's clothes. Before I know it, we're on the floor, breathless and sort of half-naked.

"Just so you know," he says, tugging at my shirt. "It's been a while."

"For me too." I manage to unzip his fly. "Except for a one night stand I just had. In my car, if you can believe it. And then the guy dumped me."

"His loss," he says. By now his pants are down to his knees. "I tell you what. After we do this…" We kiss feverishly. "You can dump me. Even the score."

"Excellent plan." His face lowers again to mine.

We kiss, this time deep and slowly. Moving closer, his left arm hoists up one side of my shirt. I reach for the other side to help. He pulls back, propping himself up, and I throw my shirt onto the chair and unhook my bra.

"Beautiful," he says.

His one hand cups my right breast. And it feels sublime. But it's strange—not to have the other one cupped, too, and I find myself touching it myself.

"Sorry," he says. "Everything takes a bit longer. I'm not the most graceful…"

"You should have seen me in the car," I say. "With the dumper. We must've looked ridiculous. The windshield actually cracked. He was so full of himself." I'm nervous talking, now, revealing too much, too soon, trying too hard.

"Maybe we should take off the rest of our clothes," Otis says, running his hand over my stomach. "That would be more than half the battle won."

"Good idea," I say.

We lie face to face, almost naked. Although Otis unbuttoned his shirt, I notice he's kept it on. It's been a long time since I've looked at a man fully aroused, and I am amazed all over again at how such an otherwise unassuming body part can make such a stunning transformation in such a short time. I take Otis in my hand at the bottom of his shaft and stroke upwards; he groans. He caresses my lower back. I climb on top of him. I rub my body up and down against his erection, and feel the deep hot rush of arousal flood through me.

"Uurrung," Otis says. I can't tell if it's an actual word or just a groan. My wetness seeps onto his thigh. He eases me over on my back with his left arm. I guide him downward, sensing by his breathing that he's ready and maybe not long for the stretch.

"I don't think I can last much longer," he says. He finds my center and starts to push, but he's too far gone and comes with a moan and an arched back, mostly onto my leg. His head falls forward and I start to rub his back.

"Sorry," he says into the crook of my neck. "That couldn't have been any good for you. If you like, I could…"

"That's okay," I say. "It was lovely. Really. So unexpected. I've been wanting to be more spontaneous in my life."

"Diplomatic and kind," he says, rolling off me. He hands me his shirt to wipe off my leg.

"First time I've ever slept with someone to get a job," I joke.

"You already had the job," he says. "Your turnips were amazing, Grace."

I laugh, reaching for my underwear and shirt. "Just so you know, Otis, I'm not really looking for…"

"Don't worry," he says. "Neither am I. It was just a crazy, impulsive one-time thing."

"Right," I say. "Just a crazy one-time thing."

"And by the way…" He pulls his pants back on and as he zips up, I notice how muscular his upper body is. "I'm going away tomorrow on a trip. Maybe that's why I actually had the courage to go through with this. Because I knew I was about to flee. I'm a coward, basically. My manager, Paul, will show you the ropes at the store tomorrow."

I gather my things and give Otis an awkward hug. Halfway to the door, I turn around.

"Forget something?" he says.

I retrace my steps and tap his shoulder with the container of figs. "I hereby dump you," I say.

The next time at the Wonder Bar, Isabelle seems distracted as I fill her in about the Mustard Seed and my fortuitous run-in with Otis. I don't breathe a word about our romp in the men's health aisle. I'd never hear the end of it, and besides, I can't stop thinking about that Bechdel test and how much time women spend talking about men. Furthermore, I feel unsettled about what happened with Otis, how bold it was and how quickly it all played out. Before I'd really started to enjoy myself, it was over.

"Only one arm, eh?" Isabelle says. "That's a big fetish thing, you know—having sex with amputees."

"*What?* Are you kidding me?" I groan. "Oh my god. He must have thought I was one of those people."

"Yeah, go on the internet sometime," Isabelle says. "There are some sick mother effers out there." She shudders. "I hate turnips."

"Not just turnips, Iz." I try to steer the conversation back to the mundane. "I'll be making signs for everything—bagels and cereal, fish fillets, lady fingers. It's like being in art class all over again."

"Whoo freaking hoo," she says, spinning her finger in mock enthusiasm.

"And get this," I say. "Otis emailed me yesterday. From wherever he is. He had to fire the plant person for embezzlement, and when he found out I had a green thumb, he added that to the job description. Almost double the pay!"

"Green thumb?" Isabelle gives me a scathing look. "Grace, you've systematically murdered every plant I've ever given you."

"Okay, so I've got kind of a greyish thumb. But I'll learn. Thank god for the internet. This is a windfall, Iz. It's steady part-time work. So I can still do my writing. And I'll actually be making some decent money for a change."

"Fish fillets and lady fingers," she says. The sarcasm's waned just a bit. "And a one-armed mystery man to boot."

"What's up? You're almost gloomy tonight," I say.

"Sorry," Isabelle says. "It's great about your new job. It's just that I'm tired and Molly's driving me frickin' crazy, and well…I had an idea."

"What idea?"

"I wanted you to write some guest posts for my blog, *Squiggle Z*. But now, with all the fruit and plants sprouting up in your life, not to mention your wild and crazy sex life—"

"Guest posts? No way. I'm not qualified."

"Of course you are. You're a published author."

"Mushrooms," I remind her. "I wrote a book about mushrooms, honey."

"You're a great writer." Isabelle dismisses this. "And you're a single woman over forty. Those are all the qualifications you need."

"I'm not just over forty, Iz. I'm over fifty."

"Exactly," she says. "The fifty-somethings need a voice, too, Grace. There're a gazillion frickin' women out there, just waiting to hear from someone like you."

"What would I write about?"

Isabelle picks lint from her sleeve. "Your life. Plain and simple. What it's like to be single again at your age. Out on the front lines, in the coffee shops, at the supermarket, out at the bars. Looking for love. Companionship. Or just sex. 'Tales of an Urban Cougar.'"

"Urban what?"

"Read this when you get home." She shoves a folded newspaper into my hand. "I'm out of here, Gracie. I really don't understand what you like about bars. On top of everything else, they smell nasty. Even without the cigarette smoke."

"Who'd want to read about some old hippie's quest for late-in-life romance?" I tuck the newspaper into my bag, still mulling over Isabelle's offer. "I can just see it now: 'Birkenstock Biddies: The Old Crone Chronicles.'"

"See, you've got the hang of it already." Isabelle takes out her mirror to freshen her lipstick. "I've done the research, Gracie. There are thirty-five million baby boomer women out there between the ages of forty-one and sixty-four. Looking for guidance, or courage. Vicarious thrills. Validation. Entertainment." She throws up her hands. "Effin' whatever."

"Effin' whatever?" I say doubtfully.

"Sooner or later, this patriarchy's going to implode. They're all going to kill each other off, the way the male lions do when you set them all loose in the den. Women have to position themselves in strategic places of power, to be ready to take over."

Isabelle leans in toward me with all the drama of a defense attorney. "It'll be a wake-up call for the old farts out there who think that after forty, we all shrivel up and disappear," she says. "Yours will be the primal war cry of older women coming out of the domestic woodwork—bad marriages and celibacy and illness and motherhood and back out into the sexual fray. You'll be leading the goddamned feminist charge, Grace. Think about it!"

"Old farts are selectively deaf," I say. "They're out there trawling for hot young chicks and the outrageous thing is, they actually get them. They can look like Quasimodo and still score, while we're all supposed to age like Sophia Loren. It's that whole beauty and the beast mythology."

"It makes you mad, doesn't it?" Isabelle says.

"Talk about double standards."

"It almost makes you want to…do something about it, doesn't it?"

"It actually does."

"So there you have it." Isabelle takes a last sip of her chardonnay. "You're hired." She starts to put on her coat. "Three new jobs in one week. And your mother says you're an underachiever."

"Where're you going?" I say. "You can't leave me here alone again. Remember what happened last time?"

"You'll be fine," she says. "Just keep your pants on, Gracie. I'm going to meet Emil at Simon's for a latte."

"Emil? So it's Emil now, is it?"

"Yes, it is." I can't remember the last time I saw Isabelle grin. "'Harvard professor gets rocks off, slumming with Medford townie.' I can see the headline now." She and the walrusy guy, a musicologist who writes books about musicians of the sixties, hit it off that first night and have met a few times for coffee. He's not half bad, for an Ivy League snoot, she says. "Oh, and Grace?" Isabelle looks down at my leopard-print flats. "Consider losing the freaky shoes."

"I love these shoes," I say.

"Fine." She groans. "Just don't drink too much. Remember now, you're on the job."

After Isabelle leaves, I take out my notebook and pen and look around the Wonder Bar. It's dark and high-ceilinged and swallows noise surprisingly well. The stools have backs and purse hooks line the underside of the bar. There's artwork on the walls. It's not great art, but it's original—an odd set of portraits of boar-like figures with long snouts, undulating necks and primordial pointed ears. Neither masculine nor feminine, they look like mutant, half-melted Vulcans, pictured in mundane settings—in a hammock, on a train platform—one's mowing a suburban lawn. At first glance, the artist's palette is depressing—

metallic greens and mustardy ochres, murky, molassesy browns. I suppose they're meant to represent something primeval in us, these eerie creatures, something base and once natural, a commentary, perhaps, on how manicured and beauty-obsessed we've become.

Bartender Jack is a no-nonsense kind of guy. He's young and lithe, runs the bar with rapid-fire, steely efficiency, crashing bottles and plates and cutting fruit like a whirling dervish, dishrag hanging out of his back pocket as he bounces around on sneakered feet. Trying to flag him down or hurry him in any way will not only *not* help the cause but may very well hurt it. Bartender Jack sees you. He has eyes on all sides of his head. At Bartender Jack's bar, you'd be well-advised to be on your best behavior.

Some of the best procrastinators are great doodlers, and that includes me. I've been working on a series of pineapples that more resemble lopsided hedgehogs. As I ponder Isabelle's job offer, I give my best pineapple a kewpie doll face and some shapely legs, add on a top hat and cane. It's true. I'm a writer. Yes, there's only been the one book, about the mushrooms, not a bestseller by any stretch, and never mind that half the market was family and friends.

I keep a copy of the *Publisher's Weekly* review tacked up on my bulletin board to remind myself that I actually did write a book once, and that the next one has to be better. I can recite it pretty much word for word.

"To the extent that a treatise on mushrooms can entertain, this one does. Grace Winthrop Hobbes brings Olga Sanoff's stunning photographs of mushrooms to life, imbuing each species with its own personality, its own peculiar attributes and quirks. The morels are 'moody, now drooping in the shade, then exultantly upturned in the sun.' Hobbes even shows compassion for the deadlier varieties. 'Let's just accept,' she writes, 'that the stalwart, mighty Destroying Angel is meant to be admired from afar, a murderer without malice. Merely a worthy foe.'"

Only the last line of the review still makes me a cringe:

"Despite the occasional indulgence in purple prose…"

Ouch. A murderer without malice? Oh well, I guess I asked for it.

But seven years later, all I've got to show for my subsequent writerly efforts is a lousy, muddled hundred or so pages of my far-from-great American novel. It's a long rambling tale about a dysfunctional WASP family set in the late sixties that spins in depressing, aimless circles, a kind of overwrought, urban *Grapes of Wrath*. Lately, I've been falling asleep during my writing sessions. Not exactly a ringing endorsement of the work. In truth, I've been feeling like anything but a writer for a good, long while, more like an imposter. This sense of never quite being the "real thing" is another female tendency I'm determined to eschew. Why is it so hard sometimes to convince ourselves that our voices are worth being heard? And so, although Isabelle's challenge terrifies me, I'm also aware that it just might save me. Of course. I won't be able to tell anyone what I'm doing for a while. And maybe never. How could I possibly explain this to my children?

I take another sip of wine for courage. I'll just have to cross that bridge when I come to it—this, the piece of advice offered most often by my proverb-obsessed mother, and not the worst one at that. The beauty of this job is that I'll be going about my regular life, but at the same time working, writing, possibly even contributing something worthwhile to the feminist lexicon. I feel a secret thrill as I close my notebook and finish my second glass of malbec. Who would've thunk it? I'm going undercover, as a perimenopausal mole.

On my way out the door, I literally bump into Fuzz coming in.

"Sherlock!" he says. "How are you?"

"Fine," I say briskly. "Completely fine."

"You look great," he says. "I like your shoes. Can I buy you a drink?"

"No, thanks. I'm done for the night," I say. "I was just walking to my car."

"I'll walk with you."

"You don't have to—"

But Fuzz has already taken my arm. "Where're you parked?" He pulls me on impatiently.

"On Shepard," I say. "Past Chez Henri."

"Ah, same spot," he says. "Were you waiting for me?"

"No, I most definitely was not," I say. "I always park on that street."

At the car door, he presses up against me. "I remember you." He slides his hands under my shirt and cups my breasts. "Oh, and I definitely remember these. I love these camisole thingees you wear."

I push him away. "I'm not doing this again," I say. "And certainly not in my car. It's cold out. And I just got the windshield fixed. And what about this other woman you've been trying to break up with, or not break up with—"

"What about her?" He tucks some stray curls behind my ear and I feel a tightening in my belly as he leans into me. "What does she have to do with this?" His breath is hot on my neck. I feel him pressing hard against my center. "You and me, right here? Right here and now?" I think of young Liam giving me the same line outside of my room at the inn in Vermont all those years back. Men are so good at living in the moment. I've got to work on that. By then one of Fuzz's hands is on the car door handle.

"Whoa," I say. "Wait just a minute."

"Why overthink this?" he says. "Admit it, Grace. You and I have a real physical connection. We rocked the car that night. You were a wild woman. You got me so hard. I can't stop thinking about it," he says.

I hate to admit it, but he's right. If there's anything my brief tryst with Otis taught me, it was that animal attraction does count. I was a wild woman that night with Fuzz. And he was as hard as a freaking rock.

"Come on. Let's get in," he says. "It's cold out here."

Talk about a feminist dilemma. On the one hand, how dare Fuzz come on to me after he ditched me over the phone? But I'm dying to have sex again, even if it's not up to last time's seven rating. What happened with Otis was sweet, but let's face it, it didn't really count. But if I give in to Fuzz's advances, won't I be betraying this other woman, going against our credo of solidarity? On the other hand, isn't all fair in love and war? Shouldn't I embrace my own carnal desires, rather than fret about some phantom woman I don't even know? But then what about my dignity? Given my newfound commitment to rechanneling my old sixties self, wouldn't I be letting myself down by giving in to this guy after how he treated me, even if he does look like Paul Newman's balding brother?

Fuzz comes in for the kiss and I succumb to the first melting sensation at the bottom of my belly, the delicious feeling of letting go. But while his tongue is exploring the farthest regions of my mouth, I think about my newfound liberty and resolve, about my new jobs and my kids and Otis and the Beatles and Perry Mason.

"You know what?" It takes everything I can muster to quell the rising heat in my body and push Fuzz away again. "This is not going to happen," I say. The little feminist fairy on one shoulder gives me a congratulatory pat, but the hot and bothered one on the other shoulder slowly crumples.

"You had your chance," I say, going around to the driver's side door. "And you blew it, buster."

When I get home, I sink into the purple armchair and read the *Globe* article Isabelle gave me at the bar. COUGARS ON THE PROWL, trumpets the headline on the front page of the Living Section. Turns out there's a new category of women out there called "cougars"—strong, independent, unattached older women who seek out younger men for casual sexual encounters without feeling Guilt or Self-Loathing or Shame or Desperation or any of the other kneejerk reactions we women have when we do things that men get away with doing all the time! Deep breath. Okay, granted—I cross my legs in the lotus position—that's not exactly what happened with me and Fuzz in the car that first night, but I'm thrilled to know there's a trendy new classification to which I may now aspire to belong.

Accompanying the article is a half-page color photo of a Fortune 500 CEO in full red business suit regalia, sitting on the edge of her desk in five-inch Jimmy Choo heels. Turns out this resplendent creature is one Sheila LaFarge. This broad's no sissy, no slouch. She makes three hundred grand a year and sits at the head of a table full of male suits and sharks and tells them what to do. And what not to do. By night she sashays among the snazziest downtown bars and restaurants and takes gorgeous younger men back to her waterfront penthouse in the wee hours to make outrageous love to her, then sends them home in prepaid cabs.

I cut out her photo and plunk it on the refrigerator with an Oscar the Grouch magnet. Okay, so I'll have to skip the penthouse and pre-paid cabs until my ship comes in. But from now on, Sheila LaFarge will be my inspiration, my mid-life love guru. I can learn a lot from her. For starters, I bet she'd never stoop to having sex in a rusty Toyota Corolla with a nearsighted, nerdy sex geek. Clearly, Sheila LaFarge never sleeps between sheets that have less than a thousand thread count. Red is her favorite color and she doesn't give a damn if it makes her look fat. Sheila LaFarge takes care of Number One, first and foremost. She doesn't take any you know what.

5

El calls out of the blue one Monday morning in early October. This is suspicious on two counts—the Monday part and the morning part. My son has never been friendly with either.

"How're you holding up, Mom?" Since Phillip and I split, this is always his first question. He says it with pointed concern, as if I'm suffering from some ghastly disease.

"I think I still have a few good years left," I say. "What brings you to the phone so early, El?"

"I want to tell you something," he says.

My ears perk up. First, if it were bad news, he would have said, I *have* to tell you something. Secondly, my son generally wants to divulge as little about himself and his life as possible. So this is huge.

"What's up?" I say.

"I have a girlfriend," he says. "Finally."

"A girlfriend?" I'm actually a bit taken aback. It never mattered, but part of me has always suspected that El might be gay. Plenty of girls have been interested, but he never really landed with any one in particular. I've long been prepared to be his most ardent, fierce supporter, leading the Proud Mothers of Gay Sons March and baking brownies for his gay fundraisers. I actually feel the slightest twinge of disappointment. "That's wonderful!" I say.

"Her name is Rachel."

"Such a beautiful name."

"She's incredible," El says, his voice nearly bursting. "I can't wait for you to meet her, Mom."

"Well…me either," I manage to say.

"When?" I've never heard such urgency in his voice.

"Bring her down," I say. "I'd love to have you visit. I've got plenty of room."

"I don't know." El hems and haws. I know how hard it still is for him to be in the house without Phillip. "We've got a big performance in December," he says. "We're pretty busy with rehearsals and all."

"She's a dancer too?"

"Yes." I hear a slight hesitation in his voice. "She's…incredible."

"You mentioned that." I decide to spare him. "Okay, I'll try to come up soon."

"Great," El says. "And just so you know, Mom, Rachel's older than I am."

"How much?" I say.

"Ten years."

"Ten years! Isn't she a bit old for college?"

"Age isn't relevant," El says.

"It isn't?"

"It's just a construct designed by our limited human imagination to cubbyhole and imprison us. In the big cosmic scene, ten years is nothing," he says. "Trust me, Mom. It's all copacetic."

"Copa *what*?"

After I hang up the phone, I pout. The big cosmic scene. Copacetic. Hrumph. Age isn't relevant? What would he know about it? Oh god. I look over at a reproachful Maude.

"I know," I say. "I'm starting to sound like my mother."

Eliot Ambrose Chicarelli. How we could have done our son so wrong in the naming department, I'll never know. There'd been three generations of Eliots in my family (Charlie is Eliot Charles, III), but neither of my siblings cooperated by producing any male progeny. Nell is long divorced after a brief and disastrous marriage to a much older man and "childless," as my mother likes to put it. Charlie and his wife Emma have three grown daughters. So I gave in to the pressure to carry on the name when the twins were born, in exchange for being able to name our daughter Maxine, a name both sets of grandparents considered coarse, if not a bit vulgar.

Sensing early on, by the time Eliot was four or five, a fey little wisp of a boy, that we'd made a mistake by giving him this prissy, WASPy name, I took to calling him simply El, thinking it had a stronger, more masculine tenor to it, like those other one-syllable boy names—Rex, Ed, Al, Joe—you know, like *Guy*. This second act of treachery and bad taste on my part only further united the grandparents against me, in their collective bewilderment that I would take my son's perfectly respectable name and reduce it to no more than a letter of the alphabet, a random syllable, a crowd noise.

"What about Jay?" I countered. "Or Bea, or Kay? Those are real names. And letters too. I had a friend in college named Dee."

El, who in those days wore firefighter boots with an orange towel cape to bed at night, took right away to his new name. "It's way cooler," he said. "And it rhymes with Hell." Ready for retaliation, we made an alliance. We'd really play it up around the house.

"What would you like for lunch, El?" I'd say.

And El would grin and say, "I'll have peanut butter and JELLy," jumping up and down on the couch, shouting his new name out loud, "Because I'm El ChicaRELLi!"

Over time, the nickname slowly took. My father died soon after. To this day, part of me feels that the truncation of my son's name was the last family indignity by which he could abide, and that I was partly to blame for his demise. When the twins were six, El tagged along with Max to ballet lessons at the Elks Hall every Wednesday. She quickly tired of the rigor and repetition of the classes, but El was a natural and continued dancing twice a week for the next five years, undaunted by the fact that he was often the only boy in a class of conspiratorial, tutued girls. But one day, after he'd just turned eleven, he came home from school and announced, "Joey Bergeron says ballet's for faggots."

"Homosexuals, El," I said. "I'm guessing Joey Bergeron isn't the sharpest tool in the shed."

"Still, I can't do dance anymore." El did the rapid blinking thing that meant he'd made up his mind.

"Why not?" I felt more heartbroken, I thought, than he did.

"Because if I keep on dancing," he said, "I can't be happy."

"But I thought dancing made you happy."

"It does," he said. "That's why I have to stop." I knew better than to argue. There's no wiggle room in the logic of an eleven-year-old. I should know. I lived with two of them for an entire year.

El put his tights and black ballet slippers into the Goodwill bag and from that day on marched bravely into the world of guy bravado—baseball cards and X-men, transformers and skateboards, high-fives and 'sup dude?' and jazzy, expensive sneakers that you waited in line for the night before they hit the stores. He joined first the badminton, and then the cross-country team in junior high. A half-hearted, mediocre sportsman at best, still, he'd made his bid to throw himself into the macho fray. And say whatever else you wanted about the kid—he could run.

El sprouted nearly five inches his freshman year of high school and made the varsity soccer team the next year. He was nicknamed *El Guepardo*—the Cheetah—and for three years, he played the part. He could've played soccer for any number of colleges that tried to recruit him, but I knew this and only I knew—that the day El Chicarelli mailed his one and only college application, early decision, to Bennington College, up in rural Vermont, an artsy, no-requirements kind of place, he was taking back his childhood, the dream he'd banished that day along with his black ballet slippers, the gentle, artistic persona he'd abandoned in order to survive in a boy's rough and tumble world. By seventeen, El had finally grown strong and brave enough to do what he'd been planning since that day when he was eleven—wait patiently to grow up, so that he could be a dancer.

Funny how the X and Y chromosomes cross paths and collide. From the start, Max had more so-called boy traits than El. She was loud and bossy and messy and daring, whereas El was neat and quiet and sensitive and unfailingly polite. I was determined not to make Max wear frilly dresses or El play with trucks and balls. I defended Max's spirit of adventure, her boldness—she the one to take apart our toasters and alarm clocks and stage Barbie warrior battles on the living room floor, perfecting the explosion noise in her cheeks long before her brother did.

Likewise did I champion El's need for order and calm, his gentle, nurturing side—he the one who put Max's dolls to bed at night, rescuing them from far-flung corners, plastic limbs splayed, hair matted, eyes rolling back into their heads, bodies often slashed and gouged after having gone under the knife of the famous surgeon, Dr. Maxine Chicarelli. El would wash them, comb their hair, put mercurochrome and Band-Aids on their wounds, dress them in pajamas, tuck them into bed. Years later, those dolls wouldn't have recognized the ferocious six-foot soccer player splattered with mud out on the playing field, his gruff voice and muscled arms—their old and loving caretaker.

So now, at fifty-three, I'm setting out to explore my masculine side, as I've always encouraged Max to do, not to let it threaten her femininity, but rather complement it. After Isabelle abandons me for Emil, and the bar for the coffee shop, I'm clearly on my own. Over breakfast one morning, I make a concrete plan. I'll go out two nights a week to the Wonder Bar for "research" sake, establish myself there as a regular presence. I want to get comfortable with going out alone, to demystify the old male bastion of the barstool. Let's face it. No man of any age berates himself for being out on the town alone, for seeking solace in a beer or a friendly chat with a stranger. A man sitting alone in a bar is not desperate or pathetic or even a drunk. A guy on a barstool is just, well...a guy on a barstool. It's the oldest legacy in the book, how some of the best jokes begin—a man simply walks into a bar.

Why can't a woman?

I also decide I can't limit my travels to just one place. Now that I'm a working columnist, I owe it to my readers to expand my bar horizons. Plus which, since I know that Fuzz's haunt of choice is the Wonder Bar, I sense it would be wise for me to maximize both my personal and professional options by extending my range. I feel certain this is what Sheila Lafarge would advise.

And so Wednesday becomes my "rogue" bar night, a chance to explore other hangouts. There's no shortage of them from Harvard Square to Alewife. The next Wednesday, even though I'm exhausted from my new work schedule, I take the plunge and get ready to go out alone. I consider calling Isabelle for an outfit consultation, but reconsider in the end. She'd only insist on my borrowing some svelte number she'd have to bring over, something in which I could never in a million years feel comfortable, like that pricey ice-blue cocktail dress she talked me into buying at some snooty boutique in the Square two years ago for a small fortune. It hangs neglected in the closet, tags still on but new smell vanished, and sneers at me. "Coward," it whispers.

As I get dressed, I try to get myself into a realistic frame of mind, an exercise that amounts to a sort of pre-emptive strike against disappointment. It's clear to me that, like everything else, this business of meeting people is a matter of odds. So here's what I figure. Of the small percentage of men in whom I might be interested, take the even tinier percentage of that already miniscule number that might be interested back. Then throw in unforeseen problems of geography, politics, personal details as yet undiscovered—closet NRA membership, halitosis, Mama's boy-itis, foot fetishism—and you're left with such an infinitesimal number of possibilities, it's beyond disheartening. I almost succumb to my urge to slip back into my QUESTION

AUTHORITY T-shirt and watch an *I Dream of Jeannie* marathon in the purple chair, but give myself a last-minute pep talk and persevere. After one final glance in the floor-length mirror in the hallway, I head for the door.

As I walk to Bar None down near Porter Square, I go over the checklist of things I meant to do before I left the house. As usual, there's room for improvement. Damn, I keep forgetting to put that lipstick I bought at CVS into my purse, a pale rose that suits my skin tone way better than Isabelle's dark hues. And I can't believe I neglected to brush my teeth after I ate all that garlic hummus. And that eight-dollar bar of organic soap that was supposed to make my skin soft and supple? Instead, it feels more like dried leather, with a lingering smell not unlike creosote.

At least I'm comfortable in the clothes I'm wearing—black jeans, a purple lace camisole and grey cashmere cardigan with a sparkly, striped scarf, blue suede boots, moonstone earrings. It's pretty much the same outfit I wore that first night out with Isabelle, with various accessory changes. To this day, Celia still says of me: "You can take the girl out of Cambridge, but never the Cambridge out of the girl." She should talk; she's turned into one of those kooky Cantabrigian octogenarians wearing knee socks with Birkenstocks all year round, striding around town with the monogrammed canvas bag she got at L.L. Bean fifty years ago, the handle in tatters, albeit, the highest quality tatters.

I enter Bar None armed with the following facts.

1) I'm a published writer.
2) My hair is not grey.
3) I can hold my breath under water for almost a minute.
4) And, as my father used to pronounce in stentorian tones: A Hobbes is nothing if not determined.

Bar None is more trendy than the Wonder Bar, which is to say, it's more expensive and caters to a younger crowd. Two more dollars for every glass of mediocre wine, and a decrease of probably a third in the over-forty population. The front corner seat is empty and I slide into it gratefully. Besides being the best spot for people-watching, it also offers the perk of having a wall to lean against. As clearly the oldest person at the bar, I feel more than entitled. It's a blissfully low-lit place. Most bars are, I suppose. A ripple of uneasiness slides up my spine. How long before I start to feel like Blanche DuBois in *Streetcar,* who refused to let Mitch see her in the light of day?

I take out my notebook and pen to write. But the creative juices aren't exactly flowing. So I prime the pump by writing down a few of my favorite jokes.

Here's the thing. A chicken and an egg were lying in bed together. The chicken was smiling and smoking a cigarette while the egg lay there looking decidedly miserable. The egg looked over at the chicken and muttered, "Well, I guess we answered that question."

And here's one of my all-time favorite jokes, a bit of a mouthful but always a crowd-pleaser.

Disillusioned by the crass and material world, a man joins a monastery and takes a vow of silence. He's allowed to speak only two words every ten years. After the first ten years, the monseigneur asks him what he has to say. "Bed hard," the man replies. After the next ten years, when he's asked again what he'd like to say, he replies, "Food sucks." Finally, after thirty long years, the two words he chooses to say are, "I quit."

The monseigneur looks at the man disdainfully and says. "I'm not at all surprised. You've done nothing but complain since you got here." *Bada boom!*

After the monk joke, I force myself to get serious. I need an idea for my first post in *Squiggle Z*, something zingy to grab my audience right away. I look around to get a sense of the crowd. I figure there're about one and a half men for every woman at the bar, but of course that's just from a heterosexual viewpoint. A friend of mine recently asked her boyfriend to marry her on Sadie Hawkins Day, after twenty years of living together. At the wedding, the groom joked that the reason she beat him to the punch was that he thought only gay people got married in Cambridge. So who knows how it all breaks down? I recently read a *Cosmo* article at the dentist's office about how much courage it takes for men to talk to women at the bar, how it's women who wield the power in the war of the sexes, how intimidated men are by our coldness and constant rejection. I decide to try and consider the scene from the male perspective. I can do that. A man hater I've never been.

Frankly, though, I'm skeptical. Men handle rejection inherently better than women. Here's my theory, hardly earth-shattering. It has three parts. First, from day one, families make their sons feel as if they're gods incarnate. Then the culture continues to imbue them with an indomitable sense of power and invincibility and they run blissfully with that for the rest of their lives. Secondly, men know how to enjoy themselves. Because they've always been *allowed* to enjoy themselves. Boys, of course, will always be boys. Girls, however, are in training from day one to be saints—selfless, loyal, sensitive, modest, nurturing. How on earth are they ever supposed to learn how to have fun? And whereas women tend to see the glass half empty, just to be on the safe side, most men opt to call it half full. Why the hell not? For a guy, if nothing works out on the romantic front, there's always sports to talk about, the endless spewing and swapping of stats and plays and trades and cars and boats and deals and fishing and all the ones that got away. And thirdly, and most importantly: boys just aren't too "swift," as my mother used to say.

We women need to have a little chat with ourselves when we head out onto the front lines. We need to land on those barstools with the simple goal of enjoying ourselves and having that be enough, without there needing to be a purpose or a game plan or a prize. And then it comes to me, the title for my first column: "The New Deal: Redefining goals and expectations on a night out alone." 'Course I'll have to come up with a sexier title, maybe "He wants: She wants," or some such fluff.

A sudden whoosh of cool air from the door announces a new arrival. Into the bar walks a dark-haired, olive-skinned beauty with glittering green eyes, five foot ten if she's an inch. As she heads for the bar, the scene slips into slow motion, as it would midway through an ad for sanitary napkins or online dating. All eyes turn, from the sports on the TV screens, from fruity drinks and menus, dinner dates and steaming plates of food, just to take her in. You can almost feel the collective, simultaneous stirring of every male member in the room.

"Dark and Stormy," the woman says to the bartender, swinging her long legs over a barstool a few seats down. "Extra thunder," she deadpans.

The bartender laughs nervously, not sure if he can deliver. I give him a sympathetic smile. Next to this gazelle-like creature, I feel like a jellyfish. We Hobbes women burn to a crisp in the sun and are prone to rare dermatological disorders. But this woman's face is as smooth and soft as coffee taffy before it hardens and her lit green eyes could guide ships home through a foggy night.

"It's Raven Mulholland," the guy next to me says, nudging his very tall friend beside him.

"Raven who?" I whisper.

"Shhh!" the guy scolds me, as if I've interrupted the last crucial play of the Super Bowl.

"The girl that used to be in those ads," his tall friend leans back to tell me.

"What ads?" I give the other guy an icy glare.

Raven Mulholland, I soon find out, is a bit of a local celebrity. In the late Eighties she was the "actress" in a series of popular TV commercials in which she regularly got squeezed out of a toothpaste tube in scanty clothing to promote a doomed product called "Dazzle" toothpaste. No surprise I missed them. Those days were a blur—of dirty diapers and broken toys, leftovers and cheery Raffi ditties that nearly drove me mad. I order another glass of wine and sit back to watch the show. Raven keeps to herself, sipping her drink, posture flawless, clearly in need of no one or nothing except her own exquisite company. But the men in the bar, now jolted out of their initial stupor, have started to twitch again.

In the space of a half an hour, three guys have come up to Raven to say essentially the same asinine thing:

"Hey, aren't you that girl who used to get squeezed out of a toothpaste tube on TV?" She offers no response, just a look that's both withering and sexy as hell. The third guy that approaches is clearly drunk and bent on trouble. The bars on this strip of Mass. Ave. don't usually attract the hardcore boozers, more often the Harvard Law School students and "yuppie" crowd, if that's still even a word. But somehow this blowhard has found his way to Raven Mulholland's side, and he is, to put it mildly—tanked.

"Hey, schweetheart, lemme ashk you something," he drawls. "How the hell'd they fit those melons into that goddamn tube o' toothpaste?" He gestures to her breasts with his bottle of beer, unsteady on enormous sneakered feet. "That hadda be some kind of wicked schpecial effects." He starts to careen headlong into her lap, just barely catching himself on the edge of the bar. "How the hell'd they frickin' do that?" he says.

"Okay, pal, that's enough," the bartender says.

Raven raises a hand to silence him, cool as a cucumber, even as the jerk persists.

"Yeah," the drunk drawls on. "I woulda thought that rack of yours woulda busted that toothpaste tube wide open." He laughs raucously. "You know what I'm talkin' about, hon?"

Raven finally turns to him and smiles. "And I'm guessing all your family jewels," she says, in a voice smooth as honey, "would've fit right into the cap."

My jaw drops. The drunk guy looks furious, and then dumbstruck, until Raven lets loose that outrageous smile. He gives in to that smile, to that face, to that body, to that dig, and starts to laugh, drunken hyena style, and then Raven laughs and I sort of laugh and while we're all yukking it up, the bartender escorts the drunk guy to the door. Raven smiles the way Popeye does after making mincemeat of Bluto, takes another sip of her drink without missing a beat. I give her an admiring nod.

"I owe you one," Raven says dryly to the bartender when he returns. "What's your name?"

"Asa," he says, resting his arms on the bar. "Would you consider marrying me? Preferably tonight?"

Raven Mulholland laughs. "Maybe tomorrow," she says.

"I can wait," Asa says steadily.

In my notebook, I write, "Note to Self: Maybe that *Cosmo* article had a point."

The rude guy next to me takes off, leaving his nicer friend one seat away. He's almost freakishly tall, reminding me of those leggy Afghan hounds that travel in pairs and walk their well-dressed owners down in the South End. His features are fine, eyes wide-set, and his silky black hair is tied back in a loose ponytail that grazes his neck. I see in him an elongated Bruce Lee. He pulls out a copy of William Dean Howell's *The Rise of Silas Lapham.*

"That's such a great book," I say.

"You've read it?" he says doubtfully.

"A couple of times." I look to see how far he's gotten. "I love the part where Persis refuses to enter the house because it was bought with blood money."

"That is a good part." He gestures to my notebook. "Are you a writer?"

"Of sorts." This is my latest, evasive answer.

"I always wanted to be a writer," he says. "It was the road not taken for me." He must be all of thirty-five.

"Which road *did* you take?" I run my hand through my hair.

"Computer science," he says with a sigh. "I'm one of the crawling masses over in the Kendall Square think tanks." He holds out his hand. "Dylan Guthrie."

"That's admirable," I say. "You're probably one of the geniuses who's going to save us all from doom and destruction one day."

"I would rather write about it," he says. "Do you write about doom and destruction?"

"Heavy on the doom," I say. "At least in what I'm working on these days. A novel set in the late sixties."

"I wish I'd lived in the sixties," he says. "All I got out of it was the name. My parents loved Dylan. And Woody Guthrie, of course."

"Are you from a musical family?"

He gives a short laugh. "Hardly," he says. "We're all completely tone-deaf. But Bob and Woodie couldn't carry much of a tune, either."

"It's true," I say. "The sixties were wild. But way over-romanticized. Believe me, it wasn't all peace, love, rock 'n' roll." Raven and Asa are now deep in conversation. Obviously, the outrageous line he threw her was worth the gamble.

"What do you mean?" Dylan says.

"All those kids were getting maimed and killed over in Vietnam and we were back here getting stoned and having sex," I say. "We thought we were doing our part, going to protests and marches, but it was mostly an excuse to get high and raise our voices." I take a sip of my wine. "I always felt like a hypocrite. The baby boomers got lost in this hazy, sunlit time warp that we've never really escaped from. And now we feel like intruders in the twenty-first century."

"That's brilliant," Dylan says, slowly nodding his head.

"I don't know about that." I'm amazed I haven't bored him to tears.

"Listen." Dylan takes one last swig of his beer. "I just stopped in for a quick pop. I play hockey every other Wednesday night out in Saugus and I've got to go. Hockey's the only thing that makes me feel somewhat…normal. I happen to be good at it. Otherwise…" He holds up the book. "I'm a bit of a nerd. What did you say your name was?"

"Grace," I say. "I didn't say."

"I feel a real connection to you, Grace," he says.

"You do?"

"I do," says Dylan Guthrie, with all the solemnity of the marriage vow. "I could see myself building something with you."

"You could?"

"I'm about to go out of town for a while," he says. "But let's make a plan for when I get back."

I look over at Raven triumphantly. Maybe this cougar stuff is easier than I thought. A giant, intelligent, soft-spoken young man with a disdain for contractions might be interested in what I have to offer, what I have to say.

And so we agree, to meet again, the first Wednesday night in November, same time, same place, same barstools. To build something. Together. Anything he has in mind. A sand castle, a bridge, a website, a tree house. I'm more than game.

I slide easily into my routine at the Mustard Seed, getting to know all of the players, the rhymes and reasons of the place, or lack thereof. I feel right at home. There's a feeling of just barely controlled chaos at the store that feels familiar and comforting, some low-level crisis always threatening to erupt. It's how life in our house always rolled. One day the dessert freezers are on the blink and the next the sprayers in the produce aisle go bonkers and cause a flood. Protesters picket outside because we carry white sugar, and a woman becomes incensed when she finds out we don't have any organic soursop. "What kind of natural food store is this?" she demands.

My art "corner," consists of a fold-up table and chair, and an old easel I found in the basement, along with a brilliant array of every conceivable color of chalk, plus some fancy new chalkboard paints I've been experimenting with. The sun streams in through the skylights and I drink endless cups of free, freshly brewed coffee. I water the tropical plants twice a week and keep the flower buckets filled. I smell the lilies and the baked chestnuts and the free-range chickens roasting on a spit. When it rains, the drops spatter comfortingly on the skylights. Classical muzac streams out of the speakers on the wall. I can't believe I get paid for what I do.

Otis's trip comes to an end. I've been grateful for the buffer time. It's given me a chance to settle in gracefully. But I can't stop thinking about our encounter in the men's health aisle and the amputee fetish thing. I wish Isabelle had never mentioned it. One Thursday afternoon, the store is buzzing with the news that Otis will be in the next day. I steel myself and try to keep my cool. We're both grown-ups. We agreed. That day in the store. It was an impulsive, one-time thing. No big deal.

But by the time I get to work on Friday morning, the day has already started out as a disaster. My washing machine broke the night before and now I'll have to take time off on Monday to wait around for the repair person. Then I find out from the store manager that I accidentally erased the first 1 in an $11.99 price marker while making a sign for shiitake mushrooms the day before, and seventeen customers got away with buying them for $1.99 a pound before a cashier finally noticed my mistake.

In addition, that random period which surprises me every once in a blue moon chose this morning to present itself with a rush of blood between my legs as I was parking the car in the store lot, and in the past hour, I've developed excruciating cramps. I don't have a change of clothes, so I'm trying to hide the stain on my jeans by wearing a black apron backward. The only comforting thought is that I'm not pregnant. It's been weighing on me that I didn't ask Otis to use a condom. And that he didn't offer. It was all so quick and surreal. I haven't been too worried. Most of those sperm never had a chance to make much of a journey except down the side of my thigh. But you never know. Sometimes you got a defiant, rogue warrior.

At about ten o'clock, Otis comes in the front door, greeting people with a handshake or a hug. Everyone seems genuinely pleased to see him. I'm up on a ladder in the produce aisle, watering the dracaena, so I have the advantage of watching him for a while before he sees me. Gone is the untucked flannel shirt and steaming mug of coffee. Gone, too, is the slightly sad wistfulness I noticed that first day. He's all business now, a snappy striped dress shirt and Escher bird tie, pressed khaki pants and clipboard in hand. Again, the sleeve which would have covered his right arm had it been there is hemmed to size and ironed crisply. I wonder if he does this task himself or if he has a designated sleeve-shortener.

Otis finally spots me and waves. I wave back, inadvertently tipping the watering can and spilling water on the floor.

"How's it going, Grace?" He comes over to the ladder, avoiding the puddle.

"Great?" I look down at him. "I can't thank you enough, Otis. I love this job."

"The sale boards look fantastic!"

"Thanks."

"Want to come down and take a break?" he says. "Have a cup of coffee?" He sees my hesitation. "Just coffee," he says with a smile.

We retire to my art corner. I offer him a cookie from my stash.

"Mmm," he says. "I love Fig Newtons."

"Not many of us left," I say.

Otis fiddles with his clipboard. "I just wanted to check in, Grace. Make sure we're okay."

"We're definitely okay," I say, relieved we've gotten this out of the way so quickly and with so little ado.

"Great," Otis says.

"So, where've you been?" I reach for a Lorna Doone.

"Idaho."

My mind draws a blank. "Potatoes?" I say.

"Lots of potatoes. And people too," Otis teases. "Real, live, upright, articulate homo sapiens. I ran into quite a few of them."

"Of course," I say sheepishly, dunking my cookie into my coffee. "Business or pleasure?"

"Bit of both," Otis says. "I went to an organic food conference in Boise and then there's this woman—"

"Ah, a damsel." I take a bite of my soggy cookie.

"She's an old flame," he says. "We reconnected online recently. I went out there to visit."

"I hope it works out," I say.

"Time will tell," he says. "I hope you don't think any worse of me for—"

"No, no, not at all!" I assure him. "You know, Otis." I finger what's left of my cookie nervously. "My friend Isabelle told me that some people really get into, well…" I look around to make sure no one's listening. "Having sex with amputees. I just wanted to say…I didn't even know that. I swear. What happened that day had nothing to do with—"

Otis laughs. "Don't worry. I didn't take you for one of those types, Grace. You haven't even asked me about my arm yet."

"Which one?" I say. "The one you have? Or the one you don't?"

He laughs. "Most people are more curious about the latter."

I have to think for a second. That former-latter construction always throws me.

I tilt my head. "When you said your arm, I guess I pictured the one you do have. I'm literal that way. It used to drive my husband crazy." I tear open a sugar packet, wondering how I'd manage with only one hand, thinking that this one, small random act is only one of thousands Otis has had to learn how to do differently.

"I wish I could say that I battled a crocodile and saved the day," Otis says. "But it's not anywhere near as glamorous a story."

"What could possibly be glamorous about losing an arm?" I say.

"I was working construction one summer in my twenties and a metal box fell on my arm," he says. "I thought I'd just have a nasty bruise for a while, but I got something called acute compartment syndrome, where the swollen muscles from the trauma block the blood flow. Basically, my arm just died. They weren't able to save it."

"How terrible!" I say.

"I was a strong, healthy kid and it shouldn't have happened," he says. "But it did. I felt very sorry for myself for a long, long time."

"I would've fallen completely to pieces."

"I did," Otis says. "But luckily, after a while, that got boring. Eventually, I picked myself up, finished college and went to graduate school, got married and had a kid, bought this store."

"How long has it been?" I say.

"Twenty-five years," he says. "Soon, I will have lived longer without my right arm than with it."

I do the math. So he's younger than fifty-three, but not by much.

"And to think that before I went in for the surgery," Otis goes on. "I was upset that I was going to miss my baseball league playoffs. Little did I know…"

"Do you still play?"

He nods. "I've learned to throw and bat lefty. And my daughter, Zephyr, inherited the right arm I used to have. She's a regular Roger Clemens."

I think of the endless Boston sporting events that have been a constant aural backdrop of my life—the drone of the sportscasters' voices, the murmur of the crowd, Johnny Kiley's staircase organ riffs, the mighty crack of the bat at Fenway. I'm enough of a Red Sox fan to know that Clemens was the all-time strike-out leader, that his nickname was the Rocket, that chicken is his favorite food and that his politics are way too far to the right for my liking. And I suspect that meeting Otis and getting this job is the best thing that's happened to me in a long time.

6

I wake up one Saturday morning in mid-October with the vague feeling that some truth revealed itself to me in a dream the night before. I've only recently begun to remember my dreams again. For years, they've been shut deep inside me, flashing in bright, distant fragments by day—a face here, a word, a smell, a nagging feeling that floats away into space—uncatchable. But for the past few weeks, my dreams have been right up there on the big screen each morning, in vivid living color, *Gone with the Wind*-like sagas starring all the characters of my life in surreal, otherworldly colors and modes. Even the Vulcan-like creatures in the paintings on the wall at the Wonder Bar have started to roam my nocturnal subconscious.

I'm briskly stirring the Irish oatmeal on the stovetop when the dream comes back to me. Nell and I were young, maybe six and nine. We'd just had a terrible argument with Celia—the kind of visceral, screaming fight you can only have in dreams, when your raging id is unleashed—and been sent to our rooms without supper. Later that night, we snuck out into the backyard and burned all the ugly clothes our mother made us wear. The next morning at the breakfast table, she told us that we couldn't be her daughters anymore. We ran away to live in the forest (actually the playground around the corner, which wasn't even there back in the day). We pricked our fingers with a black-tipped needle and took the blood oath of unloved children, built a lean-to out of sticks and mud and made our own clothes from newspaper, bark, and leaves. When we were hungry, we stole Fritos and chocolate milk from the corner store and spied on our brother Charlie through the bushes, practicing his cello in the living room, while his guinea pig, Boxer, chewed on his sheet music on the floor.

And as the oatmeal comes back to a boil, I realize what's

been bothering me—I miss my sister. In good WASP fashion, Nell and I have basically been avoiding each other since Whack Sunday, although we've both gone to a few family gatherings and pretended nothing ever happened. But the last time I saw Nell at Charlie's fifty-fifth birthday party a few weeks ago, I was shaken. She was thinner than usual and her hair was messy. Moreover, I could have sworn there was a food stain on her mint-green hoodie.

Nell's called a few times after a glass of Dubonnet or two to beg my forgiveness. And no matter how many times I tell her she wasn't responsible for the breakup of my marriage, she won't believe me. I get it. Guilt clings long and hard to us WASPs, like single socks to the dryer wall. And I have to admit that I've been taking a certain mean-spirited pleasure in knowing how much Nell's been suffering. It definitely served her right to stew for a good, long while. But guilt's slowly caught up with me too. I'm still punishing my sister, even though no true crime was committed. She's the kid standing guilty in the corner for breaking the cookie jar, unaware how badly it was already cracked. In truth, I've secretly come to think of Nell as Phillip's and my unlikely savior.

After breakfast, I walk over to Nell's apartment in Inman Square to make amends. It's a warm day and the autumn leaves are at peak brilliance. I buy lilies from the flower shop on Brattle Street to bring as a peace offering. At the rock fountain near the Science Center, I take off my shoes and sit down on one of the rocks, feeling the cool spray wash over me. A frail Brother Blue, wearing his signature blue beret, weaves his stories from the heart to anyone who will stop to listen. I remind myself as I sit there that I have no intention of hailing Nell as a savior to her face. That would be going too far. After all, Phillip was my husband and she was my sister—and a kiss was a kiss was a kiss. Not to mention the additional canoodling on the couch, which I simply refuse to let my mind imagine. But I'm no sadist (our mother more than adequately plays that role in our family) and I'm ready to bury the hatchet. Nell's miserable and I miss her, if only because without her, I've lost my lone ally against Celia, who reports approvingly that Nell's lost weight, unaware of the true cause.

I walk down Cambridge Street past the high school and the hospital, and turn onto Elm Street, where Nell lives in a sunny one-bedroom apartment on the third floor of an old Victorian. I climb the stairs, knowing the bell is broken and knock loudly on her door.

Nell's face appears in the open crack of the door. "Hi," she says uncertainly.

"I forgive you," I say, holding up the flowers. "You are officially off the wicked sister hook."

"Really?" Nell flings open the door and throws her arms around me. "Oh, Gracie. I thought you were never going to talk to me again. I'm so sorry."

"I know." I pat Georgia, a life-sized papier-mâché giraffe in her foyer, on the neck. "It's all water under the bridge now."

"But how can it ever be the same between us?" Nell says, wringing her hands.

"It won't," I say. "It'll be different." I plop down on Nell's couch, which is covered with an African giraffe print. "We're both single women now. And to tell you the truth..." I decide to throw her a bone after all. "I'm happier than I've been in years. Life is so much simpler, Nellie. I feel so...free!"

"We've got so much to catch up on!" She sits down next to me. "Where to start? How're the twins doing?"

"Max is still mad." I stretch out my legs in front of me. "I guess I can't blame her."

"She must hate me," Nell says. "I wrote her a letter trying to explain, but she never wrote back."

"Give her time," I say. "She thinks Phillip and I gave up on our family. El seems to have made more peace with it all. I thought it would be the other way around. Maybe it's because he's distracted. He called the other day to say he's got a girlfriend."

"Shut the front door!"

"Her name is Rachel and she's ten years older than he is."

"Ooh la la." Now that Nell's convinced I've forgiven her, she's slid back into her old gossipy self. "Talk about robbing the cradle!"

"Not much I can do about it," I groan. "I'm just the mom."

"Wait until Celia hears," Nell says.

"Celia's not going to hear about it until El tells her himself. Isn't that right, Nell Wilder Hobbes?"

"Okay, okay." Nell makes the motion of zipping up her lips.

"And speaking of mothers," I say. "Have you noticed that ours has been acting strangely lately? I think she's up to something."

"Stranger than usual?" Nell says.

"Yeah, she's all squirrelly and cagey," I say. "Looking dreamily into the abyss and talking about random things—teacups and such. Don't let down your guard."

"I won't," Nell says, and then, after a pause. "Did you ever tell her about…what happened that day?"

"Do you think I'm insane?" I throw a couch pillow at her, which she catches and then balances on her head. "So what's new on the romantic front?" I say. Just before Whack Sunday, I'd helped Nell get registered on Match.com.

"Nothing," she says. The pillow falls off her head. "I've been on a few horrible blind dates. And all the men I meet on my own are either psycho or married or gay."

"You've got to get out there, Nell. You spend all your time at school or holed up in your apartment or out looking for giraffe memorabilia. Come to the bar some night with me."

"I'm a sloppy drunk," Nell says. "You know that. I'd only embarrass myself. And you too."

"You don't have to get drunk," I say.

"That's what people do at bars, isn't it?"

"Not all of them," I say.

"Have you…met anyone?" she says, haltingly.

"No one…significant," I say.

"What do you mean—significant?" Nell slips into the lotus

position and lurches toward me. "You mean you have sex with random strangers?"

"They're only random at the beginning," I say, crossing my arms defensively.

"Wow!" Nell says. "Way to get revenge on Mother!"

"I'm not doing it to get revenge, Nell. This is the twenty-first century. We're modern-day women. We're allowed to have sex lives. I can't believe I have to give you this speech."

"How many guys have you—"

"Let's just drop it."

"Two?" she says. "Three?" I feel my face redden. *"More?"*

"Just two," I shush her. "Well, technically, one and a half. But there is another guy—"

"You sneaky little slut!" Nell says, throwing the pillow back at me.

"For god's sake, Nell!" I catch it neatly. She's three years younger than me, just enough to have missed the height of the sexual revolution in the sixties. "If a guy sleeps with three women, he's a stud, but if a woman does, she's a slut? Please! We're not living in the Dark Ages!"

"You're right," she says.

"Have you ever considered dating women?" I say. "You keep saying all your relationships with men are disastrous."

"Maybe I should," she says. "There'd be so much less bull-shit, so much less drama." She sighs. "I don't know. I'm beginning to think I'm just an all-round romantic loser."

"No one's a romantic loser," I say. "There's someone out there for everyone, Nell. In fact, there are dozens of someones out there for everyone."

"I haven't found even one," Nell says, settling into a slump. "And I'm pushing fifty!"

"There's a handsome stranger," I say. "I know there is. Just waiting to walk through that door."

"How will he know where I live?" Nell says.

"When you *tell* him," I say, tossing up my hands.

The light streaming in from the window shifts slightly and

a breeze from the open window rustles the curtains behind my head.

"Want some tea?" Nell asks. "I just got this ginger-peach herbal that will tame any beast that may live inside you. And I had no idea how many there were!"

"No thanks." I get up off the couch. "I made a vow to work on my novel for at least two hours every day." I slide my red espadrilles back on. "I just have one more question," I say. "And I want you to tell me the truth."

Nell nods apprehensively. "I will," she says solemnly.

"Do you have feelings for Phillip?" I say.

A look of terror crosses Nell's face for a second, but then it fades back into calm. "For those few minutes, at your house that day, I thought maybe I did," she says. "But now I never want to see him again."

"Because if you do, that's different," I say. "If you do, Nellie, then you need to tell me."

"I don't." Nell looks at me with those dewy Peter Pan eyes and of all the possible choices I have to make at that moment, the easiest one is to believe her. "I promise," she says.

Phillip's certainly not pining away. He has what Max keeps calling this "straight-up gorgeous" apartment in East Cambridge, which makes me feel as though our crooked old house is downright shabby. Maybe it's time to spruce things up a bit—get a jazzy new living room rug, or at least wash the slipcovers on the purple chair. Phillip also has a new girlfriend named Yvonne, a designer who often collaborates with his architecture firm. He calls to announce this quite formally, in the name of "full disclosure," but it's Max who gives me the real scoop. She comes over to the house one day to rummage in the attic for Halloween costumes. She's looking for something Andy Warhol slash Jack the Ripperish. We drink ginger tea at the kitchen table.

"Dad got totally snagged by that Yvonne broad," she says. "She's been waiting to pounce on him for years."

"She has?" How do my children know such things?

"Yeah, she's always lurking around his desk, all…Phil this and Phil that. Didn't you ever notice?"

"Apparently not," I say.

Yvonne is, of course, younger than I am—eight years to be exact. Max says she has an awesome sense of style and that Phillip's new apartment is starting to look like something out of a high-end design magazine. I've promised myself I won't grill my children about Phillip's new life, about his bachelor digs or any of the women he may be seeing, but it's hard not to be curious, and a bit devious.

"Interesting that your dad has a girlfriend whose name begins with Y." I figure this could only be construed as innocuous.

"That is such a random thing to say," Max says.

"Of all the letters. I'd even have guessed Z before Y. They're plenty of cool Z names—Zelda, Zena, Zola, Zadie. But only those frou-frou French names begin with Y—Yvette, Yvonne, Yolande."

Max shrugs. "It's just her name," she says. "You really can't hold that against her."

"I was just wondering…"

"Relax, Mom. She's not that pretty." Max pulls a rubber gorilla mask over her head.

"Oh." I'm not quite sure how to take this, as a slight to Yvonne or me. Or maybe both of us.

"How 'bout you, Mom, Are you 'dating'?" What is it with kids these days and their constant need to curl up their fingers to denote quotation marks? Whatever happened to good old-fashioned, snarling, straight-ahead sarcasm?

"I wouldn't say I'm dating." Unlike Phillip, I haven't embraced the concept of "full disclosure" yet.

"That's maddeningly vague." Max pops wasabi peas into her mouth through a hole in the gorilla mask. "What would you say, then?"

"Well, I have been stepping out."

"Stepping out?" She yanks the mask off her face and her bangs stand up on end from the static. "What's that supposed to mean?"

It hits me like a lightning bolt. The grand apple doesn't fall far from the grand tree. Max is as ruthless and relentless an interrogator as Celia.

"Stepping out as in, I've gone out to a few bars and met a few people," I say steadily.

"How many people?" Max's eyes narrow.

"One..." I pause. "Or two."

"And what do you 'do' with these people?" Again with the curled up fingers.

"We talk," I say. "Have a glass of wine. So far, it seems—"

"You know what?" Max grabs the Halloween costumes and heads for the door. "Forget I ever asked."

In the last week of October, I get a call from Fuzz from out of the blue, announcing that he's broken up with his "lady," as he puts it. Time to get rid of that moniker. The only female who ever wore it with dignity was the cocker spaniel in *Lady and the Tramp*. I'm completely caught off guard. I thought I'd put the whole Fuzz incident to bed, so to speak, but as his low voice streams through the receiver, the specter of that first steamy night in the car rears its tempestuous head. Since Fuzz reignited the sexual flame, I've been feeling incredibly—horny lately. Do people still use that awful word?

"It's completely over?" I say.

"Finito," Fuzz says. "She moved out yesterday. I told you things might change."

"You had sex with me while you were living with her?" I say. "That's pretty shabby, don't you think?"

"Water under the bridge," he says. It's not lost on me that this is the line I threw Nell a few days before.

"So what happened?" I say. "I thought you were trying to work things out."

"We were."

"And?"

"We didn't." I hear a trace of irritation in his voice, which he then tries to squelch. "And that's why I'm calling you now."

"So, what are you proposing?" Damn. I curse myself silently. Of all the words to use.

"I'm proposing..." He loads the word with disdain. "That we get together for a drink and get reacquainted."

In the old days I might have said, "You mean have sex?" But the new me remembers a) not to be defensive, and b) not to be a hypocrite. Who's kidding whom? I've been dying to have sex again. And again, no offense to Otis, but that time at the Mustard Seed didn't really qualify.

"Okay, one drink," I say. This time, I promise myself, it will be on my terms.

We meet at the Wonder Bar on Halloween night. Bartender Jack is dressed as Death, with a gruesome trickle of blood leaking from the corner of his mouth, and Amanda, the bar back, has a rubber axe through her head. There are giant spiders bouncing from the ceiling and cobwebs draped over the wooden booths. A haunted laugh creeps out of the wall speakers at five-minute intervals, startling me every time. I'm wearing a headband with cat ears and mascara-painted whiskers on my cheeks. Pinned to my black leggings is my tail—made from one of Phillip's old socks filled with more of Phillip's old socks—and I'm sporting a black hoody.

"Meow," Fuzz says. "Sexy kitty."

"I thought we were going to dress up," I said. "What are you supposed to be?"

"Undercover cop," he says. "Narcotics unit. FBI. I may have to frisk you later, ma'am."

"Original." Fuzz can't keep his hands to himself. He caresses my arm, my thigh, the back of my neck. And then he starts playing with my tail. I pull it away and stash it in between my legs. As much as I've been craving his touch since he called, I wish he'd show some restraint. I find PDAs revolting.

"I have ideas, Sherlock," he whispers.

"What kind of ideas?" This sounds ominous.

"Sex ideas," he says. "We're going to try for that eight tonight," he says. "I brought props."

"Props?" I say. "What do you mean, props? And by the way, if we're going to do this—"

"Do what?" His voice has turned Vincent Price creepy. "What are we going to do, kitty cat? Say it. Say it out loud. What we're going to do after—"

"Whoa," I say. "First, let's lay out some ground rules."

"Ground rules?" Fuzz abandons the sleazy voice with a groan. "It's a sin to have rules for sex."

"Guidelines, then," I say. "First off, no more sex in the car."

"Why not?" he says. "I love car sex! There's something about the smell of those leather seats, being near that warm, purring engine…"

"It's my windshield that got cracked," I say.

"All right, all right," he says.

"And we agree, just sex, right? No staying the night, no flowers, no fanfare."

"Got it."

"No other expectations or obligations." I look him squarely in the eye. Why does it feel so strange to be the one initiating this conversation?

"Absolutely," Fuzz says eagerly. Clearly, my conditions have made him very happy and somehow this disarms me. Aren't I supposed to be the one holding the upper hand?

"And as for the condoms," I say. "I took care of the first one. You take care of the rest."

The car door's no sooner closed than he's on top of me. His mouth is wet and warm, and I find myself responding. It's clear that under different circumstances, he and I would be a lousy match. Sooner or later, we'd come to blows. But sexually, there's no doubt there's heat. My body's enjoying this. My body doesn't want to stop.

"I forgot how good you feel," he murmurs, yanking off my cat tail and tossing it into the back seat.

"God, you too."

By now his hands have slid around to my back and found my

bra clasp. The kitty ear headband lands on the steering wheel.

"Okay," I say, breathless, pushing him off me. "Let's go to my place. It's just a few minutes away."

"Don't make me stop now," he says with a groan. "Have a heart, Sherlock."

"Not in the car," I say. "We just agreed."

"Just one more time." He undoes the bra clasp. "Please?"

"Okay, okay." My breasts fall forward. At least he's forgotten about his props. "You get the pants," I say. Fuzz pulls my leggings down to my ankles. I unbutton his shirt and slide it off his shoulders. One hand finds his back, warm and muscled. The other slides down to his lower belly. He moans. I feel him rise hard against my thigh and I take his cock in my hand. And I realize that I've never once called it that before, not even in my wildest fantasies. I've only just recently gotten comfortable with saying the word *penis* out loud. But what I'm holding, in my hand, is Fuzz's warm, very hard cock. And it does, in fact, appear to be throbbing.

"God, you've got great hands," he says. "Make a ring with your thumb and middle finger. Bring it up. Then down. Yes, like that. Right at the rim. Faster." I watch in fascination. I didn't think it was possible but he's actually getting bigger. He slides his hands under me and lifts my legs up to that same impossible angle. Only this time, when he enters me, it's so deep and primeval, I forget for a moment where I am and what I'm doing. And then I feel it, the first tingling when your clitoris is being played just right and the pressure builds until you almost can't bear it. I lift my body up higher with each thrust. And then it happens, with a few strong shudders and that glorious feeling of unnegotiable release. For the first time ever, I've come while having sex with a man.

"Tell me that wasn't an eight," Fuzz says afterward, panting in my ear.

"I'm with you," I say breathlessly. "Maybe even an eight and a half."

So I knew it would happen, sooner or later, that I'd run into one of the twin's friends at the bar. They're all turning twenty-one this year, legal drinkers at last, god help us. But of all the possibilities, did it have to be Elvira Moreley? Elvira and Max went to grammar school together and both ended up at the Museum School in Boston for college. This was no surprise for Max, who was an average student but a gifted painter and sculptor. But Elvira turned down a couple of Ivies to go to art school, much to the chagrin of her parents. At the time, I gave her credit for standing her ground.

People thought I was outrageous, saddling my daughter with the name Maxine, but Elvira? Who can forget "Elvira—Mistress of the Dark"—the dark-eyed vixen who hosted the late-night grade-B horror flicks on UHF TV back in the early Eighties, sporting a sexy black outfit and a beehive hairdo, cleavage beyond belief! Lying seductively on a red velvet couch, she made wisecracks about the movies in a valley girl voice. And this young Elvira is not unlike that mythic one, tall and self-assured, dark, Gothic, I guess they call it now, with a bust that makes me feel lacking in my 36 nearly-B cup push-up bra. Ironically, having come of age in the burn-the-bra era (and being flat as a board and easy to screw, as we used to so charmingly put it), I never even wore a bra until after I had children in my mid-thirties.

"Hi, Mrs. Chicarelli." My attempt to turn away is not successful.

"Elvira. Nice to see you. What is it you're studying at the Museum School?"

"I'm heavy into Found Objects. And the Destructive Arts," she says. She's wearing a massive black cape, high black boots, and black lipstick.

"You mean deconstructive arts?"

"No, destructive."

"Never heard of those."

"Basically, it's about annihilating your artistic creations in order to, like, enhance your true artistic sensibilities," she says.

"Making something and then destroying it. You know, like, acknowledging that something doesn't have to physically exist to be, like, beautiful."

"Interesting," I say. "Could you give me an example?"

"Like I made this gorgeous ceramic vase the other week. Glazed and painted it and made it all 'pretty.'" Black fingernails curl up to make quotation marks around the airborne word. "And then I, like, smashed it to pieces with a hammer."

"Goodness!" My eyes open wide.

"Yeah." She snaps her wad of gum, which flashes tangerine between her teeth. "It was awesome. I felt, like, totally liberated. My professor says it's the up-and-coming thing."

"But here's a thought." I don't know why I take the bait, why I even bother. "If the Destructive Arts become all the rage, won't all of the museums eventually be empty?"

Elvira gives me a stony look. "Maxine told me about the divorce," she says. "Bummer."

"Thanks," I say. "It's really fine, you know, a mutual, friendly kind of thing. Mr. Chicarelli and I will always—"

"Actually, I'm not surprised." She takes another piece of gum out of her enormous black vinyl purse.

"You're not?"

Elvira the Young nods knowingly. "I always thought you two had, like, clashing chis," she says.

"Clashing what?"

"Phillip has more of a cerulean aura—"

"Phillip?" I say. Since when does Elvira Moreley get to refer to my ex by his first name?

"Oh yeah, for sure," she goes on. "His aura is brilliant, luminous, very clear. While yours…" Her fingers start wiggling grotesquely. "Is more of, like, a murky pea green."

"Murky pea green."

"Yeah." She looks down at my feet. "Which is why those lime-colored shoes aren't exactly doing you any favors, if you don't mind my saying so."

"Not at all," I say. "So tell me, Elvira, what color is your aura?"

"Black," she says. "Black, through and through, like, all the way."

With, like, a streak of putrid yellow running through it, I think to myself.

Max calls me the next day. "Elvira Moreley said she saw you last night at the bar. What's up with that, Mom?"

"Word travels fast." I won't be bullied by my beautiful, headstrong daughter. I've done nothing wrong.

"You're fifty-three years old, Mom. What do you even do at the bar?"

"The same thing everyone else does. I have a glass of wine, maybe a good conversation. What's so wrong with that?"

"It's embarrassing!"

"For whom?" I say.

"Me!"

"But you weren't even there," I say.

"Elvira texted me," Max says. "She said you looked..." She nearly spits out the word. "Hot!"

"I certainly did not."

"She said you were wearing some slinky turquoise thing. Since when do you have any slinky turquoise things?"

"Well, I've been trying to branch out a little. Isabelle and I went to Filene's Basement the other day."

"Elvira said you had *cleavage.*" There it is, the final accusation.

"Well, not much, I'm afraid." Wow. That nearly-B push-up bra must be for real. "After all—"

"Yeah, yeah, I know," Max says. It's a family joke. "I got my boobs from Dad."

"Well, not strictly speaking, just from his side of the family." I hem and haw. "You know, Max, there's something about that Elvira Moreley that really...irks me."

"Irks you?" Max fake gasps. "Whatever happened to 'Why can't you be more like Elvira Moreley?—Elvira, the president of the chess club, Elvira, the National Merit Scholar, Elvira the...'"

"I never gave you that speech."

"You most certainly did!"

"Well, I take it all back," I say. "There's something chilly about that girl, Max. She lacks compassion."

"You and your love affair with compassion," Max says. "Elvira's not bad, Mom. She's just way too brilliant to have any social skills. You'll get used to her."

"Luckily, I don't think that's in my future," I say.

"It might be, actually."

"What do you mean?"

"Elvira and I are going to be each other's conceptual directors for our senior projects. So we'll be spending a lot of time together next semester."

"Since when do you need a conceptual director for an art project?"

"It's a new pairing concept at school. Intertwining ideas. Providing inspiration and support. It's pretty cool."

"What's your project?" I say.

"Mega-scale self-portrait," Max says. "Mixed media—sculpture and painting. It was Elvira's idea to use found objects. I already got a ton of cool stuff from the attic. Like that wacky old Beatles album cover and that goofy Red Sox back scratcher. Talk about fossils!"

"Wow," I say. "Sounds...intriguing."

"It's going to be larger than life!" Max goes on. "A virtual tower! Dad's going to help me stretch a bunch of canvases and I'll pile them on top of each other and then attach the objects. When it's done, it will be as big as a house!" Max puts her feet up on the dashboard. I swat them down. "And by the way," she says, "is it okay if I move back home until after the holidays? I need more space for my project. And my roommates are driving me crazy."

"Move back in?" I feel a slight drop in my stomach. I've been enjoying my freedom and the empty house so much, but it's rare that Max reaches out to me, and maybe this will mean we can finally close the door on Whack Sunday and be friends again. Sooner or later, she'll get sick of living back home. It will only be for a little while.

"Sure!" I picture the two of us drinking eggnog and making gingerbread houses with gumdrops and mini marshmallows, watching the Charlie Brown Christmas special together and singing carols. "I'd love to have you back home, Max. It'll be fun."

"Great," she says. "I'll move my stuff in this weekend. Elvira's got a pick-up truck and she's going to help. And on the bar front, Mom?"

"What bar front?" I say.

"Just behave," Max says.

It's what I've been telling her for years.

7

The first Wednesday night in November, true to his word, Dylan Guthrie awaits me at the same stool at Bar None.

"Grace!" He greets me with a hug and a radiant smile, as if I were the Queen of Sheba.

"Hi, Dylan." I start to take off my jean jacket.

"Keep it on," he says. "We're not staying."

"We're not?"

"No." He picks up a bag from the floor and ushers me to the door. "We are going to have a picnic."

"A picnic?" I look nervously over at Asa, who gives me a "beat's me?" shrug. It's become clear that whereas Bartender Jack has eyes in the back of his head, Bartender Asa has ears on all sides of his head. No spoken word escapes him. "In the dark?" I say to Dylan.

"Up on my rooftop," he says "It's a perfect night. Perhaps the last rogue gift of Second Summer."

"Very poetic," I say.

"I noticed you were drinking red wine," he says. "So I got a côtes du rhône, and some bread and cheese. Will that do?"

"Nicely," I reply. I get such a kick out of his formal, old-fashioned way of speaking. It's hardly the norm these days, especially out of the mouths of millennials.

We cut through the Porter Square parking lot and wind our way to a triple decker behind the Star Market, buffeted along by a warm breeze. Dylan motions to the fire escape. A cloudy sky cloaks a sliver of a moon. "After you," he says.

I start up the ladder, managing the climb, I hope, with some measure of grace. I'm just hoisting myself up onto the roof when my left shoe slips off. Dylan catches it in mid-air and leaps onto the roof with one long-limbed Pele stride. He takes a plaid blanket out of the bag and spreads it gallantly over the asphalt, motioning for me to sit. A billboard with that little green gecko who's everywhere these days stares me smack in the face. His spindly legs are crossed and he's drinking from a blue mug. Dylan pours me a glass of red wine.

"So," Dylan says, struggling to adjust his gargantuan legs. "Tell me more, Grace."

"About what?" I slide easily into the lotus position. My posture's better when I sit that way.

"The sixties." He takes out a joint and lights up. "I have been thinking about what you said, how you feel like an intruder in the twenty-first century. I can relate to that. I often feel as if I were born into the wrong era."

"Oh, it was my era all right." The wine's far better than what I'm used to. "I just don't think I've ever fully adjusted to life *after* the sixties," I say.

"I don't feel that I even have an era," Dylan says. "One that I belong to, anyway. Or that belongs to me. I feel cheated somehow."

"But you're on the cutting edge of all the latest technology," I say. "You may turn out to be one of the important minds of the computer age."

"I doubt it," Dylan says. "It's pretty hard to distinguish yourself. We're a virtual can of techno sardines." He takes a hit. "Anyway, I was always more of an artistic soul." He cocks his head to one side and offers me the joint. "Do you smoke?"

"I used to." Before you were even born, I think. I don't tell him that the only time I've indulged in the last thirty years is when Isabelle and I smoked a joint a few years back at her old apartment. Afterwards, we ate an entire apple pie that she'd won at a library raffle that day. As I walked home through the Cambridge Common, I was convinced that whoever had made that apple pie had wanted the last slice, and was following me with a pick axe to get revenge for our gluttony. I always did get paranoid when I got high. Oh well. I take a quick hit. When on a rooftop…

"It is true that I've embedded myself quite successfully into the corporate world." Dylan uncrosses his legs and stretches them out in front of him. "And for a while that made me feel validated. And safe. But I don't want to feel safe anymore. I want to find my own time warp to slip into."

"So you wish you'd come of age in the sixties?" The dope goes down more easily with the second hit.

"Not necessarily," he says. "But this notion of belonging intrigues me."

"Are we talking time travel here?" A siren spirals down below and the smell of cooking meat drifts over the roof.

"Virtual time travel," Dylan says. "We create virtual worlds, don't we?"

"Can't say I ever have." I take a third hit of the joint, inhaling deeply, and it all comes back to me, how to slowly let the smoke slide down your throat and fill your lungs and how the soft purple haze starts to settle. "I'm pretty rooted in this world, for better or worse," I say. "And I'm okay with that."

"Awesome," he says. I give him the under-thirty-five pass. He turns to me. "Is it true that people dropped acid and had wild orgies back in the sixties? That having a different sexual partner every night was no big deal?"

"It happened," I say. I think of Crazy Legs Campbell, who boasted at our graduation that he'd just had his fiftieth fuck. And to think I'd been his first—behind the Harvard Stadium, down on Soldiers Field Road. By the end of high school, I'd had a few unremarkable sexual encounters, but I was hopelessly monogamous from the start and the only one that mattered back then was Floyd.

"It was pretty crazy," I go on. "No questions asked, no judgments made. There was so much raw energy and freedom, so much possibility for change. It was exhilarating and empowering. But it was debilitating too. Somewhere along the line, I think we started to lose our individuality. We turned into one giant, stoned, like-minded mass. That's been kind of a problem for me." I take one last hit. "I still don't know what I want to be…when I grow up," I say haltingly, on the in breath.

"But sexually," Dylan says, "you must be very experienced, very uninhibited."

I shrug. "How do you know?" I say. "When you only have yourself for comparison?"

"Hmm." It's what Phillip always said when I threw him for a loop.

"Look at you," I say, handing him back the joint. "You're young, focused, and highly successful. When I was your age, I was living in a rundown house in North Cambridge with a struggling architect husband, a staggering mortgage, and two crying babies. You probably already make six figures and own your own condo."

"True on both counts," he says. "But sexually, I'm pretty much a novice. I was a geek in school, a total nerd," he says. "I didn't even kiss a girl until I was seventeen."

"And then?"

"And then I grew a foot and my life changed forever," he says. "Just the way my mother always said it would."

"You've got to trust your mother," I say.

He studies me. "You're very striking…in a Daliesque kind of way," he says. "You never look quite the same."

Daliesque? I can't even begin to imagine what he means by this. And I don't mention that he's only seen me twice.

"Dali was the grand illusionist," he says. "He was into distortion—limbs and objects and different points of view."

"Mmm." I still want to believe this is some sort of twisted compliment.

"He would have elongated this beautiful neck," he says, pressing his thumb into the back of my neck. "And melted this beautiful thigh." He trails a finger down my leg. "Dali found beauty in the surreal," he says. "And he made it sublime."

I reach out to touch Dylan's cheek. His mouth comes toward mine. And it must be true about very tall people and their giant appendages. His tongue reaches places in my mouth I never knew existed. And before I know it, I'm making out with a thirty-four-year-old computer genius who never kissed a girl until he was seventeen, but since then has clearly been making up for lost time. We fall back onto the blanket and Dylan dips down for another kiss.

After we peel ourselves apart, we lie on our backs and look up at the star-flecked sky.

"It's beautiful, isn't it?" I say. "Just lying here on a rooftop in the middle of Porter Square?"

"It really is," he says.

Not exactly the way Sheila LaFarge would have scripted the night, getting almost to second base on a moth-balled blanket on an asphalt rooftop in Somerville, but very much the way I, Grace Winthrop Hobbes, fifty-something cougar novice would have had it—with a nice glass of red, a few hits off a joint, some faraway memories, and only a cheeky billboard gecko as our witness...and a beautiful, long-legged man.

The weekly routine with Fuzz becomes clear. Two drinks at the bar or at his apartment, followed by an hour of sex and light chitchat, no post-coital lingering or cuddling, no staying the night, no flowers, no gifts, no babytalk, no treacly nicknames. Finally, I'm living in the present, in the NOW. That's the Buddhist way, isn't it? I feel triumphant. This is how I imagined later-in-life romance could be, all neat and tidy and rolled up into two efficient hours a week. No picking up the other's dirty clothes, taking in the other's morning breath, bickering over coffee. Been there done all that. It's a glorious, perfect arrangement when you strip it down to its essence—a man and woman coming together, just as Mother Nature intended, without the needless intervention of the mind or the heart. Finally, we're back to what we used to champion in the sixties—good old-fashioned, meaningless sex.

"I have a theory," I tell Fuzz one night. We're lying naked in bed in his sterile one-bedroom apartment in the Port—stark white walls, dull furniture and black sheets, not one jolt of color to be found except for the red of the fire alarm box. Whatever feminine touches the Termite Woman might have lent to the decor, she obviously took with her. Fuzz is jotting down notes on the sex we just had.

It's a measure of how malleable we are as humans that I don't even find Fuzz's note-taking strange anymore. Sometimes I even throw in my two cents. For instance, tonight we tried this kind of backwards-sideways thing, and at first it felt great, his entering me at that sharp angle. I even thought he was closing in on the elusive G-spot, and tried to move in such a way as to guide him toward it. But then I moved too far and he started to lose it, so the climax for both of us was anything but. Now we have to wait until next week to try something new.

"Put this in your notes," I say. "The next time we do that thing from the side, when I zig, don't zag. Just keep it steady and let me try to find my spot."

"What spot?" he mutters as he writes, *Zig, don't zag.*

"My G-spot."

"Oh, right," he says. At least he's heard of it. "Is that with a capital G? What does it stand for anyway?"

"The Promised Land." I go for the lame joke.

"No, the G." Fuzz is so tiresomely literal. "What does it stand for? Great? Galactic? Gushing?"

"In our case, it stands for yay, I just had an orgasm," I say. "Actually, it's named after some German dude named Grafenberg. How does that make any sense? What would he know about it?" I say. "Anyway, back to my theory—"

Fuzz pretends to pick up a phone. "Hello, *Boston Globe*? Get the presses ready. Sherlock Hobbes has a theory."

"If we had more sex," I say, ignoring him, "not only could we experiment more, but I bet my creative juices would flow more freely. I'd be a better writer. Or more productive at least."

"But if we had more sex…" Fuzz reaches over me to grab his bottle of Poland Springs water, which he insists on bringing into the bed. "We'd get sick of each other more quickly. And that would be a shame." His hand slides down my leg.

"I bet you were the kind of kid that rationed his Halloween candy and made it last until summer," I said. "Until the Tootsie Rolls were hard as rocks."

"I made a fortune selling it to my younger brothers," he says. "They always ate all of theirs on the first night."

"It was the only way to go," I say. "Devour it all in one fell swoop."

"And then get violently ill."

"Sometimes," I say with a sigh. He hands me the water bottle and I take a swig. "There was something about dumping out that bag on your bed and eating every last, glorious piece," I say. "Nestles Crunches and Charlestown Chews, Mike and Ikes, fireballs burning up your mouth, even those disgusting malted milk balls. Even if you did get sick in the end."

"So, what's your point?" Fuzz rolls over onto his side and props his chin up on his hand. "You wish we had so much sex that we got sick of it, sick of each other?"

"Maybe." I sit upright, not even bothering to cover myself with the top sheet. I could swear my breasts have gotten bigger since I started having sex again. And if I say so myself, they look pretty good. "Wouldn't it be incredible to go on a delirious, non-stop screwathon?" I say, looking over at him. "Just sex, sex, sex, until we were all exhausted and limp, all sexed out, just totally and completely done." My hands gesture wildly. "I'd finish my novel and you'd perfect your sex formula. And then we'd turn our backs on each other and walk away without looking back. It would be such a poetic, fiery end."

"Screwathon?" Fuzz's eyebrows spring up, boomerang style.

"Screwathon." My hands fall back into my lap. I'm done with people telling me I can't make up words. I'm a writer. That's what we do.

He pats my arm. "It's better this way, Sherlock," he says. "Trust me. Too much of a good thing and all. And we're no spring chickens."

"Why does everyone keep saying that?" I say with a sigh. For all that he thinks of himself as some wild sexual outlaw, Fuzz is in many ways so conservative—such a stickler for routine. He won't be the kind of muse I want him to be, wild and spontaneous, headlong. But at fifty-three, I'm nothing if not practical. I'll take what I can get.

I get a few tepid responses in my inbox from my first online column about women going out to the bar with a new, improved attitude.

You go, Grandma! someone writes. *Age is just a number!*

Women's hips make it hard to sit on barstools, one reader tells me.

Fucking men! is all another has to say.

One comment simply reads, *DUH!* and is signed, "Way Ahead of You in Tewksbury."

Isabelle assures me this is a respectable first outing and that things will get better as I get a sense of my audience and start to find my voice. So I vow to carry on, undaunted.

Meanwhile, I'm dutiful in my research. And after a few more weeks, I actually do start to feel comfortable at the Wonder Bar. Bartender Jack knows I like the corner seat and finagles it for me when he can, giving me notice that someone is leaving with a slight tilt of his head. There's the usual cast of characters. Palindrome Guy never seems not to be there. Turns out, no surprise—his name is Bob Hannah. Raven Mulholland frequents this bar, too, and likes to bury herself in the bar line-up, drinking bright-colored cocktails and fending off unwanted admirers. Good luck with that, I think. Chuckie D., an old timer from the neighborhood, likes to tell me about the night back in the fifties when a local boxer, Micky Smythe, keeled over dead in the front corner seat, as if to scare me away, but it only endears the seat to me more. And Chuckie F. in the argyle sweater, ninety if he's a day, tells me the same joke over and over—or anyone else who will listen—the one about the old guy sitting with an attractive younger woman at the bar, who keeps asking her, "Do I come here often?"

The reactions to me at the bar with my notebook vary. A good number of people think I'm writing a restaurant review and are disappointed when they find out I'm not that important. Those with a literary bent are curious. "Are you published?" is an invariable question, as if to ask: are you human, were you vaccinated for smallpox, are you red or green or blue? And I love the inquiry that often follows when I answer yes. "Have you published anything recently I might have read?" First, the inference that I might publish frequently enough to have written something recently that anyone might have read is absurd enough, but even more ludicrous is the asker's assumption that he or she, against all odds, with six plus billion humans on the planet, might happen to be one of the few hundred-odd people who've actually read my book about mushrooms, sitting right next to me in this very bar, at this very moment. Who do they think I am, for cripe's sake...Joyce Carol Oates?

The paranoids give me menacing glances and turn away, inching their barstools nearer to their companions, dropping into confidential whispers, as if I'm some sort of perverted voyeur and the dull half-moon details of their lives might be of salacious interest to me. Hey, I feel like telling them. I've got a perfectly good dull life of my own to tap from. I certainly don't need yours. My favorites are the happy-go-lucky optimists, who tell me their life stories and look forward to seeing themselves as characters in my next novel. And lastly, there are a good number of folks who clearly consider it pretentious to be writing in a bar alone at my age in Cambridge. On a bad night, these are the ones I agree with.

Some nights I watch Bartender Jack. When I'm a full-fledged cougar, he could very well jump to the top of my fantasy list. But that will be a long time coming, being able to even imagine a conquest as fine as this. How old is Jack? I wonder. Anywhere from his mid-twenties to late-thirties, I'd guess. He has that ageless gamin look about him—a man who will always move with the ease and swagger of a boy. What does he think of me, I wonder, this older woman with her notebooks and crazy shoes? I don't dare to venture into his mindset, even in the abstract. Bartender Jack is off limits, not just because he's so young, but because he's the mainstay of my life here at the Wonder Bar. It's a delicate balance and I never want to break it. If I were ever to give in to temptation, reach up and tug on the lobe of his left ear, as I've sometimes imagined, I'd never be able to step foot in here again.

The Wonder Bar has become my home away from home, my comfortable, dim-lit shrine. The Vulcan-like creatures in the paintings on the walls are my quiet companions. My favorite is one standing in dark profile, shoulders hunched, waving across a fence to someone or something unseen. A half moon lies tilted in a mussel-shell blue sky, and there's an owl, not resting on the limb of a tree, as you would expect, but roosting beside the Vulcan creature on the ground. The painting elicits in me the strangest sense of *deja vu*. I feel as though I've been there, at that fence, with that owl, standing next to that crooked tree, looking over—at what I'm not sure.

The Wonder Bar is my Shangri-La and Jack is my sage. I can't jeopardize any of this. Even for one touch, one taste of the sublime and wary Jack, bar towel sticking out of his back pocket, buzz cut framing his angular face. How to explain to Jack that I'm old, as tough as nails and fragile still. He won't believe me, he won't get it, that I'm old enough to be his… arghhh! I crumple up my notebook page. Is this how the cougar starts to crumble?

I set out to Bar None to meet Nell on a Thursday night in late November. There's a group of rowdy guys at the bar and the only open seat is next to Raven Mulholland. There's no getting around it. We're face to face.

"Hi." I seize the moment. "Raven, isn't it?"

She nods. "How's the book coming?" she says.

I follow her gaze to my notebook. "Oh, the book," I say. "I'm actually working on a few different things these days." I slide into the vacant seat. "You're quite the celebrity around here."

She rolls her eyes. "I wish I'd never done those stupid ads. I didn't even make much money. And now I'll always be labeled the Toothpaste Girl."

"It's not the worst legacy," I say. "Something to tell your grandkids about."

"I didn't even have the satisfaction of quitting," she says. "The toothpaste turned out to be a flop. It stank."

"How bad could it be?" The noisy guys take off, leaving behind a blissful silence.

"It literally had a bad smell," Raven says. "Kind of like camphor and wet cardboard. It wasn't long before they yanked it off the shelves."

"Yeah, I guess that's not exactly what you want in a toothpaste." I take a sip of my wine and turn to face her. "So I have to ask," I say. "What does it *feel* like?"

"They didn't actually squeeze me," Raven says.

"No, no. What's it like…" I spin my hand in circles. "To be so tall, so otherworldly?" I say. "So incredibly gorgeous? It's as if you come from a completely different planet from the rest of us."

She lets out a guffaw. "Most of the time I feel like a freak."

"That's kind of hard to believe."

Raven gives a dismissive wave of her hand. "You were here the night that drunken idiot made a scene. That's the kind of attention I usually get. I've been through so many boyfriends. They all end up being jerks."

"Even your name is exotic," I say. "How many people in the world are called Raven?"

"It's not that glamorous," she says. "My parents are just big bird people. We're Wren, Lark, Robin, and Raven. And our brothers are Phoenix and Hawk. It's totally corny, if you ask me."

"My family went for the boring, one syllable, WASPy names," I say. "Grace, Nell, and Charles." I look over at the opening bar door. "Speak of one of the devils," I say.

Into the bar walks my sister, Nell, decked out in a butter-yellow sweat suit and baby-blue parka. Raven kindly moves a few seats down to make room for her. She's no sooner relocated than Bartender Asa is by her side, talking her ear off. She doesn't seem to mind.

"Whoa," Nell whispers, watching the retreating Raven. "Who is that?"

"That," I say, "is the famous Dazzle Toothpaste model from the '80s."

Nell's face lights up. "The one who got squeezed out of the toothpaste tube?"

I throw up my hands. "How come I'm the only person on the planet who never saw those ads?" I say.

"You were kind of busy," Nell says. "With two crying, pooping babies. Damn, she's even more gorgeous in person. How can someone actually look like that?"

"Beats me," I say. "So good job, Nellie. You made it out into the big, bad world. Congratulations."

"I'm here," she says. "So show me how it's done, big sister. Show me how to snag a guy."

"You're not here just to snag a guy," I scold her. "You're out expanding your horizons. Having a good time. And if you happen to meet someone, then so be it. Just try and have fun."

"Okay, but I do need some tips," Nell says. "I'm your poor pathetic sister who married an old geezer who couldn't even get it up and then dumped me."

"Just take the plunge," I say. "Talk to that guy who just sat down next to you."

"What do I say?" she asks in a panicky voice.

"Say hello," I tell her. I move down the bar next to Raven to give Nell some space. Nell gets the conversation rolling and I give her a thumbs-up. There's some nagging feeling about the guy that I can't put my finger on. Raven and I play the "guess everything about him" game.

"Forty-six years old," she says.

"Nah, he's fifty if he's a day," I say.

"Religious?" she asks.

"Not with that hat," I say.

"Animal lover?"

"Way too neat and tidy," I say.

About half an hour later, Nell comes over, waving a napkin. "I got his number!" she says.

By then I've figured out what's been bothering me about the guy. And it's got me all roiled up. "What was up with that?" I say.

"What?" says Nell, bewildered.

"You know very well what."

"No, I don't," Nell says defensively. "What did I do?"

"That guy you were talking to looked just like Phillip!" I say.

"What?" Nell looks over at the guy, who's now halfway out the door. "He did not."

I take an old snapshot of Phillip out of my wallet and ask Raven to be the judge. "Didn't that guy who just left look just like this guy in the picture?"

Raven cranes her neck to get a good look. "Not really. That guy had a really round head, and your guy," she points at my picture, "has more of a pointy one."

"Right, see!" Nell says. "Pointy. I loved you in those ads by the way."

"Thanks," Raven says. "You really own that Peter Pan look, girl, very gender-neutral cool."

"You think?" Nell says, pleased.

"Let's let Asa be the judge," Raven says. She shows him the photo of Phillip.

"Dead ringer," Asa says, flicking the photo with his thumb and middle finger.

"See!" I say, triumphantly. I've never noticed how handsome Asa is. Olive-skinned with mahogany eyes, he has high cheekbones and a strong Roman nose. On top of that, he's perfectly proportioned. Maybe it's just because he's short that his good looks escape you at first glance.

"You were the one who told me to talk to him," Nell grumbles. "You've got this thing about me being obsessed with Phillip, but I think it's the other way around." She lowers her head.

"Who keeps a picture of their ex-husband in their wallet?" she grumbles. "I'm just sayin'…"

I meet my brother Charlie for lunch a few days later at Mary Chung's in Central Square—best Chinese food in Cambridge, hands down. He's crossed over the river from work, wearing one of his expensive tailored suits, which, at midday, brandishes barely a wrinkle. I'll never understand how I turned out to be the only frump in our family.

"We have to talk about Mom," he says, pouring himself a cup of green tea.

"Why?" I groan. "I don't want to talk about Mom, Charlie. And why are you the only one who gets to call her Mom? Nell and I still call her Mother."

"Call her whatever you want." He orders moo shu pork and I get mango chicken with cashews.

"She claims *mom* is too Norman Rockwell," I say. "Only her darling boy…"

Charlie groans. "Give me a break," he says.

"You already got all the breaks, Charlie," I say.

"Mom's losing it, Grace," he says. "We had her over the other night and in the middle of dinner she got up from the table without saying a word and wandered into the kitchen. Emma found her putting teabags in the freezer."

"She's faking it," I say. "She wants us to put her in that snazzy assisted living place out in Lincoln where Martha Coolidge went."

"I don't know," Charlie says. "She seemed really out of it. And at the end of the night, she called Emma, Gert."

"Gert was Mother's roommate in college. Look, she was wearing two different earrings a while back when we had tea. And she called me Rose. I don't think she'd washed her hair in weeks. That's what happens when you get old, Char. The marbles start dropping. Then the personal hygiene starts to go…"

"This was strange, Gracie. For a minute, she looked at us as if she didn't know who we were. I'm worried she's got the Big A."

"Oh god, she can't," I say. "She's way too…bossy."

"The Big A doesn't discriminate." Charlie slings his silver tie over his shoulder and takes an enormous bite of his moo shu pancake. "I think we should get her tested."

"She'll never agree."

"That's where you come in."

"Me?" A piece of mango slips off my chopsticks just as it arrives at my mouth. "Shoot! Why me?"

"Because you're the only one who can convince her. Nell isn't forceful enough and—"

"How 'bout you, Charlie?" I surrender my chopsticks and pick up a fork. "Why don't you do it if you're so concerned?"

"I'm way too chicken." He pours the last of his pot of tea. "You're the brave one in the family, Gracie. We all know that."

"Well, I'm the sucker, that's for sure," I grumble.

Celia and I are just finishing up our tea at Simon's the next Tuesday. I've finally convinced her to make an appointment for a check-up with a doctor (who's also a neurologist) when Isabelle walks through the door.

"Iz, what're you doing here?" I say. Celia looks over at me hesitantly. "You remember Isabelle, don't you, Mother?"

"Isabelle, of course," she says, relieved by the prompt. "How nice to see you. Don't you look…elegant." She gives me a pointed look.

"Thank you, Mrs. Hobbes. I hate to interrupt, but could I borrow Grace for a moment?"

"I was just leaving." Celia starts to gather her things. "Here, dear, take my seat. And while you're at it, could you please give Grace some fashion tips, or at least recommend a good hair stylist?"

"I've tried," Isabelle says with a sigh.

"Thanks," I say, glaring at both of them.

"I've got terrible news," Isabelle says, plunking down in the chair. I've never seen her look so agitated. "The frickin' rabbit died!"

"What frickin' rabbit?"

"The rabbit, Grace. Haven't you ever heard that expression?"

"Sure, I've heard it." I rack my brains. "You're becoming a vegetarian?" I say.

"No!" she says. "I got knocked up, Gracie!"

"Very funny." Isabelle's the queen of wry jokes, but this one takes the cake.

"I'm not kidding," Isabelle says.

"Whoa. What? When? Who?" I say, and then after a pause of confusion, "The walrus guy? Emil?"

"No," she says miserably. "Mick Frickin' Jagger."

"Busy fellow," I say.

"I can't believe it," Isabelle says. "The one time in my life I toss caution to the wind." She picks up my napkin and starts to shred it.

"What do you mean?"

"It was just that first time we had sex. For once, I said the hell with it, live in the moment, just let it happen. I must have been channeling Molly back in her derby days. You know me. I am not a goddamned risk taker."

"True," I say. "Except in the swearing department."

"Emil and I have been careful ever since," Isabelle says. "I didn't think anything of not getting my period on time. They've always come and gone as they damn pleased."

"How did you find out?"

"I was at the dentist and they were taking X-rays and they put that creepy lead coat over me and all the signs were staring at me, saying in sixteen frickin' different languages: Is there ANY chance you could be pregnant, *enceinte, embarcadero*?" She picks up what's left of my lemon scone. "Do you mind? I'm starving."

"Go ahead," I say, well after she's scarfed most of it down.

"And then it hit me," Isabelle goes on. "That there actually was the slightest chance that I might be pregnant, so I rescheduled the X-rays, went to CVS and got a pregnancy test, totally expecting it to be negative. But it wasn't negative. It was positive! The stick turned frickin' blue, Gracie! The rabbit died and now I'm screwed."

"I still don't get what any of this has to do with the poor rabbit."

"Forget about the rabbit, Grace. This is serious!"

"Sorry," I say. "What are you going to do?"

"I have no idea," she says. "But I'm not going to tell Emil."

"Don't you think it might be a good idea to…share this with him?" I remember how happy Phillip was when I told him we were finally pregnant, and then, when the news came that we were having twins, it was utter delirium.

"Whose side are you on?" Isabelle says.

"Yours, of course," I say. "But if you decide to have the baby, and unless you plan on disappearing into thin air, how can you not tell Emil? He's a tenured professor at Harvard. He's not going anywhere, and neither are you."

"I'll move to Alaska," she says.

"You hate the cold."

"I do. I hate the freaking cold." She shudders. "The thing is, I actually like this guy."

"So what's the problem?"

"I want to keep seeing him."

"What's stopping you?" I put my fingers up to my temples and squeeze. "This is a very exasperating conversation, Iz. And by the way, we are *so* flunking the Bechdel test."

"You're right. It's the hormones," she explains. "They're making me crazy. I can't make up my mind about anything. Look at what I'm wearing!" She tugs at her blouse. "Denim on denim? It's as if you picked out this outfit for me, Grace."

"I don't know who's more insulting, you or Celia—"

"But if I do keep seeing Emil," Isabelle goes on, "and I decide to keep the baby, he's going to find out."

"True," I say. "Eventually, he will find out that you're having his baby."

"*My* baby," Isabelle says defiantly, slapping one hand on her chest.

"Well, it's your choice," I say. "But if there does end up being a baby, then technically, it will be both of yours."

"Stop being so frickin' practical, Gracie. What am I going to do?"

I eat the last few crumbs of the scone. "Well, there is this old-fashioned thing people sometimes do when they get pregnant, even by mistake, and they really like each other…"

"What?" She's so rattled, she doesn't have a clue.

"They start a family," I say.

"I don't want a goddamned family," Isabelle wails. "I can't possibly be a mother. How could I bring a kid into this world who eventually would have to find out that her grandmother's nickname used to be Blow Torch?"

"She'd think it was cool," I say. "I guarantee it."

"All marriages are doomed," she says. "It's an impossible premise, spending your whole life with just one person. Completely ridiculous. Look at you, Grace. All that time with Phillip and now everything's kaput."

"Everything is not kaput," I say. "Phillip and I are the best of friends. We've got two great kids and I have no regrets."

"Freaking doomed," Isabelle says again.

8

December settles in with the first wet snow and I grudgingly turn the heat up to sixty-six degrees. Atticus and Maude take up residence next to the radiator under the kitchen window and I unearth my long underwear from the back of a bottom drawer. I can't take El's badgering phone calls anymore, so I take off one Saturday morning for godforsaken Bennington, Vermont, to meet his "incredible" girlfriend, Rachel, who, he forgot to mention until a last-minute phone conversation before I left the house, is not only ten years older than he is, but one of his dance professors!

"What?" The hairbrush I was using clattered to the floor.

"Calm down, Mom," El said. "I knew you'd overreact."

"What else are you going to spring on me?" I said. "Is she a vampire too?"

"Ha ha, very funny," he said. "What's the big deal?"

"The big deal is..." I couldn't even begin to articulate what the big deal was, but it was something. And it was *huge*!

"Once you meet her, you'll see, Mom," El said. "Rachel's just completely...normal."

"Normal."

"And besides, there's no conclusive evidence that age-gap couples are any less compatible than peer couples."

"Where'd you get that from? *Redbook Magazine*?"

"What?"

"Never mind. Oh, El," I said. "It just doesn't sound—right, somehow."

"It *is* right." El's voice was strong and steady on the other end of the line. I imagined him doing the rapid blinking thing that meant he'd made up his mind. "It's totally right, Mom. You just have to trust me."

So I did what I've always done with my son. I trusted him.

As I head to Medford and get on 93 North, I ponder the Rachel situation, still in the outraged stage. Isn't this unprofessional, let alone illegal, not to mention unethical? Approaching the New Hampshire border, I notice I'm going over eighty miles an hour. I ease my foot off the gas pedal. I must be out of my mind, with all of those bored state troopers hiding in the highway wings, waiting to pounce. As I hit the rolling hills of 89 North, I picture this Rachel person in a black sleeveless leotard seducing my poor, defenseless son on a sun-lit wooden dance floor after class or out in a lonely Vermont grove on that desolate, dark campus. It's like Transylvania up there for cripe's sake. Couldn't they spring for a few more lightbulbs with the forty grand we're shelling out each year for tuition? Again, I notice the speedometer needle wagging over the eighty mark and lift up my leaden foot. Shouldn't it be a college's responsibility to keep its faculty in line? This Rachel person has brazenly stolen my son's innocence, luring him under the guise, no doubt, of "advising" him, "helping" him with an assignment, "demonstrating" a dance move, a hand on his back, his leg, her vampire teeth poised over his neck...aaarrrrghghghg! My hands grip tighter on the steering wheel. Make the visions stop!

But who am I to talk? My face floods with heat as I remember reaching up to touch Dylan's face on his rooftop, the gecko sign looming over us and the night breeze blowing, not caring who might be watching or what anyone might think, how much I just wanted to feel his soft skin, the line of his firm jaw, how much I wanted him to touch me, how I let him kiss me and I kissed him back and how we leaned back onto the plaid blanket as the police sirens wailed.

The college entrance looms suddenly ahead on the right. I put on my blinker and start down the long, winding road to the campus. They're waiting for me by the empty guardhouse at the top of the hill, arms wrapped around each other's waists. I park the car and walk toward them, carrying a jade plant I've brought as an offering.

"Mom, this is Rachel." El can hardly contain himself. "Rachel, this is my mother, Grace."

"Rachel," I say. "It's great to finally meet you."

"Likewise," Rachel says in a crisp English accent. Wonderful. On top of everything else, she's a charming Brit.

"I asked her out six times before she said yes." El shifts his weight nervously from one foot to the other. My god, he's grown another half a foot since I saw him last and his voice is an octave lower. What has this woman done to my son? He looks so strong, so confident, so...happy. That was supposed to have been *my* doing. And who "goes out" anymore?

"Your son is most persistent," Rachel says quietly. "And very talented. It's a shame he had to give up his early dance training. He's got some catching up to do." She's ethereal, see-through pale with long black hair, a startling contrast, sylphlike and lovely. Shame indeed. Doesn't she think I know that? Doesn't she understand that El made that choice himself and that I had to respect it? That it wasn't my fault?

"I kept telling Eliot that it wouldn't be appropriate for us to get romantically involved," Rachel goes on. And there it is—the family name we gave our son and then yanked away. She's given it back to him, unsullied and noble, as it was meant to be in the beginning.

"But when I turned twenty-one last week..." El takes her in his arms from behind. "She couldn't argue with me anymore."

"I did try," Rachel says, giving me an apologetic smile.

We walk around the campus in a cold, drizzly rain—Rachel and El hand in hand, me trailing behind, feeling weepy and betrayed. I've always been of the opinion that the Bennington campus has a serious identity crisis—an uneasy mix of stark, modern buildings and old clapboard farmhouses amid fields and cement paths and scattered birches. A few lone students stroll the campus in the chilly twilight, heads tucked down and hands stuffed into shabby coat pockets. I feel as though I'm in a science fiction movie where I've just awoken to discover that the earth has been virtually abandoned. El rambles on about the story of the student who went hiking one day in 1946 and disappeared into the Bennington Triangle, inside which a special energy was believed to attract visitors from outer space. "She was never seen again," Rachel says dramatically. But I can't concentrate on any of it.

Little did I know when I sent El his birthday package two weeks before, special El stuff—Day of the Dead socks and Jordan Crane's new graphic novel, fruit slices from Brigham's, no lime, extra cherry—that it would not be me, his mother, making his day, the way I had for so long, but this...Rachel person, who instead of baking him a cake had probably made love to him instead. Probably even did both! My heart sinks. I'd even momentarily forgotten how momentous this birthday was. The twins were twenty-one now, officially grown up. Here it was then, a mother's final heartbreak. The end of the oedipal line.

We eat dinner at a vegetarian place in a neighboring town, which otherwise consists of a post office, a general store, and a one-teller bank. El and Rachel eat tofu curry with chopsticks, while I tussle with tempeh and beansprouts with a bent, two-tined fork. After the food settles, my desolate mood starts to lift. I'm determined to try and be cheery.

"You're such a long way from home," I say to Rachel. "How did you make your way to Bennington?" I have some fantastical, irrational notion that by learning how she got here, I can somehow make her go away.

"A friend told me about the job opening a while back," she says. "And I've always wanted to come to the States..."

"She's being modest," El says. "The dance faculty has been wooing her for years. All the top schools wanted her." He looks over at Rachel adoringly. "Bennington finally won out," he says. "And so did I."

"El tells me you're a published writer, Grace," Rachel says, giving his arm a pat. "That's most impressive!"

"Well, just the one book," I say.

"Mushrooms, wasn't it?" she says with a slight tilt of her head.

"Right," I say. "Mushrooms."

"Brilliant," she says, and flashes me a dazzling smile.

After dropping El and Rachel off back on campus, I stop at a Shurfine to buy a bag of Hershey's Kisses and an *Us Weekly* magazine, prepared to hole up in my hotel room for the night. From the lobby, I see a man sitting at the bar in the lounge, short and stocky, in a nice suit jacket, with a thick shock of Columbo-style hair. For a minute, I consider stopping in for a drink. He sees my hesitation and our eyes meet, and I know now how easy it all can be, how quickly it can happen. But Judy Dench looks up at me from the magazine cover with her steely, disapproving eyes and it's as if she's saying in her starchy, commanding voice, "For God's sake, Grace, give it a rest!"

Just as I'm about to break eye contact, the man at the bar motions me over. I hesitate, but the smile he sends me is so weary and unthreatening, I find myself drawn his way.

"I'm Mark," he says, as I approach him. "Care to sit and have a drink?"

"Grace," I say. "No thanks on the drink, though. I've had a long day. I'm here from Boston, visiting—"

"Your kid, right?" he says. "At Bennington? Me too. We're all here, holed up at the godforsaken Comfort Inn. I came up yesterday from New York."

"Son or daughter?" I say.

"Daughter," he says. "Rebecca. Sophomore. How 'bout you?"

"Son," I say. "His name is…Eliot. I just came up from Boston. Cambridge, actually."

He sighs. "They don't come home anymore so we have to come to them."

"It's true."

"And now they've got significant others, so basically, we've been completely left in the dust." Mark turns to me. "Remember when we used to be the most important people in their worlds?"

"Vaguely," I say, with a laugh.

"I see you have big plans for the evening." He gestures to my magazine and the chocolates.

"I'm not ashamed," I say.

"Good for you," he says. "I have my eye on a couple of Milky Ways in the mini bar myself."

"Well," I say, lifting up the bag of kisses. "Goodnight."

"Wait," Mark says. "Could I possibly…have your phone number?"

"I'm leaving first thing in the morning," I say.

"Me too," he says. "I just thought we might talk on the phone…later on. Just, I don't know…exchange pleasantries?"

Pleasantries? It hits me like a ton of bricks. This guy is talking about phone sex! Does that make him a pervert? Or is this just another part of the post-middle age sex game that's completely passed me by? Am I, in fact, just a big old WASPy prude at heart? If he called, would I even dare pick up the phone? And if I did, what would on earth would I say? Or would I just hang up and double-lock my door?

"I'm not trying to be a creep," Mark says. "Forget what I said. I was just sitting here thinking how hard it is to meet people, and go through all the motions, and how phone sex might possibly be a brilliant solution to loneliness. A way to experience pleasure, while leaving our dignities intact."

"Interesting," I say. "Have you ever done this before?"

"No." I try to get a sincerity read from his tone. And frankly, this guy just seems too dispirited to be much of a liar. "It's just the late-breaking thought of a tired, lonely guy," he says, lifting up his drink. "Cheers, Grace," he says.

I take a pen out of my purse and write my number on his napkin.

"Really?" he says with surprise.

"Will you call?" I ask him.

"If I get up the nerve," he says. "Will you answer?"

"If I get up the nerve," I say, and head for the elevator door.

Back in my room, I strip the hideous floral coverlet off the bed, take off my jeans, and climb under the covers, turning right away to the "Fashion Police" pages at the back of the magazine. *What you can do with a garbage bag, duct tape, and scissors.* That's what Madame X has to say about the silver dress Catherine Zeta Jones wore to the premiere of *The Legend of Zorro.* And about the outfit Jack Black was wearing at the Golden Globes? *It looks like an inner tube that got caught in a lawn mower.*

By the time I've devoured the Fashion Police and finished reading an article about a man who killed and dismembered his mother and kept her in a freezer for two years, all the while setting a place for her at the dinner table every night—Mark still hasn't called. I feel relieved, if a bit disappointed. Just as well, I say to myself. I rip open the bag of chocolates and dive into a juicy article about the ongoing feud between Jen and Angelina. And then I remember my friend, Dorothy, who claimed she'd rather spend the night in bed with a box of chocolate than with a man. I take out a silver-wrapped kiss and hold the tear-shaped candy in my hand.

"The battle, maybe," I tell it, yanking out its paper tail. "But not even close to the war."

Just then, my phone rings. Startled, I drop the kiss onto the sheets. I toss the magazine onto the floor and put the phone up to my ear.

"Hi, it's Mark," he says.

"You're kidding!" I say, and he laughs.

"Took me a while," he says.

"I figured you had second thoughts." I start to twirl my hair.

"I did," he says. "I had second thoughts and then third thoughts and then ninth thoughts, and on the tenth thought, I finally screwed up my courage. I mean…"

"Good for you," I say. "So… how do we…go about this?"

"We just start chatting, I guess."

"About what?"

"Well," Mark says. "I'm a banker. What do you do?"

"I'm a writer slash health food store employee."

"Interesting," he says. "What are you doing right now?"

"I'm reading *Us* magazine in bed," I say. "I was about to give up on you and eat my first Hershey's Kiss. And now I'm twirling my hair. Which people say means I'm nervous."

"You have great hair," he says. "And pretty blue—no wait, green eyes."

"Mud eyes," I say.

He laughs. "Pretty mud eyes."

"You have great hair too," I say. "And you wear loafers."

"No pennies, though," he says. "You had on striped zebra mules," he says.

"Men don't usually notice the shoes."

"What are you wearing now?" he says. "Not on your feet, but…"

Wow, I think, he's getting right down to it. I start with the facts. "A maroon T-shirt," I say. "And my Hanes nude hipster underwear."

"Nude hipster underwear."

"That's the color," I say. "The nude part."

He laughs. "Tell me about those nude hipster underwear."

I slide my hand down to the underwear's elastic. "Well, they're beige and they're cotton," I slide my hand underneath, "and they come up to just under my belly button."

"Why don't you take them off," he says.

I slide my underwear down over my toes. I can already feel myself getting wet. Just thinking about him…thinking about me. "What are you wearing?"

"Nothing," he says. "I'm lying on my back. The sheets are cool."

I slide down on my back. "I'm down to just the T-shirt now."

"If I were there," he says, "I'd slide my hands under your T-shirt and touch your breasts. Would you do that? And tell me what they feel like?"

I slide my hands under my shirt and push my breasts upward. "Soft," I say. "Heavenly."

"And your nipples?"

"Tight," I say. "I'm sliding my hand down your stomach, low. Can you feel it? Can you slide your hand down to your cock and tell me...what's going on?"

He groans. "I'm getting hard. And it feels good. Almost too good. Can you touch yourself and tell me how it feels, down low..."

"It's wet," I say. "Hot and wet." There's no speaking then, as we both go at it. I work myself to climax and I hear Mark's heavy breathing and raspy groan. Afterward, there's a long pause.

"Are you still there?" I say.

"Just barely," he says. "Wow, that was really...something."

"It was," I say. And there's another long silence.

"Well," Mark says awkwardly. "It's been a real pleasure, Grace—not exactly having sex with you. Thank you so much, and well, goodnight."

"Goodnight," I say and push the END button on my phone.

I wake up early the next morning feeling rested and calm. The only evidence of what happened the night before is that one uneaten Hershey's Kiss, smushed flat and now firmly stuck to the sheet. It must have melted under my leg in the heat of the moment. I scrape the chocolate off the sheet as best I can, toss the *Us* magazine and the bag of chocolates into the trash, and leave a twenty for the housekeeping staff.

As I start up the car, I notice an unread text on my phone. It's from Mark, and was sent in the nether hours —3:51 a.m. to be exact. *Are you married?* it simply says.

I type my answer and push SEND. The three words fly through the ethernet—*Not any more.* I delete Mark's text and head back out onto Route 9 East. And damned if Vermont Public Radio isn't at it again after all these years, playing one lilting Chopin sonata after another, as I make my way back home.

And whereas El seems to have found true love, Max, at the ripe old age of twenty-one, has informed me that she's taking a break from alcohol and sex. Of course, this begs the question of how much alcohol and sex she's already had in her young life, but I know better than to ask. Does a mother even really want to know? And even if I did, who would I be to judge?

Max has been back living in the house for over a month now. Elvira drove her over in an old pickup truck and helped her move. As the girls clomped into the house with all of Max's stuff and the rap music started to pound, I felt my heart sink just a tad. Her clothes filled two green trash bags and the rest of the truck was loaded with wood and canvases and paints and brushes, and an odd array of strange objects, all of which got dumped in the backyard but will eventually, purportedly, come together as Max's gargantuan self-portrait project. Conceptually directed by Elvira. I'm still not clear on what this means.

But it's been great to have Max back. And I'm even starting to get used to Elvira, who, as Max predicted, has become somewhat of a fixture in our lives. She's an only child and her parents often travel—her father in search of vintage antique cars, and her mother chasing the latest in nouveau art trends. Clearly, this kid is lonely. So she stays over a lot. Elvira's final project is to compose a symphony, which involves flying objects and sound waves. Max is acting as her conceptual director. Again, whatever that means.

Elvira and I have bonded over the old Elvira *Movie Macabre* videos which I rented for her at Hollywood Express. She'd never seen them before. And I was right. They are kindred spirits, these two dark Elviras. *They laugh alike. They walk alike. At times they even talk alike*... I make a mental note to rent *The Patty Duke Show* videos for the girls.

But on the Sunday when I get back from Vermont, Elvira is nowhere to be seen and Max suggests we go out for dinner at the Wonder Bar. I'm relieved, knowing that Fuzz never ventures out on Sundays (must be some sort of Philadelphian thing), and Dylan will be at his Mandarin class that night. My first thought is that Max is checking up on me. But then I remind myself that

I'm the grown-up. Or at least the more senior grown-up. Part of me feels it's wrong for us to go out to the bar together; I've never fully recovered from getting stoned with my mother back in the sixties. But Max is twenty-one now; she's legal. Although she's temporarily "off the sauce," as she puts it.

Max asks for a soda water with lime and I order a sweet vermouth. Bartender Jack serves us our drinks and I make a quick introduction. He gives Max a nod and hightails it off to the other end of the bar.

"Nice ass," she says, watching him retreat. "Too bad I'm off the market."

"That's a terrible expression," I say. "You're not a commodity, Max. And neither is he."

"Relax, Mom," Max says.

"I'm very relaxed," I say. "So what's up with the ascetic lifestyle?" Palindrome Guy is chatting with ninety-if-he's-a-day Chuckie F. in the argyle sweater, who's working on his second whiskey sour.

"What kind of question is that?" Max squeezes a lemon slice into her seltzer and squirts some into her eye. "Ouch!" she says, wiping her fingers on her jeans.

"Just curious," I say.

"Spoken like a true sixties mother," she says. "Not having sex or booze for a while hardly makes me an ascetic, Mom. And it's not forever." Max sucks the lemon wedge dry and her mouth puckers. "I just want to purify myself right now, finish growing to my strongest core, so I'll be at the ultimate peak of my powers when I begin to pursue my career path."

"I thought you were an artist," I say, trying not to sound judgmental.

"The point is," Max says. "Desire and lust are puerile, self-indulgent impulses that at this point in my life will only drag me down."

"Puerile?"

"Plus which..." Max takes a sip of her drink. "Men are so needy, so immature."

"Your dad isn't needy or immature," I say. "How is it that you've arrived at such a dim view of men?"

"He made the moves on your sister," Max says, her brow furrowing.

"He didn't mean to." I find myself defending Phillip more often now than when we were married. "Your dad and I have both made our share of mistakes, Max. I hope someday you won't feel the need to assign blame."

"I'm trying," she says with a sigh.

"I think the world of your father," I say. "I hope you and El know that."

"And yet you got divorced." She starts chewing on her straw.

"Let's not go back down that road," I say. "Your dad and I are both doing just fine."

"A bit too fine, if you ask me," Max says. "This broken, modern family stuff might be hunky-dory for you two groovy divorcés. But just so you know, it sucks for me and El."

"I know," I say. "I'm sorry." I've learned, humbly, that our assessment of our parenting is worth nothing. It's the kids' versions that count.

"Anyway," Max says. "All the guys my age are such big babies. Except for El. Maybe that's the problem, that I have such a great brother. No one else can ever measure up."

Another thing I've learned. If you are parents with strong opinions, you will have children with strong opinions. But not necessarily your own. However, on this point, we can agree.

"How are you feeling, by the way?" I say. "About...El and Rachel?"

"I'm happy for them," Max says tepidly. "Of course."

"I wouldn't be surprised if you felt a bit...left out," I say.

"Of what?" she scoffs. "El's allowed to have a girlfriend, Mom. Just because we're twins, we're not joined at the hip."

"I know," I say, my voice trailing off.

"So how's our favorite potty-mouthed feminist?" Max sits up straight and changes the subject.

"Isabelle?" I can't divulge the news about her being pregnant, but I decide this is as good a time as any to tell Max about my other job. "She started an online blog and asked me to write a guest post every now and then."

"A blog?" Max nearly chokes on her seltzer. "You're writing a post for a blog? You, who called me to help you find the DELETE key on your computer and was too afraid of copying and pasting to try it for over a year?"

"I wasn't afraid," I say, bristling. "I just didn't want to lose anything. Anyway, those days are long gone. I haven't just been sitting around eating grapes all day while you and El are away at school, you know. I'm getting quite computer savvy." I think of a lesson Dylan just gave me on how to format an outline with Microsoft Word, all the while looking over my shoulder and planting kisses on my neck. Isabelle suggested that I write outlines for my columns, so that they're not "so all over the frickin' place."

"So what's this blog about?" Max says.

"Well," I start out, treading carefully. "It's for women of a certain…vintage."

"The forty-plus-somethings," Max says helpfully.

"Right, the forty-plus-somethings." I try to buy more time. "Isabelle thought there was a need for a more mature woman's perspective, the voice of an older, single woman."

"Ew," Max says. "You mean you're writing about your love life? I thought you said you weren't dating."

"I'm not really dating." Oh god, I think, what have I gotten myself into? But clearly Max wants to avoid the subject even more than I do. We order a batch of extra crispy fries and talk about the Vulcan creatures in the paintings on the wall—Max's favorite is hula-hooping on a stage, wearing a tutu and a clown's hat, and I've grown fond of another one resting in a lawn chair listening to a transistor radio.

"I used to fall asleep with my transistor radio on," I say, starting to reminisce. "Oh, the magic that came out of that little box."

"Okay, Mom, let's not get sentimental. That's another reason I'm off booze for a while. It makes me all mushy."

"I don't mind being a bit mushy," I say.

"We've noticed," she says, rolling her eyes.

Shifting gears, we try and guess what various bar goers do for a living, based on their looks and their vibes. I figure the guy with the crewcut is a CIA agent, and she figures his companion is a Freudian analyst. One of them will ultimately end up killing the other. Quite the pair.

All the while, as we dip our fries into little Dixie cups full of ketchup, we watch Bartender Jack.

Some nights I make myself stay in. Despite all my new life pronouncements, it's hard not to feel a bit guilty about my new lifestyle, and not just because of the money I'm spending or the fact that I'm drinking more than I should, even though the new buzz is that red wine is good for you. What worries me most is that it's gotten to the point where a night at home holds little appeal. I get restless and bored. Whereas home with my family was always a haven, it now sometimes feels—not to get too dramatic, but—prison-like. Where the TV used to calm me in the purple armchair, it now seems to pale in entertainment value compared to what's going on out in the world. Even Perry Mason seems like a pedantic, predictable bore. And books? The last thing I read was that trashy *Us Weekly* magazine up in Vermont. What's happening to me? And more importantly, where will it all end?

Phillip calls one night in December to say he has good news. I feel a residual pang of guilt. Last spring, during those depressing days when we were trying to save our marriage, I'd secretly fantasize about ways to dispense with Phillip, demises where he wouldn't suffer and the twins wouldn't be too sad, an end that would have been "the way he wanted to go"—a massive heart attack after a Miles Davis concert or a lightning strike on the summit of a snow-capped mountain. Deep down, I truly must be a terrible person.

"What's up, Phil?" Now I'm pleased to feel real excitement about his good news—a promotion at work maybe, or a new house. Maybe he and Yvonne are getting married! And maybe I'm not such a terrible person after all, because I think I could handle that. I could almost be happy for him. Maybe.

"I'm going to climb all of the mountains higher than four thousand feet in New Hampshire," he says.

"Radical!" Some of the twins' teenage lingo still sticks hopelessly in my craw. "And when're you planning to do this?"

"Tomorrow," he says.

"You're going to climb all of the mountains over four thousand feet in New Hampshire tomorrow?" I say. "That's impressive."

He laughs. "Starting tomorrow," he says.

"But it's almost winter," I point out. "Wouldn't it be better to climb all of the mountains in New Hampshire over four thousand feet in the summer?"

"I like a challenge," he says. "Let's face it. Winters aren't what they used to be. And these ain't the Rockies."

"What about work?" I peel off what's left of my pinkie hangnail, which I snagged on the shower curtain the night before.

"I'm taking some time off," he says. "I asked for a divorce leave." There's not one ounce of malice in that joke.

"Good for you." I remember all the times over the years that Phillip forewent vacations, when his fledgling architectural firm was struggling to break into the black, when we needed the extra cash. "You deserve it, Phil," I say.

"Thanks. So how are you, kiddo?" I don't remember when he started addressing me this way. It seems slightly condescending. And where is that telltale tightness in his speech that made me bristle so often over the years? It seems to have dissipated, maybe even disappeared.

"I'm fine. Busy," I say. "I got a job at the Mustard Seed. And I'm still working on the old, long-suffering novel." I don't tell him about Isabelle's blog. I worry he might take the details of my new life as a condemnation of the one we once shared.

"And you know, dealing with the twins and whatnot. They're both doing great, don't you think?"

"They're fantastic," he says.

"El's really blossomed at Bennington," I say, "and did he tell you…?"

"He's got a girlfriend!" Phil says.

"Who, incidentally, is his dance professor and ten years older than he is."

He laughs. "He conveniently left out those parts."

"Figures," I say. "Speaking of girlfriends, how's Yvonne?"

"Yvonne…" His voice trails off. "Turns out I was just another design project for Yvonne. She kept saying"—he goes into falsetto—"'the pieces are all here, Phillip. We simply have to rearrange them.' As if I were some sort of goddamned jigsaw puzzle," he goes on. "Thanks for never trying to reassemble me, Grace."

"It never occurred to me," I say. "Maybe—"

"Too late now," he breaks in. "So, how 'bout you? Do you have a…boyfriend?"

"No, not really. Silly, to use those terms, isn't it, at our age?"

"Are you—"

"And Max seems to be mellowing out a bit." I don't want to go any further where he's heading. "She's back living at the house for a while. Did you hear about her monster self-portrait project?"

"Max Chicarelli. Larger than life," he says. "I hear the unveiling will be in the spring."

"What if you're still on top of a mountain?" I miss Phillip in a piercing flash that's gone as soon as it's come.

"Then I'll come back down," he says.

9

Otis brings his daughter into work a few days later. The holiday displays are up in full force, strings of colored lights on potted spruces, gingerbread house kits, menorahs, and three different flavors of organic eggnog. An instrumental version of "The Little Drummer Boy" plays over the loudspeaker. I see them walking toward my blackboard corner. Above all else, Zephyr is tiny for her seven years, a little ghost slip of a girl, wispy blond hair surrounding her pale baby face. Her arms are wrapped around a giant hat box. Otis is carrying a long, thin object in a canvas case.

"You packing heat?" I ask him.

"It's a tent," he says.

"I can set it up all by myself," Zephyr says.

"She can definitely set it up all by herself," Otis says.

"I've done it sixty-eight times," she says.

"Wow," I say. "That's sixty-eight more times than I've ever set up a tent."

"That means you've never set up a tent at all," she says.

"Zeph," Otis says quietly. "Be polite."

"You're right," I say to her. "I don't know the first thing about tents. Maybe you could teach me."

"Maybe," she says, but not with much conviction.

"What's in the hat box?" I ask her.

"My cancer wigs," she says.

"Cancer wigs?" I look over at Otis uneasily.

"I don't actually *have* cancer," Zephyr says. "But I get to wear the wigs because I've got alopecia. That's when your hair falls out."

"You *used to* have alopecia," Otis says.

"But I still like the wigs," she says. "Dad won't let me wear them to school anymore, though."

Zephyr unlatches the hat box and starts to pull out the wigs. "I've got the raccoon, the basset hound, the hippo, and the monkey." She pulls out one last wig and puts it on her head. "And this is my favorite. The hedgehog. Feel it."

I reach out to touch its quills. "Spiky," I say.

"Zephyr's hanging out with me here at the store today," Otis says.

"School's not working out for me very well," Zephyr says, kneeling down to loosen the drawstring of the tent bag. "I'm not going back."

"She's taking a little sabbatical," Otis says. "We're going to try homeschooling for a while."

"My teacher's a witch," she says. "I hate her guts."

"Zeph…"

"I don't like her very much," she amends.

"I had the meanest teacher ever in second grade," I say. "Her name was Miss Beaver. She had these long pointy teeth that stuck way out. And she twisted your ears if you forgot your homework."

"Was she allowed to?" For the first time, Zephyr looks up at me with interest.

I nod. "Back then, she was," I say.

"She was probably mad because she looked like a beaver." Zephyr pulls the tent frame out of the bag, the hedgehog wig sitting lopsided on her tiny head. "I would be," she says.

"I guess I would be too," I say.

Otis clears an area next to my easel. "Okay if Zephyr sets her tent up here?" he says. "It's out of the way and—"

"Christmas is eleven days away!" Zephyr starts hopping up and down on one foot. "I can't wait, I can't wait, I can't wait, I can't…"

"Zeph," Otis says gently.

"I have to say it eleven times!" she tells him. "While I'm hopping. Da-ad! Why'd you make me stop? Now I have to start all over again!"

"To yourself then, *uggla*." He puts his hand on her bobbing head. "Count to yourself."

After Zephyr is settled in her tent, drawing pictures of a bowl of fruit I've arranged for a still life, Otis tells me about the conference he just had at school. Zephyr's teacher was concerned because her obsession with counting things had gotten worse and the kids were starting to tease her. They'd been vicious about the animal wigs, which is why he'd made the "no wigs to school" rule. And her blunt way of speaking wasn't exactly making her any friends. The teacher recommended a core evaluation and suggested that Zephyr might be happier out of the classroom for a while. And when Otis asked Zephyr if that were true, she said yes, it was very true.

It was hard to reconcile the little girl who'd so determinedly set up the tent in my corner with the one Otis now described, the one who obsessively counted the tiny tiles on the bathroom floor every night, time after time, because she kept getting different answers, who crawled into bed with him when she couldn't sleep because the numbers ran in circles in her head and made her afraid.

"I'm really worried about her," he says. "That's why I went to Idaho."

"To see the old flame," I say.

"Right. We're thinking of giving it another try. Maggie's great. Good with kids. Very patient. She's coming to visit for a few weeks in the spring. I think it would be good for Zeph."

"Good for you too?" I say, looking up at him.

"Good for me too."

"Zephyr's such a great name. How'd you come up with that?"

"Her mom loved the Babar books," he says. "Zephir was the little monkey. We changed the *i* into a *y*."

"Where is her mom?" I ask gingerly.

Otis looks over at the tent. "She sort of… flew the coop," he says, lowering his voice.

"Where'd she go?"

"She just disappeared one day three years ago. We had no idea where she'd gone. The police got involved. It was terrible. Finally I got a call from her mother. Turns out Diana had taken a train to Chicago to visit a friend. But she never made it. They found her in Ohio riding a city bus."

"That's tough," I say.

"I knew Diana had some emotional issues when we got married," Otis goes on. "I just kept telling her she was doing great, that everything would be fine. But it wasn't fine. She was in trouble and she tried to tell me. But I didn't hear her. I didn't listen. That's my biggest regret."

"I'm sure you did the best you could."

"Diana's back living with her folks now, in New Hampshire," Otis goes on. "She's in therapy and taking meds. I take Zeph up there every weekend to visit. It's been tough on her, though. She's always had the alopecia, on and off, and it's probably stress-related, but her OCD has definitely gotten worse since Diana, well, for lack of a better word, cracked up."

"Hey, Dad." Zephyr pokes her head of the tent. "Can we stay here forever?"

"No dice, darlin.' We can't stay here forever," he says. "But we can stay as long as you like."

"As long as I like," she says, zipping the tent flap back up, "is forever."

Christmas Eve finds me with a full house. I haven't thrown a party since Max and El left for college and I'd forgotten how much work it is—shopping, cooking, cleaning, wrapping. But I feel a warm glow as I hear the first ring of the doorbell. The house looks beautiful. Max and Elvira have strung up white Christmas lights around the window frames and fresh fir garlands decorate the archway going from the living room into the dining room. Elvira made a found-object menorah featuring sticks, bark, scraps of metal, and colored sea glass—gorgeous in its hodgepodge way. It's only when I place the menorah on the old Shaker table as a centerpiece that I notice that one of the candle holders is made from half the pair of pliers I've been looking for all week to bleed the radiators. Elvira must have "found" them and dismembered them. But nothing can spoil my mood tonight. There's a fire crackling in the fireplace and the delicious smells of pine sap and chicken cacciatore mingle in the air. Max followed Phillip's famous recipe and, based on the tastes I keep sneaking with a spoon, has perhaps outdone the master.

Isabelle's the first to arrive, looking elegant in an eggplant-colored chenille cowl tunic and black leggings, with a pregnant glow that only I can appreciate. The cowl neck is another fashion trend that only works on the most elegant and assured. On most of us, it looks like a wobbly, deflated tire. Emil arrives soon after, with a bottle of wine in hand. He's traded in the tweed jacket for a navy henley polo. Isabelle has convinced him to let his hair grow out, so he looks slightly less professorial, and a bit more dashing. Celia is there in a red floral Marimekko shift she bought half a century ago, so old that now it's wildly fashionable again. Nell has forsaken her usual sweats and is wearing a pair of baby blue overalls with a white turtleneck. Otis and Zephyr round out the crowd, Zephyr in her hippo wig and Otis in red and green flannel. All told, counting Max and Elvira. We are nine.

Isabelle comes into the kitchen to help me with the hors d'oeuvres. I've roasted red peppers in a paper bag and soaked them in olive oil and garlic overnight.

"Taste one," I say.

Isabelle pops one into her mouth and groans. "Holy crap," she says. "No shit sinful!" She dumps sesame crackers onto a platter while I cut up carrots and celery. Max puts on the *Charlie Brown Christmas* album and the melancholy strains of "O, Christmas Tree," float through the kitchen door.

"Well, I've decided." Isabelle arranges the crackers in a ring around the platter. "I'm going to keep it."

"The baby?" I narrowly miss cutting off the tip of my thumb. "You're going to keep the baby, Iz?"

"I just passed the twelve-week mark," she says. "So, there's no turning back. I think I actually might want the little cretin after all, Gracie. I don't know what's gotten into me, but I think it might be okay."

"That's great, Iz. And I guess *cretin* is a step up from *it*. Have you told Emil yet?"

"Not yet," she says. "And no lectures, please. I'll do it in my own goddamned time."

"Before the due date might be good."

"How should I tell him so he won't die of shock?" Isabelle hops up onto the kitchen counter and grabs a carrot stick. "How'd you like to have to explain to your kid that her old man kicked the bucket at the very minute he found out he was going to be a father. You're the writer. What words would you drum up to tell your kid *that*?"

"I think I'm about to die of shock." I take away the plate of carrot sticks that Isabelle's devouring as fast as I can cut them, and hand her a whole one from the bag. "In all the years we've been friends, I don't think you've ever asked my advice about anything."

"Well, I'm asking now," she says.

"Just come right out and tell him," I say. "Who knows? Maybe he's always secretly wanted a family."

"No way. Emil and I are not that kind of people. We're no-kid people."

"Happens every day," I say. "No-kid people turning into kid people." I snap my fingers. "Just like that!"

"If Emil had wanted a family, he'd have had one already," she says grumpily. "He's as old as the frickin' hills."

"He's four years older than I am, Isabelle."

She ignores this. "I could send him a letter, registered mail." She dips her carrot into a bowl of baba ganoush. "Read at your own risk."

"Coward's way out," I say. "Emil seems like the sturdy type to me. Just tell him."

"I want to have some kind of lead-in." Isabelle shakes the

carrot in the air. "Something to soften the blow. And I want to explain it all in such a way that he'll believe me when I tell him he doesn't have to be involved if he doesn't want to."

"Why not?" I say. "You didn't make the kid all by yourself."

"I wasn't using birth control," she says. "That was totally irresponsible."

"Neither was he," I say.

"True," she says.

"Do you want him to be involved?" I notice that the new retro kitchen clock I bought at Tags, which has been gaining time every day, is now almost fifteen minutes fast.

"I don't know," Isabelle says. "I'm not going to be able to take it much longer living with Molly, particularly after I tell her the news. I'll have to get my own place again and I'll adapt, of course, for the kid. But I don't know if I can take it, having some guy hanging around the house clearing his throat and watching football, strewing his underwear all over the place and not even trying to hold in his farts."

"Domestic bliss," I say. "Comes with the territory. And once again, we're seriously flunking the Bechdel test."

"I don't think it counts if we're saying negative things about men," Isabelle says. "I'm so confused, Grace. About everything. I used to have this sane, logical mindset, this sane, logical life, and now it's all frickin' shot to hell. I don't know if I can handle it."

"You can handle it, Iz." I head for the living room with the plate of hors d'oeuvres. "Just tell the man, for heaven's sake."

The doorbell rings. "Who could that be?" I say.

Max sprints to the door and throws her arms around one of the new arrivals before I can even see who it is. But then I get a glimpse of El's face peering over her shoulder and the swish of Rachel's long black hair beside him. We weren't expecting them until the next day.

"Surprise!" El puts a bag of gifts under the tree and goes over to kiss Celia on the cheek. "Hi, Grandma," he says. "Merry Christmas!"

"Eliot," she says. "You're more handsome than ever. And even taller! What are they feeding you up there in…remind me where it is that you are?"

"Vermont, Grandma." Rachel comes up behind him. "I'm up at Bennington."

"And who is this young lady?" Celia says, adjusting her glasses.

"This is Rachel," El says.

"Rachel." Celia looks over at me. "Who on earth is Rachel?"

"Rachel is El's girlfriend, Mother," I explain.

"Actually…" A smile spreads over El's face and he looks over at Rachel. "As of six hours ago, she's my wife!"

"Your…" I start to sputter.

"What?" Max says. "Holy shit, bro. Talk about making a grand entrance!"

"We just did it," El blurts out. "We were talking about the future and I said the future's now and Rachel said what do you mean and I said let's just get married and so we did!"

Rachel smiles. "Eliot is most persuasive," she says.

"Congrats!" Max gives El and then Rachel a hug. "I'm really happy for you guys."

"Very, like, *wow*," Elvira says. "I feel like I'm in a sitcom."

"Mom…" The pleading look in El's eyes nearly breaks me. "We drove straight here from New York. We couldn't wait to tell you."

"You got married?" I say, still dumbfounded.

"I don't understand," Celia says. "Who is this girl, Grace?"

The anxious look on Celia's face pulls me out of my stupor. I put my hand on her shoulder. I know what I have to do. And nothing will be gained or changed by not doing it. "This is Rachel, Mother," I say. "Apparently, she and El just got married. So she's a part of our family now."

"Are you British?" Celia asks, turning her gaze on Rachel.

"I am," Rachel says. "London born and bred."

"Well then…" Celia raises her glass of sherry and says, "Congratulations to the both of you. And God save the Queen.

If, in fact, she needs saving. She always seemed like a pretty tough cookie to me."

I manage to pull myself together and rescue the baked Alaska from the oven before the meringue burns. El startles me from behind.

"Thanks, Mom," he says. "I thought you were going to lose it out there, but you didn't."

"You got married?" I wail. "Without even telling us?"

"We thought it would be easier all around." El starts attacking the reserve plate of cut-up carrots. "Rachel's parents are older and don't travel much. And her brother knew a lama in the city, so we—"

"Lama?" I said.

"Oh yeah, I forgot to tell you," he says. "I'm converting to Buddhism."

"From what?" Hasn't El always referred to himself as an agnostic? I hand him the bag of carrots. "Eat these," I say.

"It's important for Rachel." He snaps a carrot in half. "She wants to raise our kids with Buddhist values."

"Kids?" I say. "You haven't even finished college yet! You've got so much time, El. What's the rush? Your dad and I might never have even gotten married if our parents hadn't been so straitlaced."

"And look how that turned out," he says. "No offense, Mom." He lowers his eyes, then starts the rapid blinking eye thing that means he's made up his mind. "Anyway. This is different."

"How?" I lift up my pot-holdered hands in bewilderment. "I don't get it. What's so different, El? Tell me."

"You and Dad were just two random people who ended up together," El says. "I've been waiting for Rachel my whole life."

After dinner, we retire to the living room and Max suggests a game of charades. We split up into teams—me, Isabelle, Zeph, Rachel, and Otis against Max, Emil, Elvira, Nell, and El. Celia is the judge. A few rounds in, I draw a folded slip of paper out of the hat—*Bringing Up Baby*. Hah! In spite of the funk I've fallen into, I can't ignore the irony of the title.

I roll my hand around in a circle. Movie. Three words. First word. Sounds like. I point to the fourth finger on my left hand.

"Finger. Hand. Ring." Zephyr jumps up and down, shouting out guesses.

Ring. Ding. Bling. BRING. Isabelle finally gets it.

Second word. Little word. I point up at the ceiling.

Ceiling. Heaven. Finger. Sky.

I wag my finger downward, then up again.

Down. Up. Down.

UP! I point my finger at Rachel and nod my head.

"Okay, up," Rachel says. "Bring up…"

Third word. I cradle an imaginary baby in my arms.

Swing. Rock. Cradle. The guesses come fast and furiously.

I kiss the imaginary baby's face.

BABY! They all shout it out at once.

"Bring—up—baby. *BRINGING UP BABY!*" Otis shouts triumphantly.

"What's up with all the baby references?" Nell asks. "We just did *Rosemary's Baby* in the last round."

"Yes," Isabelle says, looking daggers at me. "What's up with that?"

"Everyone loves a baby," I say innocently.

"Adorable," she growls.

El and Rachel exchange meaningful looks. Her face has suddenly gone pale. "Did you tell her, Eliot?" she says.

"No!" El looks alarmed. "I didn't. I swear."

"I thought we agreed to wait."

"We did." El goes over to Rachel. "I would never…" He turns to me and says, "How did you know, Mom?"

"Know what?" There's a sudden chill in the air. I don't understand what's gone wrong. *Know what, know what, know what?* My question echoes in the air.

"Rachel's pregnant!" El says. And with that, the bubble of confusion pops with a loud, resounding bang.

Max shrieks and Isabelle laughs out loud. I'm instantly furious at them both. I cannot wrap my head around how the evening has gotten so twisted out of shape, how this lovely holiday dinner has turned into the strange, surreal stuff of bad dreams.

Rachel is sniffling. "I can't imagine why I'm crying," she says. "I'm deliriously happy, of course. They say it's the hormones, don't they?" She looks over at me hopefully.

"Hormones," I repeat dumbly.

"We didn't plan it this way." El jumps up, still beaming. "But it happened, so I guess it was just meant to be. We're just going to live each day as if it were our last, go with the eternal flow."

Go with the eternal flow? Didn't plan it? What the hell did that mean? Were you using contraception? I want to ask. Or not? Did you listen to anything your father and I ever tried to teach you? Are both of you stupid? My mind is suddenly filled with the most medieval, paranoid ideas. Did Rachel trick El? After all, she was over thirty. The ticking clock and all. Did she conveniently *forget* to take her birth control pills, *accidentally* prick her diaphragm, knowing full well how hard he'd fallen for her and what a tender heart he had? Some young women still did that sort of thing, didn't they, even in this day and age?

"We weren't planning to tell you about the baby yet," El says. "But it was as if you knew somehow, Mom, with this whole charades thing…"

I shoot Isabelle a dark look. To her credit, she looks chagrined. She can see how close I am to losing it and knows it's partly her fault. She comes over to my side and guides me down into the purple armchair. "This calls for more eggnog," she says and disappears into the kitchen. It's the last thing I want at that moment. As if sickly sweet eggnog ever solved any of the world's more pressing problems.

El can't stop talking. "We're going to move in together after I graduate this spring," he says. "Rachel will keep teaching until the baby comes and then I'll get a job in the city. She'll work part time and I'll go out on dance auditions."

Job in the city? Auditions? How naive can they possibly be? I know what kind of jobs Bennington art majors get in the Big Apple after they graduate. Waiting tables and pouring drinks. There are thousands of them, scraggly twenty-somethings serving up beer and burgers and living in cockroach-infested hovels in Alphabet City. And then throw a baby into the mix? Utter disaster!

"Mom," El says. "Say something. Please."

But I've used up all the saint in me. I've run out of patience, generosity, tact. I want to shout at El, "How could you do this to me? To us? To yourself? Your father's on top of a mountain and you're my only son and I've lost you forever in one fell swoop. And couldn't you at least have had the decency to tell me in private? But I have no game face to put on, no words left to say. So I sit in the purple chair with a stalk of celery and a glass of rum-laced eggnog and do absolutely nothing.

Rachel is suddenly all cheer again. She squats down beside me with a perfectly straight back and lays a slender hand on my arm. "You're going to be a fantastic grandmother, Grace!" she says, in her most chipper English accent. "I'm hyper in-tune to these kinds of things. I can feel it in my bones. Your caretaking vibes are deeply spiritual and entrenched. They're practically bouncing off of you."

"Are they?" I say through gritted teeth, trying to muster a half-hearted, wobbly smile.

I abstain from alcohol for the next two weeks and go on a fruit and veggie diet to cleanse my body of holiday poisons. I don't generally go in for all that deprivation and redemption stuff, but I've been wallowing in a pool of gloom since Christmas Eve and don't have much of an appetite. Might as well take advantage of that rare occurrence. Slowly, El and Rachel's news starts to sink in. I'm going to be a grandmother. Whether I like it or not. And now that I've acknowledged this fact, certain priorities have become clear. I need to stay present and healthy and strong. I need not to feel old.

By the end of the second week, I'm feeling virtuous, if still wounded. I've lost four pounds and can fit into my favorite jeans, which haven't reached over my knees in years. I wake up early each morning, unable to get back to sleep, and the only thing to do is put on my sweatpants and old Saucony sneakers and go out for a run. One morning, as I'm jogging around my neighborhood, I find myself imagining what a child of El's and Rachel's might look like—a dark-haired little girl with cat-like eyes, troublingly brilliant and heartbreakingly kind. With a be-loved, favorite grandmother.

Max, Elvira, and I are sitting in the living room one Sunday morning a few weeks into the new year, hunkering down for a two-day blizzard that's supposed to dump three feet of snow on the ground. The first straggly flakes have started to fall and I've just made us all hot cocoa. I've been privy to everyone's New Year's resolutions, but have stubbornly made none of my own. Max is going vegan until Valentine's Day and Isabelle's goal is to increase her blog's page views to a thousand per week. Rachel vows to eat more healthily for the baby (turns out she's a secret junk food addict, which gives me smug, if guilty pleasure), and Elvira has committed herself to mastering the *New York Times* Sunday crossword puzzle in ink. The puzzles will also figure into her final "Mad Hatter Symphony" project. After the puzzles are finished, she deconstructs them into piles of tiny random letters, each of which is assigned a note on a scale, and then are incorporated into the music. For someone so committed to taking things apart, Elvira also seems to get a great deal of satisfaction from putting them back together. She's sitting on the couch wearing her signature black cape over ripped black leggings, the crossword folded open on her lap. It's hard to imagine a time when Elvira wasn't a fixture here.

"What's a five-letter word for *mark*?" she says. "Beginning with G."

"Grade." Max looks up from one of her dog-eared *Calvin and Hobbes.* These books are her bibles; she reads them over and over again.

"Yes! It fits." Elvira fills in the letters with a green magic marker. "Speaking of grades, what did you get in Beckman's class?" she says.

"B plus," Max says. "How 'bout you."

"I spun a D minus," Elvira says. "The needle almost stopped on A, but then it slid into the D zone."

"That sucks," Max says.

"Whatever," Elvira says.

"Excuse me," I say, looking up from my newspaper. "What do you mean you *spun* a D minus, Elvira?"

"Beckman's Russian alphabet roulette," Max says. "You spin the wheel for your final grade. Whatever you land on, you get."

"That's outrageous," I say.

"Relax, Mom," Max says. "You don't have to do it. It's optional."

"Don't you guys have enough to worry about with all the pressure and cutthroat competition these days?" I say. "I've just been reading an article about kids cracking up from the stress of trying to get into college. It's appalling."

"Beckman says it will, like, free us up," Elvira says. "Get us off the uptight, goal-oriented grid. He says someday we'll look back on it and laugh, realize how meaningless it all was."

"Is this the same charmer you were telling me about that night at the bar?" I ask. "The one who teaches the Destructive Arts?"

"People literally, like, kill to get into his class," she says. "Max and I were lucky."

"Well, I think it's terrible, this spinning-your-grade stuff." I snap my newspaper open to the Metro section. "Manipulative and sadistic and completely illegal, I'm sure. That D minus is going to be on your permanent record now."

Max and Elvira look at each other and burst out laughing.

"What's so funny?" I say.

"Mom, chill," Max says. "No one can hold that *permanent record* bullshit over our heads anymore. We're adults now. We *are* our permanent records."

"Even, so, I have half a mind to call—"

"Don't even think about it," Max says darkly.

"What do your parents have to say about this, Elvira?"

"They don't really care," she says with a shrug. "Since I decided to become an artist, they're not that interested in me anymore."

Six letter word for indifference? Ending with Y? It's A-P-A-T-H-Y. For sure.

Fuzz keeps bugging me to have sex again in the car. "For old time's sake," he says, as if our "past" were comprised of anything more than a few months of once-a-week sex. Ever since I told him my idea about the screwathon, he plays this up when he wants to have his way. "You were the one who said you wanted more sex!" Car sex makes him hornier, he claims—brings out the teenager in him, makes him a better lover.

"Please, please, please!" he cajoles one night after we've left the Wonder Bar. I don't let on that I occasionally like car sex, too, though my back always pays the price the next day. His probably does, too, but that's another sweet side of the deal—our respective aches and pains are not one another's concerns. Fuzz will never have to massage my lower back the way I used to make Phillip do when I had period cramps, and I won't have to listen to him moan and groan his way through every I-told-you-so aging-jock sports injury. Still, I like to make Fuzz pay for car sex, one way or another, before I give in. I've never let him live down the broken windshield. Why should I? The new one leaks in a hard-driving rain.

We're sitting in the Corolla on a cold January night, waiting for the heat to kick in. Fuzz leans in for a feel and a kiss.

"Not so fast," I say. "I'm taking you on a little ride first."

"I don't want to go on a little ride." He groans.

"You have to," I say. "You're my prisoner."

"Ooh. Bondage sex," he says. "Got any bungee cords?"

"No S&M," I say. "It's in the rules."

"Okay, a short ride. But afterward, car sex."

"We'll see," I say. My children refer to this response as "the kiss of death."

First, we go on a tour of what's left of the Christmas light displays. You can always count on Somerville to keep them up for a couple of months—life-sized dancing reindeer and huge deflated Santas bopping up and down in the wind, porches draped with icicle lights and lit-up Virgin Mary's on the half shell. Then we head back into Cambridge and I take Fuzz on a tour of the three houses I grew up in, all located within half a mile of one another. We drive down Linnaean Street past my first Cambridge abode, across from the oldest house in Cambridge (1681), where they gave out plastic magnifying glasses for Halloween. My mother went into labor with Nell there in 1957, while laying a brick patio in the backyard.

We head up Washington Avenue to Upland Road, past the two houses of my misspent adolescence—the first on the corner of Mt. Pleasant, and the second on top of Avon Hill, where Charlie's comic book collection caught fire in the upstairs screened-in porch and nearly burned the house down. He used to charge us a nickel to read a comic, and a quarter for the latest "Archie" editions, hot off the press. As I peer into the lit windows of those old familiar houses, I feel a yearning for those far-away, lazy days, when there was still so much of a lifetime to go, when the thought of being old enough to be a mother, let alone a grandmother, seemed absurd.

Fuzz hums "Joy to the World" as I head down Raymond Street, past the house of the guy who won the Nobel Prize and then was found dead on a Scottish moor.

"Are you even listening?" I say.

"Every word." Fuzz waves one hand around vaguely, all the while looking at his cell phone. "Brick patios and magnifying glasses," he murmurs. "Scottish moors and comic books. You were a true Cambridge hippie. Ho, ho, ho. It's all fascinating."

"My brother Charlie got one of those cheap Beatle wigs at the Star Market." I refuse to let Fuzz ruin my mood. "He was supposed to use the Green Stamps to get the P volume of the

Encyclopedia Britannica, but he caved and got the wig instead. My mother was furious," I say wistfully. "I still put the wig on to dance sometimes. It looks like a giant hairball. Come to think of it, I haven't seen it around lately."

"Yeah, yeah, yeah," is all Fuzz has to say as we tool around in the Corolla, my pointing out landmarks while he gets impatient for sex, distracting me with kisses on my neck, stroking the inside of my thigh. Fuzz isn't the least bit interested in who or what I was before I met him. He's just not a curious guy. Like I told you, he's from Philadelphia.

We pull over onto a dark side street. I straddle him and we kiss. This is usually a sure-fire jump start for me, but during the course of the tour, I've somehow lost the urge. Nothing like nostalgia to kill the old sex drive. I pull away.

"What's wrong?" Fuzz says, sliding his hands under my shirt. "Come on, Sherlock. I went on your little trip down memory lane."

"I've just got a lot on my mind." I climb off him and plunk back down into the driver's seat. As per our agreement, I haven't told him anything about all the recent upheaval in my life, but it seems fair enough to offer it up as an excuse in a general way.

"Tell me about it." Fuzz straightens up in his seat, and I can tell he's about to launch into a diatribe about how overworked and under-appreciated he is.

"Let's just call it a night," I say. "I'm tired. I'll drive you home."

"All right." Fuzz closes his phone with a sigh. To my surprise, he doesn't argue. The spirit seems to have left him, too, and I'm instantly disarmed. Am I losing my sex appeal? Have I been letting myself go? Has my hair started to turn gray since I found out I was going to be a grandmother? The old, unbidden insecurities rush over the floodgates, but I'm way too tired to fight them. We ride in silence down Cambridge Street through Inman Square.

"See you next week," I say, as we pull up to his apartment.

"Before you go," he says, unbuckling his seat belt. "I've been thinking, Grace. About something new we could try."

"It's late," I say. The cold air floods in through the open door and Fuzz's coy, evasive tone is starting to annoy me. "Let's talk about it another time."

"I'll just leave you with one word then," he says. "One word to consider. And don't dismiss it out of hand."

"What word?" I say impatiently. "What one word are you talking about?"

"Threesome," Fuzz says, and slides out of the car.

10

Threesome? That's all I need, I think, as I walk on a snowy night to meet Dylan at the Wonder Bar a few weeks later. Another crazy minor character tossed into the already overcrowded novel of my middle-aged life. Fuzz must be out of his mind to suggest such a thing. But maybe I shouldn't dismiss it without at least considering it. That's typically what I'd do and I want to change that. Time to sashay my way out of a few more comfort zones.

I stomp the snow off my boots just inside the bar door. The delicious aroma of steak frites wafts toward me and I realize I haven't eaten for hours. Bartender Jack is hard at work behind the bar. Raven Mulholland is deep in conversation mid-bar with Dylan. *My* Dylan, I've come to think of him, but of course he's nobody's Dylan except his own, and his mother's (forgive me, whoever you are). But after a brief chat, he turns his attention to me. I guess I wouldn't think much of Dylan if he were immune to Raven's extraordinary charms. Hell, who isn't attracted to her?

"Grace, you look great!" he says, putting his hand on the small of my back. Filled with post-holiday courage and having kept off the four pounds, I'm wearing the ice-blue cocktail dress that's been hanging in the closet for two years. Those daily morning runs, begun out of insomnia and anxiety, have started to pay off.

I feel almost giddy with excitement. We're taking the T to the MFA. First Fridays are free! How long has it been since I went to a museum, let alone with someone who might actually enjoy it? Phillip wasn't much of a museum person and the kids always got bored so quickly. I haven't been in years.

It's Dylan's thirty-fifth birthday and I've written him a poem, which I plan to read to him at some strategic point in the evening which I feel sure will present itself. The poem came to me while I was running around Fresh Pond one day, stanza by stanza, all of a piece. I sat in my car in the parking lot for the next half hour, scribbling it down on a Dunkin' Donuts napkin, and typed it up on the computer when I got home. As a finishing touch, I drew a sketch of Dylan standing on his head, reading *The Rise of Silas Lapham*—whimsical and kind of Thurberesque. It's the first thing I've written in months.

We walk to the Square through the Common in the falling snow. White fire-fly lights are strung on all the trees. We pass the Lincoln statue and I slide the snow off the Civil War cannons with my glove. I remember when they used to flood the Common every winter and we'd take our skates down and zip around on the bumpy, grass-tufted ice. Hard now to imagine George Washington gathering his troops on this green at dawn.

As we walk through the ornate archway back out onto the street, Dylan hooks his arm into mine. We track the bronze horseshoes that commemorate Dawe's midnight ride to Lexington and descend into the warmth of the subway station at Church Street. At Park Street, we take the Green Line out to the Museum stop. Three sisters of varying sizes kneel on the trolley seats across from us, looking out into the dark tunnel as the train rumbles along. One of them keeps pulling another's hair behind her back. Dylan's in an unusually chatty mood.

"What happened with your husband?" he says, as we come up from underground onto Huntington Avenue. "Why did you two get divorced?"

"We just kind of ran out of steam," I say. "The kids went off to college and we both hit fifty. The intimacy had vanished from our marriage. And we couldn't find our way back to it, even though we tried. In the end, it seemed too bleak to live that way forever."

"Was it mutual?" he says.

"Thankfully," I say.

"Were you ever unfaithful?" Dylan says. "If you don't mind my asking."

"No," I say. "Well, only once, sort of…"

"Sort of?" Dylan looks over at me and then lowers his eyes. "Sorry," he says. "I don't mean this to be an inquisition."

"I don't mind talking about it," I say.

"Did he ever cheat on you?"

"I don't think so," I say. "Until he kissed my sister."

"He kissed your sister?"

"It's a long story," I say. "Why all the questions, Dylan?" Secretly, I'm pleased. It's a refreshing change from Fuzz's bored indifference. This guy seems to be curious about who I am. He wants to know more about me.

"Just wondering," Dylan says, as we step off the trolley onto the uprooted sidewalk. The wind's picked up and it's snowing even harder now. I pull my coat tight around me. The museum, lit from underneath its ridged columns, looms regal and impressive in the distance. "My parents got divorced when I was thirteen," he goes on. "I guess the odds aren't really with us. Forever is a long time."

"It's not an unworthy goal," I say. "Some people make it."

"Is that when you started going out to the bars alone?" We walk up the pathway to the museum entrance. "After you and your husband split up?"

I nod. "At first it was just to get out of the house," I say. "Then more for companionship, for the scene. I love going out at night. You get to be part of the play."

"What play?" He stops in his tracks.

"The neighborhood play, the play of life." I wait for Dylan to scoff, the way Isabelle did when I tried to explain this to her, but he just looks at me intently. "And that first night, when you came to the bar with that book," I say. "Thus began the Act of Dylan."

"Did you know right away?" he says. "That you would pursue me?"

"Pursue you?" I say. "Whoa! You were the one who said you wanted to build something. Remember?"

"That's right, I did." He turns to me as we climb the steps

to the museum. "And what is it that you think we're building, Grace?"

"Affection, maybe," I say tentatively. "Trust."

"Right." He nods his head slowly. "Affection..." His voice drifts off. "Maybe trust."

We stroll the permanent collections—Asian, Impressionists, Modern—and then grab a bite to eat in the Museum Cafe. Afterward, we head for the Dutch Art Wing, in the spirit of saving the best for last.

Ruisdael's massive painting, *Waterfall in a Mountainous Landscape with a Ruined Castle*, on loan from a private collector, takes up most of an entire wall, leaping off the canvas and into the room. You can almost hear the thundering swell of the rushing waterfall and smell the heady whiff of the fallen trees. I imagine the winds swooping through the crumbling doors of the ruined castle and feel a sudden chill.

"Look at the luminosity of that sky!" I go closer to get a better look. "And the detail on those trees. It's incredible!"

"Ruisdael was a well-respected naturalist," Dylan says. "To this day, botanists study his work. You see those dabs of heavy paint in the trees? It gives the foliage a rich quality. You can almost sense the sap flowing through the branches and the leaves."

"You know a lot about a lot of things," I say.

"Does that make me a dilettante?"

"No, a dilettante knows a little about a lot of things."

"I feel like a dilettante sometimes."

"It's a common affliction," I say. "It's tempting to pretend we know more than we do."

We sit down on a bench in front of the Ruisdael. We're alone in the dimly lit room. Whispers echo in the distance. Heels clatter down a faraway hallway. My eyes catch details of the painting I've never noticed before—another small house hidden low on the castle hill, a fish shape in the cloud above the mountain. I take the folded paper out of my purse.

"Happy birthday, Dylan," I say. "I wrote you something."
"What is it?" His eyes narrow.
"A poem," I say, and start to read.

DYLAN UPENDED

Thirty-five stories high
on which floors
are the treasures kept?
In dark corners or in knotted wooden drawers
numbers dance on the windowsill,
comets shoot off the screen,
synapses snap and crackle.
The dawn breaks,
the upshots sail
on parting waters
through the locks of the canal
Out to sea.

Turn him sideways,
he reaches farther
than he'll ever know.
The bridge
spans worlds and swirling tides
turn him upside down
and shake him hard.
Out tumbles the debris,
one sparkling granite nugget
dislodged
in plain sight now
for him to see.

There's a long silence. Dylan's face shows no emotion. He's very still. I wonder if I've embarrassed him. It's not homage, I want to tell him. Just observation.

"It came to me out of the blue," I say. "It's nothing, really; it's about your desire to belong to an era, about your many gifts, wanting to write—"

"How do you do that?" he says, taking the paper from my hand.

"Do what?"

"Make the words move like that?" he says. "When I write, it's as if I'm plunking out random notes on the piano." He looks down at the poem. "You make it all so…lyrical."

"If you're lucky," I say with a shrug, "it just comes out that way sometimes. The rest of it is mostly drudge work."

Dylan looks back up at the Ruisdael and takes my hand. "I want to tell you something, Grace," he says.

Whether it's the spicy tofu bites we ate at the museum cafe or the wine or my embarrassment about the poem or the anticipation of what else Dylan might say, Mother Nature chooses this moment to blast me with a searing hot flash. The heat starts in my chest and rises up to fill my face. Sweat forms on my brow and upper back. I can only imagine how red my face must be. I surreptitiously lift my arm to pat my face dry.

"Are you all right?" Dylan says. "You look flushed, Grace. You're sweating. What's wrong? Should I get you a drink of water?"

"No, I'm fine." I don't want to break the fragile, loaded moment. "I think they're overdoing it with the heat in here, don't you? You said you wanted to tell me something?"

"Yes, but… Are you sure you're okay?" Dylan looks down at the printed poem, then at me, and back at the poem again. There's a pained look on his face that I can't read.

"I'm fine, really," I say. "What was it you were going to tell me?"

Dylan takes a deep breath, the kind you draw before confessing."I read your mushroom book last night," he says. "Cover to cover."

"What did you think?" I say.

"It was amazing, Grace," he says.

Back at home, I unzip the ice blue cocktail dress and kick off my topaz boots. I look in the freezer for some vanilla ice cream, but the girls must have raided my stash, so I rummage in the cupboard for a random cookie or a piece of chocolate. No such luck. In a last-ditch effort, I pull open the kitchen junk drawer, and there, amongst the dead batteries and broken plastic forks and stretched-out rubber bands, is an unopened fortune cookie! It will have to do.

I plunk into the purple armchair with a long, wistful sigh. There's always the next time with Dylan, I tell myself. As long as there keep on being next-times. Maybe that's what's so terrifying about getting older, the rapidly diminishing number of next-times. My fortune reads: *Patience is a rare virtue.* Hah! Maybe for the young! Another night with Dylan has faded away, puzzling and tantalizing and lovely and unfinished. But how can I complain? As frustrated as I sometimes feel, this is my kind of romance. There's nuance and uncertainty, layered conversation, unanswered questions—rippling, welling heat. "Let the Mystery Be." That's what the song says. Maybe that was the problem with Phillip and me—there just wasn't enough mystery. Or does mystery simply stand no chance against time? I won't overthink this. I won't try to rush it, or control it, or let it make me crazy. I'll just go with the eternal flow, as El says. I don't want the answer to this Dylan riddle to be the one I seem to attach to every question I put to myself these days: because I'm old.

Dylan pursues me with such slow, milky devotion, as if we have all the time in the world. Hurry, I want to say to him, every day that goes by floats away into the hazy, amorphous past. But one thing is clear. To pounce on Dylan is not the way to land him. He's hopelessly undaunted and pure. He's moody and careful and doesn't count the moments of every day. At thirty-five, he doesn't understand the urgency and vagaries of time. He doesn't understand that in the morning I'll be grumpy and deflated, that my wrinkles and sags will be on full display, that without the benefit of a good day's work and two glasses of wine, I'm not nearly as quick-witted or generous or insightful, that his being closer to my children's age than mine really does bother me.

The last of the sugary fortune cookie dissolves under my tongue. The kitchen clock is now nearly twenty minutes fast. I glance over at Sheila LaFarge's photo on my fridge. Stay strong, she tells me. Don't overreact, don't give up, don't despair. Above all else, don't let your cowardly, weakling heart intrude. Take each day as it comes. Go out there on the front lines—take risks, engage, enjoy. Go forth and be cougarish, cougarize, encougar!

I crumple up my fortune and close my weary eyes. Maude snatches it out of my hand and runs off with it in her mouth. Atticus jumps up and settles in my lap. I bury my face in his warm fur and let the purring soothe me. And I wonder—why do I sometimes feel, after only a few months on the prowl, that I'm all cougared out?

The waiting room at the Bay State Health Center is immaculate, except for a Utah-shaped stain on the gray carpet, which I trace over and over again with my right foot. Celia sits fidgeting beside me one February afternoon, indignant at having been dragged to this "waste of time appointment," to which she now claims she never agreed. Her grey hair, as always, is cut straight just below the ears and neatly parted on the side, like the little French girls in the *Madeline* books. On her tiny feet are an ancient pair of black Mary Janes. I stifle an urge to clamp my hand around her tiny wrist, the way I used to with the twins when they were toddlers and we were approaching a busy street. I keep thinking she's going to flee.

"There's absolutely nothing wrong with my memory," Celia says, flipping idly through the pages of a lean *Time* magazine. "I remember the day Harry Truman took office. 'Democracy holds that free nations can settle differences justly and maintain a lasting peace.' Such eloquence." She raps her hand on the picture of George W. Bush on the cover. "Truman put this idiot to shame. He can't even pronounce the word *nuclear* correctly."

"You're the one who keeps saying how forgetful you've gotten lately, Mother." I knew if we called Celia's bluff, she'd change her tune. I'm only going along with this because Charlie seemed genuinely worried, and anyways, it's high time the old bird got checked out. She hasn't been to a doctor in years.

Celia sighs. "Talk to me when you're eighty-three," she says. "I have a lot more to remember than you do."

"I hope I will be talking to you when I'm eighty-three." It's not entirely true—my god, she'd be one hundred and twelve by then—but I consider it a lie of kindness and therefore forgivable. "That's why we're here," I say.

Dr. Mendoza is a handsome, dark-haired woman, alarmingly young. They all are these days. It's kind of shocking. Celia seems to have accepted this reality long ago—that the work force is largely made up of oversized children.

"I'm fine, doctor," she says. "My children insisted that I come."

"No harm in getting checked out," Dr. Mendoza says. "I'll do a physical exam first and then we'll go from there."

"Where will we go?" Celia looks over at me pointedly.

The doctor puts the stethoscope into her ears and against Celia's chest. "Excellent," she says. "You have the heart of a forty-year-old."

"And the brain too," Celia says. "Even though my children seem to think I'm losing my wits."

"Blood pressure, seventy over one ten. Good. Open your mouth please? Say ahh…"

Celia's leg jerks up when the doctor taps her knee with the rubber reflex hammer. "Would you look at that!" she marvels.

"The neurological exam won't take long." Dr. Mendoza sits down in a chair and slides over to a desk. "I'll just be asking you a series of questions."

"How long is not too long?" Celia says.

"About fifteen minutes," she says, opening up Celia's file. "Are you ready?"

"Ready." Celia checks her watch.

"First, I'm going to say three words to you, and I want you to try and remember them. Okay?"

"Fine."

"Bird. Snow. Pencil."

"Bird, snow, pencil," Celia says.

"Right. Now, tell me, what year were you born in, Mrs. Hobbes?"

"1922," she says briskly. "Warren Harding was in the White House, although not for long. He up and died of a heart attack the next year. My father bought a Pierce-Arrow Runabout in 1926, just after my brother Frederick was born. We drove it out West during the Depression. It was quite an education."

"I bet it was," Dr. Mendoza says. "What day of the week is it today, Mrs. Hobbes?"

"For goodness sake, call me Celia," she says. "Mr. Hobbes has been dead now for nearly twenty years. I never really agreed with all that *Mrs.* malarkey, but I went along with it, for Eliot's sake. He was old-fashioned that way…"

"What day is it today, Celia?" the doctor asks again.

"It's Wednesday." Celia nods her head briskly. "I have my bridge club at four o'clock." She looks at her watch again. "As long as this doesn't take too long."

"It won't," the doctor reassures her. "And what day of the week came before today, before Wednesday?"

"Tuesday."

"And what did you do on Tuesday?"

"I have tea every Tuesday," she says. "With Grace. At four o'clock. Give or take. She's often late. I told you there's nothing wrong with my memory." I can tell she's getting agitated and I touch her arm to calm her.

"Okay, let's take a short break," Dr. Mendoza says. "Do you remember the three words I told you when we first started?"

"Surely," Celia says. "There was a *bird* and then…" She

looks blankly at the door. Her voice slows and softens. "Eliot loved birds. We had a bird feeder out in the backyard. That day we saw the cardinal, he told me things weren't going well at the firm, that we might have to take out a loan..." Her hand goes up to her face, and she looks over at me. "We never did tell the children."

"Where are you right now, Mrs.... Celia?" the doctor says gently.

"We went to the bank...to see about a loan." Celia's eyes dart from the doctor to me and then back to the doctor and all around the walls of the tiny, antiseptic room—at the eye chart and the diabetes poster, and then over at the closed green door. I give her shoulder a squeeze. "Oh." She comes back to reality then. "I see we're still here." She consults her watch. "And we're six minutes behind schedule."

I meet Max for lunch at Simon's the next day. She's got an hour to kill before her next studio class downtown.

"How's Grandma?" she says.

"She got a little confused at the doctor. Just anxious, I think. They ran some tests." I keep it vague, not wanting to worry her. "Want to watch TV tonight?" I take a sip of my vanilla latte. "It's an Elaine episode on *Seinfeld* and Homer gives up drinking on *The Simpsons*. I'll make the popcorn."

"Sorry. No can do." Max slides a rogue tomato back into her pesto and mozzarella sandwich. "I've got a date," she says.

"A date? Wow. What happened to 'men are so needy' and 'growing to your strongest core'?"

Max shrugs. "I really like this guy," she says. She shimmies her eyebrows, Groucho Marx style and slides into character. "What can I tell you? His karma ran over my dogma."

"Well, that's great," I say. "Who is he, Max? Do I know him?"

"Sort of." She takes a sip of her raspberry tea. "And that could potentially be a problem."

"Why? What's his name?

There's just the slightest hesitation. "Jack," she says.

"So what's the…" It comes to me then, as I plunk out the last word, but it's not a question anymore—"problem?"

"Mom." Max waves her hand in front of my face. "Earth to Mom. Come in, Mom. Can you read me?"

"Bartender Jack?" I say. "You're going out on a date with Bartender Jack?"

"Correct."

"Well, wow…" I try to buy time, praying my sudden sense of betrayal is not showing on my face. "How did that happen?" I say.

"Elvira and I went to the Wonder Bar last week. Jack and I got to talking and we really hit it off."

She and Jack were talking? I think to myself. How could that be? Bartender Jack didn't *talk*.

"Where are you going on this date?"

"Jack's taking me to the Capitol Grille on Newbury. I've always wanted to go."

"That's a steak place," I say. "I thought you were going vegan."

"It's the Capitol Grille, Mom!"

"It's awfully pricey," I say. "I hope you're going to split the bill."

"He won't let me," she says. "Said he wouldn't hear of it."

"Well, make him, Max."

"Make him? Why? I think your feminism's running amok, Mom."

"My feminism's just fine."

"It's nice to get treated once in a while," Max says. "And besides, Jack makes good money."

"He does?"

"Yes. And he says you're an excellent tipper. Way to make me proud." She grabs her coat and gets up to leave. "I've got to get back to the studio," she says. "And then come home to change before my date. What do you think? The slutty red dress or the sexy purple one? Or maybe just black jeans and a nice shirt?"

"Wear whatever you're most comfortable in," I say. "You're

not on display. And there's nothing worse than feeling overdressed."

"Whatever," Max says. "And by the way, Mom, if anything actually comes of this Jack thing, you might have to stop going to the Wonder Bar." She hikes up her low-rise jeans, first over the right hip, then the left. "I'm just saying," she says.

I march boldly through the door of the Wonder Bar that night, senses heightened and nostrils flared. Sure enough, Bartender Jack is nowhere to be seen. A new bartender, Larry, a lumbering, doughy guy with a bushy beard and droopy eyes comes over to take my order.

"What can I get for you?" he says cheerfully.

"The usual," I say.

"Which is?"

"Cabernet."

"The Carnivore or the Freak Show?"

"I don't know. What I usually get. Jack knows."

"Jack's not here tonight."

"I'm aware of that."

"Would you like a taste of each?" Larry's unflappable patience is exasperating.

"Just give me the cheaper one," I say.

"You got it, ma'am," he says, and starts to whistle "Sweet Caroline."

Ma'am. There you have it. He's totally ruined the evening. And now that chirpy song will be stuck in my head for days.

Stop going to the Wonder Bar. Max's words keep echoing in my brain. No way. Not a chance. This is my place. I found it first. I staked my claim. I will not be banished, even, or especially not, by my own daughter. While I sit fuming, I do some deep breathing and draw a new pineapple in my notebook, sitting in a lawn chair with a transistor radio, a companion piece to the Vulcan creature painting that I've recently grown fond of. The owl painting seems to have disappeared. I kept meaning to ask Jack how much it cost. Too bad. I would have liked to have that painting hanging on one of my walls. I guess I missed my chance.

I look around the bar, watching the young people fixated on their cell phones, using them as armor against shyness and boredom, staring at the lit-up screens, fingers dancing, playing games, checking, hedging, texting. What on earth did we all do with ourselves before the technology boom? I take a sip of my wine. But aren't I as much a coward, hiding behind my notebook the way they do their phones, jotting down random thoughts, sometimes just scribbling nonsensical French phrases to make it look as though I'm deep in thought? *Le petit hibou a peur du grand aigle,* reads my messy handwriting on a wrinkled notebook page. I am the little owl and how can I not be afraid of the big eagle? The big eagle is the long, dark night and what it holds of me in it, all of my middle-aged longing and vulnerability. I'm the poster child for mid-life mood swings these days.

I read my notes from the last time I went out, a list of post ideas for Isabelle's blog: "In Defense of Ketchup"—"Bar Posture: What does it Tell You?"—"Grammar Pet Peeves." I seem to be much better at coming up with ideas than actually writing about them. Max's attack on my feminism reminds me I have to write a post for *Squiggle Z* on the subject. "The Other F Word," I'll call it. Or has that been used to death? How many times have I been asked, *Are you a feminist?* My answer always is: *Aren't all women feminists, just by virtue of being female, living and coping as women in a patriarchal world?* But I'm going to have to do better than that. I can't just ask the tough questions. I have to try and answer them.

Raven walks into the bar and sits down next to me. "Hi, Grace," she says.

"Can we talk about Brussels sprouts?" I look down at the saucer of food I've just ordered. "They used to be the most reviled vegetable on the planet, and now we're paying six dollars for a measly eight of them. They're hard as rocks and taste like they were cooked in dirty dishwater."

"Never touch them," she says with a shudder. "Can we talk about men?"

"I'm trying to do less of that," I say. "But sure."

"They're such idiots."

"Agreed." I stab my fork into one of the Brussels sprouts and it flies into my lap. "What happened?" I say.

"This guy I've been seeing said something ridiculous about how women shouldn't be allowed to drive in the city and I called him on it and he said, 'Oh, so you're a feminist?' And then he gave me this whole rap about how he was a feminist, too, and I asked him what that meant to him and he said it meant women should be allowed to vote and stuff." She throws up her hands. "In this day and age, it's pathetic!"

"They can talk about feminism all they want," I say. "But they still just say and do whatever they damn please."

"It's true," Raven says. "Why can't we do that?"

"We care too much what other people think."

"We've got to stop *doing* that!" Raven says.

"We've got to keep reminding ourselves to be feminists," I say. "Hopefully the next generation will come by it more naturally."

"I was brought up to act like a little princess," Raven says. "But I was this huge, awkward freak. And a tomboy to boot. I hated being a girl."

"I tried to break the gender barriers with my kids," I say. "But I'm not sure it worked. My daughter, Max, is out on a date with Bartender Jack tonight and she asked if she should wear the slutty red dress or the sexy purple one. That made me think we haven't come all that far."

"What did you tell her?"

"I said she should just feel comfortable."

"Good advice," Raven says, giving me a nod of approval.

I lean back against the corner wall. "I remember when Max was six and the electrician called her sweetheart and she called him a 'male chauvinist.' And I thought, Wow, her first feminist moment."

"I'm not sure I've even had one yet," Raven says.

"The night you told that guy his family jewels would fit into a toothpaste cap," I say. "That was pretty good."

"I guess," Raven says. "You've probably had a million feminist moments, growing up in the sixties and all. What was your first one, Grace?"

"Well, it's hard to say, because I was raised by a sort-of feminist." I think for a moment. "For the longest time, I always just assumed that all of my moments were feminist. But one day when I was sixteen, I decided to be brave and shave my legs for the first time. You have to understand, that wasn't cool back in those days. I took my father's razor and took it all off. It felt great."

"Whereas my mother made me start shaving my legs when I was eleven," Raven says. "She bought me these little pink razors before I even had any hair on my body. She said a lady shouldn't run around looking like a hairy ape." Raven puts her hands in her armpits and does an excellent gorilla imitation, grunts and all.

I scooch my back up against the wall, sliding back in time. "There was the time I ate my first Ring Ding. My mother was appalled. And then one day I got up the courage to admit that I actually liked a Simon and Garfunkel song."

"A Simon and what?" Raven says.

"Never mind." I'm suddenly struck by an idea. "Let's go around the bar," I say, "and ask women about their first feminist moments. I write a post for my friend's blog. I think this could be interesting."

I turn to the two young women sitting next to me—well-dressed and groomed, early twenties. I've been eavesdropping. They go to Harvard Law School—I know the cue words—Pound Hall, Harkness Commons, Cornell West, torts and contracts and liens. They speak in the crisp confident tones of those who know they'll someday rule the world. Except that every third, seventh, twelfth word is—*like*. It's worse than fingernails on a blackboard. Clearly the "like" disease does not discriminate. It's the scourge of an entire generation.

"Excuse me," I say to the young woman sitting next to me. Could her teeth be any straighter? Or whiter? "We're doing a little survey. Do you mind if I ask you a question?"

She gives her friend a dubious look. "I guess not," she says.

I lean forward. "What would you say was your first feminist moment?"

"Seriously?" The young woman looks over at her friend again.

"Seriously," I say, pen poised over my notebook.

She thinks for a moment, fiddling with a gold bracelet on her wrist. "Well, when I was, like, eight, I told my parents I was going to be on the Supreme Court someday," she says.

"And you go to the law school, right?" She nods. "So you could very well be on your way," I say.

"I wouldn't, like, rule it out," she says, exchanging a smirk with her friend.

"Okay, so here's the deal," I say. I just can't stop myself. "Might I suggest, your honor-to-maybe-be, that it's just not going to be cool when you and the other justices are up there deliberating and you say, 'I, like, think he's guilty, but, I'm like, not really sure.' Sometime between now and when you get nominated for the Supreme Court, you're going to have to stop with all the 'likes.'"

"Oh...my...god," the young woman says to her friend in disbelief.

"Right?" the friend says supportively.

"One last piece of advice," I say. "And then I'll shut up, I promise. If you're up there on the bench, and you're tempted to say *like*? If the overwhelming urge comes over you? It's better to just say *um*."

She gives me a disgusted look and turns away. Raven and I turn back to our drinks. And for this night, anyways, that's as far as the feminist experiment goes.

11

Those of us who have brothers know that one of the jobs of being a sister is to watch the brother "do things"—all kinds of contests boys regularly hold with themselves that require an audience—preferably female. Charlie used to drive me and Nell crazy. *I bet I can skip this rock eight times! I bet I can knock that sneaker out of a tree with this tennis ball! I bet I can catch all of these M&Ms in my mouth! And if I don't do it on the first try, I'll do it on the second, or maybe the fifth! Watch me, watch me, watch me!* Geez. And they say we're the vainer sex. El wasn't as bad, but I did spend a good share of my thirties and forties watching him practice his ballet moves—*grands jetés* and *pas de chats*—and then later skateboard tricks and soccer moves. Max demanded her share of attention, too, staging murder mysteries in the basement and magic shows out in the backyard. Suffice it to say, I've put in more than my share of time being an observer.

So when Dylan asks if I'd like to come out to Saugus one night to watch him play ice hockey with "a bunch of guys," my first reaction is, Why on earth would I want to do that? But I rein in the thought and try to think rationally about the question from a fresh perspective. Points to consider:

Dylan is not my brother. Or related to me in any way. This is a biggie.

Dylan wants to build something with me. And I have agreed. An ice-skating rink. Maybe?

Dylan and I have kissed. Even gotten to second base a few times. And the fact is that I would like to go all the way with Dylan. So what's a little jaunt out to Saugus to help the cause?

Dylan picks me up one drizzly Wednesday night near the end of February in his car, which reeks of sweat and pine-scented air freshener, wafting out of one of those little faux velvet trees dangling from the rearview mirror.

"Sorry about the smell," he says. "It's my hockey equipment." His gear's strewn all over the back seat—giant leg pads and a cobalt blue helmet, jock straps and rolls of black tape and a few busted hockey sticks, mouth guards, gorilla-sized gloves, and a snazzy looking pair of skates that must reach up to his knees. "I can't seem to get rid of it."

"Eau de Guy," I say. "It's a familiar scent."

"Why is it that women smell so much better than men?" Dylan says.

"I think they just wash more," I say, sliding a fast-food container out from under my butt and tossing it onto the floor.

"Right." He considers this. "They probably just wash more."

The hockey rink is vast and echoing. I remember the smells—boiled hot dogs and Zamboni fumes and stale popcorn and sweaty boys. Dylan's friends are already out on the ice, skating in circles and shooting pucks back and forth.

"Hey, Guthrie!" one calls out. "Is that your old lady? The one you—"

"Shut it!" Dylan shouts back, and then says to me, "Sorry about that, Grace. Don't pay any attention to those morons."

"I *am* an old lady," I say. "Compared to you guys."

"You are ageless," he says, caressing my cheek. "Perfectly seasoned."

I sit down on the bleachers with a cup of instant cocoa from the vending machine, cradling the Styrofoam cup in my hands. And I remember hanging out in high school with my girlfriends at our old grammar school playground and watching my boyfriend Floyd play street hockey, his muscles clenching as he whacked the ball with his stick—me thinking about how we'd have sex later that night, and melting inside. And here I am, nearly in my dotage, a silly striped scarf wrapped around my neck, picking mini-marshmallows out of my cocoa, watching my thirty-five-year-old sort-of-would-be boyfriend dashing around the ice, banging up against the boards—and hoping for the very same thing.

Dylan speeds toward me and stops with a sharp, angled tilt

of his skates. Sparkling ice shards fill the air. His cheeks are red like apples. "Did you see that shot?" he says. "It almost went in! That goalie made one hell of a save. I have to give him credit. Are you watching, Grace? Are you watching?" *Watching, watching, watching?*

"I'm watching," I say, as he skates back out toward the blue line. And as Dylan gets into a fight with a guy who checks him hard against the boards, and the sticks and gloves go flying, those old playground thrills of lust and longing fill me all over again.

Outside, after the hockey game, the rain is falling hard. Dylan's changed back into his jeans and his hair is wet and tousled. He carries his skates by their dripping, uncovered blades. His eyes are lit with exhilaration.

"I hope that wasn't too boring for you," he says.

"No, it was fun," I say. "Reminded me of the old days…"

"Which old days?" He tosses his skates into the back seat.

"When I used to watch my boyfriend play street hockey way back when," I said. "And then later…watching my son play soccer."

"You have a son?" He looks over at me in surprise.

"And a daughter," I say. "They're twins."

"What? You never mentioned them."

"I didn't?" Was this actually possible? Hadn't Dylan gotten the same earful about my kids as everyone else? And if so, why not? Had I subconsciously avoided telling him that I had two adult children?

"How old are these twins?" Dylan says.

"Twenty-one." I close the door. "Legal grown-ups as of three months ago. It makes me feel so—"

"You have to stop obsessing about your age, Grace." He stops me with a hand on my arm. "It's irrelevant."

I laugh. "That's what my son tells me."

"Well, he's right," Dylan says, looking over at me pointedly. "Wow, twenty-one-year-old twins…"

As Dylan pulls out of the parking space, I put my hand on his mile-long thigh. And by the time he's straightened out the steering wheel, the hand has slid down to his crotch.

"Whoa," he says. "Are you trying to make me have an accident?"

"Sorry." I pull my hand away. "An old reflex. You asked about sex in the sixties. We did a lot of that back in the day."

He takes my hand and puts it back on his jeans, easing the car back out onto Route 1. "Keep going," he says. "No one's ever done that to me before."

"Never?" I undo his belt buckle. Even though I'm not a big fan of oral sex, it just seems like the right thing to do. "You are a late bloomer."

"I was taught that oral sex was selfish," he says. "Just for the guy's pleasure, you know." We pass by the Hilltop Steak House, with its life-sized plastic cows grazing out front, and then the Kowloon's colorful Thai-style roof.

"It doesn't have to be," I say. "If there's…reciprocation." I unzip his jeans. "Do you want to pull over?"

"No, I'll go slowly." We pass the huge orange Tyrannosaurus Rex on the miniature golf course, with his toothy dinosaur grin. "This is such a turn on," Dylan says, his hand moving downward. "Keep going."

I didn't think it was possible, such a thing, but here it is, staring me right in the face, a veritable model Bunker Hill Monument. Bending down, I go down on him slowly. I'm reminded of something I once read in a magazine, that a good blow job was a hand job with oral embellishments. I keep going down, then up, and back down, using my hand to carry the stroke right to the base of his shaft. He makes a sound like a balloon losing air, his hands gripping tight at ten and two on the wheel. I feel his thigh muscles clench. He lifts his hips up and I can hardly breathe. Arousal spreads through me, as my mouth slowly fills with cum.

"Oh my god," he says.

I sit up again and my tight nipples graze my shirt. I'm wet

and close to the edge. I unzip my jeans and lead his right thumb to my center. The car smells like a primeval rain forest.

"Gently," I say, rocking back and forth. "Right there. Up and down. Up and down. Ever so slightly."

"That is the sexiest thing I've ever seen," he says.

"Keep your eyes on the road," I say. "I'm so close. Just like that. Keep your thumb right there. God. Keep your eyes on the road."

And as I come, with an arch of my back and a few quiet shudders, I see the windshield wipers working frantically to keep up with the now pouring rain. We climb the ramp up onto the Tobin Bridge, and by the time Old Ironsides comes into view, we're halfway back to Cambridge.

"So how's that post on feminism coming along?" Isabelle asks me a few days later. We're at the Mustard Seed, in my chalkboard corner, having a cup of coffee. "I thought it would be good to run it on International Women's Day. March 8th."

"Still working on it," I say. I was hoping she'd forgotten. That encounter with the law school student got me rattled and now I don't know what I want to say about feminists anymore. Except, obviously—just be one!

"You missed your last deadline, Grace."

"I know," I say.

"And this is just a suggestion," she says. "But I still think your posts would benefit from a bit more…focus."

"Focus?"

"More big picture ideas. Less minutia. And can the jokes, Gracie. This isn't a frickin' comedy routine."

"Didn't you like that one about Elvis and Ben Franklin and the Pope at the bar?" I say.

Isabelle gives me a dark look. "You actually have to say something, Grace. Without being preachy, of course," she adds. "You've got to make a point."

"Points aren't exactly my strong suit. I'm more of a mental meanderer."

"Which is a sure-fire way to lose your audience," Isabelle says. "The national attention span is down to about ten seconds, Gracie. If you don't snag them right off the bat, you're doomed." She pulls up my last column on her phone and reads a line. "EMOTIONAL NON-GRAVITY AT THE BAR: WHERE WHAT GOES UP DOESN'T NECESSARILY HAVE TO COME DOWN. What the hell were you even trying to get at here?" she says. "People were nodding off before they even finished reading the title."

"At the bar, all our negative baggage doesn't have to drag us down," I say. "We get to just float around for a while, in a nonthreatening, nonjudgmental environment."

"It's called drinking," Isabelle says. "Choose a few grounded points and stick to them, Grace. You can't just wander around aimlessly in your mind and throw in a semi colon here or there for good measure."

"Okay, I get it," I say. "More big picture. No jokes. No meandering. No semicolons. Less minutia. Snagging. Focus!"

"Focus," Isabelle says.

It's my turn now. I pour myself some more coffee. "And how are plans for that little chat with Emil going?" I say. "About a certain tiny humanoid that's growing inside of you and may be sporting a walrus mustache as we speak?"

"In progress," Isabelle says darkly. "They're in freaking progress, Gracie. My sciatica's killing me and I'm moody as hell. So give me a break here. Please."

"Give us all a break and tell him!" I say. "Less procrastination. Fewer swear words, Iz. More action. Focus!"

March comes in like a snarling polar bear, high winds and more snow, single digit temperatures for three consecutive days. I pull out my long johns again and unearth all the mittens and scarves I've carefully washed and put away. We're being pushed to our winter limits. Nerves are on edge and egos are frail. In the eggplant-colored house, cabin fever has set in.

I get up the courage one Saturday morning to ask Max about

her date. She's sitting on the hot air heater wrapped in a wool blanket reading *Calvin and Hobbes.* There are art supplies and audio equipment everywhere on the living room floor, random canvases, Elvira's found objects, paints and brushes and glues and fabric—the flotsam and jetsam of two twenty-one-year-old conceptual geniuses. I've gotten used to a messy house again and I'm trying to be at one with it (as a WASP I'm constantly trying to ward off my OCD tendencies), but I often dream of all those empty, cavernous spaces that were mine back in September, and I can't wait to reclaim them.

"So how did it go?" I say.

Max looks up from her book. "What?"

"Your date with Jack. I've been meaning to ask."

She folds down an ear of one page and closes the book. "I've been on three dates with Jack," she says. "And they've all been great."

"Three?" I say, alarmed.

Max nods. "He's a really interesting guy. Did you know he was in the Merchant Marines for two years?"

"I did not," I say, sitting down in the purple chair.

"And his mother was a Hari Krishna," Max says. "He was one of those kids who hung out in the street barefoot while the grown-ups danced around in pigtails and orange robes. Out in Santa Fe. He's never met his father."

"Like Isabelle," I say. "Poor guy."

"That's not the way Jack sees it," Max says. She pulls her knees up to her chin. "He says his past made him realize who he didn't want to be and therefore who he did."

"And who is that?" I say.

"Himself," she says.

I don't press it. "What did you end up wearing that first night?"

"The little black dress," she says. "I'm glad I went with my gut. It was a fancy-schmancy place. Jack wore a button-down shirt and a suit jacket. He looked so handsome." Her face suddenly darkens.

"What's wrong?" I say.

"It's weird," Max says. "I'm used to guys liking me more than I like them. But with Jack, it's different."

"Isn't it best to try for a balance?"

"I suppose," she says. "But it's so much easier to be the one in control."

"Of what?"

"The situation. Your feelings." Max starts to braid the fringe of her blanket. When she's deep in thought, she looks so much like a brooding Phillip. "With Jack, I feel so…vulnerable. This little voice in my head keeps saying, 'Don't fuck this up, don't fuck this up!' But why do I have to feel like it's all up to me? And what if I do fuck it up?"

"If it's really good," I say carefully, "then you won't."

"But how do you know if it's really good?" Max says, shaking her head back and forth.

"You just do," I say, but not with much conviction.

Charlie, Nell, and I have a meeting with Dr. Mendoza in early March.

"I won't beat around the bush," she says. "Your mother's brain imaging results confirm my clinical observations from her last visit. As you suspected…" She looks over at Charlie. "She appears to be in the early stages of Alzheimer's."

"I knew it," Charlie says, slapping his thigh.

"Fortunately, the older a person is at diagnosis, the more slowly the disease tends to progress," the doctor says. "And, considering your mother's otherwise good health, she'll likely have some time left before—"

"She's a complete basket case," Charlie says.

"Charlie!" Nell says.

"Can she still live alone?" I ask.

"For now," Dr. Mendoza says. "I don't think she's in any immediate danger to herself. But it's up to all of you now to be more vigilant, more present. Call her a few times every day. Remind her of mundane things—upcoming events, grocery lists, appointments; try to keep her grounded in the present. An actual physical check-in by one of you once a day is also a good idea."

"What will happen next?" Nell says.

"Eventually, the confusion will get worse." Dr. Mendoza has the most soothing voice. I can't think of anyone I'd rather have telling us this heartbreaking news. "She may start to wander in her mind, through space, or through time, the way she did here in the office that day." She hands each of us some pamphlets on Alzheimer's. "She may go out to do an errand and find herself somewhere unfamiliar. She may not remember how she got there. Or how to get home. This can be scary. Keep reminding her that if and when that should happen, she should call one of you. She has a cell phone, of course."

Charlie shook his head. "We gave her one for Christmas but she never used it. She donated it to Goodwill."

"Get her another one," the doctor says. "Insist that she keep it with her at all times. Teach her how to use speed dial. You'll be numbers one, two, and three. Once she gets used to it, this will be a comfort to her. Luckily, she's in excellent physical health for her age. The silver lining, if you will—"

"How long will it be until she doesn't know who we are anymore?" Nell says.

"That's hard to say," Dr. Mendoza says. "It's different for every patient. We'll just have to keep a close eye on her, and see how things progress."

"I knew she was losing it," my brother says, giving me the evil eye.

"Good for you. You get a bonus point, Charlie," I say. "Does that make you happy?"

"I told you she was acting weird!"

"Show some sensitivity, guys," Nell says. "She is our mother."

"I know how devastating this news can be," Dr. Mendoza says, closing up Celia's file. "The caretaking does eventually become very difficult. I'm glad you all have each other for support."

Out in the parking lot, we linger by Charlie's beat-up BMW. Nell lights up a cigarette.

"I thought you quit," I say.

"Don't tell Mother," she says. "I'll never hear the end of it."

"Who do you think you're kidding, Nellie?" I say. "She told me you smelled like an ashtray the other day."

"What does it matter what we tell her anymore?" Charlie says. "She won't remember it anyway."

"That's a long way off, Charlie," I say. "Can't you try to be more positive?"

"You should be number one on her speed dial, Grace." He ignores my question. "I'll be number two, and, Nell, you'll be three."

"Why am I number one?" I say. "That means she'll always be bugging me."

"And why am I number three?" Nell says. "Don't you guys trust me? Anyway, who says you get to decide, Charlie?"

"Maybe she should just move in with you, Grace," Charlie says. "It might be easier all around."

"What? Forget it," I say. "How 'bout with one of you two?"

"My place is way too small," Nell says. "She'd have to sleep on the couch. Or I'd have to sleep on the couch. No thank you."

"She's not very nice to Emma," Charlie says. "I don't think I could ask that of her."

"She's not very nice to anyone," I say. "Why does it always have to be me?"

"Calm down, Grace," Charlie says.

"I'm sick of being the one who takes care of everything in this family." I catch a glimpse of a piece of paper stuck under my windshield.

"Well, excuse us, Mother Teresa," Charlie says, yanking his tie loose.

"I took her to the doctor," I said. "And I have tea with her every week."

"I take her to the theater once a month," Charlie says. "And to the symphony whenever it's Mahler. And Emma drives her to her water aerobics class once a month. Even though she's not very nice to her. So don't act as if you're the only one—"

"I took her to the library yesterday," Nell says. "She got lost in the stacks and the whole library staff was looking for her. Afterward, she acted as if I was the one who'd wandered away. And all she ever does is badger me about my weight."

"Has either of you ever cut her toenails?" Charlie and Nell exchange sheepish looks. I've definitely got them there. "She's not moving in with me and that's final," I say. "I've got enough going on right now."

"I told you she had the Big A," Charlie grumbles, digging in his jacket pocket for his car keys.

"Will you guys ever stop treating me like the baby?" Nell says, walking toward her car in a huff. As the sun slips away behind a bank of dark clouds, we all go our separate ways. But I'm the only one going home with a parking ticket.

How long can the honeymoon last? The honeymoon Fuzz and I are on—of consensual, unfettered, no-strings-attached sex? Not forever it would seem. How disappointing to discover there's probably no such thing as a neutral, uncomplicated relationship, despite all our convictions and best intentions. On the one hand, I could care less what he does or doesn't do. But I'm inquisitive by nature. I'm fascinated by where people come from, how they got made and formed in their families, what they say to one another, what makes them tick.

And so one night as I watch Fuzz at Bar None, I see him as a boy whose father probably rode him too hard, the oldest son, the expectations set too high, leaving him now as a man who always has to prove himself, have the final word, by making a scene over his martini not being dry enough.

"I can't drink this," he says, after taking one sip.

"It's not the driest," I say, after a taste. "But I wouldn't say it's undrinkable."

"It's bloody undrinkable." He summons Asa with an impatient hand.

I refrain from mentioning how much he's reminding me of my father.

"Better," Fuzz says curtly, when a new drink arrives. Raven comes through the door and I wave.

"Thanks, Asa," I say, and then to Fuzz. "What was that prima donna act all about?"

"Way too much vermouth," he says. "He should've coated the glass and then poured the rest out. And it wasn't even properly chilled."

"His name is Asa," I say. "And you didn't have to be such an ogre about it."

"Don't be melodramatic, Grace. I wasn't being an ogre. This is a place of business. The bartender's an employee. The product was subpar and I complained. He did his job; he made it right. End of story."

"You didn't even say thank you," I point out.

"Thank you," he says, speaking down to his martini glass.

"So." I twirl my red wine around in its glass. Asa's poured Raven a drink before she even sits down. "I'm guessing you had a few issues with your father," I say.

"Wow," Fuzz says. "It's like being out on the town with Sigmund Freud. Issues with my father?" he says scornfully. "Come on, Grace. Everyone has issues with their parents. We said just sex, remember? No complications."

"Oh, relax. I'm not trying to complicate anything." I take a sip of my wine. "You should be flattered. I'm just interested in who you are, where you came from."

"I bet you are," he says.

"What's that supposed to mean?" Get over yourself, I feel like saying; you're not that interesting. Fuzz can be so damn smug. But he's right. We agreed. Just sex. I was even the one who laid out the rules. And if I'd been smart, I would have left it at that. But I'm not that smart.

"I just don't understand why we can't even talk to each other. About each other," I say. "What possible harm can come from my knowing more about you? Why is that such a threat?"

"Me, Tarzan, you, Grace." Fuzz's lame sense of humor is starting to wear on me. "That law of concrete jungle," he says, pounding his fists on his chest. With his hands all bunched up that way, they look abnormally small.

"I wouldn't mind if you were just a tiny bit interested in my life," I say. And here's where I cross the line, in spite of every good intention. The image of Dylan taking my hand in front of the Ruisdael painting looms and I let the fateful words fall. "You've never even read my book," I say.

"I hate mushrooms," Fuzz says with a shudder. "Why would I want to read a whole book about them?"

"That's not the point," I say. "If you'd written a book, I would've read it, no matter how boring it was. I would've gone home that first night I met you and looked it up on Amazon and ordered it on the spot. And even if I hadn't liked it, I would have found something good to say about it."

"Hey, I googled you." Fuzz makes this pathetic last offering with a shrug.

As we pull up to Fuzz's apartment, I look over at him and notice for the first time that in spite of having a strong jawline, he has a rather weak chin. "I'm not coming in tonight," I say. "I'm tired."

"Again? Why not?" He yanks off his seat belt. "Is this about the goddamned martini?"

"No, it's not about the goddamned martini," I say. "I just don't feel like it. That was part of our deal. We both have to be into it. And I'm not."

"Couldn't you have told me that before we went out?" he says.

"I didn't feel this way before we went out," I say. "So how could I have told you?"

"All right, all right," he says, grumpily. It's clear he's itching for a fight. "By the way, I've been meaning to ask you something. Why do you keep your eyes open when we're having sex?"

"Do I?" This is news to me.

"It's unnerving," he says. "I feel as though I'm screwing a zombie sometimes."

"Are you saying that you always keep your eyes closed?"

"I go in and out," he says. "I find it's more romantic that way."

"I like to see what's going on," I say. "It's erotic. Anyway, how do you know I keep my eyes open the whole time if you don't?"

"Okay, okay, I'm not going to argue with you," he says. "But have you thought anymore about the threesome, Sherlock?"

"Please," I say. "Right now, I can't even think about a two-some."

"I went on this website," he says. "Threescompany.com. It's very discreet. Reliable. A friend recommended it. Just take a look."

"I told you I'd think about it," I snap. "And I'll let you know when I decide."

"Fine!" Fuzz says. And pretty much slams the door on his way out of the car.

Phillip calls on a Sunday in mid-March to check in.

"Did Pawtucket Phil see his shadow?" he asks.

"It's Punxsutawney Phil," I say. "Anyway, that was weeks ago."

"Still tons of snow up here."

"Where are you?" I say.

"Chicorua," he says. "Just came into town to do some laundry. How's it going down there, Grace?"

"Everything's unraveling!" I wail.

"What's wrong?" he asks, alarmed. "Are the twins okay?"

"Technically speaking, they're fine," I say. "But Max is dating a snarky bartender and we're going to have Buddhist grandchildren and Isabelle won't tell Emil about the baby and my mother's going around the bend—"

"Whoa," he says. "Buddhist grandchildren?"

"He didn't tell you?"

"Tell me what?"

"El got married, Phillip. To that Rachel person. Without even telling us. And now they're pregnant!"

"*What?*" I hear some sort of commotion on the other end of the phone.

"They're having a baby," I say. "In September. We're going to be grandparents!"

There's a long pause. "Well, I'll be damned," he says finally.

"Is that all you have to say?"

"Give me a break, Grace, I just found out—"

"And El's converting to Buddhism. Not that there's anything wrong with that—"

Phillip laughs. "Well, we always wanted El to come into his own. I guess he's finally done it."

"Did he have to do it all at once?"

"Listen," Phillip says. "I'm at a pay phone and I'm out of change. I've got to go now, Grace. But don't worry. Everything will work out. It'll all be just fine."

"How do you know that?" I yowl. "Max is back living at home and Elvira has taken up residence too. Charlie's driving me crazy and Isabelle eats like a horse and even Emil stays over sometimes—"

"Emil?" Phil says. "Elvira? Who the hell—"

"Never mind." A recording comes on. We have less than a minute to talk. "How many mountains have you climbed, Phil?" I'm suddenly hungry for more of his calm voice and cheerful news. This is a new Phillip, reassuring and chatty. I wish I'd gotten to know him better.

"Thirty-eight down. Or up, rather." His laugh's cut short by the click of the phone shutting down.

"Ten more to go…" My voice drifts off as I hang up the

phone. I happen to know there are forty-eight four-thousand footers in New Hampshire; I looked it up on the internet.

I ask Max to have tea with Celia at Simon's the next Tuesday while I take Isabelle to the doctor for her six-month ultrasound.

"Grandma needs babysitting now?" Max says.

"Have some compassion, Max. Your grandmother has Alzheimer's. It's not fun for her, you know. She's mostly her old self still, and she'd love to spend some time with you."

"Since when?" Max says. "She never even liked me." Max has never forgiven Celia for calling her an odd child. "It was always all about El, El, El. The beloved golden boy."

"Marcia, Marcia, Marcia!" I try to nudge her out of her dark mood with the *Brady Bunch* line.

"Seriously," Max says. "What are we supposed to talk about?"

"Bring some of those sketches you've been doing in your life drawing class. They're wonderful."

"They're nudes, Mom," she says.

"Your grandmother's no prude," I tell her. "She took me and Uncle Charlie down to the Met in New York to see the Rodin statues when we were young. We got in trouble if we giggled."

"What if she freaks out on me?" Max says.

"It's not like that...yet," I say. "She just gets forgetful sometimes. Give her the occasional nudge back into reality and she'll be fine."

Max leans back in her chair. "Elvira's grandmother has Alzheimer's and half the time she thinks she lives on a ranch in Oklahoma," she says. "What do I do if Grandma says she wants to fly to the moon?"

"Fly away with her," I say. "Just make sure you bring her back again."

After depositing Max at Simon's to meet Celia, I pick Isabelle up at her mother's house. She slides into the car with an open container of hummus, which she's eating in scoopfuls with one finger. I notice for the first time that her pea coat is a big snug.

"The cravings are out of control," she says. "I went to the

Star Market last night at midnight and bought three frickin' tubs of hummus. Can you drop me off at Emil's after my appointment? I don't like to eat like a pig in front of him. He might get suspicious."

"This is crazy, Iz," I say. "You've got to tell him. You're six months pregnant, even though you're barely showing. You're having this baby in three months. Do you realize that's less than a hundred days?"

"God, when you put it like that, it's downright terrifying!" she says. "Emil has noticed how big my boobs have gotten. I don't have the heart to tell him they're not for keeps."

"The more you put it off, the harder it's going to be."

"I know, I know. Sweet Jesus on a cracker, another song with 'baby' in it." Isabelle jabs the OFF button on the radio dial. "Don't lecture me, Gracie, please."

We head down Cambridge Street toward Lechmere. "Are you going to find out the baby's sex?"

"No, I'm too scared. As long as it's human, I'll be more than satisfied."

A surge of heat swoops up through me and I open my window to get some air. I'm not entirely unhappy to still have hot flashes at my age. Let's face it, in the evolutionary scheme of things, once your eggs dry up and you stop being able to conceive, you become dispensable, obsolete. "How'd Molly take the news?" I say.

"Oh my god, she's like a rocket ship shot off to the goddamned moon. No wonder they used to call her Blow Torch," Isabelle says. "She's been online night and day, looking at baby clothes and mobiles and high chairs and cribs. When I was born, she could've cared less. But now it's like the coming of the next frickin' Dalai Lama."

"Please don't use frickin' and the Dalai Lama in the same sentence," I say. "It's disrespectful." I sneak a fingerful of hummus. "Molly's probably trying to make amends. You know, for not being around much when you were little."

"Well, she's going to have to freaking chill," Isabelle says.

"She's driving me insane." She fidgets with the lid of the hummus tub. "Speaking of which...I have something to ask you, Grace. Do you think I could possibly move in with you for a while? Just until I tell Emil about the baby and we work things out. *If* we work things out. I can't think straight with Molly on my case all the time and I don't have the money to get an apartment right now."

"Move in with me?" I nearly run the stop sign at Cambridge and Sixth.

"I won't be a bother," Isabelle says. "I'll take the attic room. I'll cook, I'll...well, I won't say I'll clean, because you know that would be a lie, but—"

"Geez, I'd love to have you, Iz, but you know, Max is still there. And Elvira, too, most of the time. El and Rachel have been coming down for weekends. And I told Otis I'd help out more with Zephyr—"

"Please, Gracie." I've never heard Isabelle sound desperate before. "Molly means well and basically I forgive her for everything," she says. "But I've got to get out of that house before I go out of my frickin' mind. And would you close that goddamned window? It's like the tundra in here!"

I suddenly see how I can leverage this. "Okay, you can stay on one condition." I roll my window halfway back up. "You promise to tell Emil about the baby before the week is out. And then you can move in with him. Or get an apartment. Whatever you two decide. Deal?"

"Deal," Isabelle says, wiping the last of the hummus container clean.

"No monkey business," I say. "No fingers crossed, no 'just three more days, just two more weeks.' No beating around the bush, no nothing!"

"No nothing." Isabelle holds up her hummus-covered little finger. I curl mine around hers and tug on it hard. "Pinkie swear," she says.

12

Otis's girlfriend, Maggie, comes to visit from Idaho at the beginning of April. He drops Zephyr off at our house on his way to the airport to pick her up. Zeph's wearing her basset hound wig with the floppy ears and sets up her tent near the bay window in the living room. She and Max watch *Duck Soup*. They've designated it "Backward Talking Day."

"Lunch for want…. you do what?" I call out.

"Soup duck!" Zeph's in fine wise-guy form.

"Soup duck…of…out fresh," I finally put it all together.

"Jelly and butter peanut, okay," Zephyr says. "Weird so sounds that."

Isabelle comes downstairs in blue silk pajamas holding an open jar of pickles. "Pickles, pickles, pickles," she says, taking a crunchy bite of a dill. "I do love pickles!"

Zephyr looks up. "Who's that?" she says, pointing at Isabelle.

"That's my friend, Isabelle." I push her pointing finger down. "She's staying with us for a little while. Isabelle, this is Zephyr."

"Like in the *Babar* books," Isabelle says.

"Except I'm not a monkey," Zeph says. "I'm a girl. With a *y*."

"Got it," Isabelle says. "The other Zephir was a boy. With an *i*."

"Right," Zephyr says. "He saved the Princess Isabella. A mermaid helped him. Her name was Eleanora. That's my cat's name."

"I like your ears," Isabelle says, taking another pickle out of the jar.

Zephyr cocks her head and looks at Isabelle suspiciously. "Are you going to have a baby?" she says. "Or are you just getting fat?"

Max and Elvira look over at Isabelle.

"Zeph," I say. "That's not polite."

"Sorry," she says grudgingly.

"Don't worry about it, kid." Isabelle dips her pickle back into the jar of juice. "You hit the nail on the old noggin'. I'm just getting fat."

A few hours later, the doorbell rings and Zephyr scoots inside her tent and zips it closed.

I open the front door. Otis ushers in a petite woman dressed in various shades of beige. Maggie is straight out of stepmother central casting—pretty, rosy red cheeks and cascades of curly auburn hair. And one of those twelve-year-old-androgenous-type bodies that will never bulge or sag. Otis lifts his hands as if to ask, *Where is she?* and I point to the tent. He kneels down and pulls down the zipper.

"Come on out and meet Maggie, Zeph," he says.

Zephyr crawls out of the tent on all fours and rests back on her knees.

"Hi," she says uncertainly, adjusting the basset hound wig on her head.

"Hi, Zephyr." Maggie squats down to be at eye level with her. "Are you a dog today?"

"Not actually," she says darkly, tugging on one of her ears.

"Your dad's told me so much about you," Maggie says. "He loves you very much."

"I know that," she says, looking over at Max uneasily. "That know I."

Maggie looks perplexed. "Backward Talking Day," I explain.

"Oh, right." She nods her head. "Right, oh," she says gamely.

"Get your stuff, *uggla*," Otis says. "Maggie and I are taking you to the movies."

"Which movie?"

"*Happy Feet*. About the penguins."

"No," Zeph says, shaking her head. "I can't watch that movie."

"Why not?"

"Sad too it's," she says.

"*Happy Feet* is sad?"

"Yes," she says. "Sad is Feet Happy."

"Okay," Otis says patiently. "We don't have to go to the movies. We'll do something else then, okay?"

"I'm Grace, by the way." I stick my hand out to Maggie.

"Otis's told me so much about you too," Maggie says. "I hope we can all get together some time while I'm here."

"Great."

"How about Friday night for dinner?" Otis says, collecting Zephyr's markers and drawings from the coffee table.

"Sounds like a plan," I say. "I could meet you guys somewhere on the Ave. And Zeph could come over and stay with the girls. How 'bout the Wonder Bar? It's a nice, casual—"

"No, not there," Otis says quickly. "How about Bar None?"

"Sure."

"I want to stay here, Dad," Zephyr says. "With Max and Gracie. Gracie and Max."

"Say goodbye and thank you." Otis pulls her up to her feet.

"You thank and goodbye," Zephyr says, looking back at me wistfully. "Again over come I can?"

"Time any," I tell her. "Time any come can you."

"Rock you!" Max calls out from the purple chair. "Girl rock you!"

I know it's a bad day when I spend most of my run around Fresh Pond composing the acknowledgments for my unfinished novel in my head, and then the glowing review that will appear on the front page of *The New York Times Book Review*. "There must be something in the water on Yerxa Road," it will begin. In a strange twist of local fate, my street has produced one MacArthur grant recipient and one Pulitzer Prize winner in the last few years. "Must be true that good things come in three…"

I know what this fantasizing means. I'm losing touch with reality. I haven't worked on my novel in weeks. And I know why. It's because I'm losing it—all that space, all that freedom I had in the fall, all that peacefulness and empowerment and calm. It's ebbing away, day by day, crisis by crisis. I have no privacy any more, no room to think clearly or breathe. The muses keep a wary distance from my messy, crowded house. There's nothing more terrifying to a WASP than encroaching chaos. And it's all I can do to keep it at bay.

Isabelle's moved up into the attic bedroom and craves lima beans in the mornings and beef jerky at night. Max has gone gluten free on Jack's advice and the limp brown noodles she serves when it's her turn to make dinner are a poor substitute for the real thing. El and Rachel (who, now that they're married and pregnant, seem to have no hesitation popping in for a day or two without notice), prefer to eat lacto-vegetarian, so I try to go along with it, even though the Buddhist prohibition against the five pungent spices—garlic, shallots, onions, leeks, and chives—really cramps my cooking style. Elvira, bless her heart, will eat anything you put in front of her. My grocery bill has tripled and I can't keep enough shampoo and laundry detergent in the house. Not to mention pickles and Pop-Tarts. I put a jar labeled "Food Contributions" on the kitchen counter and hear the plink, plink of coins dropping into the glass from time to time. Every once in a while, there's even a bill or two. Good thing I have a discount at the Mustard Seed.

I'm back to running a full household—cooking and cleaning and catering for at least four, just as I did when the twins were little. The difference is that none of my current housemates is a child. Children in a household come to understand that certain family rules and boundaries are to be respected. Adults, on the other hand…not so much. And so, the "only one Pop-Tart each per day," and the "use a bath towel at least twice before you throw it in the laundry hamper," and "wash your own dishes" rules never really stand a chance. I make a final push for a "no shoes or boots in the house" rule, even buying a couple of snazzy plastic trays and placing them just inside the front door. But the only shoes that ever seem to land there are mine, and nagging doesn't seem to work any better than it used to. The chorus of *sorry's!* gets old pretty quick. Still, they're such a cheerful, remorseful bunch of anarchists, it's hard to stay mad for long.

In spite of it all, my spirits remain high. My body's never been in better shape. The static season is over and I'm loving my hair! Things seem to be slowly heating up with Dylan, and I'm not feeling as insecure about the age gap anymore. Maybe it actually could work out for the two of us. Look at Bogey and Bacall. Demi and Ashton. Madonna and all her boytoys. (Oh, dear lord, Rachel and El!) The Fuzz thing may eventually run its course. And in the end, that won't break my heart. It's not as if I actually want to settle down with someone again. And certainly not Fuzz. But things with Dylan are on a tantalizing, slow burn—definitely cooking.

My secret, "other" life keeps me going, keeps me sane. It's thrilling to hold my carnal thoughts hostage. That I'm this close to having sex with Dylan. That Fuzz and I might actually go ahead with this threesome idea. I think dirty thoughts as I'm folding laundry, or making popcorn on the stove. Dylan and I making passionate love on a pine-needled forest floor. Fuzz crushing me in the back seat of the car, finally reaching that elusive g-spot and triggering an orgasm the likes of which I've never felt, one that would shake the Corolla to its very core. I can even imagine the soapy cinnamon smell of the phantom woman who will be part of our threesome, and fill with a mix of excitement and dread. I haven't agreed to it yet, but I think I might. I keep insisting I'm not a prude. Maybe it's time to prove it.

Dylan's at Bar None the night I meet Otis and Maggie for dinner. Full disclosure. I kind of lured him there, not exactly under false pretenses, but… Turns out he's a big fan of Emil's and has read everything he's ever written about his rock and roll heroes from the sixties. So, I just may have suggested that he stop by. I couldn't have asked Dylan outright. It's not as if we're actually a couple. But I want Otis and Maggie to see that I might have something to offer an intriguing younger man, that I've still got it. Shameful, I know. And sneaky. And cowardly. But Maggie's the kind of person that can make another person feel ordinary. And lumpy. And if not sluggish, at the very least, nonessential.

Isabelle and Emil are joining us too. Isabelle's time is up and she promised to tell Emil about the baby before the night is over. Might as well kill as many stray birds as possible with one trip to the bar. My house is getting crowded and I need some peace and quiet again.

Raven's sitting in the corner seat and I stop by to say hello.

"I think I've finally had my first real feminist moment, Grace," Raven says, watching Asa sashay from one end of the bar to another. "I'm falling for a guy who's more than a foot shorter than me. And I don't even care."

"Nice," I say approvingly. "And good for him for not caring either."

"Why does he get points for that?" she asks.

"Come on, Raven," I say. "You've got to give any guy credit who's brave enough to take you on, especially one who only comes up to your shoulders."

She shrugs. "Who're you here with?" she says.

I look over at my motley crowd. "Friends," I say.

"Couple nice-looking friends," she says coyly.

I don't take the bait. No way will I ever divulge to Raven that I've already sort of had sex with one of these men and am working on having sex with another. Or that there's a third guy out there with whom I have sex once a week.

At the table, I make introductions. We order a bunch of small plates to share—spicy meatballs, buffalo cauliflower, fried plantains with guacamole, pulled pork sliders. Maggie's hands move constantly. I get dizzy watching them flutter, from her drink glass to her hair, to Otis's arm, to the menu and back. Tonight, her outfit is a contrast in greys. For someone with such an outgoing personality, she sure likes to dress in drab. Otis is as calm as she is animated. His is a warm, easy smile. Watching him dispassionately, I'm suddenly aware of what a woman might see in him, his quiet confidence, the way he listens so carefully, his real and ready laugh. I get a flash of the day back in September when we first met at the Mustard Seed, and the vague stirring of attraction between us that grew to a feverish pitch and then got sidetracked so quickly before fading away. And I realize that, without my even being aware of it, Otis and I have become friends.

"How did you two meet?" Maggie asks Isabelle and Emil.

"Down the street at the Wonder Bar," Isabelle says. "It was a fluke. Grace dragged me out of the house that night. I never would have gone otherwise."

"I'm not much of a bar goer either," Emil says. "So it was kismet." He gives Isabelle's arm a squeeze. "It's been almost six months."

"Has it been that long?" I say. Isabelle gives me an icy glare.

"It's good that you're getting out and having fun while you still can," Maggie says. "How far along are you?"

Isabelle looks dumbstruck.

"What?" Emil says, confused.

"Oh dear…" Maggie says.

Isabelle's face blanches and her fork goes limp in her hand.

"Oh no." Emil gives a short laugh, suddenly understanding what Maggie means. "We're not…"

"I'm so sorry," Maggie says to Isabelle. "I just thought—"

"Isabelle." Emil looks over at her with alarm. "Are you all right?"

"Isabelle!" I say sharply and she finally comes to.

She turns to Emil. "It's true," she blurts out. "I'm pregnant. Six months. And it's yours. I'm going to keep it and you can do whatever you want. But it's going to be here in three months, which, for your information, is less than a hundred days. So you're either going to have to ditch me and get out of Dodge… or freaking deal!"

The deep, braying laugh of a man at the end of the bar barrels toward us. It seems to go on and on. The beer tap gushes gold and steam pours out of the dishwasher door. We all wait for Emil to stop chewing his spicy meatball, for the news to sink in, for the sheet of ice that's formed over the scene to break into tiny shards and fall to the floor and bring us all back to life again.

"Say something," Isabelle says finally.

"I'm fifty-seven years old," Emil says helplessly.

"And I'm forty-three," she says. "What the hell does that have to do with anything?"

"I thought you were using—"

"What? Birth control?" Several heads turn our way.

"Yes." Emil looks uncomfortably around the table. By then, we've attracted quite a bit of attention. "Birth control," he says under his breath.

"Except for that first time, I was," Isabelle says. "I went to the doctor the next day and got back on the pill. Did you even think to ask?"

"Don't you two want to take this over to another table?" I say.

"No." Emil looks bewildered. "No, I didn't think to ask," he says. "Of course I should have."

"Well, guess what," Isabelle says. "You didn't and I didn't and, you know what they say—shit happens."

Dylan and Otis exchange uncomfortable looks. Maggie sits there wringing her hands, looking miserable and embarrassed.

"You'll have to excuse me," Emil says, slowly getting up from his chair.

"I know I should have told you sooner, Emil." For the first time ever, I see a scared look in Isabelle's eyes. "It's just that—"

"I have to go." Emil folds his napkin and puts it down on his plate. "It was nice meeting you all." He looks dazedly around the table. "I'll be in touch, Isabelle. I'll call you soon."

"Well, that's that," Isabelle says, after Emil's left the bar. She stabs a meatball with a toothpick and stuffs it into her mouth. "The end of that ill-fated saga—Medford townie hooks up with geriatric Harvard professor. I knew it would never last."

"I'm so sorry," Maggie says, wringing her hands. "I've ruined the evening. And quite possibly your life."

"Don't worry," Isabelle says. "I might never have told him if you hadn't said that. I knew he'd freak out. I knew he wouldn't want to be a father. I'm totally prepared to do this on my own."

"Give him a chance, Iz," I say. "You just blurted it out. Look at it from his perspective. He's in a state of shock. And that 'shit happens' line probably didn't help matters."

Isabelle winces. "Well, it does," she says.

"At least it's done," I say.

"The proverbial cat let out of the proverbial bag," Otis says.

"Never a dull moment in this crowd!" Dylan chimes in. We all look over at him. It's the first thing he's said all evening.

By mid-April, the last piles of dirty snow have melted and our scraggly backyard is revealed in all of its barren nakedness. Any former vestiges of a lawn are long gone. Truck wheel ruts run through what was once my herb garden. Scruffy hedges line the back of the house and the old tire swing hangs low to the ground from a crooked branch of the chestnut tree. The crocuses, as if afraid, have just barely reared their purple heads.

Max's gargantuan self-portrait project slowly rises up from out of the bed of Elvira's pickup truck like a sculptural phoenix, canvases of different sizes piled on top of one another at different angles with various and sundry objects attached thereto. The girls have constructed a kind of primitive scaffolding around the sculpture, with ladders and planks on opposite sides. I see them out the window, moving up and down the ladders, with hammers and nails and string and glue. The Homer Simpson doll and the cover for the *Night at the Opera* DVD disappear from the étagerè in the living room and suddenly appear ten feet up on the sculpture. One of El's old soccer cleats is tied together with a black ballet slipper and slung over an image of a running cheetah. Tweety Bird's water dish is glued onto a painting of a cage. On a canvas depicting two bushy eyebrows and a Groucho Marx mustache stands a banded Cuban cigar.

Elvira's "Mad Hatter Symphony" is now almost fifteen minutes long. Her finished crossword puzzles provide the notes for each new movement. She picks them randomly from a jar the way the caller does at a bingo game and strings them all together. The most godawful noises come out of Elvira's old tape recorder at all hours of the day and night, giving new meaning to the term Destructive Arts.

The ingenious part of this plan, the girls explain to me, is that the masterpieces are moveable. Max's sculpture will be driven down to the Museum School and parked in the back parking lot, while Elvira's "Mad Hatter Symphony" plays in the background, as random objects dance along a moving clothes line on a pulley. Their professors will evaluate their work on the spot. Roving Artistry, Elvira calls it. Must be another one of Beckman's brilliant ideas. Max's abstract sculpture grows every day and I keep telling myself I should go out into the backyard sometime and really study it, to see what truly distinguishes it from being, well...just a well-arranged tower of colorful, scrambled junk—because mostly, as I gaze out the kitchen window, that's all I see.

"Has Emil called yet?" I ask Isabelle on a Sunday morning. She's sitting in the bay window with a cup of tea, the morning sun streaming in and Lauryn Hill crooning about her baby, Zion, on the CD player. It's true that since Isabelle got pregnant, there seem to be nothing but "baby" songs traversing the airwaves. "It's been nine days," I say.

"Negative." Isabelle's on her third piece of cinnamon toast. Since that disastrous night at Bar None, her belly has suddenly popped out, cartoon style, and now sits like a good-sized pumpkin in her lap. I'm making her eggs over hard on the stove, and what's left of the tofu bacon. She's taking the bottomless baby pit to a whole new level.

"This is ridiculous." I toss Isabelle her cell phone. "Call Emil and tell him to come over and face you. Or go over to his place. You two have to talk."

Isabelle catches the phone neatly. "He said he'd call. He'll call when he's ready. And if that's never, then so freakin' be it."

"He's never going to be completely ready, Iz. Help him out. You just sprang this on him out of the blue. Remember how freaked out you were when you first found out? Be the bigger person here."

"Hel-*lo*! I am the friggin' bigger person..." She puts her hands on her belly. "Look at me! Emil should have to suffer too. Let him be the bigger person!"

"Just call him, Iz," I say with a sigh. "This is getting tiresome."

"You know what's getting tiresome?" Isabelle stands up and puts her hands on her hips. "You lecturing me every other goddamned minute!" she snaps. "I told you! The ball's in Emil's fucking court and he'll call when he's fucking ready! Get off my goddamned back, Gracie!"

"Isabelle, stop!" I say, lifting the smoking frying pan off of the burner. "I can't take it anymore!"

"What?" Isabelle suddenly looks deflated and pathetic, holding what's left of the half-eaten toast in her hand. "Why are you yelling at me?" All of her bluster is gone. "I know I'm being a pain in the ass, Grace. It's all the cretin's fault. But you've got to understand—I've got hemorrhoids!"

"I'm sorry you have hemorrhoids," I say, in a calmer voice now. "But enough is enough."

"What?" she says meekly.

"The swearing, Isabelle!" I shake my head. "It's exhausting. We get it. You're wicked tough. You're wicked smart. And you don't need anything or anybody. Everyone knows that. You don't have to swear all the time to prove it!"

"At least I come by it honestly," she grumbles, flopping down on the couch. "Molly swears like a frickin' sailor, so how was I supposed to avoid that fate? And what about you? You talk as if you're living in some tight-ass Jane Austen novel. You don't think that's annoying?"

"It couldn't possibly be *as* annoying," I say.

A sporty red car pulls up in front of the house.

"Shit. Speak of the devil!" Isabelle grabs her toast and ducks down onto the floor. "It's him!"

"Who? Emil?" I turn off the burner beneath the frying pan and watch the car door open.

"Yes, Emil." She peeks over the rim of the bay window. "And there's someone with him. Who is it?" she hisses.

I crane my neck to see. Emil gets out of the car and goes around to open the passenger side door. A small figure emerges carrying what looks like a seventies-style boom box

"You're not going to believe this, Iz," I say. "It's your mother."

"What the hell?" Isabelle says, after flinging open the front door. The boom box is blaring the Bee Gees, "Stayin' Alive."

"Honestly, Isabelle," Emil says. "If we're going to have a baby together, the swearing has got to stop."

"Is that all anyone can think about?" she says. "What the frig is going on here?"

"I came to see you at your mother's house," Emil says. "I thought that's where you lived."

"I do. I did..." she stutters. "I'm just staying here with Grace for a while."

"I told him you flew the coop," Molly says.

"Molly and I got to talking," Emil says. "And we decided to stage an intervention."

"Intervention?" Isabelle shoves the last bite of toast into her mouth. "I don't need a goddamned intervention. I don't drink or smoke, or do anything unhealthy any more. All I do is eat. This kid is starving! I can't keep up with it!" She puts her arms protectively around her pumpkin belly. "How dare you two come storming over here like the goddamned riot squad? Haven't you ever heard of a little thing called a phone? And, Molly, isn't that my boom box, the one I've been looking for the past two years?" She grabs it out of her mother's hand and flicks the OFF switch. "You know I can't stand the Bee Gees!" she says.

"We're here to stake our claim," Emil says. His voice and body language are strong, a far cry from that night at Bar None, when all he could do was stammer his bewildered goodbyes. Furthermore, his shaggy hair has started to curl up at the base of his neck and he looks rather rakish.

"Your claim to what?" Isabelle says defiantly.

"My grandkid," Molly says.

"And my… kid," Emil says quietly. "I'm starting to get used to the idea." For the first time, I see why this alliance might actually work. In this sturdy walrus of a guy, Isabelle may have finally met her match.

"You can't just run for the hills, kiddo," Molly says.

"Hah!" Isabelle says. "That's rich, coming from you, Molly. You've been running away from your crap your whole life. And you," she gestures to Emil, "when I told you I was pregnant, you just walked out the freaking door!"

"I did," he says. "That was not my finest moment. But now I'm back."

"I can have this baby alone," Isabelle says.

"Yes, you could have this baby alone," Emil says patiently. "And you'd do a great job, I'm sure. But we could have this baby together and wouldn't that be even better?" He softens then. "Why didn't you tell me sooner?" he says. "I could have been there for you, Isabelle. I could've massaged your feet and made you soup and sandwiches."

"I didn't want to ruin everything." I can tell she's losing steam. Her stamina's not what it used to be. "What kind of sandwiches?"

"Fluffernutters." He goes over to her and she slumps into his arms.

"I love Fluffernutters," Isabelle says, with a groan. "Are you sure you want to have this kid with me?"

"Positive," Emil says.

"Even though you're as old as frickin' Methuselah?" she says. "You're going to have to play with it, you know, even if you have one foot in the grave."

"Wheelchair basketball," he says. "I'm in."

"And I'll tell you right now," Isabelle says, pulling away. "It's not going to Harvard!"

"How 'bout we let 'it' decide," Emil says.

"We'll see," Isabelle says, planting a blustery kiss on Emil's mouth. "All right then, Professor," she says. "Let's do this gol' darn thing." She grabs the open loaf of cinnamon bread. "You guys really think I swear too much? It's your fault, Molly. There's not enough soap on the planet to clean out that foul mouth of yours. Cinnamon toast, anyone?" She pops two slices of bread into the toaster. "I'm ravenous!"

Tonight could be the night. It's May Day, which, to my mind, has always been the ritual beginning of spring. Dylan's offered to cook dinner for me. At his place. Something has shifted since that night at the museum, and then again after the steamy Route 1 car ride in the rain. He's relaxing a bit, letting me in. I think he's beginning to trust me. Asked what I wanted for dinner, I chose spaghetti with red sauce because that's easy. I'm bringing the wine. And dessert. Meringues and Rocky Road ice cream.

Dylan's condo is small and cluttered, the top floor of a rickety triple decker, with a saggy porch in back overlooking a tiny, overgrown yard, mostly covered now by a deflated wading pool. As I climb the stairs, I remember that Second Summer night back in the fall when we smoked a joint and drank wine on the rooftop, never imagining that one day I'd be here having dinner in his apartment down below.

A computer sits on a table smack in the middle of the living room. A brown corduroy couch lines the backyard wall. On the coffee table sits a tub of onion dip and a half-eaten package of Ritz crackers. Stacks of paper and magazines are lined up on the floor. There's a black-and-white poster of Einstein tacked to the wall, next to a calendar featuring poker-playing dogs.

"I tried to clean up a bit." Dylan's just out of the shower. His hair's wet and out of its ponytail, which makes him look even younger. "But I figured it was more important to focus on the food," he says.

"Good decision." I kiss him lightly on the mouth. "Mmm," I say. "Oregano. Did you make the sauce?"

"Mama Angelina did," he confesses. "I just added a few spices."

After dinner, we retire to the couch, which smells faintly of cat pee, though I've seen no evidence of a cat. I'm feeling sexy and relaxed. And Dylan, not usually much of a drinker, is in a mellow mood after three glasses of wine. He rustles through a stack of CDs. The sound of kids playing comes from the apartment below. I wouldn't have taken Dylan for a Leonard Cohen fan. Suzanne takes us down to the river and I slide off my mustard-colored clogs.

Dylan eases me back down onto the couch. After we've repositioned ourselves, we French kiss, long and deep.

"How's the weather up there?" I know he hates this joke. But I can't resist.

"Actually, this is one of the few times when I'm at pretty much the same latitude as everyone else," he says. "When I'm horizontal."

"So, here we are, horizontal together, on your couch." I lift my hand up to his face.

"Here we are," he says solemnly. It's so hard to make him smile.

"I'm glad we waited." I brush his cheek with the back of my hand. "Until we got to know each other a bit first."

"Did we?" he says.

"I'd say I know you just well enough," I say, wrapping one leg around his thigh. "To let you have your way with me."

"I'm not sure you do," he says.

"What do you mean?"

Dylan sits up abruptly and pulls his hair back into a ponytail with a rubber band from his wrist. "I have to tell you something," he says, straightening up on the couch. "Before we go any farther."

"Tell me later." I try to pull him back down. "It can wait."

"No, it can't," he says. "I've been keeping something from you, Grace."

I sit up and straighten out my cockeyed shirt. "Okay. What's up?"

"I haven't been completely honest with you," he says. "About my life...about my work." Einstein stares at me with crazed and crinkly eyes.

"What do you mean?"

"I actually do some writing myself, from time to time."

"That's great," I say carefully.

"For a magazine, actually. *Rolling Stone.*"

"You're kidding! That's a big deal, Dylan. Not as big as it used to be. But still—"

"I just finished my first assignment." His hair comes out of the ponytail again. And then goes back in.

"Congratulations!" I say. "What's it about?"

"They hired me to research and write an article about—"

"Let me guess." I lift my palm. "The perils of being tall, beer tasting, life inside the tech world, playing hockey in later life—"

"No, no." He shakes his head. "Nothing like that." He's so serious again, so pale.

"What's it about?" I say.

The kids downstairs start to argue. *"You're a liar!"* one of them shouts. *"Am not!"* the other one counters.

"Cougars," Dylan finally says. "I wrote an article about cougars."

"I'm telling Mom!"

My brain turns to molasses. The strangest thoughts fill my mind. A pregnant tiger I once saw at the zoo, El's old soccer nickname, *El Guepardo,* a book about wolves that used to scare Max senseless. And then it hits me. My refrigerator comes into view and Sheila LaFarge's red suit and Jimmy Choo heels. Cougars. Dylan Guthrie has been researching and writing an article about cougars. About older women shamelessly chasing after younger men. Frolicking around like fools when they should be home watching *Mannix* reruns and taking their Tums. Picking up men at the bar—snickering, conniving, devious younger men who lead them on and then ridicule them behind their backs and finally publicly humiliate them. Dylan Guthrie has been writing an article about *me*.

"Oh my god." I get up off the couch, my face flooding with heat, and tears starting to well. "I'm such an idiot."

"No, you are not." Dylan tries to take my arm. I pull away. "You're an attractive, fascinating woman and I've come to care about you a great deal. I would like nothing more than to have sex with you tonight. But I had to tell you, Grace. I couldn't in good conscience go through with this—"

"I think that ship already sailed."

Dylan rubs his forehead. "For what it's worth, it's more of a sociological piece than a personal one," he says calmly. I want to smack his perfect jawline and yank his shiny ponytail out of its green rubber band once and for all and make it hurt. "I think you'll actually find a lot of it very flattering," he goes on. "And of course I'm not using your real name."

"How thoughtful," I say.

"I deserve this," he says quietly. "I deserve your anger. And your sarcasm. I expected it and I don't blame you."

"Are you asking for my permission?"

"No," he says. "I just wanted you to know."

"Will you kill the piece if I object, Dylan?"

"I've already turned it in," he says. "This means a lot to me, Grace."

"What about what it means to me?" I feel my fingernails digging into my palms. "Is that of any importance here?"

"I'm sorry." He looks at me steadily. I want to snap his head down so I can't see his traitorous eyes.

"You're sorry." The words come out scorched.

"Yes," he says. "And I will understand if you never want to see me again."

"I don't," I say.

"That will be my loss," Dylan says. "But I want you to know, Grace. I'll always treasure the poem you wrote for me. No one has ever—"

"Burn it." I quickly gather up my things. "Rip it up into tiny pieces and burn them all."

"Why?"

"It was a gift," I say. "But it's meaningless now. Just burn it."

"Why would I destroy something so beautiful?" He clearly doesn't have a clue.

"It may have been beautiful when I wrote it." I slip my feet into my clogs. "But now it's just a bunch of random, empty words." And then it comes to me, Elvira telling me about the Destructive Arts at the Wonder Bar all those months ago. And I sort of get it. "Go to hell, Dylan," I say.

"I'm an atheist," he says. "That means nothing to me."

"What does mean something to you?" I sputter.

"You're angry," Dylan says.

"Yeah, I'm mad." I feel the heat steaming out of my eyes. "For those of us who came of age in the sixties, back-stabbing betrayal is kind of a big deal." I grab the meringues and head for the door. Putting my hand on the doorknob, I turn around to face him one last time. "And you actually had the gall to think you were going to get laid after this?"

"Hope springs eternal," he says.

"You are so full of shit, Dylan Guthrie," I say, and slam the door on my way out.

13

The next morning, I wake up in a dizzy, muted rage.

"Arrange it!" I text Fuzz, before I've even gotten out of bed.

He replies with a series of question marks. "???????"

"ARRANGE THE THREESOME!!!!!" I text back in all caps.

Thirty seconds later, my phone rings. It's Fuzz, sounding like a kid who's been promised a new bike for his birthday but doesn't quite believe he's going to get it. "Really, Sherlock?" he says. "You'll actually do it?"

"Why not? What the hell." I made myself sleep on the decision after last night's disaster with Dylan, and now, in the cold light of day, my resolve is even stronger. "Might as well try for a goddamned ten!" I say.

"Yes!" I imagine Fuzz pumping his fist in the air. "Can we get a woman?" he says, as if we're choosing ice cream flavors.

"Sure, get a woman. Get a man. Get a frickin' llama," I say. "Just do it."

And so, as my world slowly unravels, everyone else's seems to be chugging full steam ahead. Max has been out on five dates with Jack and all but one of her fingernails have grown out, so I know she's happy. I've been avoiding eye contact with Jack at the bar lately. It just seems like the right thing to do. Thankfully, Max hasn't brought him home yet. I'm slowly getting used to the idea of their being a couple, but I don't think I could handle that just yet—especially after the Dylan fiasco.

Isabelle and Emil are back in love and busy planning the rest of their lives together. Emil's having renovations done at his house, so he's basically living with us. El and Rachel have more or less moved in, too, bringing more and more stuff with them each time they visit. Zeph comes over to hang out and do schoolwork in the late afternoon two times a week, Tuesdays and Fridays. And she's keeping to her word about leaving her cancer wigs at home on one of those days. Her choice. Even Elvira seems positively cheerful, helping around the house, humming snatches of her "Mad Hatter Symphony" as she goes.

I'm back to being a caretaker. And I'm good at it. That's some small comfort. Every day is a puzzle of timing and logistics, the way it was when the kids were little—taking Isabelle to the doctor, stocking up on Pop-Tarts and toilet paper, checking in on Celia, helping Zeph with her schoolwork. I get a quiet, unaccountable pleasure from fitting the puzzle pieces of everyone else's days together, grateful for the endless distractions. It's a relief to be part of everyone else's life dramas, and completely avoid my own. My latest game plan? To just keep chugging along too.

I run into Otis at the Mustard Seed one morning in early May, as I'm checking the storage closet for more chalk. We retire to my art corner for a cup of coffee.

"How's it going with Maggie and Zeph?" I say.

"Zeph hasn't really warmed up to her yet. She says Maggie's too 'sticky,' whatever that means."

"She is kind of sticky," I say.

"You think?" Otis says uncertainly.

"Not in a bad way," I hasten to add. "Maggie seems great. I'm sure it'll just take time."

I feel Otis's eyes on me. "What?" I say.

"When you start twirling your hair like that, there's usually something on your mind."

I yank my finger out of the twisted curl. "I'm fine," I say. "Just in a *What's-It-All-About-Alfie* kind of mood. My life's great. Really. I'm so lucky. In so many ways. It's just that—"

"L'enfer, c'est les autres?" he says. "You've got quite a crowd at your house these days. I'm sorry if Zeph's adding to the mayhem. But she loves hanging out with you guys. I can't thank you enough."

"I really can't blame my funk on anyone else," I say. "Although some days, I'm sure in the mood to try."

"What's going on, Grace?" Otis says.

I take a stab at trying to explain, while skirting around the actual, wince-inducing details. "I've been trying to reinvent and reinvigorate myself this year," I say. "And it's not exactly working out as I planned." How can I tell him about what's really got me down, my convoluted sex life, my frustration with my work, my mother's dementia? "My troubles are paltry, compared to most," I say. "I'll be up and running soon."

"I know you're a tough Yankee broad," Otis says. "And I'm just a lackadaisical Midwestern Methodist. But one thing I do know, Grace. You have a big heart. And you're generous with it. But you don't have to take care of the whole world. You don't always have to be good."

Easy for him to say. He's not a WASP. Not even a lackadaisical one.

"I can't believe you agreed to the threesome!" Fuzz says a few nights later, as we undress in his bedroom.

I take off my blouse and unhook my bra. "I won't say I'm not nervous," I say. "It's probably good to be nervous, though. Don't you think?"

"What's to be nervous about?" He slides his jacket over a hanger. It occurs to me that our clothes no longer land in a frenzied heap on the floor in the heat of passion. Now they get folded, draped, and hung. "It's just sex," he says.

"What will it be like, I wonder?" I say, slipping out of my jeans. "Will we know what to do with her…with each other?"

"I'm sure it'll just happen naturally," he says. "Don't overthink it."

"What if she wants oral sex?" I say. "I don't think I can do that. In fact, I'm not going to do that. I'm telling you right now."

"I'll do it," he says, unzipping his pants.

"And what will I do in the meantime? Twiddle my thumbs?

Won't that be awkward?" I sit down naked on the edge of the bed. "How will it all *work*?" I say.

"Just use your imagination." He kneels on the floor and starts to caress my breasts. "You are one brave and sexy lady and it was a lucky day when I walked into that bar. Do you know that, Sherlock?"

"I'm starting to." I absentmindedly stroke the top of his bowed, balding head.

"We should probably have a safe word," Fuzz says, looking up.

"Safe word?" I put my hands over my breasts in alarm. "What for?"

"To signal if something goes too far, anything we feel is taboo."

"I thought nothing was taboo for you."

"There're a lot of sickos out there," he says.

"Don't get someone with huge breasts," I say. "That might make me feel uncomfortable."

"I'll put that on the list," he says. He pushes me down on the bed and we kiss. I stroke his cock and he starts to get hard. I love that moment, when it begins to take on a life of its own, when you feel its dry, silky, primeval power and know how good it can make you feel. He climbs on top of me and we kiss again. I tug at his lip with my teeth and taste a trace of the French onion soup we shared at the bar.

"I hope she doesn't have halitosis," I say. "Not that it would be her fault. I'm just kind of sensitive about tastes and smells—"

"Goddamn it, Grace!" Fuzz says, rolling off me. "You're killing my hard on with all your chatter."

"Don't blame me!" I say, lifting myself up on my elbows.

"I was feeling great. And now you've got me all flummoxed." He tries to make himself hard again with his hand. "Shit. I can't get it back up. This is the beginning of the end. Viagra, here I come!"

"Calm down," I say. "It's just one time."

"No, it's not..." He looks at me uneasily. "Besides, it's easy for you. All you have to do is lie there..."

"Excuse me?"

"Whatever," he grumbles.

"You should be happy," I say. "Some guys your age are walking around with four-hour erections and blood pressure through the roof."

"I can't believe this!" He's on his knees now, still feverishly trying to make himself hard.

"Stop it!" I say. "This is so not sexy. I'm not in the mood anymore. How are we going to have a threesome if our two-somes aren't even working these days? Have your Viagra crisis on your own time." I gather my clothes and disappear into the bathroom to get dressed. And for the third time in as many months, we end up not having sex.

Nell keeps asking to come over sometime, to apologize face to face to Max. I miss her drop-in visits and I want her to feel comfortable in the house again. And I suspect that Max is at her most generous and forgiving right now, because she's in love. Nell comes over one dreary afternoon for tea. I cover up the couch with a colorful batik throw, hoping to veil any concrete reminders of Whack Sunday.

"I'm so sorry about what happened that day, Max." Nell steers her way carefully around the couch and sits down in the purple chair. "I did something terrible and I completely violated you and your brother's trust. Not to mention your mother's." She wrings her hands. "I really want to try to get it back again."

"I just can't get the picture out of my mind," Max says with a shudder. "It was horrible, Aunt Nell. Horrible!"

"It must have been truly horrible," Nell says, hanging her head.

"Anyway, it's not so much what you did to me and El," Max says. "It's what you did to my mom."

"Max..." I say.

"I just don't understand how you could do something like that to your own sister," Max says.

"I don't either." Nell starts ripping an old Kleenex to shreds. "I keep trying to figure it out. And all I come up with is that sometimes you do something on impulse, and afterward you don't even recognize yourself as the person who did it. I can't even imagine... I think I was literally out of my mind that day."

Max pulls up her legs and puts her arms around her knees. "I feel that way sometimes," she says. "With Jack."

"Who's Jack?" Nell says.

"Just a guy," Max says. "I walked out on him the other night at the bar. We were just sitting there, having a good time. He didn't do anything wrong. It was totally my problem, not his. And I don't even know why I did it."

"Interesting," Nell says carefully.

"I guess what I really want to know is," Max says, "did you kiss my dad to hurt my mom?"

"Honestly, at that moment, that was the farthest thing from my mind," Nell says. "I know it shouldn't have been, but it was."

"Because to me, the sibling bond is sacred," Max says. "No matter how pissed off I am, I could never do anything to hurt El, because he's my brother and he's the one I can always trust. If he ever betrayed me, I'd—"

"Your mom has always looked out for me," Nell says. "Ever since I was little. The last thing I would ever want to do is hurt her."

"Then why did you do it?" Max asks again.

"I think maybe..." Nell says. "I was trying to hurt myself."

Dylan's *Rolling Stone* article comes out the second week of May. The magazine's lying on the kitchen table when I come down to breakfast one morning. Isabelle's standing by the sink, eating a bowl of Fruit Loops, her huge belly sticking out of a yellow T-shirt. She's been adamant about not wasting money on maternity clothes and seems to have thrown modesty completely out the window.

"Fair warning," she says. "The monster is in the room."

"Did you read it?" The magazine cover is brim full of dead rock stars and celebrities, *Sargent Pepper* style—Elvis and JFK, Janis and Jimmie and Marilyn—the people that only ever needed one name.

"Everybody's read it," Isabelle says.

"What does it say?" I slather half a pumpernickel bagel with cream cheese and take a bite. "Tell me the worst parts first. No, tell me the best. Maybe it's better if I don't read it at all." I throw the knife into the sink. "That goddamned, conniving, gargantuan rat fink!"

"You're going to read it eventually," Isabelle says. "Just do it now and get it over with."

"Why should I give him any more satisfaction?"

"You're right." Isabelle reaches for the magazine. "I'll just put this into the recycling bin."

"Give it to me!" I snatch it away and turn to the folded down page. There's a black-and-white illustration of a woman's silhouette in profile and a line of male silhouette profiles of decreasing sizes facing her…I steel myself and start to read.

"Justine Evans (not her real name), is a fifty-three-year-old mother of twin college students. She is recently divorced from her husband of twenty-seven years. I find her on a barstool just north of Harvard Square on a warm September night. Clearly uncomfortable, but game, and endearingly clumsy, she keeps forgetting about the straw in her water glass and pokes herself in the face when she takes a sip. She has mountains of curly brown hair and sea green eyes that will grab you. Younger than my mother—still, she's old enough that she could be.

At first glance, you might say Justine dresses "young" for her age, but as you get to know her, you come to understand that this is how she has always dressed, and always will—she's a jeans and T-shirt girl. Justine is a love child of the sixties and in the way of some characters in fairy tales, has never really grown old. A self-described "intruder in the twenty-first century," she is a sometimes writer and loves books. I've brought one to the bar, *The Rise of Silas Lapham.* Who else in the world but the two of us has ever read such an obscure tome? I express a polite interest in getting to know her better and she readily agrees."

"Readily agrees?" I close the magazine. "What a jerk! He was the one who came on to me. And he's way more of a *sometimes* writer than I am. I can't read anymore. Just tell me one thing. Did he mention a car ride? A car ride in the rain? If he did, I'll—"

"What car ride in the rain?" Isabelle's eyes light up. "What happened on the car ride in the rain, Gracie?"

"Never mind." I open the magazine again and my eyes jump down to the beginning of a paragraph on the next page: "Diane Downing (not her real name)..." And then, to another paragraph, at the bottom of the next page: "Angela Delminico (not her real name)."

I feel my breath stop short. "Oh my god." I look up at Isabelle, who's drinking the last of the purple Fruit Loop milk from her bowl, suddenly acutely aware of the loud ticking of the kitchen clock, which is now almost half an hour fast. "I wasn't the only one." I close the magazine with a snap. "How many?" I say to Isabelle. "I can't look. Tell me. How many were there?"

"Just three," Isabelle says. "And you got by far the most press, if it makes you feel any better. That Angela Delminico broad was sixty-four years old! Damn, I would've loved to be a fly on that wall!"

"It doesn't make me feel better at all!" Tears well up in my eyes. "It makes me feel terrible!" I go into the living room, which is filled with dirty dishes and books and art supplies and newspapers and clothes, and toss the magazine face down onto the coffee table. "What is all this...*shit*?" I pick a banana peel up off the floor and kick an empty Ben and Jerry's container to the other side of the room. Max appears at the top of the stairs. "We're drowning in *crap* over here!" I yell out.

"What is your problem?" Max says, coming downstairs. "What's going on?" she asks Isabelle.

Isabelle hesitates. "Your mother just read something that got her upset."

"She'll know," I say in a panicky voice to Isabelle. "When she sees 'twin college students.' Can't I sue him for that?"

"She'll know what? What are you talking about?" Max reaches for the magazine. "Who are you suing? Let me see!"

I make a dive and grab it away from her. "Don't touch that!" I fold the magazine in half so she can't see the cover. "It's private, Max."

"It's a magazine," she says. "How can it be private? What's wrong, Mom? You're acting like a crazy person."

And with that stricken look in my daughter's eyes, I take hold of the horrible moment, the horrible feelings and banish them away. I stuff the folded magazine into the back of my jeans, vowing to burn it afterward and watch it turn to smoke and ash. It's just a stupid article, I tell myself, it's just a stupid man, it's just… The voices in my head keep clamoring, *It's just my stupid life.*

Zeph stays for supper that night and, sensing I'm not myself, tries valiantly to cheer me up.

"You want to talk about it, Grace?" She sidles up to me on the couch, while Isabelle and Max clear away the dinner dishes. I wonder how many umpteen times Zeph's been asked that question. How grown-up she is, at seven, to be asking it of me!

"I'm just kind of down in the dumps," I say. "I feel sort of… discombobulated."

"What does that mean?"

"All mixed up," I say.

"I feel like that all the time." Zeph picks up a Magic Marker. "How do you spell it?" she says.

"What?"

"That long word you just said. Disca…whatevermajiggy." Zeph starts to spell the word, writing it down on a piece of paper. "D-I-S…then what?"

"C-O-M-B-O-B-U-L-A-T-E-D," I say.

Zeph counts the letters silently with one finger. "Fifteen letters!" she says. "Maybe that's one of the longest words!"

"How about supercalifragilisticexpialidocious?" I say.

"That's from *Mary Poppins*," she says scornfully. "It's not a real word."

"You want to know the actual longest word in the whole English language?" I say.

"What?" she says eagerly. Zeph's the only other person around who's as interested in words as I am.

"SMILES!" I say. "Because there's a mile in between the first and the last letter!"

Zeph looks at me, almost with pity. "Oh, it's a joke," she says.

"It's kind of funny, isn't it?"

"Not really." Clearly, I've disappointed her. "No offense," she adds.

"None taken," I say.

I think we're done with our little pep talk, but Zephyr has one more piece of advice.

"We all live in the oyster, Gracie," she says.

"Pardon?"

"The oyster is the world and the walls are shiny and hard so they'll protect you." She cups her hands together to make the shape of a shell. "It's hard to open it up and get in, but once you do…" Her hands spring outwards and then close back up again. "You'll be safe inside. My mom told me."

"Good to know," I say.

"And the best part is," Zephyr goes on, "you might even find a pearl."

"Like your mom did,' I say, giving her a squeeze. "When she had you."

The next day, when I get home from work, I find El giving a dance class in the living room. He's strung up a taut rope from one end of the living room to the other for a makeshift barre.

Stravinski pours dramatically out of Isabelle's boom box. Max, Zeph, the two pregnant women, Celia, and Elvira all stand tall with their right arms outstretched. What a motley lineup! I take off my silk-covered flip-flops and take my place at the end of the barre.

"Plié! Relevé! Plié! Relevé!" El's voice strains to be heard above the music.

"Eliot!" Celia shouts out. "I can't seem to bend my knees."

"That's okay, Grandma. Just go as far as you can. Don't push it."

Zeph's wearing her hedgehog wig, her favorite. "Can I do it backward, El?" she says.

"Go for it," he says. Zephyr spins herself around. Max starts picking at her nails.

Isabelle groans as she tries to bend her knees. "Pregnant women are exempt from the low pliés," El says. "Practice your deep breathing instead."

"Max, don't hold onto the rope," El says. "Your fingers should only touch it lightly."

Max leaves the line-up and heads for the refrigerator. "Now I remember why I quit ballet," she says. "Can you say *bor-ing*!"

El heads my way, just as I'm starting to bend. "Head up, Mom," he says, tilting up my chin. "And tuck that butt in."

Nureyev ain't got nothing on the likes of us.

After dance class, El and Zephyr sit down on the couch together.

"You're a good dancer, Zeph," he says. "You've got some great moves. What else don't I know about you?"

"Well, I'm homeschooled." Zeph scooches back on the couch and sticks her legs out straight. "I have a cat named Eleanora and I used to have alopecia and now I've got OCD," she says. "I want to learn how to play the drums and I'm a little Aspergery," she says.

"Me too," El says.

"You are?" She looks up at him.

"Yeah," El says. "It's hard for me to talk to people sometimes."

"Really?"

"And make them listen to what I have to say."

"Same here," Zeph says. "My dad says we've just got to keep trying."

"He's right," El says. Their palms clap together in a resounding high five. "We've just got to keep on trying."

I freeze at my post at the sink, where I'm watering the plants on the window sill, dumbfounded. OMG! This explains so much, so many of the mysteries that have always been El's. How could I not have known this simple fact about my son? That all along, he was just a little bit Aspergery?

I go out to Bar None the next night. Muscles I haven't used—possibly ever—are aching from El's dance class the day before. I order a glass of Freak Show cabernet and straighten out the bar's inspection certificate on the wall, then lean back to watch the nightly show.

I zero in on a young man a few seats down. He has one green eye and one blue eye and I can't stop looking at him. He's telling his friend about the social mores of polar bears, which, by the way, are fascinating. Who knew that nose-kissing is the way polar bears ask to share food? Or that mama polar bears snore? But the guy's a serial "like" user and every time he says it, my linguistic hackles rise. I don't know why I'm so preoccupied with this whole "like" business. I just can't seem to let it go.

"Excuse me for interrupting," I say. "What you know about polar bears is very interesting. But do you realize how much saying 'like' every fifth word takes away from your otherwise articulate voice? It's just excess noise. There's no point to it."

"Sure, there is." The guy turns to me, not the least bit offended. "Historically, all languages have fillers like…*like*," he says. "They're not punctuation exactly, but depending on their placement, they can lend different meaning and nuance to the sentence as a whole."

"How so?" He's definitely got my attention.

"For example, exaggeration." He thinks for a moment. "'I, like, nearly died of embarrassment!'"

"Wouldn't an exclamation point do just as well?"

"Not in, like, a million years!" he says.

I laugh.

"Or introducing a quote." He slips into a drawling, preppy voice. "He was, like, get off my back, dude, and I was, like, make me."

"Whatever happened to 'he said-she said'?"

"We don't even hear all the *likes*," he says. "It's just the trademark of our generation's speech." He takes a swig of his beer. "Yours must have had one too."

"It was called *um*," I say. "And no one ever gave it such a rousing defense."

"Did you know that polar bear cubs say 'uh' or 'um' when they're content?" he says. "When they've been soothed?"

"Really!"

"In the end, isn't that what we all want?" The guy flashes me a luminous smile. "To be happy? To be at one?" he says. "It's human nature, don't you think? We all, like, just want to fit in."

"You make some good points," I say. "But I think it will always drive me crazy."

Asa comes over. "Is she giving you two a hard time?"

"Just keeping us on our grammatical toes," says the guy with different colored eyes.

"She does that," Asa says. I don't know whether it's a compliment or a gentle rebuke. But because it comes from the wise and gallant Asa, I take it as the former.

Well, I never thought I'd say this, but thank goodness for good old Fuzz. I haven't been completely abandoned and betrayed. I'm still attractive and desirable to someone. We had great makeup sex after that last sexless encounter when I walked out on him at his apartment. And he even apologized for that crack about me "just having to lie there." The old fire is back. We agreed to call a truce on arguing and just enjoy the sex. A sane and rational conversation. It all makes sense again.

Lately, we've been working on simultaneous orgasms. We've come to know our way around each other's bodies and have both gotten good with our hands. Good sex, it turns out, is largely about timing and communication. Our dialog goes something like this when we're working on SOs. And you have to imagine the comical panting and grunts and awkward body twists and turns that go along with it.

"You almost there?" Fuzz says, his breath running short.

"Just about. Oh yeah, that's good. Keep doing that, a little more to the left. I'm just about…oh, wait. Are you close?"

"I was, damnit, let me just…"

"Hold on." I scooch my body over to the left. "I'm falling off the bed."

"Okay," he says, back on track. "You good now? You ready, Sherlock? I can't last too much longer."

"No! Ouch! Wait a second."

But for a guy, at a certain point, a second is just too long.

Afterward, while Fuzz is washing up in the bathroom, I read his notes on the table next to the bed about the sex we just had.

2 much tlkg!

Gr tks 2 long 2 cum

better 2 hv sep orgms

Score: 3+ (4 xed out)

I turn randomly to another page, where I find notes on the sex we had way back on December 4th.

Awkwd. 69 nt al crked up 2 be.

Gr nt in2 oral sx. Dnt bthr. Score: 2

Oh yes, I remember. 69 was awkward and—he's right—not at all what it was cracked up to be. It's hard to enjoy the feeling when you're too busy trying to focus on the job at—hand. And I'm glad I let Fuzz know sooner rather than later, that I'm just not into oral sex.

I close the notebook and toss it back onto the table. Its yellow cover elicits some nagging thought—not a good one.

And then the depressing truth hits me! Fuzz and I are both "notebook" people—uptight, anal types who need to write everything down instead of just enjoying it—analyzing, critiquing, giving everything a grade. Neither of us has the capacity to be truly spontaneous or carefree. These are the exact same cheap notebooks I buy at CVS and scribble in at the bar. And not only that, they're the side-to-side kind, not the flip tops! As Raven would say, throwing up her hands, "Pathetic!"

Still, I can't really argue with Fuzz's ultimate grade of 3+ for our last stab at simultaneous orgasms. I'm beginning to think he's right, that the whole notion is overrated. In some ways, isn't it more exciting to witness your partner's orgasm and then let him witness yours? Or vice versa? It's a waste of pleasure to try and synchronize them—kind of like eating chocolate and ice cream at the same time.

14

I'm starting to feel cautiously excited about the threesome. We plan it for a Monday night at Fuzz's apartment in late May. I'm relieved, grateful even, that he's willing to "host" the event. I somehow couldn't bear to have it take place on my home turf, where I raised my children, where I was a wife and mother all those years. Besides, it's so crowded these days, there's no such thing as privacy any more, no secluded nooks in which to curl up with a good book, let alone host an orgy.

Her name is Allëgra. With two dots over the e. Which turns it into what, I'm not sure. As I make my way over to Fuzz's, I look again at the text he sent me with her photo from the threesome website, just a head shot—a nice-looking woman in her late thirties, early forties, full lips, dark red hair cut short, long neck and dream catcher earrings. I'm wearing the same old thing… Dylan's right on one point; a jeans and T-shirt girl I'll always be.

She's already there when I arrive, comfortably settled on Fuzz's leather couch, long legs crossed casually in tight black pants and a shocking pink cardigan that clashes wildly with her hair—a flashing neon sign in Fuzz's somber den of blacks and greys. The sweater's slightly askew, revealing the edge of one low-slung breast. No makeup, no bra. Several silver bracelets jangle on her left wrist. Beside her on the end table sits a glass of white wine. Fuzz pours me a glass of red and one for himself.

"Allëgra, right?" I put out my hand awkwardly. "Nice to meet you."

"You, too." She seems amused. Fuzz keeps clearing his throat.

"First time for you guys?" Allëgra says.

Fuzz and I look at each other and nod.

"It's gonna be great," she says and then gestures to me. "Come on over and have a seat."

I sit down next to her and before I've even had another sip of wine, she's unbuttoned her sweater completely. "Why don't you take off your shirt too," she says to me. "Maybe that will help this guy relax." She smiles over at Fuzz as her sweater slides off her shoulders.

Fuzz stands there looking uncomfortable. Emboldened by the sight of him so unsure, and Allëgra naked from the waist up, I slide my shirt off over my head and toss it onto a chair. Allëgra turns toward me, squares me by the shoulders from the back, and unhooks my bra. I sit up straighter, trying to flatten out my stomach. She brings her hands to my breasts from behind and starts to caress them, expertly flicking my nipples, which turn instantly hard. I close my eyes, starting to feel wet and tingly and lean my head back against the couch.

"Guys usually like watching two women go at it," she says to Fuzz. "Are you in that camp, cowboy?"

Fuzz nods slightly.

"I could use some attention too," Allëgra says to Fuzz. "I made it easy for you. No buttons, no bra."

Fuzz kneels down on the floor and reaches for her breasts. "I'd rather you suck them," she says, her hand moving down to my stomach. "Could you do that? It really gets me going."

It's amazing how good Allëgra is at disrobing, not only herself, but also the two of us. Before I know it, she's not only unsnapped my jeans, but somehow slipped off her own pants and unbuttoned Fuzz's shirt. It's quite the game of *Twister*, now, with Fuzz trying to put his mouth on one of Allëgra's breasts, my trying to stroke Fuzz's thigh, and Allëgra's hands all over both of us, as skilled as a Hindu deity with multiple arms.

In his best move yet, Fuzz manages to slide Allëgra onto the floor, which thankfully is carpeted. Dark brown shag.

"Pants," Allëgra says to Fuzz, taking hold of his zipper.

Meanwhile, I gamely stroke Allëgra's inner thigh while she

slides back and forth against Fuzz's leg, her knees bent behind her.

"No problem if you're not ready yet," Allëgra says, as Fuzz's pants land on the floor. "We understand. It's two against one, after all. And we got a head start." She reaches for her bag and pulls out a pale blue vibrator. "We've got backup, so don't worry. If you're only up for one of us." I look over in alarm at the dildo. "But we'll take good care of you, too," she says to Fuzz. "Promise." With that, Allëgra starts to lick his belly. Meanwhile, her hand slides in between my legs. For the moment, I forget all about Fuzz.

"Maybe this will help," Allëgra says to Fuzz, whose face registers increasing alarm. "Watching me get Greta off…"

"Grace," I say, arching my back with a moan.

"Watching me get Grace off here. She's so wet. Want to feel her? She's so hot…"

Without warning, Fuzz suddenly plunges down on top of Allëgra, knocking her off me and banging her head against the floor.

"Ow!" she says. "Easy, cowboy."

"Sorry," he says. I know from experience that he's ready to make his move.

"First things first." Allëgra reaches out to take Fuzz's cock in hand. "Let's take care of Grace here. It would be cruel, wouldn't it?" She turns back to me. "To just leave her this way, so very wet…and ready. You're close, aren't you?"

I murmur assent. She tries to roll me over on my stomach. "Lift your hips," she says. "He can come in from behind. Are you ready, cowboy? I like what I'm seeing here. Very impressive… And Grace is going to like it even more…"

"No." I roll over on my back again. "This way."

Allëgra turns to Fuzz. She's caressing her own breasts now, breathing heavily. "Grace is ready, cowboy. Give it to Grace. Give Grace what she wants and make her want to explode." By this time, I'm about ready to do just that.

Fuzz comes toward me, and I see a look of abject fear on his face, which is growing redder by the minute. Allëgra is fondling his balls but I can see he's not as hard as he was. Suddenly, he stands up and turns his back to us.

"I can't do this," he says.

"What do you mean?" I lift myself up and rest back on my elbows. Allegra doesn't seem the least bit flustered.

"Failure to thrive," she says. "It happens."

"I just can't," he says. "I've lost it. I'm..."

"No worries," Allëgra says. "Me and Grace here will just carry on. Come on back if you change your mind. Or you can watch if you like. Maybe that'll get you back in the saddle."

Fuzz pulls his pants back on and hastily throws on his shirt.

"Don't leave!" I say. Arousal is instantly dead. Allëgra pins my arms back on the floor and her tongue slips inside my ear. Ten seconds earlier, this might have turned me on, but now her tongue just feels wet and gross.

Fuzz grabs his shoes and heads for the door.

"You can't go," I call out after him. "You live here!"

I see Allëgra reaching for the dildo, which is now vibrating wildly. "Don't you want to finish what we started, Grace?" she whispers, as Fuzz closes the door behind him.

"No," I say, sitting up. "No, actually, I don't." I grab my shirt, which has somehow slid under the couch. "It's over, Allëgra. Thanks anyways. Thanks for trying. I don't think we really thought this through. I guess we're more old-fashioned than we thought. I'm sorry, we've wasted your time."

"If you think too hard, it doesn't fly." Once again, Allëgra seems unfazed. She puts her pink sweater back on and starts to hum. The blue dildo disappears back into her bag. I wonder what else is in there. It crosses my mind that this was probably what Dylan expected of me, a completely uninhibited sex goddess—ready and up for anything. But next to Allëgra, I feel like a stone-cold fish. I wonder if she'll move on now to the next adventure, with another, less uptight couple.

"I'm sorry to have dragged you all the way over here." I pull my shirt over my head and start patting down my hair. "Can I call you a cab or something?"

"No worries. I've got my bike." Allëgra takes two of the bottled waters Fuzz laid out on the kitchen counter, throws them into her bag, and heads for the door. "Too bad, though. It could have been fun, if he'd relaxed a bit, if he'd just hung in there. It could've been hot. You were certainly game. Sorry I didn't get you to Nirvana."

"Oh, that's okay," I say.

"If you ever want to try again, you know with someone else. You've got my number." Allëgra looks back at me as she opens the door. "It's always us women who have to get the gears grinding, isn't it?" she says with a shrug. "Whad'ya going to do?"

I go over to the window and look down at the street. Allëgra exits Fuzz's building with her bag slung over her shoulder. Straddling her bike, she takes a helmet from the back seat and slides it over her head. She eases the bike off its stand, and brings her foot down hard on the kick starter. It catches on the first try. Revving the engine with two rolls of her right wrist, Allëgra roars off into the distance on her vintage Norton 750—the same motorcycle my boyfriend Floyd used to ride—her dream catcher earrings flying behind her.

The next morning, I wake up, desperately hoping that the botched threesome was just a bad dream. But of course, it wasn't. And my crumpled outfit from the night before on the floor next to the bed is proof. I hear Max and Elvira bickering downstairs about who forgot to turn off the stove, as the noxious fumes of burned tea-kettle bottom drift up the stairs. Isabelle's country music station is blaring its twang in the living room. *When I see snow stains on my boot heels, I know I'm in the wrong town.* I step in a puddle of cat throw-up on my way to the bathroom and the toothpaste tube that never seemed to quit is finally utterly empty. I toss it into the trash and wet some paper towels to clean up the mess in the hall. Clearly, it's going to be a miserable day.

"Ma!" Max wails from downstairs. "Have you seen my green pants?"

After breakfast, the doorbell rings. It's Zephyr, wearing her monkey wig and carrying a backpack. I've never been more glad of a distraction. "What are you doing here, Zeph?" I say. "Are you all right?"

"I'm good," says, kicking off her sneakers. "I ran away." She makes a beeline for the kitchen table, where what's left of Max's French toast is drowning in a pool of maple syrup on an orange Fiesta Ware plate.

"Did you tell your dad?"

"I left him a note." Zeph picks up the plate with both hands and starts to lick.

"That's not exactly running away," I say, handing her a spoon.

"It's a good kind of running away," Zeph says. "Because it's responsible. And polite."

"Right." I call Otis. "She's here, Otis. She's fine."

"Thank goodness," he says. "I get very nervous when people leave the house without telling me. I'll be right over to get her."

While we're waiting for Otis, I take out a deck of cards and show Zephyr the mind-reading card trick I remember from my childhood. Zeph thinks she's got it figured out and tries to play the trick on me. But it doesn't work and she gets frustrated, brooding as she shuffles and reshuffles the cards.

"How 'bout a game of Crazy Eights?" I suggest.

"I've got a better idea." Zephyr's face suddenly brightens. "Wanna play Fifty-Three Pickup?"

"You mean Fifty-Two Pickup?"

"There's a joker too." She gets up on her feet. "I counted. The other one's lost. So it's fifty-three."

"Right," I say, relieved that she's come out of her funk.

"Ready?" she says.

"Ready!" I know how to act dumb. I've played this game before.

Zeph's hand releases the cards and they fly up into the air like a flock of birds. "Fifty-three pickup!" she says gleefully.

"Ah, shoot!" I say. "You tricked me! Now I've got to pick them all up, right?"

But Zephyr's already down on her knees on the faded Persian rug, collecting the cards, one by one—the two of clubs that landed on the corner of the mantelpiece, the queen of hearts under the coffee table, and the ace of diamonds stuck in the open door of Tweety Bird's birdcage. As she counts the cards, she sings out the numbers—two, five, six, nine, eleven, thirteen, fourteen…"

I bend down to help her.

"Don't touch them!" She throws all the cards she's gathered back up into the air again. "I lost count! You ruined it! Now I have to start all over again!"

"Aren't I supposed to pick them up?" I say. "I thought that was the whole point of the game."

"The way I play Fifty-Three Pickup," Zephyr says huffily. "I get to pick them up by myself."

I make maple syrup popcorn and we sit on the couch together, watching *The Simpsons* with no sound. Zephyr doesn't like the voices. They sound like baby robots, she says.

"Sorry I yelled at you, Gracie," she says.

"That's okay," I say. "What was it that made you so upset?"

"I was just trying to count the cards," she says.

"And I interrupted," I say. "You had a plan and then I kind of ruined it, right?"

"Kind of." Zeph squirms in her seat.

"But I didn't know what your plan was," I say. "Or how important it was to you."

"I just wanted to count the cards," she says. "I really like counting things. By myself."

"Okay, good. So now I know that." Homer bops Bart on the head with a *"d'oh!"* and I give Zephyr a bop on hers. "Maggie seems nice," I say.

"She's a baby." Zeph's more relaxed now that our little "chat" is over. "She never grows older and she doesn't even talk. She just sucks on her pacifier all day long."

"No, I mean the real Maggie," I say. "The one from Idaho."

"She's okay." She lines up pieces of sticky popcorn in rows of six on the coffee table. "But I don't want her to be my mother."

"She's not trying to be your mother, Zeph. You already have a mother who will always be your mother." I tap my hand on my knee. "Your dad seems to like Maggie a lot."

"No, he doesn't," she says sharply.

"I think he does, Zeph." Her face darkens. "Not the way he loves you," I say. "But—"

"He likes my mom." Zephyr eats the first piece of popcorn in every row, then starts in on the second. "That's who he married. So when my mom gets better—"

"Even when your mom gets better," I say. "Sometimes grown-ups just can't be together anymore. No matter how much they love you. Or each other."

"They can try," Zephyr says, and I can see that she's near tears. The monkey wig is tilting off her head. "That's what my dad says. You can always try. And you should always try and you should never give up. Because giving up is giving in."

And how on earth can I argue with that?

Otis arrives and Zephyr sprints out into the backyard to say goodbye to Max.

"Feeling any better?" he asks me.

"A bit." I blush to think—if he only knew what I'd been up to the other night in Fuzz's apartment. "Jane Austen's been helping the cause," I say.

He laughs. "That's not a sentence you hear very often," he says.

"I guess I'm more of a WASP than I like to admit," I say. "All of her worlds are so circumspect and well-calibrated. Everyone says just the right thing and all the messes get cleaned up so tidily. I find it comforting somehow."

"Doesn't sound like any world I've ever known." Otis starts

in on what's left of the sticky popcorn on the coffee table. "Did Zeph say why she ran away?"

"She said she needed some space," I say.

Otis chuckles. "Out of the mouth of babes," he says. "I'll talk to her, Grace. Make sure this doesn't happen again."

"On the up side," I say. "Zeph took the initiative to get over here by herself. That's pretty brave. I don't know if the kid I met a few months ago could have done that."

"You have a point," Otis says.

I watch as Otis picks up Zeph's stuff off the floor—her purple Crocs and her Jenga puzzle and her backpack—one item at a time, and I think, if it were me, I'd be able to pick up twice the amount of stuff in the same amount of time or the same amount of stuff in half the time—because I have two arms.

"This might be a weird question," I say. "But did you ever get a fake arm?"

"A prosthetic?" Otis nods. "I did. In the beginning I was all gung-ho about it. But it was heavy and painful and over time it just became more of a nuisance than anything else. I've gotten pretty good at doing almost everything I need to. Between my teeth, my abs, and my legs, I manage pretty well."

"It's impressive," I say.

"I still have my fake arm," he says. "He looks a lot like this guy." Otis stretches out his left arm. "He's even got some of my real hair imbedded in him. And a few freckles. I call him Harry."

"Hairy or Harry?" Otis's midwestern accent flattens out the *a*.

"Hairy Harry."

I laugh. "Where is Hairy Harry?"

"He lives in the closet on the first floor."

"Happily?"

"Harry's pretty happy," Otis says.

I laugh again. "How's Maggie?" I say.

"She's fine. She's at a yoga class," he says. "She tried to get Zeph interested, but no luck."

"Did she try that pretzel kid yoga class over at the public library?"

"Pretzel yoga class?"

"Max and El used to love it. They do a lot of animal poses and play acting. Zeph could probably wear her wigs. It's pretty loose."

"Sounds right up her alley," Otis says.

Zeph comes in from the backyard and slams the screen door. "Max wants to put my hippo wig on her art project!" she says with a grin. "I'm going to be famous now!"

Fuzz doesn't show up at the Wonder Bar for our next Monday night date. It's part of our deal not to call or text during the week unless it's important (and frankly, nothing about this guy feels important any more); so I simply let time pass. After his dismal behavior during the threesome, I'm not sure I ever want to see him again. If I weren't feeling so fragile and defeated, I might just call it quits.

There's no getting around it. I'm down. About Dylan. And Fuzz. About getting old and becoming a grandmother. About my writing. My finances. My full house. My bossy brother and addled mother. Maybe I have had it with men altogether. Sex may very well be overrated, after all. And Max was right. Men are so needy, so immature. I've almost talked myself back into a monastic life, where I will beg Perry Mason's forgiveness and resume my love affair with vanilla ice cream and gloomy nineteenth-century novels, thinking such a life has its merits and rewards…when I get a call from Fuzz mid-week.

"Well, well," I say. "Look who the cat dragged to the phone."

"Can we meet up, Grace?" he says. "We've got to talk."

"Now you want to talk."

"Yes," he says. "I do."

I don't even bother to shower and change before heading out to meet Fuzz at the Wonder Bar that night. I'm wearing the same "State Spelling Chimp" T-shirt I slept in the night before, and some old mom-style jeans that I only ever wear around the house. No way we're having sex tonight, no matter what he has to say. I'll hear him out, that's all. And if that's the end of it, so be it. I take my time walking over to the bar and arrive ten minutes late.

Fuzz is sitting in a booth in the back. "Grace," he says, with exaggerated solemnity as I walk toward him. "Hello."

"Where've you been hiding?" I slide into the booth across from him. He's ordered us each a glass of wine.

There's a long pause which I don't rush to fill. "I'm sorry I left you that way," he finally says.

"Abandoned me is more like it." I straighten out the fork on my napkin. And then I straighten out my napkin on the table. "You fled with your tail between your legs. Or should I say, your…Johnson. Isn't that one of the names you like to call it?"

"I never should have suggested that damn threesome thing." Fuzz starts scratching his head. "I don't know what I was thinking."

"You badgered me for weeks. And then you totally chickened out," I say. "You hardly even tried and then you freaked out and just up and left me alone with her. In *your* apartment. I was mortified!"

"I panicked," he says. The waiter comes over and we order two garden salads. "I just had to get out of there."

"Did you just flee out onto the street?"

"I hid in the upstairs hallway," he says. "Until I heard you both leave."

"Worse than cowardly," I say. "And remind me? Whose idea was this in the first place?"

"I just couldn't get into it," Fuzz says. "Anyway, she was creepy, don't you think? She talked too much. In that little girl voice. And I do not appreciate being called 'cowboy.' Her breasts were droopy, too, off-putting."

"Off-putting?" I say, as the waiter brings over our salads. "Not all women's breasts are perfectly shaped. My god, do you guys realize how ugly your—"

"Take it as a compliment, Grace," Fuzz says. "In the end, I'd rather just have sex with you. I love your breasts. Can't we just pick up where we left off?"

"Where was that?" I'm feeling weary and reckless. "At the corner of Sarcasm and Sex?"

"I miss you," he says.

"You miss me? Or the sex?"

"Both." Men are such quick, sure liars when they're under the gun. I've definitely only missed the sex. Fuzz's fingers play anxiously with his napkin. I suddenly realize there's more he's come to say.

"What is it?" I shake a forkful of romaine in his face. "There's something else, isn't there? In spite of all your efforts to keep it from happening, I know you, buster. Cough it up. What's going on?"

Oh, the look of terror on a man's face when he's backed into an emotional corner, when he's put on the spot. "That woman I told you about when we first met?" he blurts out.

"Ah yes, that woman."

"She's back in my life again," Fuzz says. "I wanted to be up front with you about that, Grace."

"Really?" I say calmly. "Well, good, at least we can be grown-ups about this—"

"In fact," he says quickly. "We're getting married."

What the…? My wine sloshes dangerously in its glass. Did Fuzz just say he was getting married? Weren't we just talking about our sex life, such as it was? Wasn't he just begging me to forgive him?

The lettuce falls off my fork into my wine glass and the oil in the dressing makes swirling patterns on the surface. "You mean to tell me that all this time we've been screwing every week, you've been planning a wedding?" I retrieve the wine-soaked lettuce with my fingers and pop it into my mouth. How much blinder could I possibly be? What the hell else am I missing out on in this world?

"Only since Valentine's Day," he says.

"Valentine's Day?" My brain scrambles to remember. "Didn't

you and I get together the next day? And have sex in your bathtub?"

"I don't remember." He starts to pick the mushrooms out of his salad, muttering under his breath, "I explicitly said no mushrooms!"

"Yes, we did. I'm sure of it," I say. "We went to the Half Tone for brunch and then you got some crazy idea about a bubble bath. Are you kidding me? What kind of narcissistic, depraved individual are you, anyway?"

"Grace." The bored, officious voice is back. "We said just sex, remember?"

"If I hear that one more time, I'm going to scream!" I say. "I know we said just sex. But I guess we should have included a clause in our contract that said, *No more sex if either one of us decides to get married.* Oh my god, I can't believe this."

"Grace, please—"

"You're making this so easy," I say. "I should have bowed out long ago. You are such a self-centered, pompous, boring boor!" I sputter. "This is definitely all she wrote. I hope you and the Termite Woman will be very happy together."

"Termite Woman? What are you talking about?" he says.

"Never mind." As I slide out of the booth, I feel the muscles in my newly toned stomach clench. "As my mother would say, good riddance to the riffraff."

"Don't go," Fuzz says. "Please."

"And by the way," I say, "don't think I'm going to stop coming here, just to avoid you." I struggle to right the inside-out sleeve of my sweater. "This is my bar. So you're going to have to go somewhere else, not me."

"I've been coming here longer than you have," he has the nerve to say. "That night we met, you told me it was your first time."

"Seriously?" My voice rises dangerously. Several heads turn to see what all the commotion's about. "Do you really want to go there?" I say.

"Grace, listen." He grabs me by the wrist. "Please. Sit down."

I plop back down on the edge of the leather seat. "Judy and I aren't getting married for at least another year," Fuzz says. "She has to finish her PhD thesis and you know how that goes. Please. I don't want to have to give this up until I have to."

"Well, you have to," I say. "Anyway, *this,* as you call it—turns out to be nothing, nothing at all. At this point, it's worse than nothing. We kept on saying it was just sex, just sex, but all that time it was actually turning into…nothing."

"But it was good sex," Fuzz says, with a pleading look in his eye. "It was great and we both enjoyed it. So what's the problem?"

"It wasn't good enough," I say, getting up from the table again. "It just wasn't enough."

For a WASP, the best defense against despair is constant motion. I start jogging around Fresh Pond twice, instead of once, and take up swimming laps at the Y in Central Square in the late afternoons after work. The "Black Hole" closet in the hallway finally gets cleaned out after twenty-three years of procrastination and I dare you to find even one cobweb under any of my chairs. The more and faster I move, the less I dwell on my problems. The good news is that I'm in the best physical shape of my life. The downside is that I smell like chlorine and my hair's even wilder than ever. And don't think Celia hasn't let me hear about it.

"Gracious, Grace! You look like some sort of bedraggled rodent when you come out of the pool," she says, one day when I pick her up for dinner after a swim.

"I'm going to try with all my might to take that as a compliment," I say.

"Well, I certainly didn't mean it that way." Celia sighs. "Maybe you should just cut it all off and get a nice wig," she says. "Something straight and unassuming. At least for when you go out in public."

"It's a wonder you ever let me out in public in the first place, Mother," I say.

I'm just getting changed into my bathing suit in the pool locker room one day when I get a call from Max, who's taken Celia to Simon's for tea in my stead. "Mom, I lost Grandma!" she wails.

"What do you mean you lost Grandma?" I hold my phone up to my ear while hoisting the bathing suit straps up over my shoulders.

"We were at Simon's and I went to the bathroom and when I came out, she was gone. I couldn't have been in there for more than three minutes. She just disappeared into thin air!"

"Okay, don't panic," I say. "I'll be right there. Go out and look around on Mass Ave. Ask if anyone's seen her."

I call Celia's cell phone, which goes straight to voicemail. I pick Max up in the Corolla, still wearing my bathing suit under my jeans. We drive around the neighboring streets, looking for Celia.

"I feel so bad, Mom," Max says. "I didn't think she'd—"

"It's not your fault," I say. "The doctor said this might happen. You had no way of knowing."

"We were actually having a good time." Max puts her bare feet up against the windshield and I feel my stomach go queasy.

"Easy with your feet," I say. "That windshield's kind of… fragile."

Max swings her legs back down and slides into the lotus position. "Grandma was telling me all these cool stories about the good old days," she says. "When you guys were little. And you're so busted, Mom. She said you and Aunt Nell used to terrorize Uncle Charlie."

"Ridiculous," I say, rounding the corner onto Hurlbut Street. "Charlie got away with murder."

"She told me about the time you and Aunt Nell put chocolate sauce in his belly button while he was sleeping."

"We most certainly did not."

"And how you kidnapped his goldfish, Flipper, and held it hostage for ransom."

"It was payback for all the money he charged us to read

his stupid comic books," I say. "But let me tell you something, Max. Charlie deserved every bit of it. He acted like Little Lord Fauntleroy around our house. It was our job as his sisters to keep him in line."

"Little Lord who?"

"Never mind."

"Grandma told me that Uncle Charlie was all bluster and Aunt Nell was the baby…" Max's legs shoot up to the windshield again. "And she said you were definitely the boss."

"Max!" I say. "Get your feet off that windshield!"

"Case in point," Max says grumpily, pulling her legs back down again.

I drop Max off at home and start off on the neighborhood route that Fuzz and I followed a few months before, making a tour of all my old abodes. As I turn left off Avon onto Martin Street, I feel a shiver, remembering the day, forty-two years ago, when JFK was assassinated in Dallas and they sent us home early from school. My friends and I strolled down this very street, bewildered in the sunlight, green book bags slung over our shoulders and skateboards tucked under our arms, heading for Brigham's on Mass. Ave for ice cream sodas, not yet knowing any of the terrible details. And I remember going home later that afternoon to find Celia in front of the TV set, tears streaming down her face, as the footage of the president's passing motorcade played over and over again.

I make a loop around to Linnaean and up Washington Avenue, then turn left down Upland Road. I pass the second old house, on the corner of Mt. Pleasant, and then pull closer to the third, on top of Avon Hill. That's when I see it, Celia's old olive-green Volvo, which hasn't been out of the garage in years, parked wildly askew, its rear end sticking perilously out into the street. She must have left Simon's and wandered home to get the key. In 1970, the Volvo was a shiny, sleek, new machine, one of the first fuel-injected models on the market, but now it looks dull and boxy and rusted at the seams.

The house is virtually unchanged, still painted a cool slate grey. Only the door, which in our day was a bright orange, is now a deep-forest green. I ring the bell and a young woman with dreadlocks answers the door. A toddler of indeterminate sex wearing a tie-dye T-shirt and cloth diapers comes up from behind and hugs her leg. "Mumma," s/he says.

"May I help you?" the woman says.

"I'm sorry to bother you," I say, "but…"

"Grace?" I hear Celia's voice coming from the next room. "Is that you?"

"That's my mother," I explain to the woman. "She has Alzheimer's. I'm afraid she got a bit confused. We used to live in this house, back in the sixties."

"Thank goodness," the woman says, lowering her voice. "She just wandered in through the back door. We didn't know what to do with her. I was about to call the police."

"I'm so glad you didn't," I say. "That would have really freaked her out. Thanks so much for letting her stay."

I go into the living room and there is Celia, seated awkwardly in a red beanbag chair, holding a glass of water. Her stick thin legs poke out from under her dress and she's wearing white ankle socks under her Birkenstocks. A perplexed-looking young man, prematurely grey, the woman's husband and the baby's father, presumably, is standing next to her.

"What a relief," Celia says. "You've finally come."

"Where's your cell phone, Mother?" I say. "Why didn't you call me?"

"I gave it to Goodwill," she said.

"Again?" I say. "You're supposed to keep it with you at all times!"

"Someone else will get way more use out of it than I ever will." Celia looks uncertainly around the room, at the young couple and the wide-eyed toddler. "I'm just not quite sure why I'm here," she says.

I go over and crouch down by her side. The toddler comes over and taps Celia on the knee. "Mumma," s/he says. Celia looks at the child, confused, then back at me. "We used to live here," I say. "Remember? We loved the sunporch upstairs. We practically lived in it. Dad had that fake putting green in his study and you had a garden out back."

She looks over toward the window. "I was the first one in the neighborhood to grow roses," she says.

"You were," I say.

"Your brother fancied himself a comic book impresario," Celia says, getting up out of the chair and going over to the window. "Nell lived in an imaginary world with all of her trolls. And you, Rose…when your cat Percy ate your pet mouse, Squeaky, you couldn't decide whether to be furious at Percy or console him by telling him that it wasn't his fault. In the end, you blamed yourself, for bringing them together in the first place. We held a funeral out in the backyard."

"Poor Squeaky," I say.

"Sweeky!" the toddler says gleefully, as if we've finally said something s/he can understand.

Celia looks up at the ceiling. "There was all that fuss about that rock group from Liverpool, those four scraggly boys."

"The Beatles." I stand by Celia at the window. "We watched them on the *Ed Sullivan Show*. Remember? All the girls were screaming."

She shakes her head, digging deep into her memory. "As I recall," she says, slowly moving toward the door. "They looked like ruffians and caused quite a ruckus. But in the end, they were harmless, really, rather innocent and sweet. Thank you for the water," she says to the young man at the door. "I feel so much better now.

15

A few days later, I come home to find Max curled up on the couch reading *Calvin and Hobbes,* wrapped up in her most tattered childhood blanket, which means something is wrong. I feel a pang of guilt as I realize how little attention I've paid to my daughter lately, how little interest I've shown in her life. I sit down beside her. My usual approach in this type of situation is not to ask what's the matter, but to focus on something positive.

"How are things going with Jack?" I say.

Max's face falls. "They're not," she says flatly. "He broke up with me."

"What?" Shoot, talk about a plan backfiring! "When did that happen?" I say.

"Last night," she says. "And before you get all mad and indignant on my behalf…" She puts the backs of her hands together. "He did it decently. And sooner rather than later. Which is good. He never made any promises. He told me he just didn't see it going anywhere. And how can you make someone see that if he doesn't feel it?" She shakes her head back and forth. "You just can't."

"Well, it's his loss!" I stifle the urge to rush down to the Wonder Bar and give Jack a piece of my mind. "And frankly, Max, he's not worth your little finger."

"Of course he's worth my little finger. Jack's a good guy, Mom, you know that."

"Well, clearly not good enough," I say. "And I know you don't want to hear this now, but there will be many others and they will be the lucky ones."

"I know," Max says with a sigh. "I just really liked Jack. I thought…" She looks down at the book as her brown eyes well up with tears.

"What?" I say. "What is it, Max? Tell me."

"They're all disappearing," she says, her voice breaking. "All the guys I care about. First Dad, then El…"

"They aren't disappearing." I reach out to stroke her hair. "They love you to pieces and they'll always be part of your life."

"Not Jack," she says, pulling away. "He doesn't love me to pieces and he'll never be part of my life." She wipes her nose with her sleeve.

"Well, maybe not Jack." The last strands of her hair slide through my fingers.

"Whatever," Max says, wrapping the blanket more tightly around her. "I'll get over it. It's no big deal. He just, like"—her face turns quickly toward the bay window and then back again—"kind of broke my fucking heart."

I find myself watching Otis the next day at work, expertly hefting boxes from shelf to shelf. I notice how he lifts them from the middle, so that they won't tilt off-balance and fall. I remember what he told me about the prosthetic and how efficiently he's learned to cope without it. I can't stop thinking about the fact that he only has one arm. How he's somehow made his peace with this spectacular corporeal omission, risen above it, taken his place again in the normal flow of the two-armed world. Never drawing attention to his plight, or complaining, or asking for any special consideration. And doing it all with such quiet grace.

And I can't stop dwelling on what Isabelle told me, about people who have amputee sex fetishes, and I scold myself for wondering what goes on between Otis and Maggie when the lights go out. Curiously, when we fumbled around in the Men's Health aisle that afternoon, I didn't even focus much on his missing arm, so self-conscious was I about my own limitations and flaws.

That evening, sitting in the purple chair with my laptop, after an hour of inspired procrastination, checking out every single dryer lint cleaner available on Amazon and reading all one hundred and thirty-six reviews—all so I don't have to work on my novel—I give up on accomplishing anything creative and let curiosity get the better of me. Taking a deep breath, I google "sex with amputees." I promise myself I won't look at any photos. I'll only reckon with words. Sure enough, the first entry gives it a name. Acrotomophilia: having a strong sexual interest in amputees. Not to be confused with Apotemnophilia: having a strong desire to *become* an amputee. *Huh ?!?!?* I can't get distracted by this even more alarming notion. I read on…

"A Jungian explanation for the [amputee] fetish is that it stems from a desire to resolve discontinuities in the collective subconscious by means of distorting the geometric representation of man, which traditionally involves five points, six when focusing on male sexuality, and seven when discussing incarnations of the Logos from certain religious cultures."

Say *what* now? *Wikipedia* doesn't always get things right.

I scroll quickly down the Google entries, which become increasingly less official and academic, and way more suggestive and sleazy. By the time I come across this one—"Leg amputee blond cougar gets lucky with young stud"—I've had enough. I quit Safari and delete my entire web history. For the moment, anyway, curiosity has killed this cat.

Isabelle's waiting for me the next morning in the kitchen, crossed arms resting on her now gigantic belly, sweatpants hanging low around her nonexistent hips. She throws a handful of papers down on the table. I see that it's the most recent post I wrote for *Squiggle Z* and the list of ideas I came up with for future columns. "I'm sorry to have to say this, Grace," she says officiously. "But you're fired."

"What?" I reach for the Wheatabix cereal box. "Who are you? Donald D-Bag Trump?"

"Please!" She shudders. "Don't even say that repulsive buffoon's name. He keeps threatening to run for president. The way things are going, who's going to stop him? Next thing you know that bloated, bigoted, misogynistic, ignorant reality show a-hole will be in charge of the nuke button. God help us all."

"Don't fire me, Iz," I plead.

"I'm doing this for your own good, Gracie. I thought you were getting the hang of this blog thing, but you're really not." Isabelle taps the papers. She starts to read from my latest post, entitled: *Oral Hygiene—Bar Style!*

"Let's face it—the over-fifty mouth is a minefield trap full of cracked fillings, tilting crowns, and failing implants. After weeks of observation, I've identified several categories of teeth cleaners and various techniques. There are—the Tongue Probers, the Pinky Pickers, the Gum Chewers, the Water Swishers, the Napkin Wipers, the Toothpick Pokers. Sub-categories of the Tongue Probers include the Open-Mouthed Sweepers, the Forward Tongue Probers…"

"Seriously, Grace?" Isabelle says.

"It's all true," I say defensively.

"And these other ideas," she starts reading again from another page.

"*In Defense of Ketchup*?" she says incredulously. "Really?"

"Technically, it is a vegetable," I say meekly.

She ignores me. "And this!" She raps her hand against the paper. "*What is it About People Who Wear Vests? Grammar Pet Peeves, Overheard at the Bar.*" She starts to read from the paper again:

> *Did you hear Andrew Jackson's getting kicked off the twenty dollar bill?*
> *My inheritance is out the fucking window!*
> *She was almost like a superhero.*
> *I want to assassinate my to-do list.*
> *Go East, young man. How come you never hear that?*
> *Her name was Sarah Gorges; and, man, was she ever!*

"These aren't ideas," Isabelle says. "They're lists."

"They're ideas in the form of lists." I halfheartedly begin

my defense. "I thought it was a novel idea. Saying more with less, you know? Snappy little thought bites. You've heard of *amuse-bouche?* Well, this is *amuse-tête.* Rouse the synapses. Get your audience thinking. Readers are so lazy these days."

"But you can't let them know that you know that," Isabelle says. "Readers don't like to be put down or lectured to. Know what readers like, Grace? They like it when writers do their job—putting words together in a cohesive, comprehensive, entertaining fashion—to make an article, or a post, or an essay. Capiche?"

I try to pump myself up to argue and rail. "The bones of the language are so fascinating," I say. "I thought other people might be interested too."

"No one wants to read about bones, Grace."

I flop down into the purple chair. "I guess I let you down," I say. "I'm sorry, Iz."

"Hey, you gave it a shot," Isabelle says. "And speaking of novel ideas, it's time for you to get out that frickin' manuscript and finish the goddamned thing!"

"Do you realize how daunting it is to write a whole book?" I wail. "Plucking one hundred thousand random words out of thin air and figuring out exactly how to string them together, one by bloody one, until you come up with characters that live and breathe and a story that has both an arc and a soul? Who *does* that?"

"OMG, that is such an effed-up, tight-ass way to look at it!" Isabelle says. "Don't be counting the frickin' words, Grace. Just make the ones you do choose count! You know what your basic problem is?" Isabelle stops in her tracks and shakes her index finger at me. "You're way too uptight. You want to control every goddamned word, every phrase, every paragraph. Just let it out. Vomit it all out onto the page. Purge your psyche. These neat and tidy lists are never going to cut it in an online post, much less a novel. The mushroom book was non-fiction, so you got away with it, but when you're telling a story, you've got to pour your heart and soul in it—blood, guts, semen, warts and all."

"The mushroom book was easy," I groan. "All I had to do was arrange the facts on the page and make sure they basically got along with one another."

"Don't sell yourself short, though," Isabelle says. "You brought those mushrooms to life with your writing. Isn't that what the reviewer said? Otherwise, it would have been nothing more than a boring, glossy coffee table book."

"You think?" I start to chew on my thumbnail.

"Had I not read that book," Isabelle says, in a slow deadpan, "I never would have known about the 'murderers without malice.'" Her fingers start to wiggle. "Lurking out there in the woods, just waiting for the unsuspecting—"

"I'll murder you with malice," I say, throwing Atticus's plush cat toy cell phone at her.

"Fine. Get your revenge," Isabelle says, heading for her not-so-secret stash of Pop-Tarts, stuffed way back in the cupboard under the sink. "Then unravel your tight-ass, WASPy self and let her freaking rip!"

I nod my head slowly. It's an interesting idea. "Hey, guess what?" I say. "I think we just passed the Bechdel test, Iz!"

"Well, gosh, dang, darn it!" she says, tearing open the Pop-Tart package. "Would you look at us!"

That night, for the first time since I can remember, the house is quiet. I set the racing kitchen clock back to real time and, as if chastened, it's suddenly quiet as a mouse. Isabelle and Emil take off to visit his parents in Rhode Island, and I can't say I'm sorry, because even though I know she's right, that my blog posts weren't any good, I need some time to lick my writerly wounds. El and Rachel are up in Vermont, rehearsing for their final spring dance performance. Zephyr's been spending most of her time with Otis and Maggie. Elvira and Max are out in the backyard working on their final projects. The hammers pound and Elvira's "Mad Hatter Symphony" keens and howls and skitters and screeches from the boom box. She's strung up a pulley-style clothes line back near the fence, and every day, new found objects appear on the line hung with clothes-pins—an old toothbrush, the other half of my pliers, a pair of sequined gloves. The girls practically live out there now that the weather is better and their project deadlines are drawing near.

I rummage in the liquor cabinet and pull out a bottle of fancy red wine given to Phillip by a client years ago—the one we were always saving for a special occasion. Looks as though there may be no more special occasions for a while. Might as well drink it now and drown my sorrows. I know I should stop being a self-pitying whiner and count my blessings and get back on all of the horses that have ever thrown me. But I'm still boycotting that WASP notion of *should. Should* implies that I've been dabbling in the *shouldn'ts*, and self-accusation only leads to crippling guilt. And although in general I feel like crap, I know I have nothing to feel guilty about. I've just had a run of… misadventures, let's say. The tides will soon turn. I'm sure of it. I'm not perfect by any stretch. But I'm good enough.

I decide to give myself one more night to wallow in my misery. And to do it royally. Tomorrow I'll wake up with the realization that except for my children, I have precious little to show for myself these days. My marriage ended in divorce. I'm no farther along with my novel than I was in the fall. I've lost one job and if Maggie and Otis end up together, I could very well lose the other two. They'll take Zeph and move to the Potato State and my two newest friends will have disappeared. El and Rachel won't have any time for me after the baby comes. And neither will Isabelle and Emil. Max will move to Colorado with a sullen, scruffy performance artist. And I'll never be able to write another coherent word again, one that has any beauty or depth.

Boo, hoo, hoo! I chide myself as Celia used to do when we felt sorry for ourselves as kids. Have yourself one last cry, she'd say, and get it out of your system. Then it's time to stop belly-aching and get a move on. It pains me to admit how often Celia's right. Tomorrow, I'll pick what's left of myself up off the dirty floor and wash it until it gleams and start all over again. But tonight—I'm going to get drunk.

I put on a Tracy Chapman CD and pour myself a glass of the fancy wine. At first taste, it's musty, with a peppery bounce and decidedly Ajaxy finish. Fruit-backwards, I'd say, with exceptionally wobbly legs. Just needs to sit a bit, I figure, after being stuck in that dark bottle all those years. I take out some chips and salsa for a snack and give the wine a few moments to breathe.

She's got someone with a fast car. I've got no one and a rusty Corolla. Clipping shut the bag of chips, I pour myself another glass of wine, hoping it's mellowed. But after a few sips, it's clear that the wine, like everything else in my life, has turned.

Too lazy for a shower, I spritz myself with a few pumps of rose water and put on the ice-blue cocktail dress. I notice a soy sauce stain from the tofu bites Dylan and I ate that night at the museum cafe. In an act that can only be labeled reckless and defiant, I pull on a pair of red Converse sneakers and grab a colorful Peruvian cloth belt to wrap around my waist to hide the stain. Might as well start embracing the eccentric old Cambridge crony I'm destined to become. I leave my car parked in the driveway and start walking to the Wonder Bar.

When I hit Mass Avenue, I see a trolley pull into the car barns, its ancient antennae creaking and swaying. I pass Frank's Steak House and then China Fair. The funeral home looms on the left and then the Dunkin' Donuts on the edge of Porter Square. Passing the old Sears Building, my step quickens. The irony of the beautiful spring night and my dark, edgy mood doesn't escape me. Purple cosmos and orange daylilies rule the sidewalk cracks. I smell the last of the sweet lilacs and the musky odor of marigolds somewhere. The fragrant air makes my nostrils flare and dares me to stop moping. I head for the beckoning door of the Wonder Bar, which less than a year ago was no more than a dark portal into a terrifying, alien world, but now welcomes me like a beckoning angel.

Palindrome Guy is at the bar and I sit down next to him.

"Hi, there," he says. "Grace, right?"

"Yes, right, Bob." For the one hundredth and seventeenth time, I think. "It's Grace."

"O. Grace Cargo."

"Pardon?" Having suspended my rule of no more than two glasses of wine for the evening, I order another.

"Your palindrome," he says. "O. Grace Cargo. It has a nice ring to it. Like F. Scott Fitzpatrick."

"Fitzgerald," I say. None of this palindrome stuff makes any sense to me. "My last name is Hobbes."

"As in *Calvin and...*?" he asks.

"Exactly." The third glass of wine is already nearly gone.

"So, what do you do, anyway, O. Grace?" he says. "Man, it's like addressing royalty!"

"Short answer..." I look around anxiously to make sure Jack isn't there. "I'm a writer."

"Nice," he says. "I see you with that notebook all the time. What do you write about?" The more he talks, the more I hear the Southern twang in his voice.

"Families, mostly," I say. "Mushrooms, sometimes."

"Psychedelic mushrooms?" His face lights up.

""Fraid not," I say. "How'd you like to buy me another glass of wine, Bob Hannah?"

"Sure."

"I like your shirt," I say. It's the same Strawberry Alarm Clock T-shirt he was wearing the night I met Fuzz. "That must be a collector's item by now. Where'd you get it?"

Palindrome Guy looks down at his chest, as if to remember what he's wearing. "I go to Buck-a-Pound twice a year and scoop up a bunch of jeans and T-shirts and then wash the shit out of them to get rid of the cooties. I don't pay much attention to what's on them."

"Wow," I say. "People still say *cooties*?"

"Sure, why wouldn't they?" Bob Hannah pulls out the shirt to look at the image. "I think it's a kid's toy or something," he says. "Some sort of strawberry-scented—"

"No," I say. "It was a group. Back in the sixties."

"Group?"

"Band," I say. "A rock band. 'Incense and Peppermints'? 'Curse of the Witches'? Ring any bells?"

"What kind of name is that for a band?" he says disdainfully.

"They're all terrible," I say. "Anyway, cool T-shirt. It looks good on you, Bob."

Bob Hannah grins. "Are you flirting with me, O. Grace?"

"Apparently." I'm suddenly buoyed by the great depths of my self-pity and the nearly empty bar, plus the fact that Jack isn't working tonight, just Lumbering Larry, and I don't give a fig what he thinks. I don't much care what anybody thinks any more.

"So are you, like"—Bob Hannah considers this for a moment—"trying to pick me up?"

"I believe I am." The wine's beginning to talk. "But first, one question: are you under forty?"

"Thirty-nine," he says, then calculates. "And one...sixth."

"Close enough. You're fair game then. How about we go outside and take a stroll?"

"Sure." He stuffs his hands into his jean pockets, as if I've just asked him to go throw stones at squirrels. "Cool tennis shoes," he says, as we walk toward the door.

"Where do you live?" I say, once we're out on the sidewalk. Scattered diners sit at the outdoor tables, as the cars on Mass. Ave. whiz by and the 77 bus lumbers along toward the Square. A car horn is stuck somewhere.

Bob Hannah points up to some windows on the second floor of the building. "I live right up there," he says.

"On top of the Wonder Bar?"

"Home sweet home," he says.

"No wonder you're always here." I'm aware of the slight slur in my speech and realize I'm probably only making sense to myself by now. "Because you never have to go anywhere else!"

"You got it, O. Grace." He steers me to the doorway. "Right this way."

Upstairs I flop down onto his checkered couch. "Do you have any wine, Bob Hannah?" I say.

"Just beer," he says.

"I'll take one."

"You sure?" He hesitates. "You seem—"

"I'll take one," I say.

But after the first sip of Rolling Rock, I remember that I don't really like beer, and the three and a half glasses of wine I've had are now making my head spin. I'm still clear-headed enough to know that whatever else may happen, no more alcohol can be involved.

"Okay," I say. "We got the idle chitchat out of the way. Let's not waste any more time. What're we here for, Bob Hannah?" I throw my arms around his neck.

"Not yet, O. Grace." He unwinds my arms and heads for a set of cluttered shelves against the wall. "First, we play a little game of Sex Scrabble."

"Sex Scrabble?" I look to see if he's making a joke. "Are you serious?"

"It's just like regular Scrabble. But you can only put down words that relate to sex in some way." He pulls a brown box with a broken top off the shelf.

"Argghhhh," I groan. "Way too hard."

"Not for me." He grins. "I'm the 2004 US Sex Scrabble Champion."

"What? No, you're making it up." I point a finger at him. "You're pulling my legs, aren't you, Bob Hannah? There's no such thing."

"There is." He starts to set up the board. "Come on. I need the practice. The competition begins next week. You're a writer. You should be good at this game."

"Way, way too hard," I mumble. "Anyway, I hate board games. Do you know how many hundreds of thousands of times I've had to play Candy Land in my life? Not to mention Monopoly and the goddamned Game of Life."

"Come on, O. Grace. It'll be fun."

"Okay, okay." I sit cross legged on the floor and arrange my letters on the rack. "Who gets to decide what counts as a sex word or not?" I say. "Is there a sex judge hiding in the closet?"

"*Sex Scrabble Dictionary*!" Bob holds up a dog-eared paperback.

"No way!" I grab the book out of his hand. "Every weird thing you can imagine in this world, there actually is. It's truly amazing. Who comes up with these crazy ideas?"

I win the draw to go first and put down LIP. A measly ten points. At least I got the double word score.

"And she's off like a herd of turtles!" Bob says gleefully.

"Don't be mean." I pick three new tiles, groaning every time another listless, low-scoring consonant appears. T. N. D. The best I can do with my next two turns is TIT and HARD. But then my luck starts to turn. I put down STROKE and AROUSE. And then I hit him with QUIM. Triple word score, using the Q!

"QUIM?" he says scornfully. "No way."

"Look it up," I say.

He opens the dictionary. "Whad'ya know?" he says. "It's an obsolete word for V-jay!"

"I read it once in a book," I say, adding up my points. "Forty-five."

"Nice play," he concedes. "And I'll forgive you because you didn't steal my spot." He puts down all seven tiles and scores a bingo with SUCCUMB. Sixty-seven points. "Game over," he says, rubbing his hands together. "If the creek don't rise—"

"Don't be so cocky," I say. "The creek still might rise."

He points at me with a grin. "Look at you, O. Grace! You made a joke."

"Everyone's a comedienne," I mutter. The best I can manage with my next turn is WET. Triple Letter Score on the W. Fourteen points. Better than nothing.

"I'll allow that," Bob says. "Even if it's not in the dictionary." He counters with DICK.

"No proper names!" I say.

"It's not a proper name," he says. "It's a generic word for the male member."

"All right, all right," I mutter. "I don't know how you guys walk around with those things, anyway."

My letters start getting better. Or my mind gets clearer, I can't tell. I plunk down word after word. ARDOR. THROB. SINFUL. TOUCH. And then I play what I think is my masterpiece. "There," I say triumphantly, putting down four of my tiles. "S-E-X-Y! X on the triple-letter word score and a double word for the whole thing! Sixty points. And shouldn't I get a bonus because I actually used the word *SEX*?"

"That says SAXY, O. Grace," Bob says. "Do you have an E?"

"Oh, shoot. No more Es." I finger the wooden tiles on my rack. "Fresh out of Es," I mumble. "Did you know that E is the most common letter in the alphabet?"

"Most commonly used letter," he corrects me. "Yes, I did know that." He studies his tiles, drumming his fingers on the table. "And I've got four of them," he says.

"I'm surrounded with people whose names begin with E." I babble on while Bob studies the board. "My son, for instance. His name is El, short for Eliot. Also my friend's baby daddy, Emil, and my daughter's weird friend, Elvira. Well, she's not really weird. She's kind of wonderful, actually. Did you know that I have a kid whose name is a letter?"

"No, O. Grace, I did not," Bob says. "But if you don't have the letter E, then you can't make the word SEXY. Isn't that what you meant?"

"Yes, I meant sexy." I point a mock stern finger at him. "I meant *you* are sexy. And *I* am sexy. And therefore—"

"No, I mean did you mean SEXY on the board?" he says in an exasperated tone.

"Sure," I say drunkenly. "Let's clear off the tiles first."

Bob Hannah finally throws up his hands. "Oh, man, you are drunk, O. Grace," he says, and pulls me down onto the floor.

I wake up the next morning in a swirl of panic. Scenes from the night before flash in pounding neon images in my brain, the way they do in aspirin commercials. My head is spinning and my mouth feels as though it's stuffed with steel wool. I brush my teeth with baking soda and clove oil and take long gulps of cold water from the bathroom faucet, letting the water stream over my head. Afterward, I sit on the toilet seat with a bad case of the hiccups, my dripping hair hanging down in between my legs. Atticus and Maude come in and start lapping up my puddle of shame. Well, I've gone and done it—sunk to an all time baby-boomer low.

The details of the previous night are fuzzy and scattered at best. Somehow, I made it home in one piece. But I do know that Palindrome guy and I ended up having sex and I do remember that we used a condom. Thank god. His apartment smelled like boiled artichokes and bus fumes and we played some kind of game. Scrabble. Oh my god. Sex Scrabble. He claimed he was the US champion. For a while, I thought I was winning. But in the end, he creamed me. The tiles flew all over the place. I had marks on my back and legs when I got home.

I drink another quart of water and take a searing hot shower, emerging an alarming shade of cooked-lobster red. All that's clear is that I will have to go to the Wonder Bar to make amends. The clock ticks excruciatingly slowly until four p.m. when the bar opens its doors. I leave work early and arrive just as Lumbering Larry pulls up in his car with the keys. A few minutes later, true to form, Palindrome Guy strolls in. I've still got a faint but persistent headache and I'm beyond mortified, but I have to get this done. And soon. Jack's shift starts at five and I can't possibly face him under these circumstances.

"O. Grace!" Palindrome Guy greets me cheerfully, not the least bit embarrassed. "How you feeling today?"

"I have to apologize, Bob." He sits down next to me. "I had way too much to drink last night and—"

"You sure were wasted," he says. "It was actually pretty funny. You were a riot playing Sex Scrabble. You came up with some great words, I have to say." He looks over at Larry and lowers his voice, "I mean, LIBIDO for fifty-three points?"

"I was on a roll for a while," I say.

"You sure were," he says. "But it's tough to run with the big dogs, O. Grace."

"I'm so embarrassed, Bob," I say. "I've just had this shitty week, you know, month, actually and—"

"Hey, no worries," he says with a shrug. "I love sex," he says. "I'll have sex with anyone."

"Great," I say flatly.

"I didn't mean it that way," he says. "I'm just saying, I love women. I don't know how y'all put up with us lugs."

"It's a challenge."

"Honestly," Palindrome Guy goes on. "I'm grateful every time a woman wants to have sex with me."

"Well, that's nice," I say. Maybe the sixties aren't dead after all. Here Palindrome Guy is, championing women and good old-fashioned, meaningless sex.

"And I have to say." Bob lowers his voice again. "You're pretty happening, O. Grace. Quite the cougar."

"Really?" A tiny glimmer of light infuses my dark mood. "Well, thanks, I guess… But please understand, Bob. That will never happen again."

"Understood," he says cheerfully. "You want a glass of wine?"

I groan. "It hurts even to hear the word. But let me buy you a beer, Bob. Oh, and I thought of a palindrome the other day. I forgot to tell you last night."

"What is it?" He grabs a napkin and picks up his pen.

"*Salt an atlas*," I say. "Let's say you want to spice up your life, by traveling to some exotic far-away place? What do you do? You salt an atlas."

"Doesn't really make sense," Bob says doubtfully.

"Oh, and *sit on a potato pan, Otis* does?" I realize that when he first told me that palindrome back in September, I hadn't even met my Otis yet. *My* Otis, I hear myself say.

"Still, it's a good effort," Palindrome Guy says, giving me a friendly pat on the back. "Bless your heart, O. Grace."

"I hope you don't mind my asking," I say. "But what do you actually do, Bob Hannah? Besides write palindromes on napkins and drink beer at the bar?"

"I'm an aerospace engineer," he says. "Over at MIT."

"Rocket science?" I say.

"You got it," he says, motioning to Larry for another beer.

Why am I not surprised?

16

Thus begins my *Oblomov* period, during which I succumb to the WASPs' final stage of defeat—self-imposed exile. I use up all of my vacation days and stay holed up at home for a week, reading Jane Austen's entire oeuvre all over again, the way I did one winter break in college as an "independent study," this time adding even the most obscure titles to the list—*Lady Susan, Sandition, Lesley Castle, The Beautiful Cassandra.*

It's all I can do to get up some mornings. I think of Oblomov, "the superfluous man," who took to his bed in St. Petersburg, stubbornly refusing to engage with the world. *Thank god I've never had to pull one sock on my foot.* Living in a state of indolence and torpor, he found comfort only in the memories of his childhood. At this point, I can sort of relate.

But as much as I've had a good life, I don't find it comforting to be stuck in bygone places or to lie in bed for hours at a time. The future's always been far more alluring than the past and I get Restless Leg Syndrome if I stay off my feet for too long. Even Oblomov was eventually coaxed out of bed by the beautiful, alluring Olga. And though I have no such Olga, or Oleg, in my life right now, by the fifth day of exile, I start to feel antsy. It's a good sign. Like when a healing wound begins to itch—you know you're on the mend.

I make a wobbly truce with myself—just to take each day as it comes. Square one is hardly the worst place to be. I try at least to keep my game face on. As a friend and co-worker. As a mentor and a mom. Even though my life has come to a slow, lurching halt, everyone else's is steaming ahead full throttle. Max's "Tower of Junk" now looms over the highest branch of the chestnut tree. The final Allegro Movement of Elvira's "Mad Hatter Symphony" rises up out of the jar of cut-up crossword puzzle letters and is unexpectedly, soaringly beautiful. Emil and Isabelle begin their Lamaze classes and El starts sanding the wood floor of his old bedroom upstairs. The Bennington semester is over and he and Rachel have been talking about moving to Boston instead of New York. Rachel has a standing offer to teach at BU and El could just as easily audition and wait on tables here, he says. He wants to make a dance studio. In my house. Otis and Maggie are taking a Bonsai for Beginners class. And Zephyr has finally worn Otis down and is learning how to play the drums.

By the end of seven days, my stamina, at least, has returned. It's true. I've got virtually nothing to show for my eight months of freedom and rejuvenation. Nothing but a weary, wounded spirit, a still-unfinished novel, and a house full of well-meaning, but nonetheless, ungrateful parasites, who love me unconditionally but don't listen to a word I say.

June rolls in with a string of glorious days in the upper seventies. I'm determined to get out of my funk and back on track. The sting of Dylan's betrayal is easing and I certainly don't miss Fuzz. I take out my manuscript and reread it from start to finish over the course of four hours one Sunday morning, while listening to Samuel Barber's "Adagio for Strings." And even though some passages still make me cringe, it isn't terrible.

There's something there that keeps the story's heart beating. The heroine's love of the ocean and her unwavering tenacity, even in the face of unspeakable odds. The humor of the eccentric postmistress, the trombone music that Leon plays for his grandmother, Sadie. To me, the measure of a good piece of art is that it at least begins to break your heart. And I think, when Jasper finally professes his love for Esme and throws his chess set into the river—this one just might succeed.

Isabelle's right. No wonder I've been having such trouble writing the great American novel. I'm a WASP! I've got to let myself go, take more risks, let her rip! Kind of like what I've been trying to do in my personal life this year. All of a sudden, words and ideas come out of the floodgates. I can't write them fast enough. I rip up chapters and go through red markers at a clip, editing and slashing and embellishing with abandon. The notebooks fill to the brim and spill onto my computer page. It's a wild, unbridled, chaotic mess. But finally, it's alive!

That night, feeling restless, I venture out to the Wonder Bar for the first time since my retreat. The front corner seat is empty. I order a cup of lemon tea and lean back against the wall. Still not quite ready for a glass of wine, I'm coasting on a wave of clean living and virtuosity, "growing to my strongest core." It actually feels pretty good.

I suddenly notice Otis in the back of the bar, near the door to the kitchen, talking to Sam, the owner. When he sees me, his eyes light up and he comes over.

"Grace!" It warms my heart that he seems so glad to see me. "You came out of the woodwork! We missed you!"

"Thanks for giving me the time off, Otis. I really needed it," I say. I look around to see if Maggie's with him. "I've never seen you in here before. I thought you didn't like this place."

Otis looks puzzled. "I love this place," he says.

"Strange," I say, dribbling some honey into my tea. "I don't know why I got that impression."

"I have a favor to ask," he says. "Could Zeph stay with you guys overnight next Sunday? Maggie and I are going to the Cape and then I'm putting her on a plane back to Idaho the next day."

"Sure," I say. "Fair warning, though. Zephyr's turning into a Pop-Tart addict. And Isabelle's stockpiling them, so that's not helping matters."

"If Pop-Tarts make Zeph happy," he says, lifting up his hand. "Then who am I?"

Sam claps Otis on the back on his way out of the bar. "Keep up with the painting," he says.

"Thanks, Sam. I will."

"Are you two friends?"

"I've gotten to know Sam a bit since I brought in my paintings," Otis says. "He was nice enough to give me a show."

"Great! When are they going up?" I wrap the string around

my tea bag and squeeze. "I've been looking forward to some new artwork. Although I'll be sad to see these go." I gesture to the paintings on the wall. "These Vulcan creatures have really grown on me."

"Vulcan creatures?" Otis says.

"I especially loved one that used to be there." I point to the place on the wall where the owl painting used to hang; it's been replaced by one of two Vulcan creatures tying their shoes at a bowling alley. "The one looking over the fence," I say. "With the owl on the ground beside it. And I also love the one with the lawn chair and transistor radio." I point to the canvas up near the front door. "Whoever painted these must be around my age. Those little radios fill me with such nostalgia."

"My older sister had one," he says. "I'd camp outside of her room in the hallway in my sleeping bag, listening to Wolfman Jack." He slides into voice—"I got that nice, raspy sound!"—then follows it up with a couple of yips and a long wolf howl.

"Good impression," I say. "The owl painting disappeared."

"I took it down," he says. "I wanted it back."

"You bought it?" I say. "Shoot. I was thinking of asking Jack for the price. I guess you beat me to it."

"I didn't buy it," Otis says quietly.

"What do you mean?"

"I painted it," he says. "These are my paintings, Grace. Of the Vulcan creatures, as you call them."

Dawn breaks over Marblehead!—as my high school physics teacher used to say. So that's why Otis didn't want to come here that first night with Maggie. He didn't want us making a fuss over his work. My finger drifts around the room. "You painted all of these?" I say.

"I did," he says. "And Sam just gave me some good news. A gallery owner came in earlier. She wants to buy five of them."

"That's fantastic, Otis. They're amazing!" I say. "I'm so happy for you."

"You don't look happy," he says, sitting down next to me. "You still look sad."

"I'm not sad exactly." I feel a lump lodge in my throat. "I just get such a longing sometimes. I'm not even sure what for. Do you ever feel that way?"

"I do," he says.

"What do you think it's about?" I wrap my hands around the hot cup of tea, desperate to hear what Otis has to say, the answer of the man who brought the Vulcan creatures to life on these dark maroon walls. "What do you think the longing's for?"

Otis lifts up his left hand and I think to myself, for the umpteenth time, *That's the only hand he has.*

"Everything," he says, with a one-armed shrug.

Zeph comes over on Sunday for the sleepover—hatbox, tent, art supplies, and a bouquet of flowers.

"These are for you," she says, handing off the flowers.

"Thanks," I say. "I love daffodils."

"Is El here?" she asks. "I have to tell him something."

"He's upstairs," I say. "I'm glad you two are getting to know each other. You're like two peas in a pod."

"I love Max best," Zeph explains. "But I like El because he's like me. Not because he likes me, but because he's *like* me."

"How do you figure?" I say, trimming the flower stems.

"El likes to count things by himself too."

"He does?" I say. "How do you know?"

Zeph shrugs as though the answer is beyond obvious. "I asked him," she says, starting up the stairs two at a time.

That night I make American chop suey, my favorite dish from my childhood and one of a few meals Celia knew how to cook—noodles with ground hamburger and tomato sauce. It always hits the spot. The girls toast marshmallows on the stovetop and we watch *I Love Lucy* classics. First up is the one where Lucy and Ethel get a job at the candy factory wrapping chocolates on the conveyor belt and all hell breaks loose. Then there's the one where Rickie and the Mertzes bet Lucy she can't go twenty-four hours without telling a lie and she ends up insulting everyone around her and revealing her age, weight, and real hair color. *"You've got some 'splaining to do, Lucy!"* Zeph can't get enough of it. We all just laugh and laugh. I look at the girls and think how impossibly young they are, how careless and open and free. And for a fleeting moment, I'm envious. But then I realize it's not really jealousy; it's just that damn longing again.

I wake up the next day and when my feet touch the floor, they can't feel it. It's as if my spirit has slid out of me and left my woebegone body perched on the side of the bed. The spirit Grace glides to the bathroom while I shuffle along behind. The spirit Grace slides gaily down the banister as I descend slowly behind, shoulders slumped, as if I were three times my age—one hundred and fifty-nine.

Down on the ground floor, I continue to see everything through a distant, ghostly lens. I see the vibrant, colorful signs of everyone else's lives—Isabelle's silver laptop with the Boris and Natasha sticker, Max's turquoise Pashmina scarf, Isabelle's beat-up boom box and El's camel-colored baseball glove. But all vestiges of my own life seem to have disappeared. Where's that Alice Munro book—*The Lives of Girls and Women*—that's been on the hallway table forever, the one Nell keeps forgetting to borrow? The coffee mug I left next to the sink before I went to bed? The moonstone earrings I took off when I came home after work? I'm the movie character waking up in heaven, wandering around in a daze, not realizing yet that I'm dead. Even Tweety the parakeet still has more of a presence here than I do, his ghost of a breeze swaying the empty bird cage back and forth.

I walk around the living room, picking up objects here and there, examining them as if they were relics from a newfound world. One of Elvira's black socks, one of Rachel's ballet slippers, Isabelle's monthly calendar. I pick up Max's hairbrush and bring it to my nose. Its aroma is earthy and strong. El's baseball glove smells like sweat and old leather. I pick up a white rag which reeks of turpentine, and yank it away from my nose before realizing it's my high school boyfriend Floyd's T-shirt, the one I kept all those years in my keepsake box. Now it's ripped and stained and rank with resin. I toss it onto the purple chair. The smells are almost unbearably strong; the house is making far too much noise. Every creak of the floor is like a crack of a tire iron against a cement wall. The kitchen clock is ticking again like a bomb; the trickle in the sink might as well be a geyser.

I notice a small black mass in the corner. As I approach, it morphs in and out of different apparitions: a sleeping cat, Elvira's cape, the vinyl cover for the hibachi out in the backyard. Gingerly, I bend down to pick it up. It's a moment before I identify it as Charlie's Beatles wig, which Max asked weeks ago if she could use for her sculpture. I agreed, a bit reluctantly, thinking it was fitting at least that such a relic end up on Max's "Tower of Junk." But like so many of the items originally slated to be part of the sculpture, this one has obviously been discarded too. It's stiff now with glue and paint and no one would ever recognize it for what it once was—the silly, wondrous thing that kept Charlie awake at nights with excitement. Now, all that's left is an ugly mess of matted, fake black hair. I walk over to the kitchen trash can and pop the lid open with my foot. The anguish it causes me, watching the ruined wig land on top of eggshells and coffee grounds and empty Pop-Tart sleeves, is almost more than I can bear.

I make a break for the back door, desperate to feel the open air. On my way through the kitchen, my foot hits something sharp and my body takes flight before landing with a thud against the side of the refrigerator. I've tripped over the cheese grater that Max and Elvira used to make pizza the night before, and it's sliced a few layers of skin off the side of my right foot.

"SHIT!" I yell out. Instantly, I'm whole again, back inside my body, back inside my world. "Shit, frig, frugging, friggin', SHIT!" I yank a dish towel off the refrigerator door handle and wrap it around my foot to stop the bleeding. The doorbell rings.

"Can someone answer the goddamned door?" I call out.

Everyone appears all at once, as if they've been planning an elaborate surprise and at the door will be a clown who's been hired to juggle bowling pins and make funny faces to cheer me up. Max and Elvira come in from outside just as I'm limping toward the front door. "What's good in the snack department, Mom?" Max bellows. Isabelle emerges from the downstairs bathroom, brushing her teeth with black charcoal. Rachel's doing exercises at the makeshift barre.

Max beats me to the door and opens it.

"Dad!" she says and throws her arms around him.

"Phillip!" I say. "What are you doing here?" He's not alone.

"Hi, everyone." Phillip's even thinner than usual, tanned and sinewy, and sporting a scraggly beard. You can barely make out the once red B on the brim of his favorite baseball cap. His hair's grown down past his shoulders. I've never seen Phillip so disheveled and grimy, so relaxed. "Sorry to barge in this way," he says. "But I couldn't wait to see you guys!" The woman beside him tugs at his sleeve. "Oh, sorry. Everyone, this is Heidi. We met up on the trail a few weeks ago. We've been hiking together ever since."

"Heidi." I can't believe this. My ex-husband disappeared up on the mountains six months ago and now he's come down looking like a wolf man with a woman named Heidi by his side? Really?

"Heidi, this is my family," Phillip goes on. "Nuclear and… otherwise." He looks over at Zephyr, drawing a picture near her tent, and Elvira, puzzled. "This is my daughter, Max…" He gives Max another hug. "My son, El, and his…wife, Rachel. Rachel, it's great to finally meet you. That's Isabelle over there, with the black teeth. And very…pregnant! Wow! Congratulations! And this," he comes over and plants a kiss on my cheek, "is my wonderful ex-wife, Grace."

Something inside me cracks then, when Phillip's words hit my ears and his lips brush my skin. The dam holding back all that longing I've been feeling, all that frustration and embarrassment and disappointment—breaks open wide. The roar of life around me is suddenly deafening again. Voices become loud and garbled. The hot and frothy water of all those pent-up feelings floods up through me and starts to spout, drenching the hallway, then the kitchen, slowly filling the whole house. Soon, I'll be completely underwater, racing frantically to reach the surface. The rest of them are oblivious; the rest of them are calmly swimming fish. I feel sure I won't be able to make it, can't swim far or fast enough, unless I pull the plug, until the water starts to level and the rest of them disappear down the drain, until I can reach the surface and snap my head up to catch my breath. Alone.

"OUT!" a voice cries out. It's a minute before I realize that it's mine. "Everyone out! Now!" *Now, now, now!* The echos bounce off the shocked heads of all those around me.

"Grace," Philip says. "What's wrong?" He catches sight of my skinned foot. "You're bleeding!"

"I can't take it anymore!" I start to spew. "You've all got to go!" I point to Isabelle. "You've got to go live with your boyfriend who is also the father of your unborn child!" I point at Max. "You've got to move back into your apartment like a regular college student! You two married people…"—I flap my hand in the direction of El and Rachel—"should make your way back to Vermont or the Big Apple and start your life together!" Finally, I gesture to Phillip and Heidi. "And you two should probably go back up north and finish climbing all of those four thousand footers!"

"We did," Heidi says timidly.

They all stare at me, dumbstruck and still.

Zephyr pokes her head out of her tent, where she retreated when I started to yell. "Where do I need to go?" she says.

"You can stay in your tent," I say. "Until your dad comes to pick you up."

Everyone looks over at Elvira, then, the only person I have yet to banish.

"And I guess I should probably, like, go home too, right?"

she says.

"Mom, what's going on?" Max says. "Why are you acting so psycho these days?"

"I'm not acting psycho. And I don't want to calm down. All I want is some peace and quiet. Is that too much to ask? I just want some space...I need...I just..." And with that, I collapse into the purple armchair and burst into tears.

Isabelle comes over and puts her arms around me. "Ah, Gracie. You're just going through a rough patch."

Max heads for the kitchen. "I'll make you ginger tea with honey, Mom." She turns to her father. "Can you come out into the backyard, Dad? I need your advice about something."

"Sure," Phillip says. He and Heidi follow her out the door.

Zephyr comes out of the tent and starts to straighten out the books on the coffee table. Isabelle goes off to get a Band-Aid and Neosporin for my foot. Elvira clears the dirty dishes from the living room.

"Why aren't you all leaving?" I wail. "Why can't I be by myself? Just for a while?"

Zephyr hands me one of Max's *Calvin and Hobbes* books. "Because even when you get mad and your face gets purple and your hair goes all crazy," she says, "we'll still take care of you, Grace." She takes off the hedgehog wig, her favorite, and puts it on my head. "Grace you of care take we'll," she says solemnly.

That night there is no dinner. Everyone wisely scatters. Phillip and Heidi eventually disappear and Elvira and Isabelle retire to their rooms early. Zeph and Max camp out in the tent in the backyard. El and Rachel go out to the movies. I hole up in my bedroom with my last Jane Austen book—*Lady Susan.* It occurs to me that Lady Susan was a cougar way before her time. She's a middle-aged, smoking-hot widow who likes money and sex, preferably with younger men. She's devious and smart and doesn't take any you-know-what. "I am tired of submitting my will to the caprices of others; of resigning my own judgment in deference to those to whom I owe no duty, and for whom I feel no respect." Damn, Lady Susan! Tell it like it is!

I lie awake for a while. Someone's put clean sheets on my bed and I can hear the crickets chirping. I fall asleep to the haunting voice of Joan Armatrading, "Open to Persuasion," coming up through my open window and the murmurs and laughter of the girls from the backyard. And for the first time since I can remember, I sleep soundly.

At dawn, the house is quiet. I open the back door. An apricot sunrise unfolds in the eastern sky, slowly dissolving into streaks of lavender and charcoal grey. The kitchen is strangely spotless. I put water on the stove for coffee.

Max comes in from the backyard, rumpled and yawning. "Are you okay, Mom?" Max says. "You really freaked us out yesterday."

"I'm sorry," I say.

"I guess Elvira and I have kind of overstayed our welcome, huh? We'll clear out soon. I promise."

"It's not you guys," I say, with a sigh. "It's me."

"Want to come out and see my final project?" Max's face brightens. "Today's the day. Elvira and I are about to drive downtown."

"Today's the day?" I feel another pang that I haven't been more involved, more supportive. I've been so selfish and caught up with my own woes for the past few months. And the girls have been working so hard.

I go over to Elvira's pickup truck and look up at the towering structure, which is now thirty feet tall and, at its widest, at least six feet.

"Wow, Max," I say, at a loss for words. "You said it would be as big as a house…"

"That's not it," Max says, starting to walk across the yard. "My project's over here."

I follow her over to the old, warped picnic table, and there, propped up against the chestnut tree, is a framed piece of art, four by five feet, filled to the brim with intricate, interwoven drawings. I come up close to take them in. All of the paintings and found objects from Max's life which have been growing on the "Tower of Junk" have now been rendered in elaborate, miniature detail.

Max has created an astonishing pen-and-ink world filled with the ridiculous and the sublime. I see birds flying out of a TV screen and a motorcycle revving in a bird cage. I see a red sock draped over the CITGO sign and Tweety Bird, the parakeet, floating on a cloud. I see an upside-down martini glass, mustached and dripping blood. I see pineapples dancing across a stage and a Jack of Clubs pouring Xs and Os out of a bottle, the image partly obscured by an EXPIRED stamp.

And then I start to notice the people. I see Celia climbing a flight of stairs up to the moon, holding her LL Bean canvas bag. I see a Candy Land sidewalk and a pair of soccer cleats. Beside them is a muscled calf and foot in a ballet slipper—her brother's calf, her brother's pointed foot. I search for Phillip in the drawing and there he is, standing on the rooftop of a house with many windows, leaning against the chimney and gazing out over a range of mountains. And there's Zeph, riding on the back of a galloping hedgehog, pounding on a drum strung around her neck. Elvira hovers over it all with her winged black cape, pulling a kite string of musical notes behind her.

I look for myself then, almost fearfully, and there I am, on the other side of the mountains, with my curly, squiggly hair, holding up the sun with one hand and a plunger with the other, balancing on a beach ball like a seal. And there I am again in the top left corner, brushing Max's long, dark hair, which then turns into a rushing waterfall that thunders down the side of the mountains at which Phillip's gazing. And finally, I see, weaving through the vast expanse of Max's world—a winding sea creek, filled with tiny creatures—starfish and algae and mussels and crabs. In the right bottom corner, where she has signed her work, is the title in small block letters. *The Isthmus Max.*

"I don't understand…" I look over at what I thought was the project, the work in progress I've been watching rise up out of the bed of the truck.

"My original idea was to combine painting and sculpture," Max says. "I wanted it to be massive, larger than life. But Elvira kept reminding me what Beckman's been trying to drum into our heads all year—get rid of the excess and see what's left when you do. It came to me that the sculpture"—she points over to the truck where Elvira is taking pictures from all different angles of the tower—"was just the storyboard for the final piece."

"So you…" I'm not even sure what question to ask.

"I saw that I had to distill it," Max says excitedly. "I finally got it, that the huge, sprawling mess of my life was better rendered in a more delicate, intimate frame. Once I got started, I couldn't stop. I've been working on it night and day." She holds up her hands. The tips of her fingers are covered in black ink. "What do you think, Mom?" she says.

"It's… amazing."

"But do you get it?" she says. "Do you get what I was trying to do?"

"I think you were trying to make exquisite, lyrical order," I say carefully. "Out of the beautiful chaos of all our lives."

"Pretty much," she says, slowly nodding her head. And the lump that's been lodged for days in my throat starts to break apart.

Elvira comes up behind us, an old Leica slung around her neck. "It's, like, brilliant, isn't it, Grace?" she says.

And how on earth can I argue with that?

We walk back into the kitchen. I crack eggs for cheese omelets into a silver bowl while Max goes off to take a shower. Isabelle appears suddenly from out of the downstairs bathroom, standing with one leg bent in an odd, stork-like way. She looks so comical with her basketball belly and long, spindly legs.

"Is it safe to come out now?" she says.

"Of course," I say. "I'm sorry, Iz. I was just at a very low place yesterday. I hit rock bottom."

"You're not the one who should be apologizing. We've all

behaved disgracefully," she says. "And I'm going to make it up to you, I promise. But, in a general way, would you say that we're forgiven?"

"Yes," I say. "You're forgiven."

"Good," Isabelle says. "Because my frickin' water just broke in your bathroom, Gracie. All over your nice, clean floor."

Thank the powers that be for emergencies, for the flight or fight response, for the ears and hearts and minds that instinctively heed the call. Saved by Isabelle's broken water, we all leap into action. Max takes over whisking the eggs. I call Emil and tell him to meet us at the hospital. He asks to speak with Isabelle. El goes out to start the car and Elvira starts emptying the dishwasher. Zeph comes in from the back yard in her pajamas, still yawning.

"What's going on?" she says.

"It's time for Isabelle to have her baby," I say.

"I thought she was just getting fat," Zephyr says. I look over at her uncertainly. "Get it?" she says with a grin.

"Good one!" I pour her a bowl of Rice Krispies. "Here. Eat these."

I gather up some of Isabelle's clothes and her toothbrush and iPhone and glasses and stuff everything into a Mustard Seed bag.

"Don't worry." I hear Isabelle reassuring Emil. "Plenty of babies are born a few weeks early. They do just fine. The kid's going to have your brains and my looks. So it's all good. And remember, she's not going to Harvard!"

"I hate to ask, but could you guys take Zeph with you downtown?" I say to Max. "Until things settle down a bit? I'll drive Isabelle to the hospital and wait with her until Emil comes. Then I'll head out to work. Otis will be over to pick Zeph up later in the afternoon."

"Come on, pipsqueak," Max says to Zeph. "We'll show you what college is all about." Zeph's out the door in jeans and her pajama top before she even remembers to put on one of her wigs.

Isabelle and I head down Storrow Drive, which is curiously empty on an early Monday morning. Runners jog the path along the river and scull boats slither over the water down toward the Salt and Pepper Bridge. A few lone sailboats tack back and forth from the Cambridge to the Boston side of the river. We veer off toward the Fens and snake our way over to the Longwood hospital zone.

"Well, this is it, Gracie!" Isabelle sits next to me in the front seat, her belly sticking out of one of Max's fleeces that she grabbed on the way out the door. "Can you believe it? Jesus effing Christopher. I'm going to be a mom. I hope I won't totally screw it up."

"You'll be great, Iz."

"What if the kid hates me?"

"She won't hate you."

"I'm not all that likeable," she says.

"It's beautiful thing," I tell her. "It doesn't matter. She's your kid. She's gonna love you no matter what."

"If mine turns out half as good as yours, I'll be happy," she says. "Your kids are the frickin' best, Gracie."

"Aren't they?" I say.

Isabelle's face suddenly stiffens, as she's hit with another contraction. "How far apart was that one?"

"Eight minutes," I say, glancing at my watch. "You're getting close!"

Emil's waiting at the door of the hospital with a wheelchair. I give Isabelle a hug and Emil helps her out of the car. I stand there watching them fly down the long corridor of the hospital under the neon lights. I see Isabelle turning sideways in the wheelchair and lifting up a hand to touch Emil's face. I see him stumbling, beaming, bending down awkwardly to kiss her cheek while he pushes her. The fifty-seven-year-old, tweedy Harvard walrus guy. Who fell in love with Blow Torch Murphy's bad-ass daughter from Mefford. It's a most comical and moving retreat.

17

Otis shows up around five-thirty. I'm just out of the shower and the house is empty.

"Did you get my message?" I say. "Zeph's still out with the girls."

"My phone died a few hours ago," he says, putting a paper bag on the kitchen table. "When will they be back?"

"If it's not too late for Zeph, we're going to meet them at the Wonder Bar later to celebrate. I hope you'll join us."

"She'd never forgive me if I made her miss out."

"Did you get Maggie off all right?" I say, drying my hair with a towel.

"I did," Otis says, sniffing the air. "Is that the new chamomile shampoo we just got in at the store?"

"I love it," I say.

"Smells good," he says, pulling out a chair. "Thanks so much for keeping Zeph."

"I wasn't exactly keeping her."

"Having her."

"I didn't have her either. Diana did."

He laughs. "I should know better than to mess with the word guru." He sits down at the kitchen table, looking around at the unusually tidy house. "How'd everything go around here?" he says.

"Well, Zeph was fine. But I misbehaved terribly. I had a meltdown yesterday. I completely lost it and tried to kick everyone out of the house. But it didn't work. No one listened. They all just ignored me and went about their business. And then they cleaned up my messy house and sent me off to bed."

"What's really going on, Grace?" Otis stretches his legs out in front of him. "You've listened patiently to all my tales of woe. Why don't you tell me yours?"

"You don't want to know," I say in a warning tone.

"Yes, I do."

"No, you don't. Trust me."

"I do trust you," he says quietly. "And I want to know."

I give in to the urge to tell Otis everything. About answering the door and finding Phillip and Heidi there, and feeling the dam break when Phillip kissed me on the cheek. I tell him about Fuzz and the Termite Woman and Dylan and the *Rolling Stone* article and the disastrous threesome and the night with Palindrome Guy. He listens carefully, taking it all in, not once interrupting.

"Wow," he says, when I'm finally done. "You weren't kidding when you said you were having quite a year."

"You couldn't make it up if you tried."

"And you obviously tried," he says.

"I'm trying to make sense of it all," I say. "I can't tell what's different, if I've changed. Have I learned anything? Did I have any fun? I don't even really know."

"Do you have regrets?" he says.

It's the right question. And the answer, when it comes to me, is perfectly clear. "No," I say.

The sky darkens as dusk begins to fall. A storm is forecast for later in the evening. It seems like a miracle that all this time has passed and no one has come in to interrupt my long, meandering saga. I mentally locate everyone who might come barging through the door. Zeph is with Max and Elvira. Emil and Iz are at the hospital having a baby. Rachel and El are at their childbirth class. Celia's at the library with Nell. It hardly seems possible, but Otis and I are actually…alone.

Otis digs in the paper bag and hands me a package wrapped in the Sunday comics. "I got you something, Grace," he says. "To thank you for everything you've done for me and Zephyr."

"You didn't have to do that!" I carefully peel off the tape so the wrapping paper can be used again. "A transistor radio!" I say.

"Batteries included," he says. I turn it on and hear the cackle of the AM dial. Instinctively, I turn it to 103.3 WBZ radio, which of course hasn't existed for over forty years.

"I also got you some wine," Otis says, pulling out a bottle. "It's a twist off. But a good one."

"Let's drink it," I say.

"Now?" Otis looks around the room.

"Why not?" I say. "Would that be weird?"

"Weird?" He slowly gets my drift. "No, actually, it would be…great," he says. "I've had one hell of a day."

We retire to the living room with the bottle of wine. I kick off my gold gladiator sandals and sit down on the couch. Otis sits down beside me.

"You know, I've often thought about that day in the store," he says.

"It seems like a million years ago."

"I find myself wanting to think about it," he says. "But then I remember how it turned out. And I feel embarrassed."

"We were like a couple of clumsy teenagers," I say. "But it was kind of sweet—a new start for us both. And now look at us, all these months later. I'm a jaded urban cougar and you found Maggie again."

He puts his glass of wine down on the coffee table. "I don't think it's going to work out with Maggie," he says.

"Why not?"

"It was a picture I wanted to paint," he says. "A happy family portrait, with the three of us, and Eleanora the cat. Maybe even another kid. I've been trying to bring it all to life, with just the right brush strokes here and there. But, in the end, I don't think it quite adds up."

"It'll take time for Zeph to trust Maggie," I say. "To trust the two of you, together."

"I don't think Maggie really gets Zeph," he says. "The way that you all do. When I see how happy she is over here—"

"She's part of the family now," I say.

He puts down his glass of wine. "Have you ever thought about giving it a real try, Grace?"

"What?" I say. And then I understand. "You mean…us?" He nods. "No," I say. "Honestly, I haven't."

"Sometimes I think you and I could be good together," he says.

"You do?" And then it hits me, not like a bolt of lightning, but a soft dig to the ribs. That Otis could maybe be…not all wrong. By now we're both feeling mellow from the wine. The last of the day's dim light filters in through the bay window. Just as Otis leans in for a kiss, we hear the doorknob turn. Hastily, we pull apart. It's Rachel and El, back from their childbirth class.

"Great breathing tonight, honey," El says to Rachel, and then to me. "Is there a baby yet?"

"No news," I say. "Otis and I were just about to head out."

"We were?" Otis says.

"Aren't we all going to the Wonder Bar?" El says.

"We'll meet you over there in a while."

El and Rachel head upstairs.

"I have an idea," I say to Otis, grabbing the batik throw off the couch. "I'm taking you for a little ride. Are you game?"

"I'm about to embark on a Grace Winthrop Hobbes adventure," he teases. "Who wouldn't be game? If a little bit terrified."

The Fresh Pond parking lot is empty except for Ranger Marge's golf cart and a sidelined backhoe. I slip off my shoes in the car. The stormy cover of darkness falls as we walk. The cool pavement on the path around the reservoir feels good beneath my bare feet. The blooming broomstick branches of elm and oak trees map the mauve-tinted sky. I'm carrying the throw and the transistor radio, which is cranking out two-minute Oldies at a rapid clip. Otis hums along, sometimes breaking into song. "I Fought the Law and the Law Won." Gusts of wind sway the hanging branches of the willow trees.

We stop at Little Fresh Pond and make our way to a secluded stand of birch. I spread out the batik throw on the grass. Thunder rumbles in the distance. We settle on the third hole. I lean over and give Otis a long, slow kiss. "Let's try this again," I say.

"Is this on your bucket list?" Otis says. "Making love on a golf course?"

"Someone once dared me to consider it," I say. "The idea's been growing on me ever since."

"Nice spot," he says. "Tucked away like this. We're probably not the only ones who've ever done this before."

"Probably the oldest," I say.

"We're not so old," he says, leaning back against a tree.

I take his hand and turn it over, massaging his palm with my thumbs. "What's it like to be a one-armed man?" I say.

"At first, it was surreal," Otis says. "There was this huge disconnect between my body and my brain. How was I supposed to fit the old me into this new body? It took forever for my mind to let the old arm go."

"How did it feel physically?"

"My center of gravity was way off. It was strange. I wasn't symmetrical anymore. I'd lost eight pounds on one side of my body. I kept imagining my arm was in a sling. I could still feel the tips of my fingers, and the watch I used to wear on my wrist."

"Do you ever get those phantom pains they talk about?" I stroke the soft skin of his inner arm.

"Sometimes," Otis says. "I feel jolts of electricity in my missing fingers sometimes. A pulsing in my forearm that isn't even there."

"It seems like such an injustice to have pain in a body part that doesn't even exist anymore," I say.

"Doesn't it?" He laughs.

"How about phantom pleasure?" I trace the line of his collar bone with my finger. "It seems only fair you should have that too."

"Phantom pleasure." He thinks for a minute. "Well, when I drink something cold, it's as if the liquid's flowing into my missing arm. That's a cool feeling. Sometimes I imagine a breeze blowing up against my elbow. And there's a tingling in my missing fingers when I have sex."

I give Otis back his hand. He lies down on his side on the grass, his chin resting in the palm of his hand. "Lie down with me," he says.

I lower my body, scooching my body back to fit his. He brings his arm around my waist and pulls me closer, then buries his head in my hair. "You smell good," he says. His hand slides under my shirt and starts to rub my belly.

"What was the owl painting about?" I say.

"Fear and loneliness in Watertown," he says. "I painted it just after Diana left. Zeph used to wander out into the yard and stare out over the fence. She was only four, but she knew that her mom had left our small, safe world. And she understood that nothing would ever be the same."

"Zeph was the owl," I say.

Otis nods. "The wise, wide-eyed, four-year-old owl. That's why I call her *uggla*. That's owl in Swedish. She never wanted to come back inside. She'd keep saying, over and over again, 'I wait for Mama. I wait for Mama.' She had so much faith."

"And you…"

"I was the tall, hunched-over figure beside her. Waiting and watching," he says. "With no faith whatsoever."

I unbutton his shirt. He lifts his right shoulder and I tug at the sleeve and slide it off. It's the first time I've seen what's left of his arm, tapered and neatly puckered. I stroke the ridge of his shoulder, trailing my fingers downward. "Is it better not to touch it?" I say.

"It's better if you do," he says. "As long as you're comfortable. If you're not, then I won't be."

"It's beautiful in its way," I say. "What do you call it?"

"Most people say *stump*," he says. "I prefer *truant limb*."

I run my fingers over its molded bottom and up and around to his armpit. "Can you feel that?" I say.

He nods. "It feels good," he says. "You've got soft hands."

When we're both naked, Otis lies down on his stomach. "Climb on top of me," he says.

I give his taut butt a few pats as I slide onto his back and press my warm breasts between his cool, broad shoulder blades. Skin to skin, I feel myself starting to get wet. I realize I'm humming softly at the back of my throat. I start to rotate my pelvis and he moans. I roll off him and he climbs on top of me.

"Are you ready, Grace?" Otis says. "Are you ready for me now?"

"Ready," I say, as he enters me, hard.

Afterward, we lie on our backs on the grass. I get a whiff of Chinese food from the Panda Pagoda across the Parkway. The lights from the car dealership twinkle. Cars whiz back and forth along the drive. The wind picks up as the storm draws closer.

"You know, I've actually gone on some of those computer sites," Otis says.

"Which ones?"

"The ones about amputees," he says. "And sexual fetishes. I sort of couldn't *not* look at them, knowing they were out there. When I got over being offended or shocked, I actually learned a thing or two. There was this one threesome—"

I groan. "Please don't say that word."

"It made sense in a weird sort of way," Otis says. "With a third person, there were suddenly enough limbs to go around. They helped each other out."

"Love Potion Number Nine" comes on the transistor.

"Blast from the past," I say. "Do you remember who did this song?"

"The Searchers had the hit in 1964." Otis doesn't miss a beat. "But the Clovers recorded it first in 1959."

"You're good," I say, looking over at his strong profile. "Who was your favorite Beatle?"

"Ringo," he says. "He was the only one who didn't take himself too seriously."

It's true. "Can I tell you my favorite joke?" I say. And at that moment, I make a deal with myself, that if Otis gets it—and laughs, really laughs, then maybe we *could* be good together, maybe I'm in.

"Let's hear it," he says. "I hope it's not as long as that monk joke."

"No, it's quick,' I say. "Why don't WASPs have group sex?"

"No idea," he says, shaking his head.

"Too many thank you notes to write," I say.

The laugh is unmistakably, unequivocally—real.

Just before we get back to the parking lot, the sky breaks open and it starts to pour. I put the batik throw over my head and make a run for it, sliding the transistor radio under my shirt to keep it dry. A roll of thunder barrels toward us and a flash of lightning lights up the reservoir. We quickly slip inside the car, dripping wet, and share a soft kiss.

I look up at the hill down which Nell, Charlie, and I used to sled for hours at a time on snow days, Celia waiting patiently on the sidelines with a thermos full of Campbell's chicken noodle soup, as we ran up the hill and slid back down with shrieks of glee, toes and fingers freezing—but we didn't care. I make a mental note to bring Celia over here for a walk soon, to take Zeph sledding here next winter, to stroll with the babies around the reservoir and tell them all about the birds and the trees. This is where my brother and sister and I—and then our children—ran and biked and played. This is where I've found solace while running. And peace when I needed to escape the madding crowd. This is where I first laid eyes on Otis, where I've scribbled down bits and pieces in my notebook before I lose them forever. In this parking lot. In this rickety, old car. Under this mauve and stormy Cambridge sky. This is my place. And I will bring everyone here that I love.

As I start up the car, Isabelle calls and I put her on speaker phone.

"It's a boy, Gracie! What the hell am I supposed to do with a goddamned boy?"

"Boys are great! They're just different. A bit..." I look over at Otis and smile. "Clueless," I say.

"I did it without any drugs!" she says. "Can you believe I

didn't cave and get a freaking epidural? And I'm not even a stoic WASP, like you, Gracie. Just a sissy Catholic. Poor Emil, though. He may never get the feeling back in his left hand."

"He will," I say.

"He's the most beautiful baby at the hospital, Grace. I've seen them all. There are some ugly frickin' kids in that nursery. But mine is gorgeous. He's got a full head of black hair, with one of those widow's peaks, like Clark Gable. We're going to name him Jude."

"Jude Gable," I murmur. I can just picture Isabelle and Emil's little cretin—widow's peak, Ivy League drawl, rock and roll swagger and all. I don't breathe a word about how all that first silky baby hair will likely fall out and leave them with a toothless, tiny, bald wizard, how tired she'll be in five months, how messy her house will be for the next eighteen years, how profoundly, fantastically her life is about to change. "Can't wait to meet him," I say.

We drive over to the Wonder Bar. Max and Elvira are there with Zephyr, who's sitting on her knees on a barstool, sipping a Shirley Temple. I see Max glance over at Bartender Jack with a broken smile and feel her heartache with a stab. Rachel and El are eating chips and guacamole at one of the high tables. And in a new twist, Asa is here at this bar—hanging out with Raven. She grabs my arm as I pass by. "News flash," she says. "I just asked Asa to meet my parents."

"What did he say?"

"He said, 'I thought you'd never ask.'"

The new artwork has been hung—angled, geometric abstracts, the kind of cold, sleek images that might have adorned Fuzz's dull apartment, if he were the least bit artistically inclined. The bar suddenly feels empty and bleak without Otis's Vulcan creatures inhabiting its walls.

Otis goes up to Zeph and gives her a high-five. "How was your day?" he says.

"I went to Max and Elvira's college," she says. "It's an art college. I want to go there too."

"Great."

"Max says I have to go back to real school first, though. Just suck it up and get through it. Anyways," she says, stirring her Shirley Temple with her straw. "I can't just hang out with you old farts all the time."

Otis gives her the look. "*Older* farts," she says.

"You think you're ready?" Otis says. "To go back to real school for a while?"

"After the summer I'll be ready," Zeph says. "Max and me and Elvira are going on a road trip."

"Where to?"

"New Hampshire, to see my mom. In Elvira's truck. It's a '53 Chevy. Elvira's dad gave it to her when she turned eighteen. Maybe when I'm eighteen, you'll get me a pickup truck."

"I wouldn't count on it," Otis says.

"I *will* count on it," Zeph says. "You have eleven years left to change your mind."

"Dream on, *uggla*," Otis says.

"Come on, Dad," Zeph cajoles. "Be a buddy, be a pal."

"We'll see," he says, sneaking a sip of her Shirley Temple. She bops him on the head and makes a face.

Phillip and Heidi arrive. I watch as she puts her hand on his arm and says something which makes him laugh out loud. He looks so at ease, so happy. There's a generosity of spirit that he rarely showed to me. Was it my fault that this easier, gentler side of Phillip never emerged and flourished during our marriage? Did I hold him back with my perplexing, WASPy ways? No, that had never been part of the deal. I was no more responsible for Phillip's happiness than he was for mine. So, no guilt. Just perhaps further evidence that "till death us do part," in our case, had just been a bit too long.

Asa strolls over to say hi.

"Is this your family?" he says, gesturing to my motley crew.

"Of sorts."

"They look like a good bunch," he says.

"They're a pretty good bunch." I look over at Raven, who's talking to Nell. "So, how'd you do it, Asa?" I say. "How'd you finally win her over?"

He thinks for a minute. "Persistence," he says. "Earnest, unwavering persistence. And an amazing Academy Award performance of nonchalance."

From a booth at the back of the bar comes a blaze of red. Something stirs inside me, some old memory, some rush of feeling. Two women sit talking quietly. The younger one seems familiar, but I'm certain I've never met her before. On my way to the ladies' room, I get a closer look. The older woman is hunched and wizened, her face lined with cross-hatched wrinkles surrounding warm, deep-set brown eyes. She's wearing a cameo brooch on her navy wool blazer and her cotton-candy hair is tinted blue. They're comfortable with one another, mother and daughter, I'm almost sure, both nursing tall brown drinks with limes. For a moment, I think—this will be me and Celia in ten years. And I'm comforted. But then I remember that in ten years, if Celia's even still alive, she most likely won't know who I am anymore.

It's the shoes that finally clinch it. Five-inch Jimmy Choo heels. Once again, dawn breaks over Marblehead. It's my mentor, my role-model, my warrior guru on the refrigerator held up all these months with an Oscar the Grouch magnet. Sheila LaFarge, right here in the flesh, at the Wonder Bar, having dinner and drinks—not with a dashing younger man—but with her ancient, wrinkled mother.

"What are those two women drinking?" I ask Jack when I get back to the bar. "I'd like to buy them the next round."

"Our special tonight," he says. "Dark and Stormy's. Ginger beer and rum. I'll send them over."

"I'll have one of those," Raven says.

"Me too," Elvira says.

"Me three," Zephyr says.

"A virgin for her," I say.

"What the heck," Otis says. "Make me one too."

"I'll take a virgin!" Rachel pipes up.

"I'll take you," El says, wrapping his arms around her.

Sometime during the evening, I take Elvira aside. "You're not going to light Max's drawing on fire, are you? You know, that whole Destructive Arts thing?"

"No, I'll spare it. Don't worry," she says. "It's way too gorgeous. It's actually something you might, like, want to hang in a museum someday," she teases.

"You just might," I say. "I wanted to tell you, Elvira. Your 'Mad Hatter Symphony' is really…spectacular! It's truly unique and completely undefinable. And you can't say that about too many pieces of art."

"Thanks, Grace," she says. "And thanks for letting me stay with you guys."

"Anytime." I give the noble and loyal Elvira Moreley a clumsy hug. "Don't be a stranger," I say.

Max comes up to Celia just then and puts her arm around her shoulder. "How you doing, Grandma?" she says. "Can I get you a drink from the bar?"

"A ginger ale would be lovely," Celia says. "Not too much ice, though, dearie."

"Coming right up," says Max. I watch her bravely order the drink from Jack, sliding a few bucks his way. I hear Max's voice on the couch that day when she told me about Jack. *He just, like…kind of broke my fucking heart.* And at that moment, I catch a glimmer of what the guy with one green and one blue eye was trying to tell me that night at the bar—about the word *like*, that it wasn't always without purpose. Max's "like' was no accident that day, no lazy slip of the tongue. She put it there so that she could turn her face away for that fleeting second, and then turn it back, so she could finish her thought, without crying. That's what a good WASP would do.

"She's stubborn as a mule, that one," Celia says, gesturing

to Max. "But of all my children, she's the one with the biggest heart. It's not easy being the middle child. I know. I was one too."

"That's not your daughter, Mother," I say. "That's your granddaughter, Maxine."

Celia's face lights up. She turns to me as if I've just bestowed on her the most rare and unexpected gift. "I have a granddaughter?" she says, incredulously.

Toward the end of the evening, I go up to the bar to settle the bill with Jack. "How much do I owe you?" I say. "For this whole motley crew. And the round for those two women in the back?"

"A hundred bucks," he says.

"No way," I say. "All those Dark and Stormy's and Shirley Temples? Not to mention the chips and guacamole. That's not nearly enough."

"A hundred bucks," Jack says and takes off to the other end of the bar.

Earlier in the day, I stopped at the ATM machine, which spat out twenty crisp new ten-dollar bills. Now I count out fifteen of them and start arranging them, fan-like on the bar, until I've made a full circle of glistening cash. I pluck a daisy from a congratulatory bouquet of flowers I bought for Max and place it in the center of the bills. When Jack sees what I've done, he stops in his tracks. And I could swear I detect the slightest hint of a smile. He takes out his cell phone and snaps a shot of the display, then slides it quickly back into his pocket. And then, with the deftness of a casino dealer, he swoops the bills back into one neat pile, flicks the daisy off the bar, and hightails it off to the register with the cash.

Outside, the rain keeps pouring down. The umbrellas pile up in the corner by the door. People shake themselves off like dogs after a dip in a pond. I watch a family sitting at a table, eating burgers and crinkly fries. A curly-headed toddler in a high chair bursts out laughing when his grandfather, without any notice, suddenly puts a napkin on top of his head. Beside him, a beautiful ageless girl with Down's Syndrome and golden hair tells her family a story, gesticulating excitedly with her hands. Palindrome Guy is chatting earnestly with Chuckie D., about particle accelerators, whatever those are. Lumbering Larry has shaved his beard, and when he smiles tonight, I notice he has a dimple. I watch El and Zephyr dancing to "Johnny B. Goode," a kind of improvised, monkeyshine waltz. Asa listens attentively to "ninety-if-he's-a-day" Chuckie F., as he starts in on his favorite joke. "Do I come here often?" he says, delivering the punchline. Asa grins and sends an air punch to his arm.

I look around at all of them, my family—nuclear, extended, and otherwise— for better or worse. Tonight, I'm watching my play—the play of my kaleidoscope life. I'm suddenly hit by a wave of serenity—a contentment with my zigzag lot, all that's come before and whatever's left to come. I catch Otis's eye and he gives me a smile so strong and sure, I could ride its wave for days. Yesterday, I held my breath for an entire minute in the pool. My kids are strong and solid. Celia thinks I'm Rose, but is that necessarily a bad thing? For now, we're all enduring. We're all okay. Summer's coming…and things are definitely looking up.

And after all is said and done…
It will have been a Dark and Stormy night.

Acknowledgments

I am grateful to Ann Collette for her help with the earliest drafts of the novel and Steve Monahan for his eye on later versions. Thanks to Leo, Tami, and Dave, my first and foremost bartenders and to all the night wanderers who shared their stories with me. I feel fortunate to have found a home for my work at Regal House Publishing and owe special thanks to Jaynie Royal for her guidance and support. Lastly, all my love and gratitude to Anna, Sofia, Natasha, Isla, Ian, and Sonja—the lights of my life.